Tw[illegible] in Biarritz

MICHELLE
JACKSON

POOLBEG

This novel is entirely a work of fiction. The names, characters and incidents portrayed in it are the work of the author's imagination. Any resemblance to actual persons, living or dead, events or localities is entirely coincidental.

Published 2008
by Poolbeg Press Ltd
123 Grange Hill, Baldoyle
Dublin 13, Ireland
E-mail: poolbeg@poolbeg.com
www.poolbeg.com

1 3 5 7 9 10 8 6 4 2

A catalogue record for this book is available from the British Library.

ISBN 978-1-84223 -329-0

Typeset by Patricia Hope in Bembo 10.75/14

Printed by
Litographia Roses, Spain

Note on the author

Michelle Jackson studied textile design in the National College of Art and Design and kicked off her career as a sock designer. After teaching for many years she took to writing for pleasure and hasn't stopped since. She lives in Howth, County Dublin, with her husband and two children.

Acknowledgements

I didn't realise how hard this was going to be but here goes . . .

To Paula Campbell and all of the gang at Poolbeg, thank you for letting me see my book in print and especially to Gaye Shortland for making it so much more legible for everyone else who reads it – your good humour and enthusiasm are contagious.

To my friends who waded through all sorts of writings – chapter by chapter – especially Clodagh, Suzanne, Niamh, Jill, Susan, Maria and Sarah – you had blind faith in me, girls, and thanks!

To the members of the SLC club – the champagne is on me, guys – thanks for the great nights spent with copious bottles of Merlot. Special thanks to my friend Catherine Whiteside for slogging with me through the streets of Biarritz!

To June Considine – thanks for your great support and advice when I first decided that I was going to be a writer. To Joy Lennon and Angela Forte who help keep my body and chakras intact through all the stages it took to get here. To Juliet Bressan for helping me with the 'science bits'!

Thanks to my parents, Pauline and Jim – without you I wouldn't be here! You're both an inspiration and endless source of help and support.

Finally to my husband, Brian – thanks for bearing with the endless hours spent with my laptop and the momentous glass of whiskey when I eventually finished my first novel. To Mark and Nicole – my beautiful children and muses – I would never have written a word only for you!

To you the reader and your first love

1

Friday 10th March, 9.25p.m.

"Sometimes it's better not to tell."

"What do you mean?" Kate was curious. Maybe she didn't know her friend as well as she thought she did.

"Look, some things are best kept in the past." Annabel's tongue was loose after the alcohol, still she beckoned to the waitress to bring another two glasses of the liqueur. She sat back in her chair. "Okay, maybe I did go back to Nico's room last night and have sex while you were with Brett!"

"Yeah, right!" Kate scoffed. "I think I know you well enough by now, my very married friend! And, besides, in the unlikely event that you did, you'd have told me. We spent the whole day together and even after meeting him in Bayonne this afternoon you never said a word to me! So I know you didn't!"

"Well, I was with him and I'm riddled with guilt, so don't ask me any more about it!"

Kate stared at Annabel. She did, in fact, look guilty. It couldn't be true! Could it? "You're kidding me, right?"

"No."

The waitress placed two more liqueurs on the table before them.

"Thanks," said Annabel and tossed most of hers back at once.

"I don't believe it!" said Kate.

"What don't you believe?" Annabel frowned.

"That you slept with Nico, of course!"

"Why?"

"Why?" Kate echoed, exasperated. "Because you just don't do that kind of thing!"

"Wha's this called again?" Annabel said, raising the glass of ruby-coloured liqueur to her lips in slow motion.

"Floc!"

"Well, Kate, I think I'm flocked!" Annabel drained the glass and licked her lips. She ran a hand through her dishevelled long blonde curls and beckoned to the waitress again.

Kate took a sip of her floc. "Come on! Tell me the truth! Did you really sleep with Nico?"

"Why d'you find it sho hard to believe?" Annabel was beginning to slur a little.

"Because: you're married, you don't play around, you're the sensible one –"

"Hold ish right there!" Annabel held up a hand. "I'm the shenshible one?" Realising she was slurring, she paused, and then made a big effort to speak distinctly.

"Oh, yes, of course. You're the artistic one, the exotic one – I'm the dull one, the boring one –"

"I'm not saying anything like that!"

"Yesh, you are! I've always been the little mouse and you've been the – the –" she took in Kate's long-limbed frame, jet-black hair and tanned skin, "the panther! Or sho you think!"

The waitress deposited another two flocs on the table.

"Well, Annabel," said Kate, "the fact is, in all the years I've known you, even before you married Colin, you have never allowed yourself to be swept away by passion –"

"Thatsh what you think!" Annabel drunkenly pointed a finger in Kate's face.

Kate pulled back and drained her old glass, before picking up the fresh one. "What do you mean by that?" she said, becoming irritated now at this nonsense.

"All I am saying is, maybe I have known passion, a great passion. Mush mush more zan anyone!"

"Oh? Is Colin on Viagra now or what?" Kate's tongue always sharpened the more she drank.

This cut much too close to the bone and Annabel felt quite hurt. "I had my great moment!" she said, flushing. "Before I ever met Colin!"

"Oh yes – a moment so great you never even thought to mention it to me!" said Kate scornfully. "Some great moment!"

"It was!"

"Okay, okay," Kate pretended to yawn, "when and

where – and what? First kiss, age twelve, school bicycle shed? You already told me that one."

Something snapped in Annabel. She was tired of Kate's presumptions about her sexual needs and desires, and the experience with Nico the night before had awakened a new confidence in her. "On the boat – with Damien – sho zere!"

"You dark horse!" Kate said, shaking her head. "You never told me about a Damien – who or when was he?"

"On the boat! You were there! Damien, it's always been Damien. I've always loved him. Zat's why it was so easy to marry Colin!"

"I don't know any Damien from our past," Kate declared, now more than a little upset and agitated that Annabel had kept a secret from her for all these years.

"Damien – you don't know Damien? You know him very well, Kate. You lived with him long enough!"

For a long frozen moment Kate stared at Annabel. Then her mouth dropped. She felt as if she had received a sharp blow to her solar plexus. "My dad! You were . . . no, you couldn't have been . . . you were in love with my dad?" Kate couldn't believe she was uttering the words.

"I sure was, and he loved me too. On the ferry, in the storm, all those years ago."

Kate felt as if she was going to pass out. Was Annabel only talking rubbish with the copious glasses of wine and floc inside her or was she telling the truth?

"What happened on the ferry?"

"I made love to your father, Kate!"

"Tell me you're joking, Annabel! You couldn't have!" Kate's head was shaking frantically as if she could shake the image away.

"I sure did and I'll never forget it." Annabel was relieved to be telling Kate the truth at last. "I need more drink – where's zat waitress gone?"

Kate sat there expressionless – unable to respond. If what Annabel was saying was true, she had been deceiving her for most of their friendship.

"I feel mush better after telling you at last, Kate – it'sh been hard keeping it from you all this time." Annabel gave a little hiccup. "I'm glad I told you now."

Kate wasn't able to drink any more. She put the napkin up to her mouth and pushed her chair back slowly.

"I'll be back in a minute," she said, finding it difficult to catch her breath.

She quickly walked to the toilets. Her stomach was churning inside and her heart was racing. There was no way – Annabel and her father! She couldn't hold the raclette back. She felt her dinner rise back up her throat and she spewed its contents into the bowl. Her head was dripping with sweat and she felt as if she were being choked by a pair of imaginary hands.

Standing in front of the mirror, unable to wash her hands they were shaking so much, she stared at her reflection and the tears sprang to her eyes. How could Annabel do such a thing? To her mother as well, who had been so good to her! And how could she have kept that secret all those years, despite all the memories they shared together? They'd never had a true friendship. Annabel had made a fool of her. She could never trust her again.

Walking on trembling legs, she made it back to the table but had to steady herself before taking her seat.

Annabel gave a lopsided smile, oblivious to the effect her revelation was having on Kate. She looked a lot drunker than when Kate had left her only a few minutes before.

Kate leant across the table, gripped Annabel's hand hard and stared straight into her bleary eyes.

Annabel blinked, startled.

"Annabel," said Kate slowly, deliberately, "I'm really upset. I need to know if what you're telling me is true."

"Ish true."

Kate took a trembling breath. "You had sex with my father on that ferry crossing – in the storm – all those years ago?"

"Yesh."

"You've been in love with him ever since?"

"Yesh, I have. Thash why I married Colin."

Kate let go of her hand. "But you never told me."

Annabel's eyes widened. "How could I tell you something like thash?"

It was true, thought Kate. This horrible thing was really true.

"I need to go to the loo now. You took ages," Annabel

grinned. She wobbled slightly as she stood up and went off in the direction of the rest rooms.

Kate was feeling numb. She thought quickly and knew she had to get away. Digging down deeply into her bag, she took out sixty euros. She threw the notes down on the table, anxious to be gone before Annabel returned from the toilet.

She didn't want to have anything to do with Annabel Hamilton again for as long as they both lived.

Nico was anxious to be on time for his arrangement with the Irishwomen.

"You're jumping around like a hare, Nico – relax and finish your beer," Brett said with a shake of his head.

"I told Kate and Annabel we'd meet them in Desperados," Nico said reluctantly.

"I wish you hadn't included me in your arrangements. One night with them was enough." Brett took a sip of his beer. "Anyway, we're a threesome this evening." He nodded towards their drinking companion, one of the other surfers.

"Hey, I don't want to get the blame for Nico missing out on his fun!" the scrawny Londoner laughed.

"He already had his fun with this bird last night," Brett grinned. "That's the bit I can't understand."

Nico felt awkward. Usually one night would be enough – they were used to picking up women all over Europe as they went from beach to beach – but Annabel was intriguing.

He took another drink from his glass and scanned his watch. Nine forty-five – they weren't the type of women to sit around waiting.

"Will you have another beer, mate?" the Londoner asked Nico.

"Not right now," he replied sullenly, making sure not to make eye contact with Brett. "I'm going out to get some fresh air." He stood up.

"Tell the truth. Are you going to Desperados?" Brett asked.

"I'm going to tell them that we can't make it. It's only around the corner – I'll be back in a minute."

Brett shook his head scornfully and returned to his beer.

Kate tossed the clothes into her hold-all with great urgency. She didn't want Annabel to catch her packing. It wouldn't take her long to realise that Kate had left the restaurant and returned to the hotel, and by then Kate needed to be well out of Biarritz.

The receptionist was startled to see her packed and ready to go, paying her bill at such an hour.

"*Un taxi, s'il vous plaît,*" Kate asked, and the receptionist obliged.

Kate's plan was simple – she would spend the night in one of the many hotels in Bayonne. The Ibis would certainly have plenty of rooms available this time of year. The drunken Annabel was not her responsibility and anyway she couldn't look her in the eyes after their conversation.

Suffering as she was at being betrayed by her best

friend, Kate's thoughts now swung to her father. Her insides twisted at the thought of him. How could he have done it? How could he have done it to her mother? The night of the storm. No wonder her father hadn't passed any comment when she was missing from her cabin all that night – Annabel was curled up under the covers in his! The thought repelled her so much she felt dizzy and had to sit down in the small foyer. She wanted to be at home in her small house under the gaze of the Pyrénées.

The waitress came over with the receipt on a saucer as Annabel returned from the ladies'.

"Where's Kate?"

"Your friend, *madame*? She has left."

"Left?"

"*Oui, madame*."

Why did she do that? Annabel sat down heavily and felt around under her seat until her hand fell on her bag. Where did she go? This was odd. Annabel was anxious to continue her discussion about Damien. Her mind was a dizzy haze of twinkling lights, delicious tastes, and aromas from the kitchen. She reached into her bag and put some money on the table.

"Your friend paid, madame," the waitress said.

Annabel stood up on unsteady legs and felt around for her coat that had fallen off the back of her chair. This was most strange.

"Would you like a coffee?" the waitress asked, noticing her condition.

"No, thank you. I really have to go," Annabel said, and slowly made her way to the door. She had flashes of her conversation with Kate. She had taken it very well, considering. There were no outbursts or condemnations – but where could she have gone? She carefully stepped out on to the street, anxious not to fall, but felt the ground swaying up to greet her. She couldn't remember the way back to the hotel but the steady roar of the ocean called her to take a left.

"Annabel!" a voice called but she didn't register it.

She hobbled down the road, the cobblestones feeling like pebbles in her shoes. A strong arm grabbed her from behind and she turned to see deep brown eyes stare back at her.

"Nico!" she exclaimed and flung her arms around his neck. Her legs went from under her for a second and he held her up with his arms gripped around her waist.

"It's lucky I found you, Annabel," he whispered. "You should not be on your own with so much to drink."

"'Ave you seen Kate?" Annabel was disoriented and her memory had turned to mush.

"I was on my way to Desperados," Nico said, surprised to find her in such a state. Where was her friend? "I will take you back to the hotel."

The receptionist had seen some sights that night already but was shocked when Annabel was assisted up to the desk only a short while after her friend disappeared into the night in the taxi.

"What is your room number, Annabel?" Nico asked.

"Can't remember," Annabel said, her head slumping under its own weight.

"Vingt-sept," the receptionist replied, handing the key over to Nico, judging that Annabel was in no fit state to make it to the second floor on her own.

Annabel was getting heavier with every step. Nico negotiated the bedroom door like a fire-fighter and plonked her down on the bed where she collapsed in a heap. She moaned and flipped over to the other side of the double bed.

Nico put the key down on the dressing-table and left the drunken woman in her slumber. The night before had been passionate and exciting – but maybe he had been wrong about her after all.

A few hours later the sun beamed through the window and burned onto Annabel's closed eyelids. She ruffled around the bed, unsure of her surroundings. She raised her head with some difficulty. The room was empty. She floundered around, looking for her watch. 8.02 a.m.

Where's Kate? What happened last night? How did I get back?

It was all incredibly vague – she had only snatches of memories to cling to.

But she remembered telling about Damien. Why did she do that?

She went to the bathroom in search of Kate but all of her belongings were gone. She looked for Kate's bag but that too was gone. There was a sinking feeling in her stomach. It was a nightmare. She looked around for her handbag and was grateful to find her mobile phone still sitting in the pocket. She dialled Kate's number but it rang out for a few seconds before stopping suddenly. This was serious. She really needed to find out where Kate had gone. And she only had a couple more hours until her flight back to Dublin.

She wished she could turn the clock back. Just forty-eight hours back and everything would be as it was before, as it should be.

2

Two days before

Thursday 9th March, 10.50a.m.

Annabel stared out the window of the plane at the wispy clouds against the perfect cerulean-blue sky, her thoughts drifting back to the first time she had seen Kate. It certainly didn't feel like twenty-seven years ago. They were two scrawny girls, barely teenagers, thrown together in the classroom by fate and circumstance. She could just as easily have sat somewhere else that day.

Time had left its mark on both of them. She tried to imagine how she would feel if she were in Kate's shoes. She wanted to kill Stefan for walking out on her best friend. It was such terrible timing coming up to her fortieth birthday. It was always easier for men – he had a new girlfriend ten years his junior and a baby on the way. Despite her positive and energetic nature, Kate had to be devastated.

"*Ladies and gentlemen, we will shortly be arriving at*

Biarritz airport. I ask you to ensure your seat belts are fastened and your tables are in the upright position."

Annabel looked down and rearranged her seat belt as the plane steadily started to make its descent.

The journey through Arrivals was refreshing after the hustle and bustle of Dublin airport. Her bag was on the conveyor belt in what seemed like a matter of seconds and she walked straight out to the taxi-bay where a line of cabs was waiting. The chill of winter still hung in the air – it didn't feel any warmer than Dublin had before she left. She took the Megane at the front of the line and settled into the back seat as the driver courteously put her bag in the boot.

She was prepared mentally for a few scattered houses and bars by the road, as Kate had told her they were visiting peasant country, but she hadn't expected them to be so pretty. By the time she arrived on the outskirts of Biarritz she felt as if she had travelled through a colourful painting.

As the taxi rolled up to the hotel, Annabel could hear the roar of the Atlantic Ocean beating off the seashore. The perfectly polished promenade of granite tiles sparkled with reflected light from a recent shower. To their right the bare trees bent over, their branches curled away from the gushes of wind rising off the sea. Annabel was almost in a trance at the scene.

"*Quinze euro, s'il vous plaît,*" the driver said, interrupting her meditation.

Annabel held up the digits on her right hand three times.

"*Oui, madame*, fifteen."

The driver huddled underneath his beige jacket with his curly head tilting backwards to see his passenger. Annabel dug deep in her purse and handed over the exact amount. How convenient it had become to travel to France! No money exchange. Frequent flights. Not like the old days when she travelled every summer as a teenager with Kate.

"*Merci*," she said, stepping out of the car.

The driver took her small travel-bag out of the boot and left it in front of the hotel.

Hotel Windsor: the name conjured images of a time gone by when the English upper classes frequented the resort. It was much as she had expected but the smell of the sea and the roar of the waves were more thrilling than she had imagined they would be. This sleepy little French town at the end of winter was an excellent choice for their reunion at what must be a very fragile time for Kate.

She steadily ascended the steps to the foyer, pulling her bag along without difficulty.

The receptionist was dressed in a dark suit with equally dark-rimmed glasses framing her eyes. Her black hair was pulled severely into a French knot. She greeted Annabel with a courteous smile. *"Bonjour, madame."*

Before Annabel got a chance to reply, an excited voice called her name from behind her.

She swung around, tossing her long blonde curls away from her face, and saw her friend rise up from her seat, her arms ready to embrace her, those doe-shaped brown eyes that had melted the hearts of so many men over the years glowing. Her hair was dyed, of course, because Kate's hair wasn't that black even at thirteen. The reddish-pink highlights were a bit of a shock – Kate assured her later that red was the new blonde in French fashion.

The two women rushed to each other like old lovers and held on tightly in a bear hug. Kate's pink jumper was soft as it brushed against her smaller friend's cheek.

"I can't believe you got here so quickly!" Kate said with a beaming smile. "I was just settling down to ring a couple of galleries."

"I can't believe it either – my flight was fifteen minutes early."

They stood back from each other, taking stock. They had long been familiar with the lines on each other's faces. They both looked well.

"I love the hair."

"Well, you know me. I'll try anything once," Kate grinned. "Your mac is gorgeous and I hate you for fitting into those skinny jeans!"

Annabel smiled. She was finally slimmer and trimmer than Kate. "Do you want to get lunch?"

"Yeah, good idea. Our rooms won't be ready for a while."

They left their luggage in the care of the receptionist.

"I need to freshen up first. What about you?" said Kate.

"Yeah – *toilettes* this way."

The two women moved through the small, informal lobby decked with cosy leather armchairs and ubiquitous MDF-trimmed bar. Annabel's handbag swung over her shoulder and her cream raincoat rested neatly in the crook of her other arm. She observed the multicoloured embroidered mule bag that Kate swung nonchalantly as she walked.

"When did you start to use a handbag?" she asked in amazement. She was always the one weighed down with make-up and hairbrushes and so on, and was now startled by the huge appendage carried by Kate.

"I need the make-up to hide the wrinkles. Time's finally caught up with me as we are here to witness!"

"I'm right behind you, girl!" Annabel said, holding the bathroom door open for her friend.

The two stood in front of the brightly lit mirrors, fixing and tweaking the blemishes on their faces.

"You wouldn't have a deodorant?" Kate asked.

"Sure!" Annabel said, delving deep into her bag.

There was a familiarity about the question. Even though they hadn't seen each other in nearly a year, they both appreciated the intimacy they shared. It could only be forged by years of friendship that had started when they had no preconceptions or expectations of how a friend was meant to be. Annabel was the closest Kate had to a sister and, although Annabel had two of her own, she had shared all her landmark moments in life with Kate.

"I feel much better now," Annabel said, wiping her hands clean with the courtesy towel.

The two women strode out of the hotel in search of the wonderful restaurant they felt sure was waiting for them. They passed under a Victorian walkway, beautifully decorated with wrought-iron moulding, as the sun started to peep through the clouds.

"How's Colin and the kids?"

"I swear, Kate, sometimes I wonder how they manage to function when I'm not around. Then, to top it all, Colin's not talking to me because I went to a fashion show last night – would you credit it? I spent two hours yesterday afternoon making shepherd's pie and lasagne so they wouldn't starve over the next two days and he's in a huff because I go out the night before coming away." Annabel sighed.

"He knows he'd be lost without you. Did the kids mind you going away?"

"Sam is obsessed with his PlayStation, Taylor is too busy with her horse and I told Rebecca I was getting her an art set that you could only get in France so she let me go with her blessing."

"So your kids aren't materialistic then!" Kate smiled. "What was the fashion show like?"

"It was the only place to be in Howth last night. June Stokes did MC, *Image* magazine were there and all the major glossies. I couldn't have missed it. Besides, the proceeds were in aid of the school so I just had to go, didn't I?"

Kate grinned and nodded her head.

It was so like Annabel to be found mingling mid-week with the local cognoscenti. Annabel had nothing to prove to anyone but was always trying to prove something to herself. She feared so much the loss of her Yummy Mummy status.

They came to the end of the walkway. Annabel was first to spot some locals behind a restaurant window, serving themselves couscous and chicken from a hand-painted bowl.

"This place looks nice," she said and Kate nodded in agreement.

The women sitting on the other side of the glass were startled by the two Irishwomen gaping in at them.

"It's couscous – have you had it?" Kate asked.

"Please give me some credit – even Patrick Guilbaud's has been known to serve couscous in some shape or form. To say nothing of my local SuperValu!"

"Patrick who's?"

"You've been away from Ireland a long time, haven't you?" Annabel grinned.

"Too long by the sounds of it," said Kate wryly.

A waitress welcomed the women in and placed them at a table for two at the window. The red and white gingham tablecloths gave the restaurant a cheerful ambience and the walls were painted a bright chalky blue that was set off by navy mosaic tiles. Orange lampshades shaped like tulip-heads hung over each table.

"This place is perfect," said Kate. "Red or white?"

"White or rosé."

"*Une carafe de vin rosé, s'il vous plaît.*"

"Your accent is perfect!" Annabel applauded her friend. "Do they think you're local now?"

"You must be joking. I'm always spotted as a foreigner. The gallery owners in Paris pretend they can't understand a word I say – ten years in the country and they look at me sometimes as if I'm speaking Greek!"

"How's the painting going?"

"I have an exhibition coming up in November and I have a few galleries that keep me ticking over in between. I'm proud to say I am making a living out of my work which is one major goal achieved before reaching forty!"

"I think you're fabulous. I wish I were creative."

"But you are! What about all those parents' association things you do? See, I do read your emails!" Kate's brown eyes twinkled as she spoke.

"Thanks, but to be honest they're more of an excuse for housewives to get out mid-week and drink too much wine." Annabel gave a sigh as she thought of the small world that she inhabited in Dublin.

"What about going back to college and finishing your degree?" Kate asked cheerfully. "You always said you would." Secretly she wondered why her friend wasn't bored to death with her routine.

"I wouldn't have the time. There's so much to do in my week. Then, of course, my main job as chauffeur takes up every afternoon."

Kate looked at Annabel, bemused, while the waitress poured wine from a ceramic jug into their glasses.

"You like to order?" the waitress asked.

"We'll have two of your couscous and chicken, *s'il vous plait,*" Annabel said.

"*Ah, Couscous royale!*" the waitress exclaimed and took off.

Annabel leaned forward, resting her elbows on the table, and explained to Kate: "While you're off painting your mountains in Hautes-Pyrénées, I am driving from ballet to tap-dancing and football to piano lessons. Most of the women in Howth spend half their time in the car or Jeep."

Kate couldn't hold the laughter back. "Sooner you than me!"

"Glad you're amused!" said Annabel, rolling her eyes in mock annoyance. "So how are the boys getting on?"

"Do you mean in boarding school or coping with the fact that their father has gone and impregnated his personal assistant?"

Annabel felt an 'ouch moment' coming on. She had hoped their conversation about the separation would come a bit later but Kate was frank and open, unlike Annabel's other friends – with them she had become too accustomed to skirting around the edges of delicate matters.

"Oh Kate, I've been so worried about you!"

"Me? Annabel, I will be fine and in the words of my good friend Ivana: '*Don't get mad. Get everything!*'"

"I'm so glad you're taking it this way, Kate. My

goodness, little did we know when planning this trip last year that things could change so quickly!"

"Only they don't really happen that quickly. To be honest, I could see it coming for a while."

"What do you mean?" Annabel tilted her head, surprised at the revelation.

"I mean Stefan was showing all the classic signs – away with work for longer periods than usual and not so interested in sex. Washing the pots after dinner and leaving funny receipts from places he couldn't have been all over the house."

"You poor pet!" Annabel's eyes clouded over. The mere thought of losing her secure position on the arm of Colin left her feeling shaken.

"It's not that bad," Kate went on. "I'm trying to create something positive out of it all and my paintings are shit-hot at the moment, even though I say so myself. What is it about creativity and crisis that go so well together?"

"At least you have your work," Annabel nodded. "It must be lonely with the boys in boarding school."

"The funny thing is the house has never been busier. I have a mish-mash of interesting friends and artisans living all around and we do a rota of sorts eating in each other's houses. My best friend is Fabian who does my garden and everyone else's around – you know, the one who's gay as Christmas. And did I mention Joy and Simon to you? They run a holistic centre and hold yoga retreats at different times during the year. They get some array of characters staying with them! Then I have a selection of teacher friends from my dabbling with the young French minds in the local *lycée*."

"Don't you miss the buzz of Paris?"

"I still get up there a couple of times a month and then I have a whole crew who whisk me away to the Bastille and Montparnasse to remind me of what civilised, or rather not so civilised, society is like, especially at three and four o'clock in the morning!"

"You're making me jealous. Your life is so . . ."

"French?"

"I was going to say well-rounded and balanced. I really wasn't expecting you to be so together when I got here. I'm not quite sure how I expected you to be but this wasn't it."

"Honestly, Stefan and I had been coming to the end of our time together for a while."

"You make it sound like a contract."

"Well, that's what it is, a contract of sorts," Kate said in a matter-of-fact tone.

Annabel was horrified. She picked up her glass of rosé to disguise the expression on her face.

The waitress arrived with a huge steaming bowl of couscous. "*Bon appétit!*"

"Tuck in," said Kate to her friend. "This couscous looks even better from this side of the glass."

After lunch Annabel still couldn't get the word 'contract' out of her head. The two women walked along the breathtaking cliffs that swept along the coast. Could Kate really feel that way about her marital vows after all of this time? If the shoe were on the other foot, she could imagine feeling very differently. She was defined by her status as Mrs Annabel Hamilton and she wished to remain that way until she died. She had her kids to think about, and her mother while she was still alive. They would be distraught if her marriage failed. Annabel had a lot of other people to think about in every aspect of her life and she couldn't be as flippant as Kate. But it had always been that way. Annabel watched from the sidelines as Kate went ahead and did everything she herself wanted to do.

"I think in life there are two types of people," she blurted out. "Those who know what they want and go out and get it and those who don't know what they want so they go around doing what everyone else expects of them!"

"Where did that come from?" Kate asked. "I was busy taking in the spectacular view and dodging the twenty-foot spray!"

Annabel paused. She had hardly noticed the rugged rocks in hues of yellow ochre and burnt umber jutting out of the sea.

Kate was standing at the footbridge that led to a viewing point and was considering crossing it. She beckoned to Annabel. "Will we?"

"You see what I mean. I don't know if I want to go over there and get battered by the waves but you just do it."

Kate frowned. She could sense that something was bothering her friend. "Are you okay?"

"I'm troubled by the way you called your marriage a contract actually." Annabel's voice was a pitch higher than usual.

Kate shrugged. "Hey, I think you were the one who came up with that word! Anyway, life's full of change and that's the time I was allocated to spend with Stefan, that's all."

"How can you be so matter of fact?"

"Annabel, I was married before, remember? It might only have been for a few months but when Harry died I dealt with it and I had two babies waiting to be born inside me."

Annabel felt naïve and inadequate next to her friend who had experienced so many different facets of human life.

Kate sighed. "Have you ever known me to be without a man . . . well, apart from now?"

"Apart from now? No, actually."

"There you go. There's someone better out there just waiting for me. I did love Stefan, I was with him long enough, but to be honest he wasn't the love of my life and you know that."

Annabel knew exactly what Kate was saying. More than that, she understood exactly how that felt, but unlike her friend she couldn't admit it to anyone, hardly even to herself.

Then out of the blue Kate dropped a clanger – she

was always one for throwing in that extra bit of information that left Annabel with her jaw dropped.

"I saw him in Toulouse, you know, about three years ago," she said in a calm voice. "He was doing a refresher course on the Airbus. He's a captain now for Airjet."

"You mean Shane?" Annabel asked quietly but with wide eyes.

Kate didn't flinch – instead she stared out at the rolling waves.

"I heard he moved to the southside," Annabel continued. "His wife's from Dalkey. I haven't seen him in years."

"He told me all about his wife. He was only just married and still fiddling around with the thin gold band on his wedding finger. It didn't sit comfortably, he said. Do you know it had been ten years since I'd seen him? He hadn't changed a bit. He still rocked me."

"I can only imagine. How did you happen to meet him?"

"I was visiting a small gallery that Fabian told me about. It was a Saturday. I had just parked the car and was walking along when I saw him . . . in a red T-shirt and jeans like he used to always wear."

Annabel wondered why she hadn't heard this story from Kate before now.

"He walked straight towards me as if we'd arranged to meet. It was so bizarre. He had three hours until the flight simulator was free and he was looking for something to bring back to *Natasha.*"

"Easy does it, girl – I can hear the cattiness in your voice."

"I'm sure she's a lovely girl. She'd have to be, for Shane to marry her. I hated listening to him talk about her though. I'm such a hypocrite! I had a husband and two strapping boys at home and I was so jealous of this woman who I'd never met."

"So tell me, what did you do?" Annabel asked, dipping her head forward.

"We had the most wonderful lunch . . . then I gave him a blow job!"

"You didn't!" Annabel's mouth dropped open.

"Of course, I didn't," Kate grinned. "But the thought did strike me! It was three bliss-filled hours spent recalling the old days. We sat in a cosy brasserie drinking coffees and staring into each other's eyes like we were sixteen again. I even drove him back to the airport for his flight test. He said he comes down to Airbus at least once a year for his annual line-check."

"Did he contact you after that?"

"He texted me the next day when he got home to Dublin, then I rang him about a week later and we must have been on the phone for a good hour. There was a gap after that, then he texted. I returned a message but no reply. I did text him later on that year to wish him a Happy Christmas but he didn't answer."

"It was probably a bit too much for him," Annabel suggested.

"It was probably a bit much for both of us. I couldn't

concentrate on my work or anything else for that matter for at least six months."

Annabel was shaking her head slowly in disbelief. "Why didn't you tell me this before?"

"I guess I was having mixed emotions after seeing him again. The only way I was going to cope was to try and forget him."

"Did it work?"

"What do you think?" Kate said as she let out a sigh. "Hey, it's a pity we didn't have a bit of a snog though!"

Annabel grinned. She hadn't heard that term in a long time. "I thought you might have – I mean, you've been a bit of a slapper in the past after all!"

Annabel was the only person in the world that Kate would take this kind of jest from.

"Annabel, you know I've been faithful to Stefan since the day I took my wedding vows. And look where it got me! Mind you, I had a bit of a problem on the run-up to the wedding day, didn't I?"

"You put me through hell," Annabel recalled. "There was I, starving myself for months, preparing to be the perfect bridesmaid, and then you go and tell me about that gallery owner and your passionate fling over a pile of canvases in his studio!"

"Christophe was some mover. My one and only older man. Boy, am I glad I copped on though! He would have just turned sixty this year. The thought of that!" Kate scrunched her face until it contorted, in disgust at her own behaviour.

Annabel stared at the sea and didn't respond.

"You okay?" Kate asked again.

"Sure." She turned her head and, frowning slightly, asked, "But you were happy with Stefan when you met Shane, weren't you?"

"I was always content with Stefan and he paid the bills which gave me the freedom to paint. He supported my sons as if they were his own. But if I were to do it all again I sometimes wonder . . ."

Lost in her thoughts, Kate walked across the stone bridge leaving Annabel standing at the wall and gazing at the turquoise ocean crowned with rolling white-horse waves.

"They were never like this on Dollymount strand," Annabel said out loud, but she was the only one to hear it.

Her mind was transported to the June of 1983. Everything was different that summer. She could clearly picture Kate and Shane on the silver sand, her in a little cerise bikini looking like "The Girl from Ipanema" and him in his T-shirt and Levi 501 jeans . . .

Annabel didn't mind being on the sideline. She liked Shane's friend Josh and since the boys were best mates the foursome fell into place nicely. Josh was easy company and put no pressure on Annabel although it was plainly obvious that he fancied her. Annabel had a passion of her own for a man who was unobtainable so she happily passed away the idle summer days with the protection of Josh at her side.

Kate sprang off the blanket. "Come on, race you to the water!" she said to Shane.

"I haven't got my trunks with me," he laughed.

But Kate was already off and running towards the incoming tide.

The current was deceptive in Dublin Bay and the friends usually only swam in a crowd. It was windy and the wave crests rushed in with ferocity. The three pals left behind on the seashore sat on the tartan rug and laughed at their hardy friend. Kate dived in and was quickly engulfed by an incoming wave. She bobbed out of the water and swam into the next wave. Beyond it, she raised an arm in the air, and the others waved back. She turned and the next wave broke over her, then she was out of sight for a while.

Annabel noticed a look of concern in Shane's eyes.

"Is she okay?" he asked.

"She's a strong swimmer. She's fine," Annabel assured him.

"She's been gone under the waves a long time."

"Look, there's her arm. She's okay."

Shane jumped up, ripped off his chunky white boots and ran to the water's edge with his socks and the rest of his clothes still on. He waded into the sea as quickly as he could until he was waist-high in the water and then catapulted his body forward, diving beneath the waves. He surfaced and began to swim strongly out to sea, pausing now and then to look for Kate. She came out of the water beyond him for a few brief seconds, then disappeared again. Shane frantically swam out further. It wasn't made easier by the fact he was still wearing his clothes.

Kate erupted out of the water like a mermaid, her body glistening in the sunshine and her long dark hair clinging to the back of her neck, droplets of water spraying off her skin.

"I knew I'd get you in here somehow!" she cried with a wicked smile.

Shane was so relieved that in mock annoyance he grabbed her and tried to disrobe her of her bikini but she was too quick in the water for him and he had to chase her all the way back to the sand dunes where the others sat laughing.

"You're drenched! Now you'll have to take your clothes off!" Annabel grinned.

Shane sat in a pair of wet underpants while they ate Mars bars and drank Coke, the staple diet of the summer.

Kate had Shane enthralled with her every move.

Annabel had to admit she was a foil to Kate's charms as well. While Kate was out there in the sea causing the commotions and making everyone fall in love with her more, Annabel stayed on the sideline and that's the way it always was.

Annabel and Kate meandered down the curved sidewalks past the town square and neo-Gothic church. They passed an antique merry-go-round that had been entertaining children since bygone days. Every side street was dotted with *pâtisserie* shops, chocolate *ateliers* and boutiques.

"Shall we?" said Kate as the two approached the huge department store, Galeries Lafayette.

A cornucopia of delights awaited them on entering. Displays of exquisite handbags and scarves took up their interest for much too long.

"If we stay here any longer we'll never get upstairs to try anything on," Annabel said, ushering her friend up to the escalator.

But Kate was distracted en route. "What do you think of this?" Kate held a stripy multicoloured wrap up to her face.

"Very Bohemian and art college – you *are* tapping the door of the big four-O, may I remind you!"

"There you go, taking the wind out of my sails. Come on, onward and upward!"

Kate was only joking but Annabel winced at the comment. Yes, she was the more conservative half of the relationship but that's the way they always had been.

They finally made it to the moving stairs. The women's New Season range was waiting for them on the first floor. Annabel rummaged through a rail of early-season shirts and tops. She threw the turquoise and rich-sienna garments over her shoulder.

"Are you in the fitting room yet?" she called out.

"Yes, Mum!" Kate replied.

"This should do you for starters," Annabel smiled, passing the clothes through the gap at the side of the curtain.

"I hope *you're* going to try something on?" Kate called from under her cotton cover.

"Plenty of time for that when you're sorted out," said Annabel. She grabbed at a pair of chocolate-brown Capri pants. They would be perfect.

"Are you still a Size 12 in jeans?" she asked Kate.

"You are too cruel, Annabel Hamilton! I resorted to a 14 earlier in the year. I can't stand people who lose weight when they get divorced. I ate tons of chocolate for weeks."

It was ironic, Annabel thought. In their twenties it was Annabel who was fighting off the pounds but now she was the trimmer and fitter of the pair. But those extra pounds somehow only served to make Kate more voluptuous than ever. Life was never fair!

Annabel passed the Capri pants through the curtain.

"Oh no!" Kate said with a gasp. "You're not going to make me put those on?"

"Trust me," Annabel replied.

When Kate emerged from the changing room, Annabel applauded her own powers of colour-coordination. It was one of the paradoxes of their relationship that the artist looked better when dressed by the pragmatist and it was some consolation to Annabel for having such a seductive friend.

"I have to say I love them though in a million years I'd never have picked them off the rail for myself," Kate said. "Do you remember that time in Prisunic – it was one of our later trips to France? You got me to try on that floral sundress? I wore it for years."

Annabel remembered that holiday well. That was the summer of '85 and that trip to France was the most special journey in her life. How could she forget it?

"Annabel, what do you think? Am I deluding myself here?" With her hands in the air Kate gave a twirl, displaying her new ensemble. The contrast of the patterned blouse and brown pants was very flattering.

"No, no, not at all – you look fabulous. And I'm going to buy it for your birthday present."

"Well, then, you'd better get looking for something yourself, so I can buy it for you!"

Annabel sifted through the next rail trying to yank her thoughts back from 1985 with each slide of the coat hanger. "You know, I don't see anything here at the moment. We can come back tomorrow or we might see something somewhere else."

"Are you sure?" Kate asked.

"Positive," Annabel assured her. "Let's go for a coffee or a drink in one of the cafés that we passed on the main street."

When they got out on to the main street they were spoilt for choice. The thoroughfare was littered with lots of cosy chocolate, coffee and cocktail bars. Annabel spied an advertisement for Leffe beer, one of her favourite treats whenever she visited France. Kate followed her into the charming bar and they sat at a small round table with a view of the road outside.

"Do you remember drinking this in Britanny?" Kate said as the waiter put the large bulbous glass of frothy brown beer in front of Annabel. "It's strong stuff – I don't know how you do it."

"How could I forget?" said Annabel.

"We really had a great time on those trips," Kate sighed. "Remember my dad letting us get vodka in the duty-free? Mum would've had a fit if she knew what we were up to."

Annabel nodded silently. "Those holidays were special," she agreed.

"It was great having you along. My little brother was so painful. It was like having two holidays when we took the car on the ferry with my dad and then later met Mum off the plane with little Philip. I can't believe he turned out to be such a pillar of virtue."

"Did you tell me that he got a new job now? That he's a registered psychologist?"

"Yes, and working for the Department of Health. He's still married to Gloria, God love her."

"No kids yet?"

"Mum said they're trying – it's the IVF road. I feel sorry for them both." Kate paused. "I'm so glad you came on those holidays – you know, you were better than any sister could have been."

Annabel smiled at the compliment but that wasn't exactly how she had felt when she was accompanying Kate on those family excursions.

"I'm lucky that your family brought me!"

"What about the night of that storm on the ferry? Will you ever forget it?" Kate said with amusement.

"No, never!" Annabel shook her head but the reasons she would never forget that night were very different from Kate's.

"I felt bad leaving you in the cabin on your own but that French guy was the cutest holiday romance I ever had," Kate said with a mischievous grin as she got to her feet. "I have to go to the loo. Back in a sec."

Annabel was glad to be left alone for a few moments. She hadn't been on her own in the cabin and she would never forget that night as long as she lived.

Suddenly she was nineteen again. . .

The ferry tossed and turned like a pea in a pot of boiling water. Most of the passengers were spewing the contents of their stomachs into the many latrines dotted around the ship or were trying hopelessly to sleep. Under the barrage of waves that smashed relentlessly against the cabin's porthole, the lovers lay entwined in their forbidden embrace.

Annabel was finally with him. She had known since she first laid eyes on him that he was The One, but she never dreamt that it would come to this. The circumstances were somewhat unusual but she hadn't conjured up the force seven gale. She was here now and for this moment everything was perfect. It could never last. It would probably never happen again, but it was so much better than the innocent fumbling she had experienced with boys in the past. Now she knew what it was like to really make love.

She dribbled her fingers along the fine hairs on his chest and felt him shudder under her touch. He raised his head slightly.

She lifted her head off his chest and turned around until her gaze met his.

"Oh Annabel!" he said in a tone of despair and sorrow and love, mixed together like a potent cocktail.

"I love you," she replied. "I've always loved you."

Again he replied but this time with a sigh. "Oh, Annabel!"

She blinked back the well of tears that was starting to fill up in her eyes. She knew the answer but she had to ask him . . .

"Where will we go, when there's no storm to protect us?" The words rolled off her tongue as she repeated them quietly, twenty years later.

"Have you started talking to yourself? You're only turning forty – it's a bit early for senility to be setting in!" Kate said jokingly.

Annabel was shaken out of her trance by her friend's return. "Sorry, I didn't hear you come back."

"Do you fancy getting back to the hotel?"

"I wouldn't mind a shower," Annabel replied, keen to wash the thoughts she had rekindled out of her head.

"You can have a long luxurious bath – no kids pestering you this evening!"

"It's been total bliss sauntering around all afternoon like this," Annabel agreed. "What are our plans for later?"

"We could always check out the casino after dinner."

Annabel was well acquainted with Kate's love of slot machines. They would end up there regardless.

The foyer of the Hotel Windsor was littered with

surfboards and broad-shouldered young men in wet suits who were briskly taking their keys from reception and bounding up the stairs.

"I didn't think the view would be this good inside the hotel!" Kate smiled a wicked smile at Annabel.

"You're insatiable," Annabel berated. "Give yourself a chance – you've only been husbandless a couple of months!"

"We haven't got time to be sensible. Mind you, I can't remember ever being sensible. That's why I was so lucky to have you."

Annabel smiled at the compliment but wondered how sensible she really was. Nervous, yes, cautious definitely, but sensible was not how she felt. Kate on the other hand was the opposite. Annabel could predict her moves no matter what the situation and nine times out of ten the result would turn out to be wacky or adventurous.

An athletic surfer in his twenties, his mop of sandy hair burnished from the salt water and sun, passed close by Annabel. She couldn't help staring at his muscular physique. What would Colin say if he saw her looking at him?

"What a dish! I think we have to find out where these young guns are going tonight and that's where the fun will be," Kate whispered in her ear.

"Are you going to lead me astray, as usual?" Annabel asked.

"Always," her friend assured her.

3

A couple of hours later the two women were sitting in front of a gin and tonic and Martini with ice, in a little bistro next to the hotel.

"We haven't seen any surfers yet," Kate observed.

"I hope they don't go to bed early," Annabel replied, getting into the swing of their self-indulgent night out.

"We're probably old enough to be their mothers," grinned Kate.

"You know, I get a shock every morning when I look in the mirror. I have to ask myself who this middle-aged woman is," Annabel said despondently.

"I know exactly what you mean," Kate nodded in agreement, "and it can only get worse."

"Lots of women around Dublin are going under the knife – would you consider it?"

"Ten years ago I'd have said no way, but you can never say never."

"Colin thinks it's great and said he'll even treat me to a course of Botox."

"The cheek, and him like a wrinkled bulldog!" Kate said in horror.

"Colin's holding his age well," Annabel said defensively. "Isn't he?"

Kate couldn't win this one, so she wasn't even going to try. "He looks very well, Annabel, but you're a stunning woman that he's very lucky to call his wife – don't forget that."

Annabel always felt confident and buoyant after spending time with Kate. She wondered if Kate was able to say the same about her in return.

"Don't look now but Sandy Hair is at three o'clock," Kate said, leaning over her gin and almost knocking it in the process.

Annabel turned her head instinctively and fixed her gaze on the dishy surfer who was accompanied by an equally attractive dark-haired friend. He seemed to recognise them from the hotel and casually waved over.

Kate gave a little shake of her wrist in return and leaned forward until she was almost on top of Annabel.

"Is that not a bit keen?" Annabel said, arching her eyebrows. "They'll think we're two desperate oul' ones."

"I know what I'm doing. They scrub up well, don't they?"

"That's the luxury of youth," Annabel said, nodding her head in agreement.

"Ah, yes!" Kate tossed back the remainder of her

drink. "However, I hate to say it but I'm famished – will we go?"

"Seems like a shame now that there's a bit of entertainment. But one good thing about turning forty – you learn to get your priorities right."

They left a ten-euro note on the table and wandered out into the night. The town was hushed and sleepy, unaware that it was meant to provide an entertaining ambience for its guests. Each restaurant that they walked past seemed emptier than the previous one.

"Maybe that fish place we saw earlier has some atmosphere," Kate suggested.

The streets were quiet all the way down to the seafront and the two were surprised to see only three tables occupied in the brightly lit seafood restaurant.

"We really are offseason, aren't we?" Annabel noted.

Things were looking up however as the sandy-haired surfer and his dark, tanned, friend seemed to have taken a short cut and were approaching the restaurant door.

"Hi, again!" the sandy-haired one said in a strong British accent.

"Hello," replied Kate who now definitely had the surfers' cards marked.

A small rotund waitress in a striped dress and pinny ran up to the four in a flap, as if the restaurant hadn't catered for such a large crowd that night.

"Une table pour quatre?"

Sandy Hair looked back at the women and raised his eyebrows slightly.

"Would you like to join us?" he asked.

Kate didn't give Annabel a chance to answer but Annabel would have been more surprised if she had. She had always made the decisions for both of them.

"That would be very nice, if you don't mind?" Kate said with a wicked grin.

The waitress ushered them down to a table at the window, covered with a crisp white linen tablecloth. The setting was nautical in inspiration with ship's wheels and ropes decorating the walls.

"I'm Brett, by the way," Sandy Hair said, offering his hand to Kate and then turning to shake hands with Annabel.

"And I'm Nico," his friend said. He sounded quite English but there was an Italian accent breaking through. He shook hands with the women.

"I'm Kate and this is Annabel."

Annabel gave Kate a churlish look, implying that she was well able to speak for herself.

"Are you girls down for the surfing?" Brett asked.

"Do we look like surfers?" Kate giggled.

"To be honest, no!"

"We're just getting away from it all. Annabel lives in Ireland and I live in Hautes-Pyrénées so we don't get to see that much of each other. Are you guys on vacation?"

"We're training for the European Championships in Feurteventura," Brett answered.

"So you're professional?" Annabel asked, trying not to sound too impressed.

"We do the circuit in Europe and the States," said Nico. "We don't get to Australia every year – only when it's a major championship."

Annabel was beginning to wonder what these two hunky guys were really like, sitting with two strange older women. Were there no girls their own age in Biarritz on a Thursday night? Maybe they had ulterior motives and the idea of no-fuss sex and a mature woman was a novelty! The conversation was spirited, washed down with two carafes of wine and four bowls of delicious mixed seafood.

"Fancy finding somewhere with a bit more action?" Kate asked.

"Desperados," Brett suggested. "It's where all the surfers go,"

"'*Why don't you come to your senses?*'" Kate joked.

Brett looked at her, obviously taken aback.

"Sorry," Kate laughed. "I guess you're too young to remember The Eagles."

"Oh! Right," said Brett.

They pushed their seats back and all stood up together.

"I think we're the couple of Desperados here," Kate whispered to Annabel when the guys moved out of earshot.

Languidly they walked along the shoreline, all wrapped up well against the cool evening breeze.

Brett walked alongside Kate, matching her strides step for step.

"Whereabouts in England are you from?" Kate asked flirtingly.

"A few places actually, but at the moment my dad lives in Poole and I stay with him when I go home. My mother lives in Gibraltar with my stepfather."

"Poole's nice, I've been a couple of times – my first husband was a sailor."

A smile developed on Brett's face. "You make it sound like you've had an array of husbands," he said with a hitch of his eyebrows.

"Well, no, I mean, maybe . . . my first husband died and my second is in the process of becoming my ex-husband."

"An experienced woman," he grinned.

"Really, I'm not that interesting. That's just the way it is." Kate was feeling embarrassed, an emotion she usually didn't experience. "So are you married?"

"Crikey, no way, I'm only twenty-eight! I'm married to my board!" Brett laughed.

"So will you be tied up with your board for life?"

"I guess so – I mean there are guys in their forties still winning championships!" he said, shaking his head incredulously.

"Really? That's very old," Kate said with a smirk. "Have you been to the casino yet?"

"I do all my gambling on the waves." His bright blue eyes were twinkling as he spoke and a mischievous grin was developing on his face. He was remarkably like Shane in appearance. He had the same cool tone to his voice but with more arrogance and less sensitivity.

Kate glanced over her shoulder to see where the

others were and found them walking slowly behind, deep in conversation. *This could turn out to be a cosy little foursome, just like the old days!*

Nico and Annabel had been chatting quietly, feeling quite relaxed with each other.

Suddenly he reached out and took her left hand in his, rubbing his index finger around the diamond solitaire and gold band. "How long have you been married?" he asked.

She politely let her hand slip gently through his grasp and rubbed her palm off her jacket. "Do I look very married?"

"You want me to answer?" Nico asked with a coy smile.

"I wouldn't have asked you otherwise." Annabel threw her head back and laughed. It had been a long time since she'd flirted with a man.

"I hope you don't mind me saying this, but you seem to be afraid. I don't know of what."

"Maybe I'm afraid of surfers," Annabel smiled.

"Ah ha!" Nico flashed his gleaming white teeth and his eyes widened as if he had made some sort of discovery. "Maybe you are afraid of yourself."

Annabel frowned. This Latin man was touching on a nerve. How dare he? He had only known her a couple of hours. "Are you sure you're Italian? Your English is better than mine."

"I lived in Oxfordshire for a few years as a child," he grinned. "Okay, okay, I have to admit my mum is

English but I like to keep Italian pronunciation for some words."

Suddenly her phone vibrated in her pocket and she stood still while she took it out. She saw her home number flash on the screen.

"Excuse me," she said to Nico and answered it. It was Colin. "Hi, honey . . . yes . . . I left them in the top drawer beside the hob in the kitchen . . . I definitely did . . . Are the kids all right?"

Nico walked on briskly, anxious not to appear to be listening to Annabel's conversation.

The bulletin from home went on and on.

"No, I didn't arrange anything for definite . . . I wasn't sure . . . but my mother said that she would baby-sit if you wanted to go out tonight . . . all right, see you Saturday. Bye!"

Colin put the phone down without saying goodbye to his wife. It was most unsatisfactory to be left organising a sitter for his usual Thursday-night pint in the golf club. He ignored the cries of his children from the living-room and picked the receiver up again. If he had to speak to his mother-in-law he would – she did come in handy and let him off the hook when he wasn't available to be with his family. A man of his standing and position deserved his little breaks, he thought, as he pressed the buttons on the phone.

"Lily, it's Colin – Annabel said that you might be available to baby-sit tonight – I have an engagement at the golf club . . . yes, she's getting on fine . . . I agree . . . about half an hour? Thanks, Lily, see you then."

Colin put down the phone and brushed by Sam who had been staring at him from the other side of the kitchen counter.

"Are you going out, Dad?"

"Your gran will be over to mind you in a few minutes, all right?" Colin said without turning to look at his son.

Sam stared at his father who was now busily making coffee from his beloved espresso-maker. He wished his dad was like other dads – the ones that went along to watch their sons play football on a Saturday morning. His father was a stranger to him in many ways, a tall man who breezed in and out of the house on his own terms while his mother held everything together. Sam had been looking forward to this night for weeks – he knew that with his mother away it would be a good chance to spend some time with his dad. Nervously he decided to give it a go and speak out.

"Don't you want to stay in tonight, Dad? We could do something?"

Colin turned around and looked his son straight in the eyes. "My dear boy, you know I always go to the club on Thursdays. Maybe we can have a chat tomorrow night."

Sam knew that there would be no chance of spending time with his father then. "You always come home late on Fridays."

"That's right – I have to go to a business meeting after work." Colin's mouth widened weakly in a half-smile. "Maybe when your mother gets home on Saturday she'll bring you somewhere that you like?"

Sam nodded. He didn't know why he kept trying with his dad. The whole thing was pointless.

Breathless and seething after the call from Colin, Annabel caught up with Nico.

"Where's this bar?" she said. "I need a drink!" She wasn't in any mood for discussion. She wished she hadn't taken the call. Thank God she had organised an *au pair* at last! It was only a pity that she wasn't there already.

"Are you all right?" the gorgeous half-Italian enquired.

"Fine. Come on – let's catch up with the others."

Under the black cloak of evening the four entered the bar with its brown wood panelling and globular wall lights. Rows of booths were fitted in by the walls and groups of a very young clientele dotted the seats.

"This is the only place with a bit of life in it, by the looks of things," Kate said, taking her coat off.

"It's not exactly salubrious," Annabel observed.

"You mean it's not Howth Golf Club?" Kate jeered.

Annabel was careful not to make any more comments that warranted a snide remark. As usual Kate's repartee was sharpening under the influence of alcohol. It was set to be another night of flirtation and teasing like so many they had shared in their youth and Annabel would put money on the odds of Kate hooking up with Brett.

A couple of hours later Annabel got the nod she was expecting. In the ladies' toilet Kate asked the question that had been asked of Annabel so many times before.

"Do you mind if we use the room for a little while?"

"Kate Cassaux, I can't believe you're turning this girls' weekend into a sordid bout of passion with a younger man!" Annabel berated her.

"Please, please, Annabel! He's yummy and it's been ages since I had a good shag. I swear we'll be quick."

Annabel could only laugh at Kate's request – things had changed little in all these years, apart from the fact that Annabel wasn't going to be paired off with Kate's fella's friend this time.

"Okay, I did think we were too old for all this but it would make it like old times. I'll give you an hour and a half. I'm not very tired anyway and I need another drink or two – I had a lousy chat with Colin after dinner," Annabel sighed.

"If I were you, I'd give Nico a go – he's a bit of a dish, Annabel."

"Yes, but I'm not you. I'll stay down in the bar and chat to him if I have to, but one and a half hours is the absolute max, okay?"

"I'm so lucky to have a friend like you," Kate grinned.

When they returned to the table Brett took his jacket and handed Kate her coat with an air of urgency. As they left, Annabel sat down beside Nico and gave him a shallow smile to indicate that she was not interested in the same entertainment for the evening as her friend.

"Would you like another drink?" he asked.

"Why not? Looks like we won't be rushing back. Bacardi and Coke this time, please." If she was going to be stuck with this handsome stranger she might as well relax and enjoy herself.

Kate rocked from side to side in the hotel foyer, dizzy from the kisses the nape of her neck was receiving. The receptionist wasn't flinching, apparently familiar with such scenes as the night developed.

"*Chambre vingt-sept, s'il vous plaît,*" Kate asked and an involuntary squeal escaped from her lips. She grabbed Brett's arms which were twisted around her waist and pushed them away. "Wait a minute," she chastised him.

That only seemed to fuel his passion more as he snapped the key from the receptionist's hand. They ran to the small lift and, embracing, threw themselves against the burgundy leatherette walls. His hands caressed every inch of her body but, although she was enjoying every second, she still had the wherewithal to press the button for the second floor. As the lift doors opened they collapsed entwined onto the red pile carpet in the narrow hallway.

Kate relished his stamp-like kisses that stuck to her face. "We have to get up," she giggled and they crawled on their knees to the bedroom door.

Shakily, Kate put the key in the lock and sighed with relief as it turned. She couldn't wait to get her hands on him in privacy. She flipped the light-switch on and turned around to find him stripping off his T-shirt. Kate's eyes fixed on his rippling bronze muscles. She moved slowly forward and smelt a sweet mixture of salt and sweat. She felt an overwhelming desire for him take over, as he started stripping her clothing off piece by piece.

"Would you like to go for a walk?" Nico asked, noticing that Annabel's glass was now empty and feeling that an alternative surrounding was required to use up the time.

Annabel nodded, stood up and put her coat on anxiously. Silently the couple braced themselves as they walked out into the crisp atmosphere. The roar of the ocean seemed louder as the town was now hushed and quiet.

"Let's go down to the sea," Annabel beckoned and Nico smiled his approval.

Soon they were walking along the beach. In the distance the tall beacon cast its light around the shore and back out to the wide gaping black of the sea. Sporadic beams of light shining from the top of the lighthouse guided their eyes from the imposing Hotel du Palais across the cliff face. Every now and again the waves crashed forcefully in their relentless battle to reach further up the beach.

"It is a good noise, huh?" Nico said, stopping still for a moment.

Annabel stood beside him and listened carefully to the cacophony of energy filling her ears.

"I like it," she said, nodding her head.

"I think, Annabel, you are a lady of many secrets."

"What gives you that impression?" she asked, puzzled by his comment.

"You seem as if you are hiding something – or someone."

Annabel was amazed at his astuteness. There was no harm in telling him about Damien – she would probably never see him again after tonight.

"Maybe I have someone, or did, but it couldn't be," Annabel smiled.

"Come now, surely you don't think there's only one person for you! I believe I could be happy with many different women!"

Annabel pursed her lips and frowned, until she resembled a stern schoolteacher. "Nico, I'll be forty in two weeks and I can honestly say, hand on my heart, that there was only one big love in my life. Yes, I am happy with my husband and could have been happy with someone else but you only get one bite of the cherry."

Nico frowned in a naïf attractive way, unsure what she meant by a bite of the cherry.

Annabel gazed into Nico's brown eyes and wanted to kiss him. His eyes were not unlike Damien's, but were more youthful than his. They stood, gazing into each other's eyes, with only the sound of the ocean as a reminder that they stood on a beach. She felt a wave of emotion rush over her – echoed by the sound of the waves crashing on the shore. Something had flipped deep inside. She didn't feel like the mother-of-three wife-of-Colin as she stood next to this handsome young man.

She looked away. "Do you mind if we go back to the hotel?" she asked abruptly.

"That's okay." Disappointment was heavy in Nico's voice. He had secretly hoped she would be mellowed by the symphony of the waves.

They returned to the promenade and walked slowly along it until their hotel came into view, the tension between them building with each step.

Nico held the door open as they entered the hotel. Inside, he caught her by the wrist so she could move no further. Then he leaned forward and softly whispered in her ear.

"Please, come to my room."

Annabel closed her eyes. She needed to be transported back to the cabin on the ship. She desperately wanted to feel adored. Her lovemaking with Colin had become stale and routine, and the strong and sensual way that Nico was gripping her wrist left her feeling powerless.

"Okay," she murmured softly.

She stood quietly next to Nico on the ride in the lift to his room. Betrayal was an emotion she didn't relish and she felt like an adulteress even before the lift came to a sudden stop. The smell of salty wetsuits and surfing equipment wafted around her as he opened the bedroom door.

"It's in a bit of a mess," he said, scratching his head and looking around the untidy room.

"It's okay," Annabel assured him. She was feeling her age as he settled the bedcovers and kicked the clothing that lay on the floor under the bed.

"Would you like a drink?" he asked, pointing to a bottle of Kahlua on the dressing-table.

"Why not?" Annabel shrugged.

Nico rushed into the bathroom where he found two glasses that he proceeded to rinse. He filled them to the brim with Kahlua and handed one to Annabel who was feeling every minute of her thirty-nine years. She took a sip and put it down on the dressing-table. Again their eyes met as they had done on the beach and Annabel knew this time that she wanted him. It was too late to change her mind. The feelings of guilt were overtaken by lust. No one would ever know and she would be back in the lobby before Kate. She took Nico's glass and placed it down beside hers. She felt as though she was possessed by someone else, a cooler more confident version of herself that had never really existed.

Staring into his eyes she slowly undid the buttons on her blouse one by one. Images of Colin and her children started to flash before her. Was she really going to do this? As she reached the final button, Nico could contain himself no more and took her nervously in his arms. Annabel surrendered to the emotions sweeping over her as Nico slowly and gently kissed her neck and face. She tried, but found it hard to blank out the picture of Damien that suddenly appeared in her mind's eye as she felt Nico's tongue travel to her ear and back to her lips.

"Let me take this off," she pleaded and she slipped off her shirt and bra with alacrity. Nico peeled off his T-shirt and proceeded to kiss her nipples as she arched her back and embraced the sensual experience.

Slowly they removed the rest of their clothing and in the heady few moments that followed they found themselves entwined on Nico's bed. Annabel felt a shiver up her spine as he entered her. It had been a long time since she had felt such excitement while making love. He fitted like a glove and his rhythmic moves matched hers perfectly. She found herself rushing to a climax before him and shuddered under its force. Nico came shortly after her and collapsed onto the space beside her.

"Bellisimo!" Nico exclaimed.

"Now I know where the term 'Italian Stallion' comes from!" Annabel laughed.

Any tension between them had been washed away like the Atlantic tide. Annabel felt rejuvenated by the experience. She had been denying herself passion for too long.

Nico raised his head from the pillow and stared at her profile.

"You really are a beautiful woman, Annabel. Why so sad and unfulfilled?"

Annabel wished the ground would open up and swallow her. She didn't want any post mortems or dragging up of emotions. She had committed adultery and not for the first time. The best thing to do now was to pretend that it had never happened.

"We'd better get down to the others," she sighed.

Nico looked at her in disappointment. "Maybe we have time for one more? Please?"

"I think we'd better go," she said as she started to get dressed.

The small bar in the foyer was speckled with a variety of surfers and tourists. Kate and Brett approached the bar, breathless and exuberant from their brief union.

"You were quick," Annabel grinned at Kate, noticing that her friend's blouse – the one they had recently purchased in Galeries Lafayette – was on inside out.

"Have a beer, mate?" Brett asked Nico.

Nico nodded. Brett turned to ask the women if they would like a drink but paused when he found that they were having a quiet exchange.

"Actually, would you mind if I went to bed?" Annabel was saying to Kate in a muted tone. "I'm kind of tired," She was anxious to have a shower and try and wash away her infidelity.

"Not at all – I'll call it a night too," said Kate and she turned and grinned at Brett. "Guys, we'll leave you to it. It was really nice meeting you!"

Brett and Nico nodded at the two women.

"Goodnight, Kate, it was very nice meeting you too!" Brett grinned mischievously.

Nico smiled at Annabel. "Maybe we'll bump into you tomorrow?"

"Maybe," Annabel replied.

The two men leaned against the bar counter on their elbows, and watched Kate and Annabel as they walked slowly over to the lift and stepped inside.

As the doors closed Kate waved a final goodnight to the boys.

"Go on then . . . was he worth it?" Annabel joked, trying to divert her own thoughts from what she had just done.

Annabel woke first the next morning. The shutters kept out the brilliant sunshine.

"How's the head?" she murmured over to Kate.

"Fine, I think," Kate whispered. "Was I dreaming or did I have a surfer back here last night?"

"That was no dream. It was a Class A type night out with Annabel and Kate. Kate scores and Annabel gets the friend to keep her company."

"I'm sorry, Annabel," Kate sighed. "You'd think I'd have more sense –"

"Don't say 'at my age'," Annabel interrupted. "If that's what it takes to prove we're not over the hill I'll go along with it any time." She jumped out of the bed and started to peel off her pink silk pyjamas. "So, where are we going today?"

Kate put her hand up to her head, shielding her eyes from an invisible light. "I was thinking we should go into Bayonne – it's only ten minutes on the bus."

"I'd love a go on a bus," Annabel giggled. "I can't remember the last time I was on one."

A short time later the two friends were squeezed into the narrow seats two rows from the back of the bus.

"This is great," Annabel beamed.

"Wait until you see this place! It's lovely," Kate said excitedly.

The twin spires of Bayonne Cathedral jutted up from the cityscape as they approached the town. Rows of impressive well-laid-out streets guided them towards the banks of the River Adour. Kate rang the bell on the pole beside her and the bus slowed and stopped.

They stepped out and strolled over to the river.

"This place is gorgeous!" Annabel sighed, looking out on the gushing water of the River Adour. "I love the view. Can we have breakfast around here?"

"Over there – it's nice enough to sit outside – what do you think?" Kate pointed at an open square by the river.

The two sat on the comfortable cane chairs under the large green umbrellas of the Café du Théâtre. A handsome waiter in a formal waistcoat strolled over and took their order of hot chocolate and croissants.

"It's so perfect here. I feel like doing something crazy today," said Kate.

"I think you did something crazy last night!" Annabel replied. *And so did I!*

"That was called maintenance," said Kate. She still had a twinkle in her eye from the encounter.

"So where are you going to drag me after the croissants?" Annabel asked, pretending fear and trepidation – which in truth she did feel to some degree.

"Not sure yet but there's definitely something out there waiting for us."

After breakfast they sauntered through the meandering streets until they reached the magnificent Bayonne Cathedral which towered above their heads. They paid it a brief visit, the artist in Kate habitually drilled into grasping every opportunity of a new source of inspiration. Droplets of coloured light dappled the floor tiles from the tall narrow windows.

"It's so cold in here," Annabel complained.

Kate realised that these sorts of sights didn't appeal to her friend. "Come on, I'm sure you'd much rather be in Galeries Lafayette," she said, linking Annabel by the arm.

"Am I that shallow?" Annabel winced.

"I'd never use that word for you. It's just a matter of taste! And different talents." She mused a little as they walked, then, hoping her friend would not be offended, said, "But, you know, you should think about developing those talents – you were clever in school and maybe you could use that brain of yours to do something for yourself now."

"I really would love to study again, now that you mention it. But, like I said, I have no time . . ."

"I always thought you should have finished your degree, Annabel. It's no burden to carry. It's probably the only sensible thing you *didn't* do." Kate raised an eyebrow.

"Maybe I will get around to it," said Annabel, then added pensively, "I might be able to use my two years before dropping out as a springboard."

"Life begins at forty, Annabel!"

They wandered down a hairpin bend and found themselves back at the river's edge. The buildings were tall and painted sugary tones of pink, almond and pale blue. Coloured shutters framed long narrow windows that went up four or five storeys. The muddy water of the river flowed slowly, dividing the town in half. Along the walkway tall streetlamps were decoratively surrounded with trailing flower baskets. Annabel was entranced by the scene and got a shock when Kate let out a wild squeal.

"I don't believe it! It's a sign!"

"What's a sign?"

"Look!" Kate pointed at a shop painted a garish tomato-soup red. The huge window was littered with pieces of paper covered with fantastic imaginative designs. "This is exactly what I was looking for and they have a picture of the Third Eye."

The Third Eye comment made Annabel take notice. "What is that place?"

"It's a tattooist's parlour and it's the perfect activity for us before lunch."

"You must be nuts, Kate!"

"I've never been more serious in my life."

Fifteen minutes later Annabel was lying on a tatty, black-leather chair that had spent a good deal of its life supporting terrified dental patients. Her right leg was wrapped around a grungy tattooist's arm and he was etching an image of the Third Eye slowly and carefully onto her inner ankle. His dreadlocks would have reached down to his elbows but were tied back in a massive knot resembling the ropes on the huge fishing trawlers in Howth. At least that's what Annabel was fixing her thoughts on, anything other than the needle pricking her ankle. She was trying to remember giving birth and decided this didn't hurt any less.

"I don't know what Colin is going to think about this!" she cried with tears trickling down her cheeks.

"Don't mind him. No one will notice it on your ankle," Kate assured her.

"I hope you're right. You've had me do some crazy things over the years, Kate, but this takes the biscuit."

Half an hour later Annabel slid shakily off the chair. Her ankle no longer stung but she felt numb and jelly-like from the thighs down.

"Your turn, Kate," she said, with the only feeling of pleasure she could muster from the experience.

Kate took the needle like a professional and casually looked through a catalogue to focus her attention off the pain when the needle touched against her bone. Kate jumped off the chair after only twenty minutes with her tattoo complete.

"Hey, how come he did it much quicker on you?" Annabel moaned.

"That's because he was only repeating what he had done a few minutes earlier," Kate grinned.

"No wonder you made me go first," Annabel sulked.

"I made you go first because I knew I'd go through with it and I didn't want you chickening out!"

Kate did have a point and Annabel wasn't going to argue it.

"Well, what do you think?" Kate flexed her foot this way and that.

"I really like mine, not so sure about yours!"

Kate laughed. She liked the cheeky Annabel that was emerging with the new tattoo.

They paid the young tattoo artist and, with their new decorations, the two continued their trek through the town past the most unusual shops.

They stalled at an army surplus store.

"Look, a bullet right through the top!" Annabel gasped, holding up a World War II German helmet. "There are even numbers and battalions listed on the belts and boots."

"It's a bit like a graveyard," Kate nodded. "I've a friend in Paris who would love to get her hands on this stuff. She's always doing sculptures with historic pieces."

Annabel sighed as she stood there gazing at the German helmet in her hands. "I really need a career, Kate. This break is making me realise that I spend too much time living through my kids' activities."

"Is there anything stopping you?"

"Colin, for one," Annabel sighed. "He'd hate me to study. He likes the wife-at-home routine."

"This is your life, Annabel, and maybe it's time you started realising that you've got to take the bull by the horns. You've only got one life."

"I thought you believed in reincarnation?" Annabel asked in surprise.

"I do, I do, but you know what I mean," Kate mumbled and slipped her arm through her friend's once more. "Come on. Let's get lunch."

They were spoilt for choice as they took a shortcut through the bustling market spotted with chic little eateries full to the brim with lunch-time customers.

"Colin asked me to get him some pâté – he says the French keep the best and export the crap."

"I hate to say it but I have to agree with him," Kate nodded. "They do the same with the wine."

Kate had never liked Colin. It was probably the only stumbling block in her relationship with Annabel. What a pity Annabel hadn't finished her degree! Then she would never have met him . . .

Annabel's father had died while she was in the second year of her course at college and, as she was the only one at home, her mother was very dependent on her. She couldn't let her mum pay for the remainder of her education and there were debts that her sisters left behind from their degrees before emigrating to the four corners of the world. So she did the dutiful thing and left her arts degree course in University College Dublin and got a job. A small number of positions became available in the Bank of Ireland a while later and she jumped at the opportunity to earn a steady income. She made some good friends but every now and again escaped up to Thomas Street to the decadent underground parties Kate frequented in Art College.

Days after getting her first-class honours degree in Fine Art Kate set off on a Boeing 747 for New York. The spontaneous artist had a placement organised in a posh downtown gallery and set off to take on the world, leaving Annabel with a big Kate-shaped hole in her life.

Annabel floundered around Nassau Street in her Bank of Ireland uniform five days a week but relished Fridays, as all the girls in the bank did. They usually went to O'Neill's Pub. One particular Friday, however, she found herself enticed by two of the girls to the Horseshoe Bar in the Shelbourne Hotel. It was the sort of place only professional people frequented but she agreed to go under duress, and the influence of three bottles of Stag.

Annabel looked great in the pencil-thin skirts and broad-shouldered business jackets that were so fashionable at the time and she turned many heads that evening in the bar. Her blonde hair was tied back neatly in a knot and her hips swayed as she walked carefully in her pointed court shoes.

Colin was over by the fireplace with a cigar and pint of Smithwicks in his hand, looking like a man ten years his senior. His hairline receded deeply but Annabel had always liked the mature look. He spotted her the minute she entered the room and made a beeline straight for her.

"Let me get you a drink," he said, his arrogance and forwardness bowling Annabel into quiet submission.

She listened for two hours to him telling how much money he made and what a fantastic position he had in KPBM and how he was about to be made the youngest partner in the company's history. It wasn't love at first sight by any means but he wooed her with an intensity that finally wore her down. The courtship lasted two years and true to his predictions he did become the youngest partner in the company. It was a time in Ireland before the Celtic Tiger raged and men of such means were few and far between. Annabel's first home with her new husband was a large four-bedroom detached house with spectacular views over Dublin Bay and there weren't many girls who could boast such security and luxury. All she had to do in return was live her life by Colin's book and her children followed as compensation. She felt that it was the right thing to do. And with her older sisters abroad but their debts still in Dublin, her mother was delighted with the match. Everyone was delighted with the match – except Kate.

"Would Colin like this?" Kate asked, holding up a pot of Landes Foie Gras.

It was certainly packaged to please and the cream ceramic pot was reusable and would suit Annabel's kitchen very well.

They ambled along the spotless terracotta tiles, breathing in the pungent aromas from the array of cheeses and cured meats. The stalls were set in a rectangular high-beamed hall with a wooden roof. Rows of ripe colourful vegetables and floral displays made the shopping experience pleasurable to the eye.

"Will you stay in France? The lifestyle seems to suit you," said Annabel as they strolled through the stalls.

"Yes, it does. But I'd like to go back to live in Ireland sometime soon. The only thing putting me off is the boys' Granny and Granddad Macken. It's hard enough putting up with them coming here once a year. I swear they still haven't forgiven me for remarrying after Harry's death."

"I have never understood that. You were left a widow at twenty-eight years of age – surely they didn't expect you to live the rest of your life alone?"

"Harry and I were tempestuous at the best of times. I sometimes wonder if we'd have killed each other if we were still together. There were moments of such extreme love and desire and then others when if I was given a length of rope I'd have happily strung him up."

"Well, eloping off to the Caribbean the way you did didn't exactly please either your parents or his." Annabel too had felt let down when she got a phone call from Jamaica informing her that her best friend was now Mrs Macken. Kate had forgotten their childhood vows to be each other's bridesmaids, but at least she got a chance to be her bridesmaid not too long later.

"Harry was always going to be a sailing bum, jumping from yacht to yacht. I never saw it at the time." Kate's mouth widened slightly.

"Look at what you got from your marriage though – your two beautiful sons," Annabel said reassuringly.

"I don't think I ever told you we had a row that day, before he left for his slot in the Fastnet. I had just found out I was pregnant and he was furious. He said he didn't want to be a father."

"Kate!" Annabel was aghast. "You never told me!"

"What was the point? Everyone was in mourning after he fell off the boat. I thought it was better to say that he wanted a family like I did."

"He'd be very proud if he saw them now," Annabel comforted her pensive friend.

"Do you know, I think he would!" Kate replied, her spirits lifted by unfolding her secret. "Now, how dare you be so serious! Let's get some wine inside us."

On leaving the market, they doubled back up a side street and were tugged into the Café Bayonne by the alluring décor and aroma of delicious Basque gourmet food.

A little black-haired waitress with thickset eyebrows welcomed them in and they took the only table for two, in a corner by the window. Paintings of bullfighters decorated the bare stone walls. The girls settled on the wooden chairs and found the string-woven seats surprisingly comfortable.

"Une carafe de vin rosé, s'il vous plaît," Kate ordered.

"Did you notice everyone in here has jet-black hair?" Annabel whispered when the waitress was out of earshot.

"This is the capital of the French Basque region. The people are totally different here to those in the rest of France. Did you notice the white and red everywhere?"

"Now that you come to mention it, yes." Annabel was amazed that it had taken her so long to make the link. Red and white bunting hung from the coatstand at the back of the restaurant and the Basque flag was displayed above the wooden bar.

"Confit of duck looks good," Kate said, licking her lips.

"I might go for a salad," Annabel said, her eyes scanning the menu.

"That's why you're a size ten and I'm a fourteen."

"What does it matter?" Annabel smiled, secretly delighted at the remark.

"Do you have to work hard to keep your shape? I've given up!"

"I go to the gym at least three times a week when the kids are at school and then I play tennis another morning, so I suppose I am fairly fit. I had to give up the glass of wine with my dinner – that was really piling the calories on."

"I'd rather die than give up my wine in the evening," Kate grinned.

"But you're an artist – it probably helps you paint," Annabel nodded.

"I do most of my work early in the mornings; the light is better. So down to more interesting matters – have you any gossip from the old homeland?"

Annabel had to stop and think for a while. "Well, since our twenty-year school reunion, there've been about three divorces and even a complete swap-over."

"I don't believe you!" Kate was aghast and hardly acknowledged the waitress as she placed a carafe of rosé and two glasses down on the table.

"You like to order?" the little waitress interrupted with her hands resting firmly on her hips.

"Eh, yeah," said Annabel.

"Go on, live a little!" said Kate. "Have the confit of duck!"

"Okay – the confit of duck and house salad, *s'il vous plaît*," Annabel said to the waitress.

"*Même, s'il vous plaît*," Kate said, turning her attention swiftly back to Annabel. "You know, things have definitely changed from the Ireland I knew."

"It's unrecognisable!"

"I know now why I always get Mum and Dad to come over to France! Mind you, it's just been Mum lately – Dad's not keen on flying as you know."

Annabel felt a blush rise in her cheeks.

"Do you ever wish you'd lived abroad?" Kate asked. "Though you're hardly going to try it at this stage."

"I'm a home bird, me. After Dad died I always felt I had to look out for Mum. I mean, Vicky and Lucy are hardly going to look after her from Washington and New Zealand."

"That's what you get for being the reliable member of the family," Kate berated her jovially.

"I don't mind. It has its benefits – Mum is only around the corner, and she's great for baby-sitting."

"How does Colin feel about his mother-in-law being in such close proximity?"

"It suits him because he doesn't get home before eight most nights and then he plays golf all day Saturday. We really only get to talk on a Saturday night and most weekends we are entertaining or going to other people's for dinner. Sunday lunch is always in the golf club and then he reads the Sunday papers and I bring the kids for a swim." Annabel sounded listless. She ran her finger along the rim of her wineglass before taking a sip. "That's the routine."

"I know you've carved a comfortable life for yourself, Annabel, but are you not a bit bored?" Kate leaned over the table and stared intensely at her friend.

"We don't all want to be living in different places with contractual husbands," Annabel quipped. Kate's remark had really hurt and, although she felt she was a bit harsh in her response, she did not need judgement from her Bohemian friend.

"I didn't mean it like that, Annabel. Come on, you know me well enough by now!"

"Yeah, sorry," Annabel said, shaking her head. "Maybe you touched on a nerve."

The dark waitress arrived with a basket of bread in the crook of her arm and a plate of lunch resting in each hand. The carafe of wine was refilled once more and by the time they had sated their appetites the world was a much mellower place.

"So how's the tattoo?" Kate asked. "Still sore?"

"A bit." Annabel pushed her chair back and had a quick peek at her newly inked ankle. "I think mine is bigger than yours, Kate."

"Optical illusion," Kate smiled as she took her leg out from under the table and put it next to Annabel's. "You have skinnier ankles."

The two laughed – both high on the fact that they were spending this precious day together.

"I can't believe I'm here at three o'clock on a Friday afternoon. Taylor has to be collected from piano at this time," Annabel grinned.

"Sounds like you deserve a break," Kate smiled. She took a sip from her wine and turned her head sideways to look out the window as a familiar figure came into view. She started waving furiously, to Annabel's amusement.

Suddenly a towering figure became clear from the other side of the glass. Kate beckoned at him to join them.

Nico appeared to be limping slightly as he made his way over to the women's table. He took a chair from an empty table and dragged it over to theirs.

"Fancy meeting you again," Kate grinned. "We've only just ordered lunch – would you like to have some?"

Nico smiled over at Annabel. He looked even dishier in daylight.

"No, thanks, but I'll have a drink with you, if I'm not interrupting."

"Not at all," Kate beamed. "Sure he isn't, Annabel?"

"It's nice to see you again," Annabel smiled coyly. She moved around nervously on her chair as the mixed emotions of lust and guilt came back to haunt her.

"So what brings you to Bayonne?" Kate was keen to find out if Brett was with him.

"I went to see a doctor about my knee. I stretched a ligament this morning which has put an end to my surfing for this week," he sighed.

"That's a shame," Annabel said, as she took a sip from her glass.

"Do you drink rosé?" Kate asked, as she filled an empty glass on the table.

"Yes, thank you," Nico said, taking the glass from her and raising it in the air in appreciation.

"Is Brett out riding the waves?" Kate asked.

"He has been surfing since nine o'clock this morning," Nico informed her. "He is one of the fittest guys I know."

I'll vouch for that, thought Kate. "So, Nico, have you got any plans for later?"

"Not yet."

"Do you want to meet up like last night, and maybe we could get to the casino this time?" Kate giggled.

"Sure!" Nico smiled over at Annabel who was remaining very quiet. "We're meeting some guy for a drink after dinner – so, about nine thirty?"

"That sounds good," Kate smiled. "Why don't we go to Desperados again?"

"That's fine," Nico said, looking anxiously over at Annabel. "See you later then."

Annabel nodded as he disappeared out the door.

"That was a bit of luck, wasn't it?" Kate grinned. "I think he's got the hots for you, Annabel!"

"Oh, come on! Don't tease!" protested Annabel, feeling very ill at ease.

After they had eaten Kate ordered coffees which they dawdled over.

"Do you want to go back to Biarritz, or stay here?" Annabel asked.

"I'm happy to go back, if you've got everything you want," Kate said.

The two women, complete with tattoos and a pot of foie gras to show for their excursion, sat silently on the bus. There was no need to talk. They were as comfortable in each other's company as they could possibly be.

This holiday was bliss. Annabel was fretting a little about the situation with Nico but decided not to allow that spoil this precious time in Kate's company. She would cross the Nico Bridge when she came to it that evening. Now she was happily looking forward to putting her tired feet up back at the hotel – that tattoo did ache in fact! – a luxurious leisurely bath, then perhaps a stroll on the promenade and a drink in a stylish bar, before enjoying another relaxed and intimate evening meal with her dearest friend.

Luckily for her present peace of mind, she had no inkling of the catastrophe that was to befall their friendship in the wake of that evening meal, or that the handsome young surfer and her episode of guilty passion were the very least of her worries.

4

Saturday 11th March, 11.15a.m

Kate couldn't concentrate on her novel. It had been an enthralling read on the journey to Biarritz but it seemed dreary on the return leg. Everything seemed different, including how she perceived her relationship with her father and how she felt about her parents' relationship. She was hurt by what her father had done. But she was even more hurt by her best friend. The fact that it was over twenty years ago that she had betrayed her and never said a word rubbed salt into the wound. She must have been laughing at her all this time.

Underneath the rhythmic hum of the train's wheels Kate faintly heard her mobile ring out. She took it from her pocket and was thankful for caller identification. She switched it off immediately on recognising Annabel's number. How could she talk to her ever again?

It was hard to remember back to the ferry trip across St

George's Channel – twenty years was a long time. If only she hadn't gone off with that French guy that night . . .

Annabel was in the tiny shower when Kate turned the handle on their cabin door the next morning.

"I'm so sorry for disappearing all night," she said sheepishly through the little bathroom door.

"That's okay!" Annabel called out. "I had a great night's sleep."

"Annabel, I think I'm in love – that guy is the most delicious creature that God created!"

Annabel stepped out of the bathroom dripping water and drying her hair with an off-white towel.

"What about poor Shane?" she asked.

"Annabel, what Shane doesn't know won't hurt him – anyway I keep telling you that ours is a non-jealous type of relationship."

"You mean he's so crazy about you he'll forgive any mischief you're likely to get up to?"

"Annabel, you make me sound like a slapper!" Kate berated her.

The appalling nerve of her! thought Kate now. When all this time Annabel was the slapper! She wanted to go to Annabel, roar and shout and scream at her but decided that it was best for the moment to let it all settle down – until she figured out what to do.

Back in Biarritz, Annabel gave her key slowly over to the

receptionist. Her head throbbed and her stomach ached and she realised that it was more than a hangover that had her feeling this way. She then handed over eighty euros to cover her half of the bill.

"I hope you had a nice stay?" the receptionist beamed.

"Lovely, thanks," Annabel gave a wry smile in return. "Could you call me a taxi for the airport, please?"

"Of course."

Annabel waited in the small foyer where only two nights ago she had stood with her best friend and the two surfers. If only she could turn the clock back. She vaguely remembered Nico putting her to bed the night before but wasn't bothered about him. She was no longer concerned about any guilt she might carry home after her indiscretion. All she cared about was Kate and explaining her story properly – without the influence of alcohol. If Kate realised how much Annabel adored her father maybe she would feel differently. There was nothing sordid about their love affair and they both did what was best for their loved ones in the end. Surely Kate could see it from their point of view?

A taxi driver entered the foyer and the receptionist pointed over in Annabel's direction.

"Bonjour," he said with a nod of his head and took her case with great courtesy.

Annabel sat silently in the back of the Mercedes Benz all the way to the airport. She was used to travelling in Mercs – Colin always drove one as his company car. She was going back to the life she knew so well. But everything seemed different now. She'd had a brief sample of what she'd been missing all these years, the other night with Nico. That passion had never been there in her relationship with Colin – and now the thought of making love to him again sickened her right through to the pit of her stomach. She would love to have the guts to do something about it but it would mean giving up so much – security, position, comfort. At the moment, though, none of those seemed very important. All that really mattered was Kate and making amends to her.

The car pulled up to the Departures Hall and Annabel paid the driver his dues. The airport was so small and convenient that in only minutes she was passing through the tiny duty-free, after checking her bags in.

"*Mesdames et messieurs, votre vol pour Dublin est près á l'embarquement,*" a voice called over the Tannoy.

Annabel joined the small queue. Most of those around her were business people with briefcases in hand. Not many holidaymakers this time of year.

Inside the plane, the cabin crew were allocating passengers to their seats. Annabel stood back – next to the cockpit door. She was in no hurry to be seated, or to return home to Dublin for that matter.

Just then the captain squeezed out through the cockpit door to make his final arrangements with the red-cap for take-off.

"Annabel!"

She turned her head and was confronted by Shane Gleason, looking spruce in his black uniform with four gold bars on his cuffs.

"I don't believe it," she said as she threw her arms around his neck and they embraced warmly.

"Well, you're a sight for sore eyes, Annabel – you look great!"

"The way I feel this morning I don't think that's true! But you don't look too bad yourself, Mr Gleason," she grinned. "Who'd have thought all those years ago on Dollymount strand that we'd meet this way . . . and hey, I was just with Kate! She lives in France now."

His eyes lit up on the mention of Kate's name. "I met her a couple of years back. I suppose she's busy with her husband and the boys?" He gave a grave nod of his head.

"Actually, she recently split up from Stefan," Annabel said.

"Really!" He looked pleased at this news. "I mean, that's terrible!" He shook his head. "God, Annabel, there's so much I'd love to talk to you about! If this was pre-9/11 I could have you up in the cockpit and we'd have a great old chat but we have to be so careful now with security regulations."

"That's okay," Annabel smiled.

"I have to go – talk later?"

"Sure."

Shane took his paperwork from the red-cap, who was anxious to sign off the passengers and avoid any delay, and went back into his tiny cell-like cockpit.

Annabel took her window seat and started to read her copy of *Hello* magazine. But she couldn't concentrate on anything much as she could hear Shane's voice over the intercom.

Shane and Kate. Maybe she could get the two of them in touch again. He'd seemed very interested when she mentioned that Kate's relationship with Stefan was over. Meeting Shane was a godsend. She needed a way to break back into her friend's life.

The Airbus settled into a cruise at thirty-eight thousand feet and Annabel ordered herself a brandy and ginger ale. So what if it was only eleven-thirty in the morning? She had done something far more decadent the night before. She always associated flying with brandy and today she needed it more than usual. She wasn't sure if the drink would help her hangover but it couldn't make her feel much worse.

She crossed her legs and the tattoo on her ankle caught her eye. It was the only physical link between herself and Kate and she was so glad now that Kate had made her go through with it. They were meant to be friends forever, and the engraving on her ankle was testament to it. She reached down and brushed her fingers over the marks. The Third Eye was very significant to them both – since the very beginning of their relationship.

"Is there anybody sitting there?" Annabel asked, standing with her mousy blonde curls and pressed school uniform, before a table for two occupied by a single girl.

The girl looked up from under her mop of black hair to see who the voice belonged to.

She clearly wanted a table to herself so she could spread her books and bag around, but the class was filling up and she was going to have to share her table. Without answering, she moved her bag off the chair and stuck her head back into her book.

Annabel didn't know it at the time but Kate was still angry with her parents for leaving their lovely home on the other side of the city. Thirteen was a horrible age to start all over again and make new friends.

"Hi, I'm Annabel. I'm new to Howth – all the other girls seem to know each other, don't they?" She gestured around the room at the girls sitting on the edge of desks and huddled around each other, relaying the news from the summer holidays.

The girl looked up at Annabel once more and grunted. "I'm Kate," she said.

"I love that drawing on your bag – is it meant to be the sun?" Annabel asked. She was delighted to have someone to talk to, no matter how reluctantly.

Kate clicked the roof of her mouth with her tongue. "It's The Third Eye," she droned.

Annabel didn't want to ask what the Third Eye was, but she would make it her business to find out when she got home, that evening.

"What date is your birthday?" she said instead. "I'm an Aries – March 24th."

Kate looked sick and Annabel wondered why. She didn't know that this didn't suit Kate's plans at all. She wanted to be the interesting girl at the back of the class that nobody would talk to because they were afraid of her – but this mousy-looking girl seemed intent on changing that. Was this perky girl going to get the hint or not? To make matters worse they had something in common – Kate was an Aries too.

"Cabin crew, your seats for landing, please," Shane's voice called over the intercom.

An air stewardess scurried over to Annabel shortly before the tall ESB towers in Dublin Bay came into view.

"The captain would like to know if you're able to meet him for coffee after we arrive in Dublin airport?" she said, with a bat of her long curly eyelashes and pursed-pink lips.

"Tell him I'd love to!" Annabel replied.

5

The wrought-iron gate seemed heavier now to open than ever before. The gravel pathway crunched under her feet as she drew near the turquoise front door. God, I love this place, she thought. The mountains hung like a velvet drape behind her charming *gîte* and she let out a sigh of relief now that she was finally home. The larks were singing an accolade in the cypress trees for her return.

"Let me help you," Fabian urged, taking the key out of her hand and putting it into the lock for her.

"Thanks," Kate replied. "It was great to see you at the station."

"Serendipity, *ma chérie*," Fabian grinned. "And we are blessed with more than our fair share living in this beautiful place. Are you not exhausted from your trip to the ocean?"

"I grew up by the sea, don't forget!"

"*Mon dieu,* but of course. So tell me everything," Fabian said with a flick of the wrist to his fringe. "How was your friend?"

"I need a coffee and cigarette first," Kate said with a shake of her head.

"But, Kate, you don't smoke any more!"

"I'm taking it up again, Fabian," Kate replied mysteriously. "I swear, you think you know someone and then . . ."

"Say no more until we are sitting down and you are able to tell everything." Fabian developed a spring in his step as they entered the cosy interior with rich burgundy tones on the walls and shiny black tiles on the floor.

The long-limbed Frenchman opened the weighty pine door that led into the kitchen. Kate followed anxiously, in a rush to put the percolator on and accelerate the telling of her tale.

"So, is Annabel still as delicious as that photograph you showed me?" Fabian asked, again brushing back his long black fringe with his fingers and making his nose appear even more prominent than when the hair was draped down over his face.

"Don't pretend you fancy her, Fabian!" Kate said scornfully. "You're talking to me, remember? And maybe it's time you told the rest of our friends that you're gay – most of them suspect it anyway."

Fabian was taken aback at Kate's sharp tone. "*Chérie,*" he said with a shake of his head, "I can still appreciate a good-looking woman, can't I?"

Kate wiped her brow and her right eye with her hand. It was a habit she had carried with her through life since she was a small child. Her brother Philip had fired a stone at her from his slingshot, missing her right eye by millimetres but cutting the skin under her eyebrow – she resorted to soothing it whenever she was stressed.

"Fabian, I am so sorry. I didn't mean to offend you. You are truly one of my dearest friends – if not the dearest at this very moment in time!"

"So what is it that has you in such a state? Tell Fabian!" He tapped the table with his fingernails as he sat down on one of the solid pinewood chairs.

Kate paused in her coffee-making and gazed at him earnestly. "You know when you think you know someone, and then they go and do something that's completely out of character?"

"It happens all the time," Fabian said remorsefully, sucking in the cheeks on his already skinny face.

"Exactly, but not with someone you've known for most of your life!"

"Ah, but that is just it," Fabian said with a sigh. "My own parents went off on a whim around the world and left me with my grandmother – I was only eleven."

Kate stopped still for a moment in bemusement. "You never told me that! I always thought your mother was ill and that was why your grandmother brought you up!"

"*Chérie,* I am not one to dwell in self-pity," he said with a shrug of his shoulders. "Please continue."

"Well, we both had a bit of a fling with these two surfing guys –"

"Would I have liked them?" Fabian asked mischievously.

"Definitely! I was straight up about my interest in Brett –"

"Nice name," Fabian interrupted again.

"Please, Fabian," she said, finding it difficult not to smile. "It turns out, while Brett and I were 'dancing in the moonlight', Annabel and his pal were at it in his room."

"And what is wrong with that?" Fabian smiled.

"Absolutely nothing – apart from the fact that she didn't tell me! We ran into her guy the next day in Bayonne and she never said a thing until later that night – after a few drinks she blurts it out . . ." Kate had to compose herself before divulging any more. "And then . . ."

"Yes?"

"And then . . . then she said that she slept with my father years ago . . . and had the audacity to say that she loved him!"

Fabian still wasn't fazed. "I slept with my friend's father too when I was only seventeen!" he informed her, not quite seeing Kate's view on the situation.

This was information she really didn't need to know. She reached up and scratched her head vigorously with both of her hands.

"Don't you see my point?" she almost screamed. She flopped down on one of the pine chairs as tears started to fill her eyes.

"Of course, I do," Fabian said in a more serious tone. "But it was a long time ago, and is it really worth losing a friend over one little, how you say – discrepancy?"

"That's just it," Kate sighed. "I'm not sure how long it went on for, or what exactly the relationship was about. And, I mean, did . . . did she seduce him . . . or did he seduce her?"

"You mean you left Biarritz without talking it through?" Fabian was surprised.

Kate nodded.

"Maybe you need to talk to Annabel properly if this is upsetting you too much," Fabian said, putting a consoling hand on his friend's arm. "Now, where is that coffee you were about to make me?"

Kate gave him a weak smile as she stood up again and went over to her granite counter-top. Maybe she was overreacting but she couldn't hide her true feelings. Her whole quality world had been rocked and she didn't know how she was going to make it better again.

Shane waved at Annabel from the cockpit as she followed the air stewardess on the pedestrian walkway.

"The staff canteen is on the first floor," the pretty uniformed girl told Annabel.

The rest of the journey to the tiny dining-room was silent.

"Tea or coffee?" the stewardess asked when they entered the canteen.

You must get so sick of saying that, thought Annabel. "Coffee, please," she replied.

The stewardess clip-clopped over to the Burca boiler and filled a styrofoam cup with water and a spoon of

Nescafé instant coffee. She rested it down on the table in front of Annabel.

"The Captain will be here soon," she said, and slipped away as quickly as her high heels could take her.

The Captain! Annabel thought. Even though she had witnessed Shane in his working capacity first-hand, she still found it difficult to think of him as a captain of a plane. The Star Ship Enterprise maybe, but not a real plane.

No sooner had Annabel opened her magazine than Shane came through the swing-doors. He rushed over to Annabel and gave her a kiss on the cheek before sitting down beside her.

"Sorry I'm dragging you to this place but I only have a little while – I'm off to Birmingham in half an hour."

"The lifestyle of the jet-jockey!" Annabel teased.

"It's not such a glamorous job any more – Airjet have seen to that!" Shane groaned. "But it pays the bills! So, tell me, how's Kate?"

"She's looking great and her paintings are flying, excuse the pun, out of all the top galleries in Paris!"

Shane shifted around anxiously on the seat, keen to ask the next question. "And what did you say about her marriage?"

"Stefan found himself a younger model, his PA to be precise, and he and Kate have an amicable divorce of sorts in process. She's happy to be on her own. She talked about you though!"

"I suppose you guys were reminiscing about the

good old days on Dollymount strand!" he said with a grin.

"She still thinks very fondly of you and was disappointed when you lost touch after meeting in Toulouse."

"That was entirely my fault," he said, as he rubbed his forehead gravely. "Her number was on my old phone and I never changed it over. To be honest, I could have got it easily from her parents but . . ."

"Why didn't you call her again?" Annabel felt she knew what his answer would be but needed to ask him nonetheless.

"Honestly? I was only recently married after I met her that time and I couldn't stop thinking about her." His furrowed brow showed strain as he spoke from the depth of his heart. "The few times we spoke afterwards I'd be daydreaming about her for days, weeks!"

"Not a good preoccupation for a newlywed!" Annabel agreed. "If it's any consolation she was in a right state too. She said she couldn't paint for six months after meeting you."

Shane jerked his head back with surprise. "She said that?"

"What is it with you pair?" Annabel sighed. "You were always the couple most likely to get it together. What went wrong?"

"I think I pressurised her, Annabel." Shane's head lowered. "She was a free spirit, as we both know. I never minded her little flirtations or flings but when she went off to the States that time after college she never asked me to join her."

"She said that you didn't want to go away!" Annabel was puzzled by this revelation.

"We'd been together for a long time and she wanted to do her own thing." Shane turned his head and looked out at the sky through the only window in the canteen. "It took me years to recover."

"It must have been hard," Annabel replied sympathetically.

"I'll never forget hearing about her first marriage." Shane turned his head back until he was looking straight at Annabel again. "I was so mad with her! Kate does first and then thinks later!"

"I know what you mean," Annabel nodded. She reached into her purse and pulled out her mobile phone. "Look, why don't I give you her number now? I know she'd love to hear from you."

"I will be down in Toulouse for a line-check next month," he said pensively.

"Why don't you give her a call?" Annabel urged gently.

Shane reached into the pocket of his blazer and pulled out his Nokia. "What is it?" he grinned and got ready to tap Kate's digits into his phone.

A few minutes later he was disappearing through the swing-doors. Annabel took a sip from the now cold cup of coffee. She hoped that he would ring Kate but only time would tell.

She sighed. She didn't relish the thought of returning to Howth. She missed her kids but couldn't honestly say she was looking forward to seeing Colin.

The journey through Arrivals felt longer and lonelier than usual. A Toyota Avensis was at the top of the taxi rank and she sat heavily on the back seat as it drove through suburban Dublin. It had been a lovely surprise meeting Shane like that, but she felt sick every time she thought of Kate. She really needed to talk to her. But maybe it was best to give her some space and try to call in a few days.

The taxi rolled up the long driveway on the sunny side of Howth Hill until Annabel could clearly see her Edwardian mansion. The bay windows, complete with blossoming pansies and petunias dripping from the sills, were a favourite feature of hers. She longed for a bath in her luxurious en suite but knew that duty would call the minute she opened the hall door. Colin's car was nowhere to be seen and, as it was a fine day for a round or two of golf, she didn't need to be Miss Marple to figure out where he was. Her mum's Polo parked beside her Jeep in front of the large double garage told her a multitude.

"Thanks," she said to the driver as he opened the back door of the car for her. "How much?"

"Twenty euro," the driver said and nodded his head in appreciation as she handed him twenty-five and told him to keep the change.

The front door opened and her two youngest

children ran out to greet her. Rebecca was still in her tutu from ballet class and Taylor was all dressed up for a birthday party.

A kindly-faced woman with silver and blonde streaks in her hair came through the door and waved to Annabel.

"Hi, Mum!" Annabel called, still embracing her little girls fondly.

Lily came down the steps and gave her daughter a kiss on the cheek. "Did you have a nice time, love?"

"Great, thanks!" Annabel would never be able to tell her mother the truth.

"And how's Kate after that terrible marriage break-up?" Lily asked solemnly.

"She's doing grand," Annabel assured her mother.

"You are so lucky to have such a fine life, Annabel," Lily said with a shake of her head, "with such a solid and reliable husband."

"Yeah!" Annabel tried to sound convinced. She had a brief flashback to the hotel room in Biarritz and Nico's rippling biceps.

How was she going to cope now that she was back?

6

The crisp mountain air blew gently in through the top window in Kate's bedroom. She pushed her duvet back as the sunlight streamed in. She was glad she had left the shutters open for a change. It felt so good to wake in the comfort of her room. The roses on the walls and the bedcover were like old friends and far more reliable than the friend she had left behind in Biarritz a couple of weeks ago. She had to decide what she was going to do today. A call to her solicitor to check up on the divorce proceedings and maybe some lunch with Joy and Simon who lived next door – that would set her up nicely.

The more Kate tried to forget about Annabel, the more the image of her father and friend together flooded her head. There was no getting away from this, and sooner rather than later she was going to have to speak to them about it. She couldn't even contemplate painting at the moment.

After a leisurely shower she wrapped herself up in her cosy bathrobe and descended the stairs. She threw open the hall door on her way to the kitchen and found a fresh baguette on the doorstep. She smiled and thought of Fabian as she picked it up. He often left one for her before he went to work. She had a lot to be thankful for.

As she smothered the sliced baguette with homemade strawberry jam she felt a sense of calm and relaxation set in. Life was good in the Pyrénées and she had a lot of good friends.

Her thoughts were interrupted by the phone ringing loudly. She took a quick bite from her bread before answering and mumbling a "*Bonjour*" to the person at the other end of the line.

"Kate?"

"Mum!" Kate quickly gulped back the bread and tried to catch her breath.

"How are things? Did you have a good time in Biarritz?"

Kate pondered briefly – there was only one answer she could give her mother. "Yeah, I had a great time with Annabel – so what's new with you?"

"Well, I've had a bit of bad news."

Kate had never heard her mother sound so aged or anxious. "Mum, what's wrong?"

Betty didn't know how to tell her daughter. There was no easy way to do it so maybe it was best just to say it right out.

"I have a tumour, love."

"You have *what*?"

"I have a tumour," Betty said again.

"What kind of tumour? Where?" Kate was shaken. She stared at the floor in disbelief.

"It's on my left breast. I'm going for an operation next Tuesday, but I don't want you to worry."

"How can you say that, Mum?" It was so typical of her mother and Kate wanted to shake her for her selflessness. "It's malignant, isn't it? I'm coming over straight away."

"They have found some cancerous cells but honestly, love, there's no need to bother. I'll be grand." Betty had been afraid this was how her daughter would react but she owed it to her to tell her before the operation. Kate would never have forgiven her if she had hidden the news from her.

"Jesus Christ, Mum, let me be there!"

Betty sighed. "Well, if you must, love, but I really will be okay. It – it will be a mastectomy but the doctor said the breast is the best place because they have great success with curing it. Mrs Kelly down the road is completely recovered and she had the whole radiotherapy thing and all."

Kate knew that they would have been able to tell a lot from a biopsy. The speed that they were carrying out the process didn't make it sound good.

"Look, Mum, I'll be there tomorrow. I might even take the boys out of school."

"But there's no need to fuss, Kate! I'll be grand."

Kate wanted to scream at her mother. "I'm not fussing, Mum! I just want to be there!"

"If you're sure it's no trouble, it would be great to have someone to look after your father."

That bastard can look after himself, Kate thought. "I'll call you later, Mum, when I get a flight organised."

"Okay, love, but promise me you won't fuss?"

"I'll see you tomorrow. Talk later," Kate said and she put the phone down.

Nothing could have prepared her for this. She'd seen it happen to so many other people but so far she had been fortunate not to experience cancer first-hand with any of her own family members. This was her time and she had to be with her mum. An uneasiness descended on her as she thought about her father. How was she going to feel when confronted by him in Dublin? She would have to keep her new knowledge to herself. Her mum was the most important person in the equation now and she was the reason she was going to Dublin. It couldn't have happened at a worse time but there is no good time to deal with something as horrible as cancer. Kate felt as if someone had thrown a bucket of cold water over her head. Her dear sweet mother who had been such a wonderful and caring force in her life was about to undergo a terrifying ordeal – Kate wondered if she was going to be able to cope with this as well as everything else that was happening around her. To top it all, she had the new exhibition to work for and painting was the last thing she felt like doing.

Annabel glanced at her watch. Nearly time to pick her

up! The extra pair of hands would give her some free time to research the Open University's courses. Colin hadn't been keen on the idea of an *au pair* in the beginning but she managed to convince him that all the stay-at-home wives needed back-up, especially with their driving duties.

"I'm going to collect the *au pair* after the school run," she informed him now.

"She's not coming already!" he said, looking up from his breakfast newspaper.

"I told you months ago and reminded you when I got back from Biarritz."

Annabel hated the way Colin forgot most of the things she told him. She wondered whether he did it on purpose or if it was because he felt that anything she said wasn't of any great importance. Looking at the creases on his forehead she felt certain that it was the latter.

"This is only temporary, mind – if she causes any interruptions in the running of this family she'll have to go," he said, shaking his head gravely.

Annabel thought it best not to reply. She had learnt over the years that it was the best way to deal with her husband when he was like this – which was most of the time. The running of the family in every detail was up to Annabel. Colin hadn't a notion of the work that she did day in day out. Even her absence for the two days in Biarritz seemed to glide over his head. He thought nothing of getting her mother to do the jobs that he should have been doing.

She grabbed her bag and, going out, slammed the front door behind her. Then she strapped Taylor and Rebecca into the car, breaking a fingernail in the process. Sam had already left for school a short time earlier on his bike. He was at that age where he was keen to exert his independence.

Her BMW Jeep swerved as she approached the turn for High Grove Primary School. It was the only acceptable educational establishment to send the local four-to twelve-year-olds to.

She kissed her daughters goodbye as she handed them over to Jean the Lollipop Lady outside the school gates. They could make their own way into class from there.

The trip to the airport was as quick as could be expected for a Monday morning. She never beeped at other motorists but was sorely tempted when a Hiace pulled out in front of her on the motorway, causing her to swerve into the next lane. She had no idea why she felt so anxious now that the time was here and she was actually getting an *au pair* and the much-needed help in her household. An uneasy feeling started to flutter in her stomach and she had to chastise herself for being so concerned. She was after all getting what she wanted!

The arduous task of finding a space in the carpark took twelve minutes – then she hastily made her way to Arrivals.

"Damien, it's almost a quarter past nine!" Betty called down the stairs. "Kate's plane will be arriving soon!"

"I know, love!" Damien sighed. He rubbed his rough chin slowly and considered having a quick shave.

"Don't be late!" Betty called again.

"I won't!" Damien sighed again.

There was no way he could go upstairs and attempt to see to his stubble now. Betty was the type of woman who never let up when she got an idea into her head and now that Kate's plane was due to land in less than an hour he couldn't be seen to be tardy. He had spent most of his married life ignoring her little outbursts and continuing to do his own thing, much to her chagrin. But since she'd been diagnosed with a tumour he felt he had to do as she wished. Deep down in a place where he seldom let himself travel he wondered if it was some sort of punishment. The guilt he felt for his little affairs and discrepancies over the years was coming back to haunt him now.

He grabbed his tan pigskin jacket from the cloakroom under the stairs and pulled it on. His car keys were on the hall table where he always left them. He tossed them in the air as he briskly walked to his Saab. With his Ray-Bans on and seat belt fixed he was ready.

"Thank God, Kate's coming home," he sighed to himself. Nobody heard.

Annabel was almost on her toes peeking over the sea of people waiting for passengers in Arrivals. From her photo, Annabel recalled that the girl had a mop of curly black hair and big brown eyes, but she figured many of the young women coming off the Madrid flight would have those features. After a break in the steady stream from behind the glass doors, Rosa Gonzalez finally appeared. She was wearing a red raincoat (Annabel had forewarned her about the Irish climate) over skinny jeans and knee-high boots. She had the face of an angel – a classically Spanish angel with penetrating dark brown eyes and hair the colour of jet. Annabel knew instantly that she was going to get on with this young woman.

"Annabel?" Rosa said from behind her trolley which was laden with four suitcases.

"Rosa!" Annabel smiled and gave her new house-guest a welcoming hug. "Did you have a good journey?"

"*Si*, I mean yes, *gracias!*" Rosa blushed under her olive skin.

"We are only a few minutes from Howth," Annabel informed her. "Let me help you with that trolley."

The two walked through the barrage of bodies in Arrivals and outside to the zebra crossing that led to the carpark. The red man was flashing on the pedestrian lights but the green man was due to show up in ten seconds.

Damien had to park in Carpark C at the other side of the airport and hoped his daughter wasn't already waiting for him. After trekking through Carparks B and A he walked up a few steps until he was on the road outside Arrivals.

In the near distance he spotted a familiar figure with

a foreign-looking girl. He wasn't sure at first but when she turned her head slightly and her long blonde curls bounced around her shoulders, he was. He hadn't seen her in a long time but she was as beautiful as ever. It was Christmas some years back that she had turned up at his house in Greenfield Close to see Kate, with an infant in her arms and two small children at her feet. Betty was the centre of attention on that day as she fussed over her daughter's friend and her young children and Damien had been glad of that. He couldn't keep his eyes off Annabel even then. She was as charming and natural as usual, paying equal attention to all the members of Kate's family who filled the room. Surely when she went home that evening she wondered how she had ever given herself to an old man like him!

Now she was so close, so close and yet so far! He felt a desire to rush over and talk to her, but what would he say? There was always going to be that tension between them and he had learned to accept it. He decided instead to stand still as he watched her pay her parking ticket and disappear into the vast multistorey carpark.

Damien rubbed his large strong hands through his hair which now had more silver threads than sand running through it. He always wore his hair longer than most men in the construction business. But then, it was a long time since he had come home from work with concrete under his fingernails. His business had boomed with the Celtic Tiger and he now employed over one hundred staff, not including all the foreign nationals that were on contract. His new-found wealth hadn't changed him and he still liked to don a hard hat and mingle with his staff on the numerous building sites that had work in progress all over the city.

When he was sure Annabel was well out of sight he ventured into the Arrivals Hall. He towered above most of the people waiting for passengers to arrive. It was a great advantage and he spotted Kate easily as she walked briskly out, pulling her case behind her.

He waved and grinned but she didn't respond though she was looking straight at him. As she approached him, he reached out for a hug but was surprised when instead she handed him her case.

"It's great to have you home, love," he said, kissing her on the cheek.

"Pity it's not in better circumstances," Kate replied abruptly.

She bit her lip as Damien looked at her searchingly. She was going to have to be careful not to take out her angst on her father over the next few days. His affair with Annabel needed to be addressed at some stage but not while her mother was facing such a critical operation.

Rosa had never seen so many beautiful houses together before. There were many affluent areas in Madrid but the fact that Howth was surrounded by the sea made them all look even more stunning.

"I hope you like it here," Annabel said, aware that the young girl had been silent for the best part of the journey.

"It is very nice, Annabel," she smiled.

"I'll show you around the house and then we have to pick Rebecca up from school. She finishes at one thirty, so there's plenty of time for all that."

At the house Annabel showed Rosa to her room and gave her time to unpack. Then she went down to the kitchen for a cup of tea before organising the rest of her day. She wanted to try and call Kate again. If only she would talk to her! She wondered if Kate was thinking of her in the Pyrénées. Then there was the matter of her birthday at the weekend. If there was one person she wanted to speak to on that day, it was Kate. And it was Kate's birthday on Sunday. Her thoughts were disrupted by the telephone ringing.

"Hello . . . oh, Melissa, hi . . . no. . . yes, I was just collecting her. She's lovely . . ." Annabel strummed her nails on the counter top while listening to Melissa's shrill voice go on and on. She could clearly see her painted eyelids and heavily coated lashes in her mind's eye. Melissa's hair was platinum blonde and even at night she sported a pair of designer sunglasses on her head. "Well, why don't you call in after school pick-up . . . this weekend?" She sighed silently at the thought of her birthday. "Well, I was planning on a meal with Colin on Friday night . . . oh, I didn't realise that was on . . . at least Simon tells you about his golfing weekends . . . okay, we can go to Ella's for dinner, that would be nice . . . see you later."

Annabel hung up. She was extremely disappointed to hear from her friend instead of from him that Colin had planned a golfing trip, especially as it coincided with her fortieth birthday. He'd had two weeks to inform her but he was obviously still aggrieved that she had been away with Kate.

The sound of footsteps traipsing through her tiled hallway reminded her that Rosa was in the house.

"Would you like a cup of tea?" Annabel asked. "I'm just about to have one myself."

"Thank you, but you 'ave coffee?"

"Of course, whatever you like."

"Please show me where everything is – I need to learn," Rosa smiled.

Annabel was so glad that the girl was showing initiative – the last thing she needed was another child in the house. All the irrational fears that she felt on the road to the airport drifted away. Rosa was going to be a great help.

The journey to Greenfield Close, Clontarf, had been silent for most of the way. Kate was trembling as they approached the large red-brick house in the corner of the cul-de-sac. She wanted to see her mother so much but was secretly afraid.

Inside, her father carried her suitcase upstairs, leaving her in the hall. Kate was startled by the thin frail silhouette she could see through the glass door of the kitchen – could her mother have lost that much weight?

The door opened and Betty came out to greet her, her smile padding out her hollow cheeks a little.

"It's so good of you to come over, Kate," her mother said, relief showing all over her ash-grey face.

"Mum!" Kate exclaimed, unsure exactly what to say. The change in her mother's physical appearance since Christmas left her gobsmacked.

"I've just put the kettle on," Betty said, trying to make everything seem as normal as possible.

Kate followed her mother into the kitchen which was always the nerve centre of the Carlton household. This was where Betty had spent most of her working days since Kate could remember. She was always there for her children and even now, with both of them gone, she spent her days waiting for them or Damien to come home. Kate felt a surge of regret for her mother and the way she had nurtured her family so well while her father was fraternising with a girl half his age.

"How are you feeling?"

"I'm absolutely fine," Betty said, brushing the unaddressed issue aside. "How was your journey?"

"It was a typical Airjet flight. Much the same as getting the Number 42 to Abbey Street!"

"Oh, Kate!" her mother giggled. "I do so miss your sense of humour!"

Kate found it difficult to see the humour in anything at the moment. She wasn't trying to be funny. "You never told me exactly when you found the lump, Mum."

"Oh, it was ages ago, but it didn't hurt or anything," Betty said in her usual dismissive way. "It was the size of a pea at Christmas but it's been getting bigger ever since."

Kate's mother was from a different era and there was no way she would give her any more details than that. It would be all 'tea and biscuits' until after the operation was over.

"Can I help in any way?" Kate asked. "I may as well make myself useful."

Betty's eyebrows arched. "Could you get me a few things in SuperValu?"

"No problem, Mum." Kate was delighted to have a task to do.

Betty scribbled a few notes onto her notepad by the sink and handed the list over with a fifty-euro note.

"You can take my car," she said with a nod.

"Do you want me to go now?" Kate asked in surprise – she hadn't even had the cup of tea her mother had offered.

"I want to do a bit of a tidy-up here," Betty replied distractedly. She always found it easier to focus on housework when she felt anxious, which was most of the time.

Kate felt it was best to obey her mother's wishes, whatever they were. Each footstep her mother took was laboured and painful despite her attempts to be normal. When she removed her buff-coloured cardigan, Kate noticed a swelling around her left breast. She was taken aback. It was the size of a tennis ball.

Kate turned around as she heard her father enter the kitchen.

"Your bag is upstairs in your room," Damien said.

"Thanks," Kate said. "I'm heading out now – Mum wants me to go to the shop – but I shouldn't be more than an hour."

"Oh, okay!" Disappointment was crisp in his voice. "Oh, I saw Annabel at the airport with a foreign-looking girl. Does she know you're home?"

Kate winced at the mention of Annabel's name. She quickly pulled herself together before her father noticed her reaction.

"I haven't had a chance to call her," she said. It was easier than explaining why she hadn't been in touch.

"Such a lovely girl, Annabel," Betty chirped.

Kate thought she was going to be sick.

"I'll be back soon!" she called, taking the car keys off the table and walking briskly out of the house.

SuperValu had changed little since her previous visit to Dublin. She found a one-euro coin for the trolley and took her chances in the aisles of the shop. She wasn't out of the first section, the bread section, before she heard someone call her name.

"Kate? Is that you, Kate Carlton?"

She turned around to find Maeve Jenkins pushing a trolley with a toddler strapped into the seat.

"Maeve, hi, it's Cassaux now," Kate said, smiling genuinely for the first time all day. "You look well! How are you?"

"Great, thanks," Maeve grinned and then nodded down at the toddler in the trolley. "Well, knackered actually –

having kids is exhausting! Now I know why all the seventeen-year-olds were spitting their sprogs out no bother, while we mums in our late thirties are crumpled up in agony."

Kate laughed. "But look at the experience you bring to parenthood!"

"Shag that!" Maeve said. "I'd give anything for a night's sleep. I don't know how you managed with twins!"

"You forget I was only in my twenties," said Kate. "But I was still exhausted!"

"So, how's your dish of a French hubby? Sorry for calling you Carlton – old habits and all that!"

"About to become my ex-hubby, but he's still a dish!"

Maeve grimaced. "God, Kate! I'm so sorry to hear that."

"It's okay," Kate smiled – she secretly loved shocking people.

"I'd better dash, Kate," Maeve said quickly. "So I'll see you on Friday night, for Annabel's bash?"

Kate tried not to act surprised. "Yeah, sure."

"It was good of you to come over for the night, but then again, you guys were always best friends," Maeve smiled. "It's great that Melissa told you about it – I didn't think she knew you!"

"There you go!" said Kate and added vacantly, "Good old Melissa."

When Maeve disappeared out of view Kate felt a rush of anxiety creep up her neck and manifest itself in a rash. She hadn't a clue what bash Maeve was talking about and she didn't want to know. Kate hoped that Maeve wouldn't tell Annabel that she was in town – but that was unlikely.

She whizzed around the aisles, flinging tins into the trolley and keeping an eye out for anyone else who might know her. She had enough on her plate coping with her mother's operation, without having to deal with bumping into Annabel.

The next day Kate and Damien drove Betty to Cornhill Hospital. It had an excellent reputation for the successful treatment of cancer but that was little solace to the three members of the Carlton family as they silently drove up the long gravel driveway to the Patients' Admissions.

"Have you bought enough bin-tags to cover the next couple of weeks?" Betty asked Damien as the car drew up to the front of the building.

"Yes, dear," Damien sighed. "Kate got four yesterday, remember?"

"There's just so much to plan before something like this!" Betty added curtly.

"It's okay, Mum," Kate interrupted. "I'll make sure the house is kept just the way you like it until you get back!"

"It's such a relief to have you here," Betty sighed. "Thanks, love."

"There's no need to thank me," Kate said in a businesslike manner as they stopped. "Just concentrate on getting better, okay?"

Betty nodded. Her eyes reflected the strain she had

been carrying around inside for months. Her roots had been redone the day before and her make-up was on as always – but somehow the illness echoed through her face.

Damien opened the boot and took out his wife's small case. Kate carried in a bag filled with fruit and bottles of water which she left at the reception desk. The three waited for Betty to be checked in.

"This is a nice place," Betty said, trying to be upbeat about her situation. "I always said if I ever had to have anything done this is the place I'd go."

They were lucky that the private hospital had agreed to take her so quickly, but Betty was adamant that she wasn't going to a large public hospital like Beaumont. Kate looked on as her mother filled in the required forms with the precision and care with which she approached everything she did.

"I'm ready now!" she said.

A mixture of emotions churned inside Kate as she hugged Betty and watched her walk away with the aid of one of the nurses.

"Are you not going with her?" she asked her father.

"No," he said quietly. "She said she wanted to go on her own."

"That lets you off the hook then," Kate replied snidely.

"Kate! That's not fair!" His daughter's remark wounded him deeply.

"Just bring me home, would you?" she snapped.

The journey back to Greenfield Close was more

silent than the outward journey. Kate wondered how long she would be able to keep her secret from her father. She fumed inside at the fresh thoughts still in her head of him and Annabel. Now, with her mum like this, she had to at least be civil to him when she really wanted to lambaste him. She knew that she would get her chance at some stage to tell him what she really thought of him but it would have to wait. Everything in her life had to wait until her mum was better. A horrible thought flashed into her head for a moment. What if she didn't get better?

7

Annabel hung up. Every time she rang Kate's French number nobody was home and she couldn't manage to reach her on her mobile either. She picked up the receiver again and dialled a different number. She booked an appointment with Daniel for two o'clock. He would breathe enough life into her hair to get her through her first day of being forty.

"Would you like me to do anything for you this morning?" Rosa asked, disturbing Annabel from her thoughts for a moment.

"No, thanks, Rosa," she replied absent-mindedly. "Why don't you take the afternoon off? You've been a great help."

"*Gracias,* Annabel."

The phone rang out and Annabel lifted it promptly. "Mum, hi . . . thanks . . . I don't have to collect the kids today. They're going to friends . . . I'd love that . . . why don't we meet in the Golf Club at one? Yes . . . I've given her the afternoon off . . . okay, bye!" She put the phone down and decided to do something positive to pass the hour until she met her mother.

It was a beautiful day for March and Annabel could feel the optimism of summer in the air since the clocks had been put forward an hour. A walk along Howth pier was just what she needed. She changed into her runners and set off through the colourful village that was now a vibrant commercial centre with a vast array of restaurants and gift shops to attract the incoming tourists. The Irish Sea lapped gently against the concrete walkway as she started her stroll down the pier. Outside the harbour mouth Lambay Island sparkled like a jewel, a rich assortment of purple and green hues. The sun was surprisingly bright for so early in the year and Annabel slipped her sunglasses onto the bridge of her nose. The waves made gentle gushing sounds that reminded her of Biarritz and Nico – and his Adonis-like physique. The memory of their passionate liaison was so far removed from her life in Howth she found it hard to believe that it had really happened. She turned her thoughts to Damien. The memory of him helped her get through the days when she questioned why she was spending her life with a pompous prat like Colin. Turning forty meant little to her now, especially since a meal in Ella's with Melissa Bond was all she had to look forward to.

In the distance a familiar figure was walking towards her. He looked considerably older than the last time she had seen him, but that was at least five years ago. A tall lean woman with peroxide-blonde hair walked at his side. It was Philip.

Annabel quickened her step. "Philip, Philip Carlton!" she shouted, waving as she called.

He held out his arms affectionately as she approached. His hair had thinned beyond recognition and he had put on some weight but his eyes were still the same.

"It's great to see you!" Annabel said enthusiastically, giving Kate's brother a bear-hug. She turned to the woman at his side and extended her right hand. "Hi, Gloria, I'm Annabel – we met briefly a few Christmases ago in the Carltons'."

"Hi, I remember you, Annabel," Gloria replied with her distinctive American twang. "How are you doing?"

"Great, thanks, are you guys over on a holiday? I was with Kate only a couple of weeks ago and she never mentioned that you were visiting."

"My mum's ill. Did Kate not tell you?" Philip asked in surprise.

Annabel shook her head. "No – oh my God, what's wrong?"

"She has breast cancer," Philip informed her sadly. "I'm surprised Kate hasn't been on to you. She was operated on, on Tuesday."

Annabel shook her head. "Where's Kate?"

"She's here," Philip replied. "She came over on Monday."

Annabel realised that Kate had no intention of phoning her. It made perfect sense now why her phone was never answered in the Pyrénées.

"I had no idea. It must have been really sudden!"

"Yes, she went for a check-up last week and they insisted on operating quickly."

"Has it been a success?" Annabel couldn't believe she was asking these questions.

"Unfortunately, they have to do more tests," Philip said sombrely. "They're afraid it may have spread."

"Poor Betty!" Annabel said, covering her mouth with her hand.

"I'm sure Kate will ring you in the next day or two," Philip assured her. "It's all been a bit manic in Clontarf since I got home. Kate has no plans to rush back to France."

"I can't tell you how sorry I am, Philip."

"Thanks, Annabel. I'll tell Kate that I bumped into you."

Annabel leaned forward and embraced him warmly. "Goodbye, Gloria," Annabel said sadly, giving her a token hug too. "Bye, Philip."

The couple continued on their walk and Annabel returned home to collect her car. She didn't hear the sea or smell the salt on the way back – her thoughts were of Kate.

She drove slowly and distractedly to Howth Golf club.

Her mother was there before her and had already ordered a club sandwich and a Caesar salad.

"Poor, Betty! I can't believe it!" her mother said on hearing the news, shaking her head.

"Neither can I."

"It's strange that Kate didn't ring you – isn't it?"

"I guess so, but she must be under a lot of pressure." Annabel certainly hadn't the courage to fill her mother in on the details of the row with Kate.

Lily was deeply moved by the news. Betty and she were close in age and they were not unalike in character either.

"Do the doctors think they can cure it?"

"Philip was pretty vague and I didn't want to delve too deeply."

"I'd like to give her a call but it's so difficult to know what to say," Lily said sadly. "I want you to find out where she is so I can send her some flowers."

Annabel gulped. How was she going to find that out without ringing the Carltons' house?

"Why don't you send them to Greenfield Close and then she'll have them when she comes out?"

Lily nodded her head vacantly but in agreement with her daughter.

"I'd better order some lunch, Mum." Annabel was keen to change the subject on seeing the effect the news was having on her mother.

It was Betty's wish that the house was kept spick and span while she was hospitalised, and fulfilling her wishes was the only thing keeping Kate's thoughts away from the severity of her mother's condition. She had become accustomed to cringing when her mobile phone rang in case it was Annabel, but she needed to keep in touch with the galleries in Paris while she was away so now she took a quick look. The number wasn't familiar, so she answered quickly before it turned onto her voice mail.

"Hello!"

"Hi, Kate?" Shane said nervously – it had taken him a couple of weeks to get the nerve to dial her number.

"Yes?" she recognised his voice straight away but didn't want to believe it was him.

"Kate, it's Shane!"

"What a surprise! How are you, stranger?" Her voice lifted an octave. A bolt of lightning would have been more expected than a phone-call from Shane Gleason.

"I bumped into Annabel on a flight a couple of weeks ago. She said she was with you in Biarritz and gave me your number, so I thought I'd give you a buzz!"

Kate tried to steady herself. A shiver ran up the back of her legs and she sat down to recover from the pleasant surprise.

"Good to hear you!" she said. "God, it's been a while!"

"Too long. I'm sorry I didn't keep in touch after the last time we met up," he said apologetically. "Time goes by so quickly."

"It's okay," Kate sighed. "Actually, I'm having a manic week – Mum's in hospital – she has cancer."

"Oh, no, Kate!" The shock was clear in Shane's voice. "I'm so sorry to hear that!"

"She's had surgery but we still don't know if it has spread."

"Is there anything I can do to help out?"

"There's nothing anyone can do at the moment, I'm afraid."

Just hearing his voice again was soothing away the awfulness of the past few days.

"Was it sudden?" Shane was panicked and wished he could reach down through the phone and hold Kate.

"Pretty much so – she only went for a check-up last week and this week she's in Cornhill after a mastectomy."

"Are you coming home?" he asked.

"I *am* home. I'm in Clontarf at the moment. I was trying to distract myself by doing housework."

"You, housework?" he said in surprise.

"I know! I'm going mad, Shane," Kate sighed.

"Can I call out and see you?" he suggested – he hoped that didn't sound inappropriate. "I really want to help."

"There's nothing you can do." Kate paused – was she really talking to Shane? Somehow the whole conversation was beginning to feel a bit like a dream. "But I would like to see you."

Shane felt nervous and excited at the prospect. He needed to show Kate that she was still someone he thought about and, at the risk of sounding soppy, he said what was on his mind. "It's your birthday on Sunday, isn't it?"

"You remember!" she smiled.

"Yours is probably the only birthday I do remember. I don't even remember my wife's."

"How is she?" she asked curiously.

"She's fine," he said briskly, anxious not to dwell on the fact that he had a wife. "When is a good time to call out? I'm on the other side of the city now."

Kate could feel a lump develop in her throat – she needed to lighten up.

"You'll have to get your visa before you cross the Liffey," she teased. It felt so strange to be talking with Shane but she didn't want the conversation to end.

"It's okay. I have a dual passport. What about tomorrow?"

"Actually tomorrow would be good. Philip and his wife are over until Sunday and that frees me up a bit."

Where would be a good place to break the ice? he wondered. "Will I come out to the Close?" he suggested.

"Yeah. Do you still remember the house?"

It was a loaded question and one that didn't need answering. Both conjured up pictures of afternoons spent in an ecstasy of adolescent fondling in Kate's bedroom.

"I don't think I could ever forget your house, Kate!"

"Is eleven too early?" Kate asked cautiously – excited at the prospect of seeing him again. It was so unexpected and yet just what she needed.

"Perfect, see you at eleven."

"And Shane . . ."

"Yes, Kate." His tone sounded like chocolate in stereo.

"I'm really glad you rang."

"So am I," he said sincerely, then hung up.

Kate stared at the phone. She felt shock and exhilaration mixed together at the prospect of seeing him again. It was good of Annabel to give him her number but then again she would be meeting him as a married man which could prove painful – especially after coming so recently out of a separation. Why was her life like this? It never rains but it pours, she thought, and something inside told her that her life was going to get even more complicated.

"Have a nice night," Colin said, his arms laden with golf clubs. "Simon and I will be back on Sunday."

Annabel nodded at her husband from the hallway where she stood watching him fill his Mercedes with his bags for the weekend. His yellow Pringle jumper and white pompous pants screamed fuddy-duddy golfer at her. He could easily be mistaken for a man ten years older.

"It's a shame you aren't staying around for my birthday." Annabel felt she had to say it, even though part of her was glad that he was going away.

"You'll have a much nicer time with the girls!"

"I'm only having dinner with Melissa!" she said, bitterness brewing in her voice.

"Oh, yes, of course," he replied, stepping back into the hall. He dragged the long strands of his thinning hair over his almost bald head and then leaned forward, giving Annabel an awkward peck on the cheek. "Happy Birthday!" he said as he took a package out of his pocket and handed it to her. "I hope you like them."

Annabel thought he had forgotten to get her a gift and took it in surprise and relief. She opened the jeweller's bag that held a small red velvet-covered box. She snapped open the lid and fingered the diamond studs resting on the tiny tray. "Thanks, Colin, they are really sweet!"

"There's a carat in each earring, so don't lose them!" he guffawed.

Annabel wanted to throw them in his face but decided it was best to say nothing. He always ruined gift-giving by hinting at the cost. When he gave Taylor those shoes with the wheels he insisted on her wearing the logo sticker on the outside so that everyone who saw them knew that they were the genuine article and not fakes. He was worse than an adolescent at times and his total lack of awareness of the fact was even more unbearable to take.

"Bye, and be good," he called, his countenance beaming at her through the tinted glass of the car.

Annabel leaned against the frame of the front door and watched him drive away with a mixture of disgust and relief.

"Will I give the girls a bath?" a voice called from behind.

Annabel turned around. "Yes, Rosa, that would be good," she nodded. "I'll be going out in a couple of hours."

She had plenty of time to shower and apply her make-up – she wanted to look her best. Ella's was a trendy bistro in the middle of the village and it wasn't unusual for the cognoscenti of Howth to gather there on a Friday evening.

A while later, Taylor and Rebecca ran into her bedroom smelling of soap and dressed in their pyjamas.

"Are you going out?" Taylor asked.

"Yes, darling, but I won't be late."

"How come we didn't get to sing you 'Happy Birthday' and blow out any candles?" Rebecca asked innocently.

"We can do that tomorrow evening if you like." Annabel knelt down until she was at eye-level with her youngest child. "We can go to Casa Pasta with Gran – you love it there, don't you?"

"Yummy, Mummy!" Rebecca threw her arms around her mother.

Funny, Annabel thought to herself. She didn't feel like a Yummy Mummy tonight. Instead she felt every minute of her forty years.

Rosa came into the bedroom, armed with books. "Would you like a story?" she asked the girls and they followed her out of the room.

Annabel went into her son's bedroom to bid him goodnight but he was fixed in front of the TV screen playing with his PlayStation.

"Night, Sam!" she called.

"Bye, Mum," the lad replied, not looking up from his game. "Happy Birthday!"

"Thanks, Sam." Annabel could see her little boy turning into a teenager before her eyes.

She grabbed her coat and house keys and set off into the cool evening air.

It had been a sad day and she planned to lower a bottle of Cabernet Sauvignon to get through the evening – and make her forget the awful night in Biarritz when she had made a fool of herself and lost her best friend.

She rambled down the hill to the cosy restaurant. As it came into view she noticed more bodies than usual through the foggy glass. The door was made of walnut-coloured wood and smoked glass and she had to lean heavily against it to open it. When she stepped inside the lights went out for a moment, giving her a shock.

"*Surprise!*" shouted a harmony of voices.

Then the lights came on, illuminating the gaily painted bistro until every face in the restaurant was visible. Each and every person in the bistro was female and associated in some way with Annabel.

Melissa dashed over and hugged her extravagantly. "Happy Birthday! I managed to get everyone here tonight!"

Annabel was gobsmacked. "I don't know what to say, Melissa!"

"Don't say anything," Melissa grinned, handing her a glass of red wine.

Annabel scanned the room and waved at the various women dotted around the long U-shaped table that had been specially prepared for her birthday dinner. For a brief moment she thought she saw Kate over in the corner but then realised it was only Maeve Jenkins. One by one the guests came over, bearing gifts in expensively decorated packages. Each manicured and pampered woman was as beautiful as the one before. Annabel noticed that a couple of girls she was friendly with were missing – this group had all been handpicked by Melissa and reflected the Who's Who of Howth rather than the women Annabel really liked. As she sat down at Melissa's right-hand side with Leslie Godkin (another mother of force at High Grove School) at her other side, she realised that she wasn't really like any of these women. Maybe she looked like them and dressed like them and she probably did much the same things as them as she went about her daily business – but that was where the similarities ended. Annabel couldn't say, hand on her heart, that these women were her friends – none were like Kate.

Annabel picked at each course in turn and drank copious glasses of red wine.

Towards the end of the evening, Maeve Jenkins came over and sat down by her side.

"Maeve, it's good of you to come," Annabel said, sounding like a broken record.

"I wouldn't have missed this for the world," Maeve grinned. "Melissa was planning tonight for ages."

"She's too good," Annabel agreed, anxiously. A surprise party was not exactly the way she wanted to spend her birthday but she felt obliged to show her gratitude for all of the trouble that Melissa had taken organising the occasion.

"I was wondering when Kate is going to show."

"Kate?" Annabel asked, with a glimmer of hope that her night would truly be made special in some way.

"Yes, I bumped into her in SuperValu."

"When?" Annabel was interested to know every detail.

"I think it was Monday, actually," Maeve replied pensively. "Yes, it was – I was doing the pick-ups from ballet."

"Did you tell her about this evening?" Annabel asked anxiously.

"Yes," Maeve replied, "but I took it she knew. I thought that was why she was home!"

"Her mother has cancer, Maeve," Annabel informed the surprised woman. "Maybe she didn't feel up to it." She hoped that explained her absence but deep down realised that Melissa probably never informed her of the party and Kate wouldn't have come even if she had been told.

"I don't believe you!" Maeve said, aghast. "She never said anything about her mum to me! She told me she was getting divorced though. God, she must be in the horrors!"

"It's a tough time for her all right," Annabel agreed. She secretly wanted the ground to open up and swallow her.

"It makes you appreciate how lucky we are when you hear things like that, doesn't it?"

Annabel nodded. "I'd better do some mingling, being the Birthday Girl and all!"

"Of course, off you go!"

Annabel knew the night wouldn't be complete without Moët and true to form, as she looked around, Melissa was popping the corks. She beamed across at Annabel as a huge pink birthday cake decorated with dozens of sparklers and candles appeared from behind the kitchen doors. Annabel fixed a false smile on her face to the strains of 'Happy Birthday' and hoped she could make it through another couple of hours before she could escape to the refuge of her bed.

Butterflies flitted inside Kate's stomach as she woke the next morning. She tried to picture Shane's face and grinned when she caught his image in her mind's eye. She jumped out of bed and ran into the shower. The warm water was refreshing and massaging against her body. She dried herself off and dressed in a pair of jeans and the top Annabel had bought her in Biarritz. She knew she looked well in it and her disgust with her friend didn't extend to her powers of colour co-ordination. She threw herself on the bed and picked up the phone to make her first call of the day to her mother.

"Hello," a bright voice at the other end of the line replied.

"Hi, Mum," Kate said cheerfully. "How are you feeling today?"

"I'm feeling really well. I haven't a pain or an ache. They really are marvellous in this hospital. I'll be out of here in no time."

"Yes, Mum." They were giving her mother morphine

in tablet form and it was no surprise that she was feeling so well. "I won't be in until later tonight. I'm meeting up with Shane Gleason, would you believe!"

"Oh, dear sweet Shane, what a lovely boy!" Betty sighed. "I'll never forget the day you broke up with him. He was the nicest fellow you ever brought home."

"I have to say I agree with you, Mum."

"That will be lovely," Betty said. "How's your father coping?"

Kate cringed. She was finding it increasingly difficult to be civil towards him and had to keep reminding herself that there was a much bigger picture than her father's affair with Annabel to be considered.

"Dad's up on the site in Lusk – he'll be in to you sometime this afternoon and Philip will be in this morning."

"You don't need to keep visiting – I'll be home soon," Betty said.

"We miss you, that's all." Kate was choking as she spoke.

"You have a lovely day, and if you don't get in to see me don't worry," Betty said firmly.

"Okay, Mum, bye!"

"Bye, love!" Betty smiled to herself as she hung up the phone. There was little would give her more pleasure than to see her daughter with Shane Gleason. Hindsight is twenty-twenty vision and it was unfortunate that her daughter didn't realise all those years ago how suited she was to the tall gangly youth.

Kate went down to the kitchen and fixed some toast and a cup of coffee. Her father had left a copy of *The Irish Times* on the kitchen table for her. He was being considerate but that didn't help.

She checked her watch and it was a few minutes past ten – Shane would be here soon!

Annabel's head ached as she opened her eyes. The bottle and a half of red wine followed by copious glasses of Moët had helped her get through the night but she would have to get through today with the consequences. The company she had kept the night before had left her feeling depressed. She had been living in a cocoon for years and it took two days in Biarritz with Kate to show the gaps that needed to be cracked open. From the outside her life seemed fulfilling and complete but deep inside she realised that she had been selling herself short for years. She was capable of much more.

She jumped out of the bed and threw on her pink silk dressing-gown.

"Rosa!" she called.

"*Si!*" Rosa replied. She was already downstairs in the kitchen feeding Rebecca.

"I have to do some research on the internet this morning – could you mind the kids for an extra couple of hours?"

"Of course!" Rosa called, stepping out of the kitchen.

Annabel pulled a cream fitted jumper over her head and her skinny jeans over her legs. She zipped her knee-high boots up and went straight for the study. She hit the Google website as Rosa came in with a cup of tea.

"Do you work, Annabel?" she asked.

"After I get myself educated – I will, Rosa," Annabel replied.

The young Spanish woman looked at her curiously as she put the cup down on the desk.

"Thanks, Rosa," Annabel smiled.

She felt genuinely good for the first time since leaving Biarritz.

8

Kate looked up at the clock on the wall. Ten minutes past eleven. She was feeling restless. When the doorbell rang, she jumped to her feet and rubbed the palms of her hands along her thighs. She straightened her back and walked anxiously to the hall door, then opened it briskly.

"Hi, Kate," he said nervously.

He looked gorgeous.

"Hi, Shane, come on in." Kate stood back into the hallway.

He hovered for a moment, unsure whether he should kiss her or not. Kate made the decision for him and opened her arms for an embrace. They hugged and Shane kissed her gently on the cheek. She got a strong whiff of his pheromones and breathed them in deeply.

"Do you want a cup of tea or would you like to go out?" Kate asked.

"Let's go into town – fancy going to Bewleys like we used to?"

Pink blushes appeared on Kate's cheeks. She always thought of Bewleys as their place. In the eighties there was nowhere else in the city to get a good cup of coffee.

"That's a great idea," she grinned. "Just let me get my coat."

Shane waited in the hallway, studying the new wallpaper and finely polished wooden floorboards.

"Betty keeps this place well," he commented on Kate's return. "Still as house-proud as ever?"

"Absolutely," Kate sighed. "But in all these years she has never wanted to move – despite numerous attempts by Dad. He built that lovely new development overlooking Claremont beach –"

"The Oaks?"

"That's the one," Kate nodded. "But Betty wouldn't move. She's very sentimental about this house."

"I can understand that," grinned Shane. "I'm sentimental about it myself!"

Without answering, Kate gave him a knowing glance. They were standing in the very spot he had come to collect her from on so many dates, so many occasions – from her debs dance to walks in the park.

Kate picked up her keys. "I'm ready," she declared.

He opened the door and they stepped outside. She slammed the front door shut and followed him to a sporty black BMW convertible that was parked outside the driveway.

"Very nice," said Kate.

"I love it, I have to admit."

"Can we have the roof down?" she asked, like a child being presented with a new toy.

"Why not? It's not a bad day," Shane smiled, opening the car door for her.

They whizzed by the towering chimneys that billowed smoke over Dublin Bay. The water was a deep ultramarine and lapped high along the promenade where people were jogging and walking in the spring sunshine.

Kate looked over for a brief moment at Shane's strong profile. The breeze was skimming off the top of his blond hair – now peppered with grey – causing it to ruffle. He had changed little in over twenty years. He threw her a fleeting look that acknowledged he was in a time-warp.

"What's the parking like around Grafton Street?" she asked.

"We'll get a space in BT's – it's so damn expensive nobody stays there for long."

Kate had been in the carpark once before on a flying visit some years back. Shane parked the car and ushered her towards the shiny aluminium lift. When the doors closed they jigged around nervously, watching and waiting for the other's next move.

"Do you ever get freaked out in lifts?" Kate asked, breaking the silence.

"I wouldn't want to be claustrophobic in my profession, would I?" he grinned.

"Dah! How silly of me!" she grinned.

"I wouldn't mind getting stuck in a lift right now

though!" He raised his left eyebrow as he had a habit of doing after a roguish suggestion.

"You're a married man, I'll have to remind you," Kate berated him.

The doors opened and they ambled slowly down Wicklow Street, taking a right turn onto Grafton Street. Street sellers had bedecked the footpath with handcrafted jewellery and mobile-phone covers.

"This city is thriving, isn't it?" Kate remarked. "So different to the one I left in the eighties."

"It sure has changed, but not always for the better," Shane said enigmatically.

"What do you mean?"

"I mean people are far more materialistic, more rushed. And as for the Land of Welcomes!"

Kate nodded. "I do read *The Irish Times* on the internet – I know what you're saying."

"Do you ever regret leaving Ireland?" he asked, his eyebrow raised again – it was a loaded question and Kate pretended not to understand what he meant.

"Do you ever wish you had left?"

"I asked first!"

"*Touché!* I don't think so, not really. I've met a lot of interesting people over the years and I enjoy the French way of life but then again . . ."

"Yes?" Shane felt a revelation was coming.

"I seem to like the familiar around me at the moment. The past is more important, more relevant in some ways when I assess what I need to be doing next and especially with the prospect of losing Mum." Kate sighed after such a profound statement. "Does that make any sense?"

"It does. Here we are – and it's just as well – I'm desperate for a coffee. Wait until you see what they've done to this place – it's cool."

They were greeted by a slender blonde girl – probably Polish but definitely Eastern European – who showed them over to a quiet table in the corner, underneath the newly refurbished stained-glass window.

"This is gorgeous!" Kate nodded approvingly as she sat down on the plush velour seats.

"What are you having?" Shane asked, his eyes skimming the menu card on the table.

"A latte and a Danish, even though I probably shouldn't!"

"What is it with women? Why the hell shouldn't you have a cake?"

"A moment on the lips – a lifetime on the hips," Kate grinned, clicking the roof of her mouth with her tongue.

"Fellas put weight on too," Shane observed. "You should see me jogging for Ireland, a couple of weeks before my medical." The mood was buoyant and Shane didn't want to ruin it, but he felt the need to ask the question that was hovering over them like a thick sea mist. "How's Betty today?"

"Doing well," Kate nodded. "Her spirits are high. It can't be easy after losing her breast like that. She's up to her eyeballs in morphine, of course. So that helps!"

"Is there anything they can do for her?"

Kate lowered her head and bit her lip.

"Dad's going in to talk to the doctor this afternoon. They'll have the results of all the tests today."

Shane looked longingly into Kate's chocolate-coloured eyes. He wanted to dive in and touch her soul, massage any hurt and take away any grief that she might be hiding deep inside.

"How long will you stay here?" he asked, partly in reference to her mother's illness and partly out of self-interest.

"I might make a flying visit back to France next week to get some stuff and collect some of my references – although I doubt I'll get much work done over the coming weeks. I intend to stay here for the duration of Mum's illness. I discussed it with Dad and he wants to bring her home."

"I think Damien would need some help all right," Shane agreed. "He could build a skyscraper but finds it difficult to change a bed."

Kate felt a pang of regret – why did she let this wonderful man slip out of her life when he knew her better than anyone ever did and possibly ever would again. It was so easy not having to explain about her family and the way she really was.

"Exactly. It won't be easy but I can always delay my exhibition by a couple of months."

"I'd love to see your current work."

"It's changed considerably since you last saw it."

"I loved the series of lilies."

"When? How did you see them?" Kate asked in surprise.

Shane tapped the side of his nose with his index finger mysteriously.

Kate frowned. She hated it when he teased her – sometimes.

"After we met in Toulouse, I visited that gallery in the Bastille that you told me about," he revealed. "It was sensational. I wanted to buy them all!"

Kate was flattered.

"I have the catalogue still." He grinned like a schoolboy telling too much and embarrassed by his own obsession.

"I am surprised," Kate beamed. "Art was never your thing."

"I know talent when I see it," he said with a wink.

"Now that's more like the Shane Gleason I know," Kate quipped.

Maybe he thought about her more than he let on. She knew that she had carried secret thoughts and dreams about him for a few seconds of every day that they had spent apart.

Annabel took a break from her web-surfing to make a sandwich. After buttering a roll in the kitchen, she tried Kate's mobile again but it was switched off. She wanted desperately to ring her parents' house in Clontarf but didn't want to make matters worse by speaking to Damien. Kate really would be mad if she thought they had spoken to each other.

She felt frustrated too about her web-search. She had flicked through so many degree courses all morning, without finding anything that enthused. She was beginning to doubt whether she wanted to go back and study at all. A pattern had emerged though: every time she hit a website that interested her, it had something to do with food. Eventually, as she went from site to site, she realised she wasn't looking at colleges and universities at all but restaurants. She had certainly accumulated a vast knowledge of food while doing those weekend cookery courses in Ballyasgor over the last few years.

Now, her buttered roll in hand, she glanced over her shoulder at the stack of books by Jamie and Nigella and all the other gods and goddesses of cooking that rested on her kitchen shelf. She took a coriander and lemon hummus that she had made the day before out of the fridge and spread it generously on the roll.

It was then that it hit her like a bolt out of the blue. Why was she going back to college when she could start a little business doing something that she really loved? Her mind went into overdrive as she looked around her fridge at the quiche she had made a couple of days earlier, and the crisp salads she had neatly arranged and packed into the shelves. It had been staring her in the face for ages. She felt a rush of excitement run through her. And she wouldn't have to go too far to find a place to sell her goods either – the Farmers' and Fishermen's Market in Howth was the perfect point of sale for her home-made produce.

She grabbed her bag and set off for SuperValu. She had pricings to do. For the first time in years she was truly excited about something that she was doing for herself. Maybe it was true that life begins at forty!

Damien pulled up to the doors of Cornhill Hospital. He got out and slammed the door of his Saab, then strode through the clinical glass doors to hear of his wife's fate.

Dr Harrold opened his office door as he heard Damien's boots tread heavily on the linoleum outside.

"Come in – take a seat," he said, gesturing at the chair in front of his desk. He sat down and cleared his throat, as was his habit when he was about to break bad news. "I'm afraid your wife has come to us very late in her illness," he began. "The cancer has spread to her liver. We could have done more if –"

"I know what you're going to say," Damien interrupted. He wasn't one to pussyfoot around when something had to be said and he knew that advanced liver cancer was very serious. "Realistically, how long are we talking about, now that you have had time to do the tests more thoroughly?"

"The only thing that might have been possible would have been a liver transplant, but unfortunately the cancer has spread to some other organs now."

"I don't think Betty is going to want another operation," Damien said with a shake of his head. "Especially since there's no guarantee it would do much good."

"You wife is very ill but I hope that she will be with us until July or maybe August," Dr Harrold said, nodding solemnly.

"And minimum?"

"She is in severe pain – we are administering drugs every four hours." He hesitated, not wanting to give the worst-case scenario. "It could be considerably less if her system doesn't react well to the drugs."

"I want to take her home," Damien insisted.

"Of course," Dr Harrold agreed. "But you may need some help."

"I have discussed this with my children already and we are getting a nurse."

"That's a good idea," the doctor nodded. "I strongly advise that you tell your wife immediately what I have just told you – she knows I'm seeing you – she insisted that we talk to you first. We usually like to give the prognosis to the patient directly but if you'd prefer to deal with it yourself . . ."

Damien nodded. "Yes, I would." He couldn't keep it from her any more and it was something he had to do on his own. "When can I take her home?"

"Tomorrow?" the doctor suggested.

"Can you arrange for a nurse?" Damien asked, his voice now quivering.

"My secretary can give you the number of an agency on the way out – it is probably the best thing to do."

Dr Harrold escorted Damien to the door and bowed his head before shaking Damien's hand.

"Thanks," Damien said gravely, and started the short walk down to Ward 3C.

Betty was sitting up in the bed reading a recent copy of *Woman's Way*. Her powder-blue cardigan was draped loosely around her shoulders and covered a satin nightie dappled with roses. If it weren't for her deeply yellow jaundice she could have looked serene and pretty for her sixty-two years. Her face brightened as Damien entered the tiny ward – she put her magazine down and patted the bed.

"Hello, love," she smiled, holding out her arms as he leaned forward to kiss her gently on the cheek.

Damien perched himself on the edge of the bed, careful not to sit too far back on the mattress and crush his wife's legs.

"So when am I going home?" Her face beamed for the first time in months.

"Maybe tomorrow," Damien tried to smile.

Betty propped herself up higher against the pillows on hearing the news. "Fantastic!" she said, clasping her hands together in delight. "The staff are lovely but I really need to get home to my own bed to get better."

Damien gave a shallow smile. "You're still very sick, Betty."

"Don't go all morbid on me," she chastised. "I'll be fine when I get home."

Damien looked deeply into her sunken pupils surrounded by sickly yellow skin. There was no talking to Betty once she had her mind made up about something. She had bulldozed her way through life but now she would have to succumb to the ravages of the cruellest illness.

"Of course you will," he agreed. "But Betty," he went on with difficulty, "I was talking to Dr Harrold just now and it looks like the cancer has spread to your liver and . . ." he had to pause – he couldn't believe he was saying these words to his wife, "there may be other secondaries."

Betty's mouth opened slightly, her lower lip quivering. "I will be all right when I get home," she replied adamantly.

"There is a chance that with more operations they could –"

Betty pressed her index finger up to his lips. "It has spread, that's all I needed to know."

Damien swallowed hard. "We all want you home but you have to consider the opportunities you are missing by not letting them operate again."

"Bah!" Betty patted down the bedspread. "I don't want any more operations. They've taken my breast – there'll be nothing left of me if I stay here any longer!"

Damien hadn't the strength to argue. The next few weeks were going to be difficult enough. He reached out and took her skinny hand in his. He clasped it tightly with his other hand on top. "We'll get through this," he sighed.

Suddenly she wasn't feeling so defiant any more. The tears started to trickle slowly down her cheek – first from her right eye, then from her left.

"I don't want to die," she whispered.

Then Damien saw a look in her eyes that he hadn't seen in a very long time. A mixture of defiance and fear wrapped up in one.

She had batted those eyes on the day he had proposed and he had worn the mantle of the dutiful husband ever since. Now looking at her, he felt more than pity. She had probably been miserable for most of their married life too.

Shane beckoned at the Polish girl to bring over the bill.

"Thanks," Kate smiled. "That was really nice."

"Fancy a wander round the Green?" He tilted his head slightly, hoping she would agree to spend the afternoon with him.

"Yeah, great!"

Kate loved St Stephen's Green. They had spent many a lazy afternoon on their school holidays feeding the ducks and philosophising on life. They were no different to most teenagers then and felt they were an authority on every subject. Stephen's Green was where he had told her that he loved her for the first time as she lay with her head on his denim jacket in the newly mown grass, he leaning over her slightly, resting on his left arm . . . then those eyes, those penetrating blue eyes that looked at her across the table now . . .

"Kate? Kate, are you okay?" A puzzled expression creased his face.

She awoke from her trance with a smile. "I'm fine. Let's go."

He stood back from the door and let her walk through first. She brushed by his arm for an instant, skin touching skin, and felt a shock shoot through her body. The nameless faces rushing around them in the café and on the street seemed to be operating in a different timeframe. She knew they couldn't touch each other overtly – this was his hometown and he had a wife and friends that could pop out from the woodwork at any moment. But she longed to touch his fingers, his face. The small talk had been covered in Bewleys. They approached the arch that led into the Green in silence. Shane put his arm on the small of her back as they walked through the gate and she felt a shiver race up her spine.

"It's been a while since we've been in here," she commented.

He leaned down and whispered in her ear. "Eighteen years, give or take a month."

The bushes were bursting with foliage and every corner of the Green showed the promise of new life and the impending summer. The ducks wandered out onto the pathway, quacking their demand for bread.

After a few minutes' silence Shane spoke. "Are you happy, Kate?"

"Funny question, but in general I think I am. I mean my poor mum is ill and I've still got to tie up the loose ends of my marriage but I feel good – even turning forty tomorrow doesn't bother me!" She couldn't mention Annabel or Damien and they were, of course, a source of deep unhappiness.

"You always were an optimist."

"And what about you, Shane? Are you happy?" Kate looked up straight into his eyes.

He stared back, unwilling to answer at first. Then he turned his head and gestured over to an empty park bench. Kate took his cue and sat down on the wooden seat.

"Well?" she asked again once they were both sitting comfortably, close to each other.

"I don't think I'm ever happy." His tone was melancholy.

"Jesus, Shane, you've a great job that anyone with an ounce of sense knows is money for old rope, you've a lovely wife . . ." She stopped, waiting to see the reaction in his face. He was motionless. "You are happy with Natasha, aren't you?"

"Yeah, she's a great girl," he nodded.

Kate was secretly disappointed. "So why aren't you happy?"

"I don't know." He started to shake his head. "There's this constant weight drags me down for no reason and I just go into myself."

Kate knew what he was talking about. She had pushed it to the back of her mind but now that he mentioned it she remembered – it was one of the reasons why she hadn't asked him to join her in the States when she left college.

"What do you think it is?" Kate asked. "Some latent trauma from a previous life?"

"I'm afraid of losing things that are important to me." He spat out the words as if they tasted bitter on his tongue. "I'm not sure but I think it goes back to losing my dad so young."

"That can't have been easy." She put her hand on top of his and gently tried to brush away his pain with soft strokes.

"But look at you, Kate. How do you do it?" Shane tilted his head in admiration. "You've had a fair few dints over the years and here you are at the height of it and you're still upbeat."

"It's just the way I'm made, I guess!" She didn't know how to answer properly.

"It's one of the things I love about you."

They both sat still and silent. He hadn't used the past tense. Kate didn't want to read into it but she felt him look at her the way he used to and she froze.

"Maybe we should head back," she gulped – loud enough for him to hear.

The conversation was entering a dimension that she felt unprepared to deal with. She had to sort her own feelings out carefully before she could dive in too deeply with Shane.

He seemed disappointed that their day was over so soon but acknowledged her suggestion with a nod.

The car roof stayed up as they drove back to Greenfield Close. Damien's Saab was parked in the driveway and Kate hovered on the seat of Shane's car, glancing at the front door every now and again.

Shane didn't wait to be asked in – he could see that she was keen to talk to her father.

"It's been really great seeing you, Kate." His mouth widened as he looked into her eyes one more time.

"Thanks for a lovely day, Shane." Kate appreciated his tact and gently touched him on the cheek before getting out of the car.

"Can I ring you again, while you're here – and see how Betty is?"

"Of course. It's always good to see you."

She got out of the car and slammed the door shut. He gave a short wave and swung his car around before speeding off down the road.

Kate hesitated for a moment as she walked up the drive. She knew that her father would have all the facts after speaking to the consultant and part of her didn't want to hear the final analysis of her mother's operation.

Her father's silhouette was clear through the glass of the kitchen door as he sat at the table.

"Kate, is that you?" he called.

"Yeah," she replied as she opened the door. She went in and sat down opposite him. "How did you get on with the doctor?"

"The results are what we expected," he said with a shake of his head. "It's spread to her liver and other organs. I can't believe it, Kate." Tears welled up in his eyes.

Shock filled her but the thought of him betraying her mother with her best friend helped her to fight back the tears. She didn't want to hold her father. A few weeks ago she'd have hugged without reason but now she didn't want him touching her.

"When is she coming home?" she asked.

"Tomorrow."

"I'll get her room ready," she said coldly. "Then I'm going out for a walk."

Damien was stabbed by his daughter's lack of warmth. This was not like her. Was she angry with him for some reason or was it just her way of coping with the impending loss of her mother? Then a darker thought struck him as he stared into the distance. Had Betty at last told her the secret that they had kept from her all these years? Was that the source of her anger? It had been his wish to tell his daughter the truth when she turned eighteen but Betty was the one who insisted that she didn't need to know. Had she now changed her mind? Dare he bring the subject up and ask Betty? But, if telling Kate was still the farthest thing from her mind, he would be distressing Betty greatly by even mentioning it. Perhaps he had better keep quiet and just see what would emerge.

9

Annabel licked her fingers clean. The sun-dried tomatoes were definitely an excellent addition to the recipe.

"Annabel, you have been cooking all day!" Rosa gasped.

"I've been really enjoying myself," she said, handing the spoon over to Rosa to taste. "What do you think?"

Rosa nodded approvingly as she licked the back of the spoon. "That is very good."

"I'm going to make hummus to sell in the Sunday market!"

"Very nice," Rosa said, amused that a woman in Annabel's comfortable position would want to cook for other people. "I go see to the children."

Annabel continued packing her savoury delights into plastic containers. She chuckled to herself as she pictured Melissa's face on hearing about her new venture. She and all the other local wives would be horrified. She only had one more day to wait before the market, when she would do some research into setting up a stall. She felt a tingle of excitement about this new scheme that sent her blood racing through every sinew in her body. But even better than the thought of the horrified look on Melissa's face was that of the look on Colin's when he found out!

Her daydreams were interrupted by the familiar ring of her house-phone.

"Hello?"

It was Damien.

She braced herself on hearing his voice. "Damien, hi! No, this is a good time, how are you?" She froze for an instant on recalling Betty's illness. "How's Betty? Oh, I see." Poor Damien! "Kate? No . . . no . . ." She hesitated for a moment. She had to tell him something to explain the fact she was not in contact with Kate. "Kate hasn't been in touch," she said quietly. "I've been trying to ring her but we had a bit of a falling out in Biarritz and since then –"

"About what?" Damien interrupted sharply.

"Oh, it was nothing," she said hurriedly, "nothing important . . . I'll try to ring her again. When is Betty home?" She hoped he'd drop the subject and she wouldn't have to tell him about her foolhardy confession to his daughter, but he rapidly circled back to the subject of Kate again. "I promise I'll keep trying to contact her," she sighed. "Will you give Betty my best wishes? Bye, Damien."

She stared at the receiver as she put it down. What was going on with Kate? Was she actively avoiding her?

Chances were that she was distraught about her mother's illness – and surely her father's affair was of little importance in the context of that? But no matter how much she tried she couldn't get the feelings of guilt to leave.

Damien shook as he put the phone down. It had been an attempt to try and find out what was really troubling his daughter but the conversation with Annabel had only left him more disturbed. What could those two possibly have quarrelled about? In all the years he had known Annabel, she was the most solid and trustworthy friend that Kate had. He had never even seen the girls argue. It must be pretty serious for them to fall out totally. A thought flashed into his head and he pondered about the chances of Kate finding out about his affair with Annabel. Surely not. No one knew except Annabel and she would never have told Kate without his agreement. In any case, she would have told Kate years ago if she was going to at all. But it would explain why Kate seemed so angry with both of them . . .

His thoughts were interrupted by the hall door opening and Philip and Gloria entering the kitchen.

"Dad," Philip said with a nod of his head, "what's the word?"

"Hi, Damien," Gloria droned.

"Kate's gone out for a walk. I've already told her." He swallowed hard. Relating the bad news to his son was even harder. "It's bad news . . . it's definitely spread to her liver and maybe to some other organs."

"Shit!" Philip cried out loud. He brought his hand up to cover his mouth. He fought to control himself. "Is she coming home?"

"Tomorrow," Damien nodded.

"I'll put the coffee on," Gloria said, feeling inadequate.

"Where did Kate go?" Philip asked.

"Dollymount strand."

"How is she?"

"Not good. Philip . . . have you noticed anything strange about her since you got here?"

"She's going through a divorce, Dad, and her mother could be dying," Philip said, shaking his head. "Give her a break!"

"But she isn't taking it out on you!" said Damien.

Philip leaned back against the frame of the door in a mixture of disgust and anger with his father. "And she isn't taking it out on you either – this isn't about you – none of it!"

Damien felt the harshness in his son's words like the slap of a whip – maybe he was in shock.

Gloria rushed over to her husband and combed her fingers gently through his hair. "You're upset – don't say any more," she whispered softly into his ear.

Damien looked at his son and his wife and wished that he could achieve a fraction of their intimacy with someone. He couldn't honestly say that in all their years of marriage he and his wife had ever been united. It was no wonder that he had resorted to numerous liaisons to fill the gap.

It had been a wonderful, horrible day. Kate's stomach was

in a knot as she twisted and turned in bed. The glimmer of moonlight poked every now and again through the gap in her bedroom curtains. She had dreamt of spending a day with Shane, like the one that had just passed, on the lonely nights when Stefan had started coming home later and later. She used to work in her studio until midnight and then retire for the night with a book before her thoughts would drift off in his direction. But those imaginary days were different to the one she had just spent. Shane was much the same in so many ways but she was aware all through that he had a wife that he was going home to. Would it have been a different type of day if they were both single?

Hanging over her were images of her mother in Cornhill Hospital. How must she be feeling tonight? She felt helpless and wished she could do something more proactive for her. Her stomach churned slowly and she felt herself retch slightly. Her father had recently installed an en-suite bathroom and she was glad of that now. As she approached the white ceramic basin she spewed up the contents of her stomach, missing the tiled floor by centimetres. She knelt down and held her forehead. It was no surprise that her day should end this way. She glanced at her watch and saw that it had turned midnight nearly an hour earlier. She was forty.

Shane tiptoed quietly into his bedroom. Natasha was curled up under the bedcovers like a cat. She didn't make a sound and Shane undressed silently – careful not to wake her. He shimmied under the covers and hit the switch on the bedside lamp. Through the curtains a sliver of moonlight shone in and he sighed. He wasn't sure what he had expected to achieve by meeting Kate today. He needed to know what his true feelings for her were but now felt even more uncertain. He loved Natasha. He looked over as her body rose and fell gently with each breath. But there was no passion in their relationship. She didn't look at him the way Kate did. She didn't enthral him the way Kate did. There was only one Kate.

Shane pulled the covers up over his shoulders and turned his back to his wife. He didn't want to feel the same way as he had after the last time he met Kate. He was a glutton for punishment. As thoughts of Kate slipped through his mind he realised he was back to square one – probably worse than the last time.

Annabel curled up in a tiny ball on the large empty bed. Thank God Colin's away, she thought. She had been shaking since Damien rang. She could still see the look on Rosa's face as she entered the kitchen. *The girl must think I'm crazy.*

He was the last person Annabel had expected to hear from and it was only after she put the phone down that she realised there was so much she wanted to ask him. He was kind but businesslike. Did he ever think about their time together the way she did?

She turned over, more restless than she had been any night since the fiasco in Biarritz. She could always try to ring him again! But Betty would be home tomorrow and anyway, it was already tomorrow. It was Kate's birthday.

It hit Damien like a dart. He had forgotten all about her birthday. Then he gave a deep sigh. It was unlikely that was the reason behind Kate's strange attitude towards him but he couldn't think of anything else. Kate was never fussed about her birthday and he never remembered it. He had always relied on Betty to get a card for their daughter. She would even sign it on his behalf. That wasn't all he would miss about Betty. They had muddled their way through the years well enough, considering the lack of ardour on both sides. There was no way they would have got married at all if she weren't already three months pregnant.

But then, if they hadn't had Kate, he would never have met Annabel. She was like a flame that sparkled briefly in his life. There had been other women who had caught his eye but no one compared to Annabel. But he had to let her go – it was the right thing to do. Just like marrying Betty was the right thing to do at the time.

10

Kate's insides were rumbling and she wasn't able to eat her breakfast for the third morning in a row. She had to brush her teeth twice before she got rid of the nasty metal taste in her mouth.

She ran her hands over the soft pillowcases and straightened the bedclothes on her parents' bed. Her father had moved most of his clothes to the spare room. Kate thought it was probably the best thing to do. Her mother would be tender after the operation and needed the space for comfort. In all her years it was the last thing she thought she would be doing on the morning of her fortieth birthday. The phone rang in the distance but she ignored it. It wasn't her house.

"Kate!" Damien called up the stairs.

"Yes," she replied.

"It's the boys!"

Kate rushed to the small white ornate phone that rested on the bedside locker.

"Hello!" she answered impatiently. "Ciarán, David, it's great to hear from you!"

She listened to them sing 'Happy Birthday'.

"You're little pets to remember."

They told her that her present was in the post – they had to redirect it to Dublin.

"Thank you, boys. How is school?"

She listened to them tell how well they were getting on in football and they were both top of the class in maths. "How's your English?" she asked. The giddy twelve-year-old boys guffawed at the other end of the line – they were always getting into trouble for using colloquial phrases.

"Your gran is very sick and I'll have to stay in Dublin a bit longer than expected, so you may have to come here for the Easter holidays."

The boys seemed pleased that they were going to Dublin. There was no point in telling them how ill their gran really was, yet.

"Okay, calm down and I'll see you soon. Your professor will give you your tickets. Bye, boys, and thanks for remembering!" She knew that it was their housekeeper who would have organised the call but it was lovely to hear her sons' chirpy little voices. She longed to see them and hold them. Sometimes she questioned her decision to send them to boarding school. It was good that they were twins. At least they had each other.

"I'm on my way to get your mother!" Damien called up the stairs.

"I'll be here!" she shouted back.

The day had been all worked out. She would cook a traditional roast and they would have family lunch like they used to. It would be like some sort of last supper as Philip was returning to England in the evening. She felt poignant that all this should happen on her fortieth birthday. Philip would have Gloria at the table and she would be on her own. She felt a pang of need, wishing that Shane was available. She wished it was the day before when he had sat by her side and massaged her ego. But she had to get through the day on her own. She wondered about Annabel. She certainly would have got the hint by now – especially as they hadn't made peace before her birthday last Friday.

She patted the bedcovers one more time before leaving her mother's bedroom.

When Betty appeared in the hall she looked better than before the operation but Kate suspected that the reason behind it was the drugs that she was taking.

"It's so lovely to be home!" She turned to Damien. "Put my bag up to my room," she ordered and he climbed the stairs without uttering a word. "How have you been getting on?" she smiled at Kate.

Kate embraced her mother gently, careful not to bang into her tender torso. "It's great to have you home."

Philip and Gloria appeared from behind the kitchen door and welcomed Betty warmly.

"I'll have a cup of tea first before I take a little rest," she beamed.

Kate knew the next few months were going to be unbearable. Her mother liked to be the one rushing around doing all the household chores for everybody. She would be so miserable when she was unable to do anything herself.

Even though it was Rosa's day off, she accompanied Annabel and her children down the twisting pathway that led to the fishermen's harbour. The brightly coloured marquees attracted visitors and locals alike.

"What do you buy here?" Rosa asked.

"Homemade breads, jams, pâtés, cakes and so on . . . some stalls do speciality coffees and you can even get handmade jewellery."

"Can I have a chocolate bunny?" Rebecca begged.

"We'll see," Annabel replied, knowing full well that her daughter would get one as always on a Sunday morning.

Although Annabel had taken the short walk many times to the market she felt an air of anticipation about this trip. She had to find out who organised it and how to get a stall. This was the start of a new and exciting venture that would give her life a sense of identity and achievement. She fancied herself as providing the stall that sold the best hummus and people travelling from all over Dublin to buy her wares. It was only the start, something small, but something for herself, where she wasn't known as Colin's wife or the children's mother.

Rebecca and Taylor were already at the counter where the delicate chocolate animals on a stick were sold. The Frenchman on the other side of the counter recognised Annabel as a frequent customer.

"*Bonjour, madame,*" he smiled. His dark moustache widened as he took her money.

"Good morning," she greeted him. "How are you today?"

"It is not raining so we are good," he replied with a shrug of his shoulders.

"I was wondering if you could help me? I need to know who organises this market."

"That is Seán Doonan – he will be here at half past three to collect money from traders who are in arrears."

"You wouldn't have a number for him, would you?"

The Frenchman shrugged again. He took his mobile phone out of his breast pocket and read out a phone number.

Annabel was quick to take the details down and was careful to thank him. After all, she could be working alongside him in a couple of weeks.

"Annabel, Annabel!" a voice called in the distance. The shrill singing quality meant it could only belong to Melissa.

Annabel turned around and caught a glimpse of the glamorous mum with her scrubbed and polished eight-year-old daughter and five-year-old son.

"Hi, Melissa, thanks again for the other night," she said once Melissa was within earshot.

"That was my pleasure!" Melissa sang. "Wasn't it a fabulous night!"

Annabel nodded. "You did way too much," she insisted. Way too much!

"Have you bought anything nice?" Melissa asked in her subtle enquiring tone.

"I'm actually doing a bit of research, Melissa," she said reluctantly. "I'm thinking of setting up a stall."

"Really?" Melissa was agog. "Doing what?"

"Making hummus and salads to start, then maybe quiches."

Melissa let out a little squeal. "Now you are teasing me!"

"No, honestly," Annabel replied earnestly. "I want to start a stall with my own produce."

"But why on earth would you do that?" Melissa asked, shaking her head in amazement.

Annabel had her answer ready. "A hobby."

"But you already play tennis!" Melissa gasped, showing how truly flummoxed she was by the revelation.

Annabel grinned internally, careful not to give any more away.

Shane straightened the lapels on his crisp white shirt.

"Where are you off to today?" Natasha asked, pulling herself up in the bed.

"Double Paris," he said as he knotted his tie in the dressing-table mirror. "I'll be back at about eight o'clock,"

"I'm going to Avoca for the day with Trudy."

"Have a good one," he said, leaning over the bed and planting an awkward kiss on the side of her cheek.

He had hopped out of their bed anxiously ten minutes earlier, on seeing that she was still asleep. She had opened her eyes as he shook the last drops of water from his body after his shower. He didn't want to be in a position where she expected them to make love. Her demands were getting more and more frequent in her anxiety to get pregnant and he was beginning to feel like a stud stallion every time she suggested making love. He grabbed his wallet from the bedside locker and put it into his back pocket as was his habit.

"See you later," he smiled at his wife.

"Have a good day, and be careful!" she called, combing her long golden hair back with both her hands as she lay splayed out on the bed.

She smiled smugly to herself. She loved being a pilot's wife. She loved it even more than she did Shane if she were being honest. Shane had been dating her friend Maria when she spotted him on a flight to Rome and she carefully had changed around her timetable for the following week to ensure that she was on all his flights. She cornered him on an overnight and told him about Maria's little exploits with the other captains on the fleet. He was putty in her hands. Natasha was always good at manipulating people and getting what she wanted and now that she had the house and sports car of her dreams she was bored. A baby was the next accessory that she desired and as her sister had given birth two months before, she was losing patience with the whole pregnancy process. She ruffled down lower in the bed. Yes, she was a lucky girl. Shane could afford to get a full-time nanny to help her after the baby was born so that her lifestyle wouldn't be too impinged upon. Natasha had it all worked out.

Shane could honestly say he was glad he was working today. He would have less time to think about Kate and how she was spending her birthday. Breakfast was a cup of black coffee and a banana before he sat into his BMW and made the arduous journey along the M50 to Dublin airport. He hit the radio controls on his dash and felt his world rock beneath him as Boston drummed out from the speakers. 'More Than a Feeling' was always their song. He hadn't heard it in years and it was particularly moving to hear it today of all days.

He reached out to his mobile handset resting on the dashboard. Before he could consider what he was doing he hit her name on his phone and waited while it rang.

One ring, two rings, three rings – he felt a jolt as he heard hello at the other end of the line.

"Happy Birthday, Kate! I couldn't let the day go by without wishing you the best."

"Shane, thank you!" Kate answered with a mixture of surprise and pleasure.

"How are you getting on?" he asked. "Doing anything special?"

"My mum's just arrived home from hospital actually but she's chatting to Philip and Gloria. What are you up to today?"

"I'm going to Paris – twice."

"I wish I was going with you – I'm really missing the boys."

"It must be hard. How is your mum?"

"She's bearing up okay but we had bad news – the secondaries were confirmed and there is no way she wants another operation. They aren't even sure if it would do much good."

"Jesus, Kate, I'm sorry to hear that." He was genuinely saddened. "Poor Betty!"

"We're all still in shock."

"Listen, I'm off tomorrow – is there anything I can do to help?" Shane wanted to see her and console her personally.

"I could do with getting out for a walk in the afternoon sometime if you feel like dropping out," she suggested.

"About three?"

"Sounds good," she said, nodding even though she knew he couldn't see her.

"I'll be over at three then. Happy Birthday again."

"Thanks, Shane."

Kate switched off her phone and walked with a spring in her step back to the kitchen. She had received two nice phone calls to cheer her up so far. Deep down she wanted to hear Annabel's voice but pride wouldn't allow her to take a call from her friend, even if she did phone after all the rebuffs.

"Who was that, dear?" Betty called down from her bed.

She's still got a good pair of lungs, Kate thought. "Shane, Mum," she called. "He was asking for you."

Betty smiled to herself. He was definitely the most handsome boy that Kate ever brought into Greenfield Close. She could understand what Kate saw in his mild and gentle ways. He reminded her so much of Liam in appearance. But Liam was really a wolf in sheep's clothing, as Betty had to find out the hard way. It was ironic that Kate should be attracted to someone similar to him.

Betty had settled for Damien and he had given her and her children a good life, but at times she still thought of Liam and today was one of those days. She was saddened that she would never see him again. Maybe in the next life . . . She would put on a brave face for her family and friends but deep down inside she had resigned herself to the ravages of cancer.

"Will you have a cup?" Kate stood at the bedroom door holding a china mug filled with piping hot tea.

"I didn't hear you come upstairs." Betty manoeuvred herself carefully up in the bed. "I'd love one."

Kate placed it down on the bedside locker.

Betty patted the bed, encouraging Kate to sit down. "Tell me about your date with Shane."

"It wasn't a date, Mum!" Kate rolled her eyes. "He's married."

"Well, so are you, technically."

Kate was surprised by her mother's attitude. "We went for a coffee in town and then a walk around the Green. That was pretty much it."

"Did he look the same?" Betty was becoming animated.

"The same – I mean, he has a little grey around his temples. He looks well."

"He was the one," Betty nodded.

"Hang on, I did have two husbands," Kate said. Even though she agreed with her, she was confused by her mother's reaction.

"There's only ever one though!" Betty grimaced.

Kate had never heard her mother talk like this. "Well, of course you think that because you were lucky enough to find Dad!"

Betty hesitated and for a terrible moment Kate wasn't sure how her mother was going to react. Then Betty just nodded – leaving Kate confused.

"If you get the chance to be with him again, grab it, Kate!"

"He's married, Mum. I'm not a home-wrecker."

"There are worse things than wrecking a marriage," Betty said, the words sounded bitter in her mouth. "You could stay in a loveless one."

"Well, I'm about to sort that out – Stefan and I will be divorced by the end of the month."

"He was never right for you, Kate. You were on the rebound and you had the boys. You should have come home that time."

Kate squirmed as she recalled the barrage of demands that the Mackens, her husband's parents, had made on her from another country. There was no way she could have raised her sons under their grandparents' watchful gaze. "I did what I thought was best at the time, Mum, and the boys are fine."

"Get them out of boarding school and bring them home, Kate," Betty pleaded.

The words hung in the air as they left Betty's mouth. They were the wishes of a dying woman and Kate knew that she could not ignore them.

"I'll think about it, Mum, but France is their home, and mine."

Betty nodded. "You must do what you think is right, but if you get the chance to be happy with Shane again, take it! Grab it with both hands and don't let go!"

Betty's eyes were fixed on Kate's.

Kate had never seen her mother look so intense. It made her wonder what secrets Betty was taking to the grave with her.

The front door swung open as Annabel was walking down the stairs.

"I didn't expect to see you home so early," she exclaimed.

Colin's furrowed brow told a multitude. His golf clubs were flung onto the maple-wood floors with a crash.

"Where are the kids?" he grunted.

"I'm taking them for a swim with Rosa."

He didn't reply but instead went out to the car to get the rest of his stuff. Annabel swallowed hard. She hated it when he was like this. No one on the outside knew that this was the price she had to pay for being his wife. If she had a means of supporting herself she could do something about his moods, have the strength to stand up to him. He often treated her like one of his apprentices in his shiny office in the IFSC. At least they could move job to get away from him.

Rosa came out from the kitchen with Rebecca in her arms.

"Colin's home – we may as well go soon," Annabel said.

On his return to the hall, with another large bag, Colin changed his expression like a light switch. "Rosa, good to see you! I hope Annabel has been looking after you well?"

"Oh, yes, Mr Hamilton!"

"Rosa, I told you, call me Colin!"

It really annoyed Annabel to watch her husband turn on his bogus charm in this way – who did he think he was fooling? He always did it with attractive women and his friends' wives.

"We're going now," Annabel said curtly. "Is Taylor ready?"

"Don't let her get grumpy with you, Rosa," Colin snorted. "Just tell me if she's being bossy."

Annabel wanted to hit him over the head. She had little enough power or decision-making in the house when he was around, and now he wanted to mess up her relationship with the *au pair*. It was just as well Rosa was so nice. Annabel hoped she could see through his shallow ways.

She drove efficiently but silently to the pool. Rosa sat in the back with the girls, playing Nintendo DS. If only she could do something more positive. She remembered she needed to call the guy who organised the market and, while she was stopped at a traffic light, hit his number on her hands-free kit.

"Seán Doonan," he answered.

"Hi, my name is Annabel Hamilton and I was wondering what the procedure is for setting up a stall in the Farmers' Market in Howth?"

"What do you produce?"

"I make hummus and salads but I would like to do more . . ."

"You could be in luck. The harbourmaster has increased the space available for stalls. I could give you a twelve-foot-square area for eighty euros per week."

"Oh, really, I think I'd be very interested in that."

She let him talk on about the rental costs and overheads – she would definitely be able to finance it from her housekeeping and use the profits from week to week to build the business up. "This all sounds great. When can I start?"

"Next week if you like," he replied.

Annabel couldn't believe there was a space free so soon. She would have a lot of work to do during the week to get ready. She couldn't make the produce too early or it would go off. Little butterflies gathered in her stomach as she pulled into the carpark of the leisure centre. Things had changed since her two days in Biarritz – but it wasn't all negative.

Shane checked his watch. "Good," he said out loud.

Again the weather was smiling on him as he crossed

the toll-bridge and arrived on the northside of the city. There was a familiarity, a type of homecoming, that accompanied this symbolic journey across the River Liffey. Now that he was meeting Kate who was wrapped around so many of his happiest memories he felt even more exhilarated and excited. Their last meeting had been full of tension and unspoken moments of embarrassment. Today would be different. They had wiped away the cobwebs of their relationship and now he had a chance to get to know Kate the woman. He felt deep down that he was in serious danger of falling every bit as much in love with her as he had with Kate the girl. If he were to be really honest with himself, he had never stopped loving Kate.

He pulled his car in at Vernon's off-licence and picked up a drinkable Chilean red that had a screw-off cap for convenience. He took two plastic cups from the counter-top and smartly made his way back to the car where he promptly flicked the switch on his dash. He didn't want to turn up with the roof down. Kate wouldn't be impressed twice!

Kate checked her hair in the bathroom mirror on realising that it was almost three o'clock. The pressures of looking after her mother, and the impending art exhibition that she wasn't doing any work for, were starting to show. Her usually tanned face was looking pallid and tired, and she was still off her food.

The doorbell rang and she turned sharply, anxious to answer it.

"Is that Shane at the door?" her mother called.

"Yes, I'll get him to say hello when we get back!" Kate hollered, running down the stairs.

This was Kate and Shane time and she didn't want to share him with anyone else.

She pulled back the door and he looked even better than the last time he had called. He was wearing a checked shirt that made him look broader than usual.

"Hi, Kate," he smiled.

"Stay where you are," she whispered. "I'm getting my bag."

She returned in an instant.

"Bye, Mum!" she called and was gone before Betty had a chance to try and get down the stairs.

"You brought the weather with you from France," Shane remarked.

"It has been nice, hasn't it?" Kate stalled for a moment. "Do you fancy taking a stroll down Dollymount strand?"

Shane visibly flinched as she said it. "We had some good times down there, hadn't we?"

"Like the time you saved my life!" Kate teased. Shane's agitated expression told her to stop the charade. "I love winding you up – sorry, Shane."

He smiled. He could never stay cross with her for long. "Hey, I've a bottle of vino in the car – will we take it with us?"

"Yeah, and we can take the car over the wooden bridge and leave it by the statue," Kate said with a nod.

Shane parked the BMW by a bank of rocks and they

braced themselves before facing the brisk wind that rose from the shoreline.

"God, it's so beautiful here," she sighed.

"I love this time of year as much as the summer," Shane agreed.

Kate looked at him from under her fringe. "I appreciate it now – more than all those years ago. We grew up in a lovely place."

"I still find it hard to get used to the southside to be honest. Natasha's the southsider." He sounded doleful.

"She wouldn't move?"

He shook his head. "Her folks live around the corner from us and she keeps harping on about how handy it will be when we start a family."

Kate was visibly jolted by his words. "I didn't realise . . . I mean, of course you must be hoping for a family." She felt a hard lump build in her throat as she uttered the words.

"I shouldn't really be talking about it but we are meant to be . . ." he paused, "trying! God, I hate that expression!"

"So you're both sure it's time?"

"She's dead keen but I'm still getting my head around the idea. It's strange but I always thought it would feel different – deciding to start a family. I have to think of her and her needs though."

"And what about your needs, Shane? It's a big step and childrearing should not to be jumped into lightly." She could see the concern etched all over his face.

"I mean, we are married long enough now – she's thirty-two and under pressure, I guess!"

"I didn't realise she was that much younger." Kate felt a wave of jealousy sweep over her.

"She might as well be twenty-two at times, I swear!" He stopped when he realised he was saying too much. "So, on a lighter note, what did you get for your birthday?"

The day had come and gone, and apart from a stripy top from Gloria and the promise of a gift from her sons she had nothing to show for it . . . except of course Annabel's birthday outfit in Biarritz . . . .

"It was a difficult day actually . . ." She paused.

"I can only imagine . . . with your mum coming home from hospital and all that."

"It's okay," she said with a shake of her head. "Hey, I treated myself to a tattoo when I was in Biarritz!"

"Can you show it to me? I mean it's not on your right nipple or anywhere like that, is it?"

Kate gave him a playful thump on his upper arm. "It's on my inner ankle."

"Let's see," he urged.

Kate reached down and unzipped her ankle boot. She balanced precariously on one foot with her tattooed leg raised off the ground as she slid down the sock until the flesh underneath was bare.

"The Third Eye!" he exclaimed.

"Well done!" Kate applauded. "I'm impressed that you recognise it. Annabel got it in the same place."

"I don't believe it! You got her to get a tattoo!" His expression showed his surprise.

"Sure I did." Kate pulled up her sock and zipped up her boot.

"So how is Annabel these days?" he asked.

"We . . . eh, had a bit of a falling out in Biarritz actually and haven't been in touch," Kate replied vaguely.

"Not even for your birthday?"

"I'd rather not go into it."

Shane knew when it was best not to delve any deeper. If Kate wanted to tell him anything, she would do it in her own time. But he was amazed that the girls had fallen out after all the years.

The sea breeze carried them further down the strand until they reached a wall of rocks that had to be scaled to continue along the beach.

"Which way do you want to go?" Shane asked.

"I'm no expert but those clouds gathering over there look like they have rain in them. Will we go back to the car?"

Shane nodded. "We can tackle the wine there if you feel up to it."

"Four o'clock in the afternoon, on Dollymount strand with a bottle of wine – sounds familiar?"

Shane grinned.

"Only we drank Black Tower and Blue Nun in those days," Kate smiled. "I'd forgotten about them – now there's a blast from the past."

"Didn't I tell you I have Blue Nun in the car?"

Kate didn't know whether to believe him or not. "Do you still drink that?"

"Really, Kate, we aren't so wine ignorant in Ireland any more!" he laughed as the expression on her face softened.

The car was warm after the cool April breeze had blown away the cobwebs.

"*Voilà,*" Shane exclaimed as he handed over a plastic cup and screwed open the Cabernet Sauvignon.

"Thanks," Kate said, taking the half-filled cup. It tasted tart on her tongue but was acceptable nonetheless.

"Cheers!" Shane tipped the lip of his plastic cup off Kate's and they drank a couple of mouthfuls in silence.

"It's weird being here like this, isn't it?" he said.

Kate nodded. "It's a bit surreal all right. But it also feels so natural being with you again."

Shane took a deep breath and let it out slowly. "I've had trouble thinking about anything else except you for the last few days. Not a good idea when you're coming into runway one-zero in Dublin airport on a busy Sunday night."

Kate blushed at the thought of Shane seeing her face on the instruments in the cockpit.

"You've been a constant in my mind too." Her brown eyes widened as she turned and leaned her head against the neck-rest.

Shane propped his cup into the holder on the dashboard, then turned to meet her gaze. "How did we manage to get it so wrong?" he sighed.

"Maybe we didn't get it wrong. Maybe this is the way it's meant to be." She gulped quietly, not really believing her own supposition.

Shane couldn't resist touching her any longer. He lifted his right hand and gently brushed it off her left cheek, pausing for a moment before removing it from her face. The heat from his touch melted Kate's skin. She closed her eyes – willing his next move. His scent strengthened as she felt his breath against her cheek and she braced herself before he softly placed a single warm kiss on her lips. When she opened her eyes his face was as close as it could be.

They both closed their eyes and kissed again, this time with impatience and longing bound tightly together. The sweet taste of wine and saliva mingled until they dissolved into one another, drinking and tasting with relish. Neither could tell how long they had been kissing when they eventually stopped.

"Jesus!" Kate exclaimed, her knees shaky and her mind heady from the experience.

Shane was breathless with eyes dazed. "What are we going to do?" he asked, looking out at the sea, afraid to look at Kate again.

"Get a room?" Kate suggested half in jest and half in all seriousness.

"I mean, what are we going to do with our lives, Kate?" Shane's tone was solemn. He was wearing his heart on his sleeve and didn't want to make light of the situation.

"Well, I'm not quite divorced and you are still married, so there isn't much choice at the moment," she muttered resolutely.

Her words cut him. "Let's take other people out of the equation. What about us?"

His tone was serious and sincere. He felt as though he had crept to the edge and one word from Kate could tip him over or save him from the life he had chiselled out for himself. Kate swallowed hard, unsure of the right answer to give. "I'm not going to be responsible for breaking up a marriage," she said. "We've only met twice in as many years – we need to put it in perspective."

His heart plummeted. "Are you telling me that kiss meant nothing?" he asked with glassy eyes.

Kate shook her head. It was time to be totally serious. "You know how that kiss felt! But we have to be sure. Spend more time together."

"You don't understand." Shane picked at the leather on his steering-wheel. "Natasha wants a family and I don't want that to . . ."

He didn't need to finish. Kate understood what was going on inside his mind. She put her hand comfortingly on top of his.

"If it's meant to be, we will be together."

"Wasted time," he said, shaking his head. "For Natasha too."

"You can't jump out of Natasha's arms into mine after a couple of days. We have to be sure and we both have stuff to sort out. I live in France; my sons are

French. We can still continue to see each other until we are both sure."

"I am sure, Kate. But I'm concerned that you mightn't be. You're the impulsive one jumping from marriage to marriage. Why won't you take a chance on us?"

"Because, Shane, you are different. You are my dream. You are the one." Her words were articulated clearly and carefully. "If we get together, it has to be perfect."

Then he understood.

11

"There's no bloody way a wife of mine is selling anything behind a stall, like some sort of traveller!" Colin shouted.

Annabel grimaced. "It's a hobby," she replied quietly. "Something for me."

"You have the kids, and a bloody *au pair* and, and what about tennis?"

Annabel wanted to cry. Is that all Melissa and Colin thought she was good for – bloody tennis!

Kate braced herself for the landing – relieved that she was going home at last. Betty was comfortable for the time being. Little had changed in her condition since Kate had arrived in Dublin over two weeks ago. The rollercoaster of emotions she'd had to deal with following her mother's operation and after meeting Shane had left her exhausted. He was there at the airport to see her off but was evidently longing for her return. She was high when she was in his company and lonely when they were apart. The intensity of their love was different to any other she had experienced. It was right that they hadn't slept with each other yet. He was still married and their love had to be uncontaminated by any sort of betrayal, if it was going to last.

Toulouse airport was a breeze to walk through. She carried a small case and was in Arrivals in minutes. She spotted Fabian's tall and lean figure in the distance. His black hair flopped from side to side as he rushed to greet her.

"*Chérie, mon dieu,* but look at you!" he exclaimed. "Give me a hug. You look awful!"

Kate couldn't help but smile. She had missed him like a brother. In many ways she felt closer to him than to Philip.

"It's been a bit mad, Fabian – how are things here?"

"You missed nothing, *chérie*, but we all missed you!"

Kate smiled as Fabian directed her to his Renault.

"Now, your mother first, how is she?" Fabian asked in his usual manner of drawing information.

"Stable. It's terminal as I said on the phone but we have to make her as comfortable as possible. She could last six months but –"

Fabian raised an eyebrow. "She won't?" he finished her sentence.

Kate shook her head silently.

"And what about Annabel?" Fabian probed. "Are you friends again?"

"I haven't spoken to her."

The third degree was the last thing she needed from her friend.

"This is the time you need to talk to her – you need all of the support you can get."

"I spent a bit of time with an old friend actually," Kate revealed, anxious to change the subject.

"Tell Fabian," he ordered.

"He's an old boyfriend."

Fabian gave an acknowledging nod. "Continue!"

"We've met a few times over the last couple of weeks and we still have feelings for each other."

"Fantastic!" Fabian smacked his lips. "That is just what you need, *ma chérie.*"

"I'm not so sure, Fabian," she sighed. "He's married."

"Ah!" he groaned. "I hate it too when I meet a nice guy and he is married!"

"Shane – that's his name – wants to leave his wife and make a go of it with me."

"Problem solved!" Fabian said as he gave the steering wheel a triumphant thump.

"You know, Fabian, I've done a good bit of thinking. I feel I need to take stock of my life."

"You cannot let this Shane slip if he is so special. You must act – *vite*!"

"I know this doesn't make sense because when I'm with him I am happier than I have ever been in my life, but . . ." she paused.

"What is this but?"

"There is something stopping me." Kate ran her hand

over her forehead. "Some little voice ringing inside telling me that this is not the time."

"You are forty now – not a baby any more!" Fabian informed her gently.

"I know. Thanks for your card by the way."

"I am only sorry I couldn't give it to you in person," he said, reaching into the breast pocket of his calico jacket and taking out a long slender package. He handed it over with his eyes still firmly fixed on the road ahead of him. "For you!"

Kate opened the navy-blue box and revealed a silver chain with a disc dangling from it. Imprinted on the circle was an enamelled image of The Third Eye.

"It's beautiful! To match my tattoo!"

"No, *chérie*, I bought it months ago – long *before* you showed me the tattoo you got in Biarritz! It was at the market in Pau and when I saw it I had no choice but to buy it for you."

Kate gulped at the coincidence. She stared at the pretty necklace and gently caressed the glazed image. She thought of Annabel – she was a huge loss in her life. Now she was going to lose her mother too. She rubbed her right eyebrow in a gesture of comfort. She wished she could wipe away the butterflies that were starting to dance in her stomach.

"Did I tell you?" she said hesitantly. "Annabel got the same image tattooed to her ankle while we were in Biarritz."

"It is a good symbol to get. The Third Eye is the

home of our deepest and truest emotions," he said sincerely. "I hope you make it up with your friend, Kate, and I hope you find happiness in your fortieth year."

"Thank you, Fabian," she said, stroking his cheek with the back of her fingers. "It's very thoughtful of you."

Halfway through the journey Kate was feeling queasy and she realised that the butterflies were more of a physical manifestation. She begged Fabian to stop. He pulled off the motorway and into a lay-by. She was retching from deep inside her stomach and had to hold onto the car door for support when she eventually dragged her heavy legs out of the car.

"My poor Kate, you are still upset?" Fabian leaned out over the passenger seat as he watched his friend vomit on a patch of grass.

"I don't know what's wrong with me, Fabian," gasped Kate. "I've been feeling like this for the last couple of weeks."

Her legs wobbled as she sat back into the car.

"I'm exhausted all the time, as well."

Fabian handed her a tissue to wipe her mouth. "You need to see the doctor, *chérie*. There is a lot going on for you."

Kate usually tried not to resort to conventional medicine but she had to agree with Fabian – she wasn't coping. A trip to Dr Borel wouldn't take long.

Later that evening she took the short walk to the village

surgery. Dr Borel was standing in the doorway of his room with his spectacles resting on the tip of his nose.

"Everybody is well today!" he grinned at Kate as she approached him from the empty waiting room. "Come in. I am glad of the company."

The small country practice was friendly and informal and suited Kate.

"How are you, Madame Cassaux?"

"Doctor, I have been having a bad time . . ." She told him of her divorce, of her mother's illness and the trip to Dublin, and the pressure of producing work for her impending exhibition.

"I will check you out," he said, taking the blood pressure monitor in hand. His manner was reassuring and Kate felt relief as he took her arm. When he was finished measuring her blood pressure he gave her an empty bottle.

"Can you give me a sample, please? Then I want to check your bloods."

Kate went into the tiny closet off his surgery and returned three minutes later.

The doctor had a bottle of urine analysis sticks ready to dip into the yellow liquid which he did quickly and discreetly by the sink. The final tester was a small plastic wand which he dipped into the urine. He then washed his hands and returned to the desk with a small grin on his face.

"Madame Cassaux, yes, you do have a condition."

Kate braced herself. She imagined how her mother

must have felt when she visited the doctor for the first time after finding the lump on her breast. She didn't want to think about the prognosis. Who would look after her children now that her mother only had months to live? She couldn't and wouldn't leave her boys with her father.

"You are going to have a baby!"

Kate's mouth dropped. This couldn't be happening. This was the sort of thing that happened to adolescents when they drank too much or took drugs. This should not be happening to a woman who had just had her fortieth birthday.

Dr Borel leaned forward and touched Kate on the arm.

"Mrs Cassaux, are you all right?" he asked gently.

Kate twitched slightly in her seat and shook herself down. "Yes, Doctor, it's just a bit of a shock."

Kate's head was spinning. Biarritz! What possessed her to be so careless? In her wild days she always had a condom in her handbag. It was obligatory – like her lip-gloss and wallet. How could she have been so irresponsible? She didn't even know how to contact the father. Hell, she didn't even know his second name. What was she going to do?

"Really, Annabel," her mother chastised. "I don't know what's wrong with you. There are plenty of women who would love to be in your position. Colin is an excellent provider for his family – you're really showing him up."

"But this isn't about Colin or my family, Mum," Annabel sighed.

"Is this all about turning forty? Because some people's hormones do start to go a bit ditsy."

"Mum, why can't everyone just let me get on with it? I love making food and I want to see if I can make a go of a little business on my own."

Lily shook her head in dismay. She didn't have quarter the resources or income that Annabel now had when she was rearing her family and she couldn't understand her daughter's actions. She had assured Colin that she would talk some sense into Annabel but now, on the evening before the market, it looked as though it was too late for that. She had never known Annabel to be so strong-minded about doing something on her own. She had always found it easy to steer her in the right direction before.

"Will you have a cup of tea, Mum?" Annabel was anxious to change the subject.

"Go on then, a quick one. It's getting late."

Annabel poured the water from the kettle into her blue and white china teapot.

"Have you any news about Betty?" Lily asked.

"I haven't been speaking to Kate," Annabel replied awkwardly.

"Whyever not?" Lily demanded. "This is the very time you could be helping the Carltons out, instead of running around doing silly markets."

Annabel sighed. Was her mother ever going to drop

it? "I have been trying to ring Kate. I told you she doesn't answer my calls."

"She's probably noticed you've lost the plot too," Lily replied sarcastically.

Annabel clicked the roof of her mouth with her tongue.

"What was the row about exactly?" Lily probed.

"I don't want to go there, Mum. It's just something that happened years ago."

"She's always been a very good friend to you," Lily droned on. "You should be investing time into your friendships instead of –"

"Don't say it, Mum," Annabel interrupted. "Just don't say any more."

"Come around, now!" Kate pleaded. There was no one else in the world that she felt she could talk to at this minute. A few weeks ago she would have lifted the phone to Annabel straight away but now she didn't even have her.

Fabian knew the difference. He knew when Kate was really upset or just throwing a tantrum. He jumped into his Renault, almost forgetting to turn the headlights on in the twilight. When he got to her backdoor it was worse than he had expected. Kate was already dressed in a housecoat. Black tracks from her mascara slid down her cheeks.

"*Chérie*!" Appalled, he rushed to her side. "What is wrong? Is it your mother? Tell me *vite*!"

Kate ran the palm of her right hand up over her nose, then searched distractedly for a tissue. Fabian took some kitchen roll from the counter-top and handed it to her. She still said nothing but used it to wipe the tears away.

"Kate, please," he whispered softly.

She looked up at him. Her eyelids drooped at the corners. "I'm pregnant," she uttered.

"*Mon dieu!*" Fabian was aghast – this was a complication of massive proportions. "How did this happen?"

"It happens when a man and woman have sex," she said, laughing briefly.

"But who is the father?" he asked, wide-eyed, throwing his arms in the air.

Kate sat speechless. Her mind flashed back to the Hotel Windsor and the bronze nubile body belonging to the young surfer. She hadn't slept with Stefan in over a year. She hadn't slept with Shane because she wanted to wait until it was right. Until he was free.

"There is only one person who it can be!" She sobbed heartily into the snotty piece of kitchen roll. "The surfer in Biarritz!"

Fabian took a sharp intake of breath. He jumped up to get her a fresh piece of tissue paper. "Here, Kate," he said, handing the tissue over. He felt inadequate to handle this situation – his gay friends didn't have pregnancy complications as a rule.

"Do I tell him he's going to be a father? How am I even going to find him to tell him? What am I going to do?"

"You could ring the hotel to get in touch, I suppose," Fabian suggested.

"Oh, yes, of course . . . but they might not give me his number and even if they did, would he really want to know? He told me himself that he was married to his bloody board!"

Fabian tenderly caressed the side of Kate's face. He hated to see anyone in this sort of pain, least of all his dear friend. There was one solution which would definitely solve her problem.

"You don't have to have it," he suggested gently.

She knew instantly what he meant and it had been the first thought that crossed her mind on hearing the news in the doctor's surgery.

"I was reared on Catholic guilt – I never thought I'd ever have to contemplate something like an abortion," she gulped. "Especially at my age."

"That is another reason why you may not want to take the risk of pregnancy."

"I've only just turned forty – lots of women have their first baby at my age," she snapped.

"Sorry!" he winced.

"No, Fabian, *I'm* sorry," Kate said softly and she stretched out her hand to hold his. "I can't believe this is happening to me, just when I thought I was getting back on track with Shane."

"Well, maybe he won't mind?" Fabian flicked a wrist in the air.

"I think two sons from a previous marriage is enough baggage, don't you?"

"Kate, you have to think about an abortion. It is not a good time with your mother so ill and all the other things happening in your life."

Kate knew that Fabian was right but she didn't know how she could handle it at the moment. There was too much going on and this was the last straw.

"Fabian, I know this may sound strange but I really thought I would never get pregnant again. I mean nothing happened for Stefan and me. I thought there was something wrong with him. Then when he got his assistant pregnant I thought there must be something wrong with me."

"But you have the boys!"

"I know but I thought maybe that was a fluke!" she groaned. "Anyway, this is not something I can just wipe out like a bad hairdo. Besides . . . I always wanted a little girl and maybe . . ."

"Too many problems for one night, *chérie*," Fabian sighed gently. He stroked the side of her face, then pushed her hair back behind her ears. "I am going to make a nice bath with a lot of bubbles for you and then I will pour you a glass of wine and bring it to you there, okay?"

"Thanks, Fabian," she replied softly. "I'm so lucky to have you . . . but would you mind making a cup of tea instead of some wine? I've been feeling ill all week after drinking wine and now I know why."

"Of course," Fabian smiled. "A cup of tea it is."

Shane crept quietly through the dimly lit house. He'd been in Barcelona and Glasgow earlier. He threw his keys on the kitchen table and went over to the tap to get some water. He missed her like a limb already. It hadn't even been a full day since she left for Toulouse but he was counting down the hours until she returned.

"Shane!" Natasha's lyrical voice called from upstairs.

Damn, he thought – she's awake.

"Yes?" he hollered.

"Would you bring me up a glass of water?"

"Yes, up in a minute."

He carried the glass up the stairs, all the time thinking and wondering how he was going to get out of sleeping with his wife for yet another night. It was nearly two weeks since they had last made love and she was watching her ovulation dates carefully.

"I've been trying everything to stay awake," she smiled. "Thank God you're home. Come to bed quick!"

Shane felt an incredible pressure bear down on him as Natasha stared at him like he was a prize bull. He definitely didn't want to make love to her now. As each day passed he questioned whether he ever wanted to make love to her again.

"I'm really tired," he blurted out. "Do you mind if I stay in the spare room?"

Natasha sat up in the bed. "Yes, I bloody well *do* mind! What is wrong with you this last week, Shane?"

"I'm really busy in work – I'll be fine."

"You're always really busy in work, so what is really wrong? We're trying for a baby, and we need to be having sex to do that!"

Shane put his hand up to his forehead. He hadn't wanted to say anything to hurt Natasha, but he couldn't let her go on with false hope. His feelings had changed and he didn't want to bring a child into the world with her while he was so uncertain.

"Now is not a good time."

"Why isn't it a good time?" Her voice was starting to quiver. "This is very fickle of you. You can't just turn around and say, I don't want a baby this month but I did four weeks ago!"

Shane knew she was right but there was no easy way of saying it. "I'm not as sure as I was last month and I just want a bit more time to get used to the idea," he gulped. "That's all."

Natasha flumped back on her pillows as if she had been given a sharp slap and she didn't like it one bit. She was good at getting what she wanted and Shane had never reneged on anything that he had promised her before. She would make him pay for this. "Go into the damn spare room then! I don't want to look at you at the moment!"

Shane was glad of the escape. Serious guilt was beginning to settle in his stomach. He needed to be braver and figure out a gentle way of letting Natasha down. She had done nothing wrong and he had to think everything through before he finished his marriage.

The spare room smelt dank and lonely. He felt he didn't deserve any better for hurting Natasha. He warmed up as he snuggled under the covers and images of Kate flooded his head. He prayed for a solution to his dilemma. He wanted Natasha to be happy and Kate to be back in his life full-time but had no idea if any of it was possible.

Annabel placed the last batch of hummus into the large cardboard box and closed it.

Rosa was still in her pyjamas and she had Rebecca by her side.

"Thanks for looking after the kids," Annabel smiled at the Spanish girl. "Bring them down later to see their mum at work!"

Rosa nodded and set about preparing the children's breakfast.

Annabel slammed the door of the Jeep and set off for the harbour. It was only a quarter past eight and already most of the stall-holders were rigging their canopies and stands. She settled beside Marcel, the French chocolate-maker, who gave her a friendly wave.

"You got a stall then!"

"Yes, thanks," she beamed. "It's great."

"You are lucky no rain today, and sometimes the wind – *puff!*"

Annabel smiled. The market traders were warm and welcoming, waving at her from all directions. Business was slack until about half past ten, then the people swarmed like bees around a honeypot.

Annabel sold the first carton of hummus with pride. "Thank you," she said politely, taking the five-euro note from an elderly lady with a tartan carrier bag and giving a coin back in change.

Then she was thronged with customers for three hours and didn't notice the time pass.

Rosa eventually arrived with the girls in tow. The girls skipped over to their mother, excited and amused at seeing her in her new role.

"Where's Sam?" Annabel asked Rosa.

"He wanted to stay at home with his PlayStation," Rebecca informed her.

"It's going well here. I can't believe it but I'm nearly sold out. I didn't make nearly enough."

"Would you like me to get you a cup of coffee?" Rosa asked, pointing to a stall over on the other side of the road.

"That would be lovely. Actually, can you get me a latte?"

Her daughters ran behind the stall and started pointing at the box full of blue and brown euro notes.

"Mummy, you're very rich!" Rebecca said.

"Thank you, darling! Yes, Mummy made that money today!" Annabel said proudly.

When Rosa returned she took the paper cup from her appreciatively. She hadn't noticed the cold setting into her hands until she held the warm cup and she understood why so many of the traders were wearing fingerless gloves. She tittered to herself as she pictured Melissa seeing her in this new guise.

"I will take the girls to the playground, Annabel."

"Thanks, Rosa," she said gratefully. "See you later, girls!"

"Bye, Mum!" her daughters called as they walked away.

She watched them getting smaller and smaller until they were specks in the distance.

By four o'clock Annabel was getting tired and she only had a few cartons of hummus left. Some of the larger traders were closing up their stalls and getting ready to go. Then, out of the corner of her eye she spotted a familiar figure walking towards her stall. He was the last person she expected to see at a market like this but he was on his own and wandering, like a lost soul, from stand to stand.

It took a few moments for him to recognise his daughter's friend in such unfamiliar surroundings but he was sure it was her when she waved at him. He strode over to her stall with speed and alacrity.

"Annabel, hi, I never expected to see you here –" Damien paused nervously. "Well, at least not behind a counter."

Annabel grinned bashfully. "It's my new venture, part of turning forty and doing something for myself."

"Good for you," he said and pointed down to the small hexagonal containers filled with different pastes. "What is it?"

"Hummus. That's lemon and coriander and that's sun-dried tomato –" She stopped when she realised the futility of the information she was giving. "You're not a big hummus man, I'd imagine."

"More your steak and chips!" Damien agreed with a nod, brown eyes twinkling. "I'm only here because Betty wanted me to get a special jam that apparently I like!"

"Did you get it?"

"No!"

They both laughed, pleased to be meeting on their own terms and not in connection with Kate.

"I hope you didn't mind my ringing," he said then, seriously. "I'm worried about Kate."

"So am I," Annabel sighed.

"I really need someone to tell me what's going on with her. Philip thinks I'm being self-centred but I feel she's acting like her mother's cancer is my fault." Anguish showed in Damien's voice.

"I think she must be very stressed," Annabel nodded. She hoped her guilt didn't show. "How is Betty? I couldn't believe it when I heard the news."

"She is in denial. She thinks she can fight this cancer but the disease has eaten through most of her organs – it's a very hard time."

"If there's anything I can do . . ."

Damien nodded his head appreciatively. "How is life for you, Annabel?"

"Picking up since I started doing this!" she smiled. "It's busy with three kids but I needed to do something that wasn't based around them and their activities, if you know what I mean."

"Good for you. I hope it's a great success." Damien pointed at the small cartons again. "And judging by the way these have sold, it looks like it is already."

"Fingers crossed!" Annabel was consumed with pride. Damien had changed little in all the years she had known him. He still managed to make her feel good in a way no one else could.

He stood back from the counter. "I'd better head," he said.

Annabel nodded. "It was good to see you."

He turned to go, then hesitated and turned back to her. "So you and Kate quarrelled over something trivial?" he asked awkwardly.

"Yes," Annabel mumbled, avoiding eye contact. "It was nothing worth quarrelling about – but you know how it is – hurtful things get said."

"Well, I hope you make it up with her, whatever it was."

"So do I," she replied. *So do I.*

Kate sat up in the bed and glanced at her reflection in the dressing-table mirror. She barely recognised herself. Had this happened because she turned forty or was it because she was pregnant at forty? It had been Stefan's idea to have the mirror against the wall at the end of the bed and she decided there and then to move it.

Fabian was a rock, she loved him dearly, but the one person she really needed help from at the moment was gone. Annabel was the only person she could speak to about something as traumatic as this. She had managed to block her out in the hustle and bustle of everything else going on but, sitting on her own in the Pyrénées, she missed not being able to pick up the phone and hear her friend's voice at the other end of the line. The sense of loss filled her until tears started to trickle down her face. She thought she had cried enough the night before but that was probably only the beginning. Decisions had to be made, things had to be done and she didn't know where to start.

Annabel would have told her gently and firmly how to tackle this situation. She closed her eyes and tried to picture Annabel's face. Should she have the baby or abort it? They were really the only two options open to her. Financially she could manage a baby on her own. The exhibition would pay for a nanny and support her for eighteen months. She thought of Stefan and wondered if the news would affect his feelings on the settlement. He was happy to give her the house at present as she was the injured party but if he discovered that she was pregnant he might not feel so generous. Then there was the overriding matter of Shane. There was no way she could tell him the truth at the moment. She wasn't sure how he would take the news.

"Oh, Annabel, I miss you!" she cried out loud. "Why did you have to sleep with my father?"

Her crutch was gone. She would have to sort her life out on her own in future. She felt more alone than she had ever felt in her life.

Rosa spread a dollop of home made strawberry jam on her toast.

"What are your plans for your day off?" Annabel asked as she started to clear the breakfast plates away. Rosa had already taken the children to school.

"I might go into the city and maybe visit the Guinness, eh, Hoop Store?"

"The Hop Store. That's a great idea, Rosa," Annabel

agreed. "You'll find it very interesting. Colin, can you give Rosa a lift into town so she can get the Luas from Connolly Station?"

"I can do that," Colin said, lifting his head from a pile of papers that he was checking over. "I'm going in about ten minutes."

"Thank you, Colin," Rosa smiled coyly.

"I'm playing tennis in ten minutes," Annabel said as she slipped out the kitchen door. "Have a good day, you two."

Colin grunted without looking up and Rosa nodded her head.

"So, how are you liking Ireland?" Colin asked, his tone lightening now that his wife had left the room.

"Very well, thank you." Rosa's cheeks turned pink. "I think I am lucky I have good family."

"I think we are the lucky ones getting you to look after us, Rosa," Colin snorted. "Do you want to go now?"

"Any time," she smiled.

Colin swaggered out to his Mercedes coupé with his briefcase swinging by his side. Rosa was impressed to be having a ride in his car at last. As she opened the passenger door, the smell of leather from the plush cream seats wafted in the air.

"Belt up!" Colin chortled, as he slipped on his seat belt.

He put his foot hard on the accelerator, revving the engine in his attempt to make an impression on his passenger. It wasn't often that he had such an attractive woman in his car, apart from his wife.

Rosa's mini-skirt rode up as she sat back into the sporty seat, giving Colin a good view of her long slender legs.

"How old are you, Rosa?" Colin's words rolled out of his mouth of their own accord.

"I am twenty-one but soon I will be twenty-two." She flashed a smile across at him showing her pearly white teeth off to their best advantage.

Colin could feel himself becoming aroused. This Spanish girl was an absolute cracker. He fancied himself as something more than a father figure to the girl. Young women nowadays were far more mature than when he was in his twenties. His eyes wandered up her legs again as he stopped at another set of traffic lights.

"Have you got a boyfriend in Spain?" He couldn't control the words as they jumped out of his mouth.

"Yes, well, I did have a boyfriend. He was thirty-two but not with a good job. I like older men but they must be a success." Rosa batted her eyelids carefully at Colin.

Colin could feel his erection harden as the car behind beeped him to move – the lights had turned green.

"I think you're right," he nodded. "Women are more mature than men and should look for an older partner."

Rosa ran her right hand up and down her thigh slowly and rhythmically, causing Colin's breath to quicken.

"We are almost at Connolly Station," he announced, half relieved that she was getting out of the car. He hadn't felt as aroused in a very long time.

"You have a very nice car, Colin," Rosa said raising her skirt to show just enough thigh as she stepped out. "I will see you this evening?"

"Yes, Rosa." Colin panted slightly and craned his

neck to look out through the passenger door. "See you later. Have a good day!"

Colin parked his car in his personal space in the IFSC carpark and walked awkwardly to his shiny office on the seventh floor.

His secretary, sitting at a desk outside his room, watched her boss loosen his collar and tie.

"A cup of coffee," he said as he passed her by.

"Of course, Mr Hamilton," she replied dutifully. He didn't usually come to work looking so ruffled.

Rosa flicked through the rails in AWear on Grafton Street. She had to find the right top – definitely a plunge neckline. He would be putty in her hands before the week was out. She put a red jersey halter-neck up to her chest and smiled. That was the one. She had a smart black mini that would finish it off perfectly. Her wedge heels made her much taller and her long legs would have him hypnotised. He was certainly dim enough to fall for her. She made her way over to the counter to pay for her purchase.

The cream paper bag swung freely in her hand as she sauntered down the street.

"Hello, dear!" a voice called from behind. "Rosa?"

She turned around and saw Lily waving at her.

"Hello," Rosa said with a saintly smile and a flutter of her eyelashes. "I was buying some clothes."

"That's nice," Lily said. "I was just looking to see if there was anything in the mid-season sales myself."

"It is so nice to meet a friendly face." Rosa smiled.

"You poor dear, are you homesick?"

"A little," Rosa shrugged.

"Would you like to go for a cup of tea?" Lily paused for a minute, thinking that her company might not be appreciated. She was more than a generation too old to make good company for Rosa.

"Yes, that would be nice. I miss my grandmother so much."

Lily's heart melted. What a sweet girl!

"Now this is my treat," she insisted as she slid the tray of lush pastries and tea along the self-service counter of the Kilkenny Design Centre. "This shop has lots of typically Irish handmade products."

"It is very nice," Rosa nodded.

They took seats at a table overlooking Nassau Street and Lily talked incessantly about her daughter and son-in-law.

"She is such a lucky girl, my Annabel, but I wonder at times if she appreciates her Colin."

"He is a nice man but Annabel is a good person," said Rosa.

"Yes, yes," Lily agreed flippantly, "but I worry about Annabel. She is never happy. For all she has, she seems to drift through her life and there is always an absence of joy about her."

Rosa smiled inwardly. It was as she had expected. There was no great love between Colin and his wife. It appeared that it had never really been there.

12

Kate packed her suitcase resolutely. She wasn't sure how long it would be before she returned to her oasis in the mountains. The week had flown by and she wasn't nearly as organised as she had hoped she would be before returning to Ireland. She did have a lot of the groundwork of her divorce sorted so that was one positive thing. Stefan was going to be co-operative. The tiredness that went with pregnancy wasn't abating and she hadn't done any painting. She had cancelled the exhibition until some time later. The curator of the Gallery in Paris was very nice about it but explained that he had a business to run and didn't have any space on his calendar for at least fourteen months. A German lithograph artist had filled her allocated space in November already.

Her mobile rang out. She knew it was Shane. She had only been able to speak to him sporadically all week.

"Hi, you!" she called lightly down the phone.

"I'm so looking forward to seeing you. What time is

your flight in?" he asked anxiously. "I changed my shift around so I could collect you."

"That's sweet of you, Shane, but my dad's collecting me."

"Kate!" he groaned. "You can't do this to me. I told you I wanted to get you."

"Please, Shane," she sighed. "I have to see to my mum first. I'll call you when I get settled."

"Of course," his voice dropped as he tried desperately not to show his disappointment.

"This is going to be a hectic time. I did warn you. Mum is deteriorating much more rapidly than we expected. I don't know how I'm going to find her."

"Look, if you need me –"

"I know where to get you," she interrupted. "I really have to go now. I can hear Fabian at the door."

"Okay, talk later."

She didn't say goodbye as she turned her phone off. Fabian wasn't at the door yet but she needed some time on her own. She brewed up a pot of tea and sat and sipped while she did a mental check that she had everything she needed before returning to Dublin.

Shane bit at the nail on his ring finger. It was a habit that he hadn't given in to in years but it seemed like the only thing to do at present. All of his calls to Kate had been awkward since she returned to France and he was miserable.

"Who was that?" Natasha asked on entering the kitchen.

Shane jumped backwards, startled. "One of the guys from work," he mumbled – he hated lying to her. "I was meant to be playing racket-ball with him this afternoon." Oh God, he hated this! If only there was a way he could be with Kate and not hurt Natasha!

"Shane, I think we need to talk," Natasha's voice was quivering. "What's going on?"

Shane was motionless. There was nothing he could say to Natasha at present. The woman he needed to talk to was brushing him away. It made him yearn for her even more. Instead of the initial joy he felt after their first weeks together, the week away from each other was breaking him apart.

"Shane, are you even listening to me?" Natasha's eyes filled. "What is it?"

Shane looked at his beautiful wife, her skin like porcelain and hair like honey. It had taken him years to find her. Natasha had filled the gap that Kate had left vacant. But with Kate back in his life he saw his wife in a different light. He used to enjoy the constant demands she made on him. Now he felt like he was being strangled.

"I need some time on my own," he blurted out. "I'm not happy."

Natasha panicked. "Shane, what –"

"It's not you. It's me. I'm so sorry," he stumbled over the words. "I'm just not happy with *me*." This was sickening – he needed so much to tell the truth.

She moved forward until she could touch his arm but he took a step back.

"I need some space at the moment," he appealed.

Natasha started to shake with anger. In the five years she had known Shane Gleason, she had never seen him like this. She was always the one in total control in their relationship. He had recently been promoted to captain and she was in her second month in Airjet when she first set eyes on him. Plenty of the other air stewardesses had made a play for him but she was the lucky one, the one that he wooed so charmingly. Their wedding was perfect. Her dress had cost nearly as much as the reception and he was insistent that nothing was too good for her. They made such a handsome couple. Everybody agreed. Everybody said they were the perfect couple.

She had turned their four-bedroom cottage in Dalkey into a home fit for the pages of *Home and Country* magazine. Even her spies still working in Airjet were adamant that he wasn't like the other captains. He never swapped rooms during the overnights.

Shane's face was pasty and pale now. He was almost like a statue, his gaze showing no emotion.

"Please, Natasha, I just need space to work something out."

There was no way she would plead or beg. She just wasn't used to him wanting something on his terms and it irritated her immensely.

"I'm calling my mother!" she erupted. "I'm taking her to Eternal Springs until you find yourself!" Her brow furrowed, putting five years on her pretty face.

Shane let out a loud sigh. The beauty farm was a

regular retreat that she and her friends visited. "That's probably for the best at the moment."

"I can't understand you – it's like living with a stranger this past few weeks," she sobbed, then turned on her heels and stormed out of the kitchen. Her pride was seriously dinted and she would do what she usually did when she was cross with him. Visit Josh!

She was right, of course, he thought. He *was* a different person. Kate was back in his life. Telling Natasha that he had changed made him feel like he was doing something proactive – moving his relationship with Kate on a little bit more. But if he was doing that, why wasn't he feeling better? He hadn't felt this miserable in years.

Damien rushed up to his daughter as she walked through Arrivals. He leaned forward and gave her cheek a brief kiss. He felt comforted by the contact with her.

"Hi, Dad."

"Hi, love," he replied, the strain of minding Betty showing on his face.

"How's Mum?"

"She's very subdued and tired. I suppose it's to be expected." Damien took his daughter's suitcase which was a lot bigger than the one she had brought only a few weeks before. Kate had an open ticket this time – neither of them knew when she would be returning to France.

Kate watched the fields of maize flash by as they sped along the M50. She hadn't felt very creative since the weekend in Biarritz – for lots of reasons. She tried to recall what it was like to see the world through an artist's eyes.

"I met Annabel at the market in Howth – she's after setting up a stall," Damien said lightly, curious to see how Kate would react.

"I don't want to talk about her," Kate retorted.

"I think she's keen to be friends with you again."

"She told you!" Kate was shocked.

"Yes. I'm surprised you haven't made up." He paused but Kate just glared at him silently. "She said it was over a trivial matter."

With relief, Kate realised Annabel hadn't told him everything. She really didn't have the energy to go into it with her father right now. Her brain had gone to putty since she discovered that she was pregnant.

Damien looked across at his daughter in the passenger seat. "Kate, you look exhausted. Are you sick?"

"I'm sick of Annabel and I don't want to discuss her again."

"Whatever you wish." Damien grimaced. After a silence he said, "Your mother sleeps through most of the afternoons."

"That will be the drugs," Kate replied in a matter-of-fact manner. "How is the nurse working out?"

"She's a nice girl and your mother likes her, so that's the main thing." Damien turned to his daughter. "When are the boys coming over?"

"Sunday."

"I can't wait to see them," Damien said and he really

meant it. His bright and cheerful grandsons were the perfect diversion for his family at the moment.

"Neither can I," Kate nodded.

Saturday had gone from being one of the quieter days in the Hamilton household to one of the busiest. At last things calmed down a little. Taylor was at horse-riding and Rebecca was at ballet. Sam was on a day's orienteering excursion to the Wicklow Mountains and Colin was upstairs getting ready for golf.

"I'm popping out to get some more ingredients for tomorrow," Annabel told Rosa as she rooted out the shopping bags from under the stairs. "The weather forecast is good so it's going to be busy at the market."

"I will stay here until the children return," Rosa nodded.

"Thanks so much," Annabel smiled. "They are both being dropped back by friends' mums."

"Okay."

"Bye, Colin!" Annabel called as she pulled the front door closed behind her.

Colin was intent on giving himself a close shave and didn't reply. A well-worn yellow towel covered the lower half of his body and was wrapped loosely in a cumbersome fold around his waist.

Rosa crept quietly up the stairs. She slipped into her bedroom and stripped off her clothing, then grabbed a white fluffy bathrobe that Annabel had lent her. She carefully slipped her mobile phone into her pocket before setting off on her mission.

Colin usually used his en-suite to shave but this morning he had brought all his paraphernalia into the main bathroom after taking a bath. The door was ajar and Rosa took a deep breath before giving a gentle knock. She had deliberately left a bottle of conditioner on the second shelf of the storage cabinet.

"Yes?" Colin grunted.

"Excuse me, Colin," Rosa said shyly. "I left my shampoo in this bathroom. I need to take a shower."

Colin's eyes wandered over the draped robe that every now and again showed flashes of bare tanned skin. Rosa's black curls were wild and tangled around her shoulders. He stared at them as she reached up to the cabinet, longing to touch them.

Rosa turned around and lowered her head, flashing an acquiescent glance.

"Colin!" she gasped. "You have a lot of muscles!"

Colin straightened his shoulders. "Oh, I'm a bit out of shape at the moment – I've been meaning to get back to the gym," he chuckled.

Rosa stood rigid – she had no intention of moving. Now was her chance. She loosened the belt on her robe until her peach-like breasts were visible.

Colin's jaw dropped. He wasn't sure how to react. Apart from the rare visit to a few lap-dancing clubs with the guys from work and the odd prostitute while he was in Europe on business, he had remained faithful to his wife. An opportunity like this didn't often come his way and his initial reaction was to pounce on the picture of beauty in front of him. It never occurred to him to wonder why such a beautiful voluptuous young woman would desire a middle-aged man with a wide midriff.

"Where's Annabel gone?" he asked.

"To buy some things for the market."

Colin grinned and slipped his hand under Rosa's bathrobe. He firmly cupped her right breast in his left hand.

"You know, I think that market stall of Annabel's is a great idea," Colin sniggered as he lurched forward and slipped his tongue into Rosa's mouth.

Rosa let the rest of her robe slip off her shoulders until she was completely naked.

"Take me to your bedroom," she whispered into his right ear.

Colin didn't need telling twice. He walked backwards, holding her as they stumbled into the room and flopped onto the bed.

"You're like an angel," he muttered as she slithered down the bed and took his penis firmly in her hands before wrapping her lips around it.

Colin moaned and groaned his way to orgasm. When he was finished Rosa politely wiped her mouth on his yellow towel that was now flung on the bedroom carpet. She crawled up the bed until her naked body was next to his.

"You are the most beautiful creature I have ever laid my eyes on," Colin panted.

Rosa smiled. Her plan was going perfectly.

Kate wasn't ready to speak to Shane yet. She was in

Dublin seven hours but had ignored his two attempts to call her. She felt cruel but needed to get clarity in her own head before she made any arrangements.

"Kate, could you bring up a hot-water bottle?" her mother called.

"Coming, Mum!" Kate would have to try hard to be the dutiful daughter and not let her own condition affect the care she needed to provide for her mother.

As she poured the water from the kettle into the narrow opening of the water bottle, her mobile rang out again. She knew she had to answer it this time. She stretched across the worktop and grappled with the phone.

"Hello."

"Kate, I've been trying to reach you all day."

She quivered on hearing his voice. "Sorry, I've been with Mum. The nurse has gone and Dad is out."

"Are you okay?"

"Yeah, fine," she sighed listlessly. "Look, I'll call you back later tonight."

"Kate, I really need to talk to you!" The urgency was clear in his voice. "I've told Natasha I'm not happy."

Kate froze. She didn't need this type of pressure at the moment – especially when she didn't know what she was doing with her life. "Come out in the morning then."

"I can't. I'm going to Edinburgh twice. But I should be back by two o'clock."

"Okay, two. Come at two." Deep down she loved him

and wanted to tell him that she was pregnant, that she was needy. But she couldn't.

"I can't wait to see you, Kate!" Shane's voice lifted now that they had an arrangement made.

"I've missed you too," she said truthfully.

Two o'clock came around too soon. No amount of hairbrushing or make-up could prepare her for meeting him. The fact that she was carrying some stranger's child put a different emphasis on her priorities. How could she tell Shane, who was willing to give up his marriage for her, that she was pregnant with another man's baby? A man that she had slept with so impulsively? How could she explain when she had refused to sleep with Shane in the weeks since they had become reacquainted? She hadn't a clue how she was going to approach this afternoon.

When he eventually rang at the front door she felt a nervous vibration run through her body.

She threw the front door open and her eyes met his. His mouth widened and he opened his arms. She put her head on his shoulder, feeling comfort and peace for the first time since she had left him at Dublin airport. He stroked her hair gently and kissed the top of her head.

"God, I have missed you," he whispered.

"Me too," she sighed softly. "Take me somewhere we used to go. I need to feel young again."

"You are still young," he said, moving away from her slightly so he could see her eyes more clearly. "Forty is the new thirty."

She smiled but said nothing as she took her keys and handbag.

They drove through the neatly arranged streets and avenues on the southside of the city until they reached the picturesque town of Enniskerry. There was only one place he could be taking her.

It was a bright and breezy April day but warm enough to be June. He hoped they would have the waterfall to themselves. There were no coaches lining the carpark as there would be on a summer's day. Shane parked his BMW in a corner under an oak tree. He turned to look at Kate but her gaze was fixed on the steady stream of foam gushing down the side of the hill. The roar of the water grew louder when she opened the car door.

"I love that sound," she said, turning to Shane who still had his eyes firmly fixed on her.

"So do I." He was in a daze now. The pain of the last week had dissipated. "Let's go."

They ambled like two teenagers afraid to get too close as they approached the pond at the bottom of the cascade. The water was crystal clear and cool.

"I wonder can you drink it?" she mused.

"I would think so, as long as you drank it before it went further downstream."

"Come on. Let's walk along the ridge like we used to," she beckoned.

They trod on the stepping-stones, carefully avoiding the narrow stream that carried the overflow from the pond. Kate almost slipped on some moss but Shane was close enough to grab her by the arm and save her from getting wet. They climbed the rough pathway until they were on a height overlooking the vast woodland that covered the valley. Surrounded in a sea of green they felt like Adam and Eve, free from the prying eyes and ears of the rest of the world.

"I love this place so much!" She breathed in the air.

"Why do you think I brought you here?" he grinned.

"We share something very few people ever experience, don't we?" she declared.

"Ah, hum," he agreed.

"Do you think it's because you were my first love?"

"Lots of people marry their first love and they're miserable," he said, shaking his head. "I think it's more than that."

"So do I. Do you know, over the years I could often feel your presence with me? Even when I hadn't seen you for years? It's a strange spiritual kind of thing."

"I know what you mean," he nodded. "It's like you're always there, even when you aren't. Why did it take us so long to find each other again?"

"Maybe the timing wasn't right," she hesitated. "Maybe it still isn't."

"Don't say that, Kate. I'm banking on it being the right time. I know it's not fair on Natasha but she's young and beautiful – she'll find someone else."

"It's not that," she replied. She felt his words were flippant. Natasha was an unfortunate casualty caught up in the Shane and Kate saga.

The wind blew up, causing her hair to dance in the breeze. A few hairs stuck to her lips and Shane gently brushed them away.

"What is it, Kate?" he asked gently. "Something has happened. I can sense it, I know you too well."

"I can't say."

"Is it Annabel? Is it something to do with your row? We have her to thank for getting together, remember. If I hadn't met her on the plane from Biarritz we'd both be lost to each other still."

"Please don't push me, Shane."

He folded his arm around her shoulders and she leant in against him.

"I wish we could just stay like this forever," she sighed.

"We will be together, Kate."

The conviction in his voice soothed her. She closed her eyes and embraced the moment. The future was as uncertain as it had always been.

Annabel stood at the gate of the school waiting for Rebecca to appear in the yard. Rosa had a hair appointment fixed for one o'clock and Annabel was angry that Colin had given her permission to take it on one of her allocated workdays. Rosa was very flexible though at the weekends and Annabel felt that she had to give the girl some leeway. However, the power issue with her husband had to be resolved. Colin had been making life as difficult and uncomfortable for her as he possibly could since she had started the market stall.

"Annabel!" a familiar voice called over the heads of the five-year-olds that bobbed along the pathway.

"Hi, Melissa," she smiled a wry smile. "How are you?"

"Great, absolutely fab," she said with a jingle from the bangles on her wrist. "Listen, I have Sophie's birthday party next Sunday and I need a favour as I'm turning it into an adult drinks party when the parents come to collect."

Annabel knew exactly what Melissa was at. Jack Owens' daughter was in Sophie's and Rebecca's class and, although he wasn't an A-list Hollywood star, he had appeared in plenty of A-list movies over the past decade. He was now revered as one of Ireland's most important celebrity actors. Annabel wouldn't say it straight out to Melissa but everyone knew he was in town and taking a rest in between movies. It would be a perfect opportunity for Melissa to home in on him.

"Sundays aren't great for me, Melissa," Annabel sighed. "I don't get finished at the market until nearly six."

Melissa's face changed hue and a scowl appeared on it. "Annabel, you're not letting a market stall take precedence over what could be the drinks party of the year!" She blinked her eyelids slowly, thinking that would be enough to set Annabel straight. "I need you to make some of that delicious salmon roulade and then some of those yummy salads. Enough for forty?"

Annabel knew that Melissa had no intention of paying her for this work. She might offer to contribute to the cost of the ingredients but that would be it. Then the penny dropped and she realised why she was included in Melissa's circle of friends. She wondered why she had put up with Melissa for so long. She really disliked the woman intensely and using her daughter's birthday party to get a celebrity into her house was a perfect example of her mercenary character. What were the woman's priorities? She had never said no to Melissa before over anything but the stall was important and she got a real kick out of it for herself.

"I'll have to pass on it, Melissa, sorry," she replied firmly. "I'm committed to this new enterprise and I have to see it through."

Melissa jerked her head back in disbelief. Annabel had never denied her anything she had asked of her before.

"I thought I could rely on you, Annabel!" Melissa was incensed. "I'm really very disappointed – it's very late notice for me to get anyone else!"

"I have commitments, as I said," Annabel replied, even more firmly this time. Her new voice was growing stronger as she uttered each word. She was sick of being around women like Melissa and being part of their shallow lives, watching who was doing what, where and when. None of it mattered. None of them were real friends. None of them were like Kate.

13

"Are you comfortable, Mum?" Kate asked.

Betty nodded her head. She took the bowl of soup from her daughter and sipped it slowly and carefully. Her cancer was becoming more aggressive as each day passed and she was deteriorating at a frightening pace. She found it difficult to hold down solid food any more and was taking a morphine injection twice a day.

"The boys will be here later."

"I'm looking forward to seeing them," Betty croaked. Her voice was affected along with many other faculties. It was difficult to believe that only a few short weeks had passed since her operation. "Have you seen Shane?"

"A couple of days ago – he's asking for you."

Betty nodded but didn't smile. "How do you think your father is?"

"Don't worry about him, Mum – he's fine!" Kate was exasperated with her mother's concern over her father.

"He's a good man – Damien. Make sure he's happy when I'm gone."

Kate wondered what had brought this on. Her mother had started constantly referring to her father's good qualities. The fact that Kate knew about Annabel made it all the more difficult to take.

"Don't talk like that, Mum – you're not going anywhere," she lied. "Anyway, I wouldn't worry about him." And she smiled as she wiped her mother's brow, using the blue flannel cloth that lay constantly in the dish beside her bed.

Rosa tiptoed into the garage, knowing that Colin was cleaning the heads of his golf clubs. He often did it on a Monday evening after playing golf at the weekend. She slid her hand around his waist and made him jump momentarily. He spun around and smiled when he saw Rosa's dark brown eyes dancing at him.

"Where's Annabel?"

"She has gone out to her mother's."

"And the kids?"

"The girls are in bed and Sam is in a friend's house."

Colin's mouth widened, the gaps in his teeth making him look eerie in the half-light of the garage. "How would you like to make out in a Mercedes?" he said, pointing over at his car.

"Ah, ha!" Rosa nodded her head in agreement.

The next ten minutes dissolved in a flurry of underwear-throwing, panting and groping. Finally it was over. Tiny beads of sweat had formed along Colin's shiny forehead, just above his eyebrows. He blinked twice then looked over at the passenger seat where Rosa was straightening her clothing.

"You are something else, Rosa," Colin leered. "I had no idea how much fun it would be having an *au pair*."

"I like being an *au pair*," she said flirtingly. "But I want to go back to Spain to study in October."

"Oh, really?" Colin was surprised. "What do you want to study?"

"Law."

"Don't you need good exam results from school?" Colin presumed that, with her good looks, Rosa couldn't possibly have a brain as well.

"I have excellent results. I can study any degree but I need to get the money first."

"How much will it cost you?"

Rosa put her finger up to her cheek and looked up in the air. "With my living expenses, I will need ten thousand euros a year."

"It's all money. That's the way of the world," Colin said harshly.

"Yes, Colin," Rosa smiled. "I am glad you see it that way, because I need that money before August and I hope that maybe you could lend it to me."

"That's an awful lot of money," Colin said with a shake of his head.

"Not for you. I have seen your bank accounts."

"Have you been snooping in my study?" Colin was appalled.

"I was cleaning for Annabel and . . ."

Colin scowled. He could sense the change of atmosphere in the car. The pretty little *au pair* had turned into a cool calculating operator. This was obviously something she had planned all along. "Are you blackmailing me, Rosa?"

"Really, Colin, how terrible to say such a thing!" Rosa's English was now perfect. It was very clear that she hadn't come to Ireland to improve her language skills.

"What if I don't *lend* you this money?" he said.

"Annabel will be very upset . . ."

"I could deny it!"

Rosa took her mobile phone out of her pocket. She had expertly video'd the scene in Colin's bedroom and his face turning purple as he reached orgasm.

"You are very clever." He nodded his head, half in awe of the brains behind the pretty face. "Okay, say I *lend* you this money. What guarantee do I have that you will stay until October?"

"I give you my word," she grinned.

"Well, if you are staying I would like us to continue this little arrangement until you leave. If you could guarantee an evening like this three times a week, we would both be getting what we wanted."

"Two times," Rosa bargained.

Colin held his hand out and Rosa shook it faintly.

"Hey, you!" Kate smiled down the phone.

"Can you escape for an hour? I could call in on my way back from work," Shane suggested.

Kate took a deep breath. She loved the spontaneity that Shane oozed but now was not the right time.

"The boys are coming home today. My dad's gone to collect them now."

"I'd love to meet them."

Sometimes Kate felt like she had a pin always at the ready to burst Shane's bubble. "There's plenty of time for that, Shane. Give me a day. But I really do want them to meet you."

"Of course," he replied.

What was it with the women in his life? To make matters worse, it was getting more and more difficult living with Natasha. She was trying every trick in the book to make him pay for his actions. She had stopped doing any of the household chores that she used to do to try and fill her day. Instead his credit card was chock-a-block with debts from the local beauticians and boutiques. Her mother had called him on the way to work one day and lambasted him down the phone-line for upsetting her daughter. It wasn't going to be easy, whatever he did. But Kate was his main concern. He wanted to be there for her every step of the way. He had silently considered moving to France. Airjet had a base in Toulouse and he was senior enough to request a transfer.

"I'll call you as soon as we get organised, okay?" Kate desperately wanted to see Shane but he had to learn that her boys were the most important people in her life.

"Great, byeee," he said light-heartedly.

Kate sighed. Her condition had improved since

returning to Ireland and she wasn't as sick in the mornings. It was such a relief as it could have gone on for weeks or months. The baby was probably well settled in there and apart from the sleepy hour which usually hit around five in the evening she was having no other symptoms.

"Mummy, Mummy!" two loud voices called up the stairs.

Kate dashed down to the hallway and flung her arms around her sons. They seemed to have sprung up inches in the time she had been apart from them.

"How are my big guys?" she asked, ruffling their smart brown haircuts with both of her hands.

"Where's Grangran?" Ciarán asked.

"She's upstairs but you will have to take it easy, guys – she isn't well."

The boys dashed upstairs and she followed. They loved their grandmother. She always presented them with money on their arrival and it usually sufficed for the duration of their holidays.

Kate stood in the doorway of the bedroom, watching her mother embracing the boys as they sat on her bed.

"My boys! I wouldn't know you both." Betty beamed. "Look how big you have grown since Christmas!"

Kate was glad that Betty had spent Christmas in the Pyrénées with her and the boys as it was more than likely her last time.

Betty handed her grandsons fifty euros each from her tan leather handbag that she kept beside the bed at all times.

"Mum, that's too much," chastised Kate.

"Please, humour me." Betty's eyes said that it would probably be the last time she would be able to give money to her grandsons and Kate felt a sudden pang of loss.

"Okay, guys, go downstairs and wash your hands – you must be starving," Kate ordered. She stood in the doorway and smiled at her mother who smiled weakly back. Time had crept up and given her mother a sharp shock.

"Kate!" Betty's mouth quivered.

"Yes, Mum?" Everything that her mother now said was of the utmost importance.

"Treasure every moment you have with those two boys. Get them out of boarding school. They will be grown before you know it."

Kate nodded. She had been convinced by Stefan that boarding school would make men of her boys but now she realised that he probably wanted them out of his way. She didn't want to miss out on another day with them after seeing their bright shiny faces as they came bounding through the hall. She would have to see what they wanted to do and everything else would work itself out after that.

She followed them down to the kitchen where her father was buttering bread for them and placing thick slices of honey-roast ham on top.

"You've become very domesticated in the few days since I was away," she commented.

"I'm glad Betty is letting me do things – she never let

me into the kitchen before in case I made a mess," he said, neatly stacking her medication next to his vitamin pills. "It's ironic really that now she has to."

"Can I have some juice, Granddad?" David asked as he levered himself onto a chair and tucked into his ham sandwich.

"Thanks, Dad," Kate smiled. It was the first time she had smiled at her father since Annabel had made her revelation.

Damien beamed back at his daughter. Was this a sign that Kate was thawing in her mood towards him? He was exhilarated by the familiar smile on his daughter's face.

"Hey, guys, do you want to go to the park?" he asked.

"Yeah," Ciarán and David answered together, as was their habit.

"Why don't you take a rest, Kate? The nurse will be here soon," Damien suggested.

"No, Dad, I want to come to the park with you."

After the nurse arrived the four packed into Damien's Saab, taking the scenic route to St Anne's Park.

"Mum, when are we going to see Annabel and Sam?" Ciarán asked. That would usually have been one of the boys' first ports of call.

"Annabel is away, darling," she lied, watching her father's face for a reaction. "We can go see them next time you're over."

Damien looked over sharply at his daughter. He was increasingly curious to know what had come between such good friends. And more than a little fearful . . .

"That's not fair. I wanted to play with Sam," the young boy sulked.

"Mum, why is Grangran in bed in the afternoon?" David asked. He was always the more sensitive half of the twins.

"Grangran is very ill. She won't be with us next Christmas." Kate didn't know how to tell her sons that she was going to die soon.

"Where will she be?" Ciarán asked.

"Heaven, boys." She looked over at Damien who was listening to every word of the conversation but anxious not to participate in this particular topic. He was going to be a widower far sooner than he could ever have imagined. "She'll be in heaven."

"Hey, Annabel," Maeve said cheerily. "How is the stall going?"

"Hi, Maeve, great, thanks," Annabel nodded. She was hopping from one foot to the other to stave off the chill of the cool breeze creeping in from the sea.

"I'll buy two cartons off you."

Annabel took the hummus with basil and hummus with sun-dried tomatoes from Maeve and packed them into a brown-paper bag. "That's eight euros – no, actually, they're on the house."

"This is a business, Annabel – you can't go around giving your produce away."

Annabel shook her head but Maeve was more forceful, pushing the money into her friend's hand.

"Any word on Kate's mum?"

"I haven't heard a thing," Annabel said with a shake of her head.

"I might give her a call. I suppose you heard about Melissa's bash next weekend?"

"Yes, but I can't make it because of the stall."

"I'll bet that really pissed her off," Maeve said with a grin.

Annabel nodded. "I only realised how much she used me as her personal caterer when I said I couldn't help her. I haven't even been invited to the drinks later on."

Maeve smiled. "I only humour her too." She looked around to make sure that nobody else could hear what she was about to say. "You know, Annabel, there are a lot of shallow people in this town and Melissa's probably the queen of them all. You're better off only seeing them in small doses."

Annabel liked Maeve. She kept herself to herself. "Do you fancy calling around for coffee with the kids after school tomorrow?" she blurted out. Herself and Maeve had never been very close but she felt the desire to get to know her better and she was a genuine person who didn't judge people by what she could get from them like Melissa and her cronies.

"I'd love that – about two fifteen?"

"Great and don't feed the kids. I'll have homemade sausage wraps for them."

"I'll look forward to that. Thanks, Annabel. I'd better get going. John hates me spending too long at this market. He says he needs open wallet surgery after I've spent more than an hour here."

Annabel chuckled. "Take care and see you then!"

Annabel smiled to herself at the arrangement. She needed a good friend more than ever now that she didn't have Kate to ring any more. Her thoughts were interrupted by her ringing phone.

"Hi, Annabel. How are you?"

She recognised his voice instantly. "Shane, hi! What a nice surprise!"

"I hope I haven't disturbed you."

"Not at all. I'm standing here at the market, selling hummus."

"Hah?" he grunted in surprise.

"It's a long story. Did you call Kate?"

"Yes, that's what I'm ringing about actually. I've seen quite a bit of her these last few weeks and I'm concerned about her. Is there any chance we could meet for a coffee sometime?"

Annabel was intrigued. "Sure, could you come out this way?"

"No problem."

"What about after three tomorrow?" Annabel suddenly remembered Maeve. "No, wait, I forgot I've got a friend calling. How are you on Tuesday?"

"I'm finished work at eleven on Tuesday and I could call straight out to you."

"Great. Do you know where I live?"

"That would help, wouldn't it?"

"I'm up at Summit Green, third house on the right-hand side. It's called Highfield."

"See you about eleven thirty?"

"Perfect."

Annabel slipped her phone into her pocket and took a pot of hummus from an elderly lady with a lilac rinse in her hair.

"That will be four euros, please," said Annabel affably as she put the carton into a paper bag.

"Really!" the old dear exclaimed with a strong west-Brit accent. "I came down here to buy provisions – not to get robbed!"

Natasha's hair was perfect after the wash and blow-dry. She slipped her sunglasses on her pert little nose as she left the salon and got into her Mazda sports car. She ran her French-polished nails along the leather steering wheel and adjusted her new crossover dress that had left little change out of four-hundred euros. She knew exactly where she was going. Josh always took his break at three o'clock on the days that he worked and it was one of his perks as manager that he had a private room on the top floor of the gym.

She breezed past the young lad in his tennis whites at reception, causing his head to turn. Walking straight to Josh's office, she opened it without knocking on the door. Josh's head was slumped over a pile of papers. His red vest and white shorts showed his bronzed figure off perfectly. He turned suddenly, startled by the intruder.

"To what do I owe the pleasure?" he grinned on seeing who the intruder was.

Natasha scowled. "Upstairs now!"

It was part of the game that they played with each other. She loved being the pursuer and he loved being the pursued. Josh was her personal trainer. They only made love on her terms and when she wanted it. She had a great body and a pretty face and Josh wasn't one to miss out on any opportunity to be with her.

They discreetly took the back stairs to his apartment and made love vigorously on the large three-seated couch. Neither spoke. They moaned and groaned their way to orgasm, copulating as if their lives depended on it. Natasha jumped up when they had finished and quickly tied her dress around her. Josh leaned back on the couch, still naked, clasping his hands behind his head.

"Are you rushing off again?"

Natasha turned around sharply. "Why don't you get dressed?"

"I thought you liked my six-pack – isn't that why you keep coming back for more?"

"Don't flatter yourself," she huffed. "You're convenient and available."

Josh smiled. He knew this woman's style. The usual charming approach that women took while chatting him up didn't work. Natasha was a smart girl and knew exactly what buttons to press to turn him on. She was also great in the sack. She'd be around again and again.

Maybe even someday she'd be looking for more. Josh was willing to bide his time.

Shane was calling around at four to meet the boys. Kate recalled the first time that he called to bring her for a walk on Dollymount strand. It was a fresh Saturday afternoon in April nearly twenty-five years ago. She could still recall the powder-blue hippy dress with little bells that hung from the ties around the collar. Some poor woman or child in India had possibly laboured for weeks on weaving the fine fabric and embroidering the details in gold thread. When he came to the door he showed more understanding than most guys his age, commenting on how well she looked. It was evident that he had spent just as long getting ready by the whiff of Brut aftershave that wafted past her as she opened the door. He probably had all of five or six hairs to shave but he had carefully removed them before meeting her.

She felt more anxious now than on that day. The stakes were higher and she had her sons to consider. What if they played up and didn't like him? Lord knows they were powerful opponents of anyone when put together. The plan was to take them to the pictures and then for something to eat in one of the burger joints that they were kept well away from in boarding school.

"We are going to meet a very old friend of mine from a time when I wasn't much older than you guys," she had informed her sons. "I want you to be very nice to him."

"He had better be very nice to us!" David had piped up.

When they saw his black BMW drive up to Greenfield Close, Shane was already home and dry.

"Your friend's got a great car, Mum," Ciarán called from the upstairs bedroom window where they had been waiting.

"Will he take the roof off?" David shouted down the stairs.

"We'll see," she called up to them on her way out to greet Shane on the driveway.

"Do I look all right?" Shane asked nervously. She noticed he had tried to spike his hair up in an attempt to appeal to the boys' sense of cool.

"They aren't going to care what you look like, silly! They're two little boys. Your car has passed the test anyway and that's much more important." She smiled reassuringly.

Two bright faces with wide boyish grins waited at the front door as Kate and Shane walked up the short driveway.

"Boys, this is Shane." Kate introduced him with an air of formality that the boys found amusing.

"Which one of you is David and which Ciarán?"

"I'm David," they both said together.

"Now, boys, you mustn't tease," their mum berated them. "This is David, and Ciarán has the dark freckle on his left cheek. But you'll remember him better by his red T-shirt for today."

"Don't give our secrets away, Mum," Ciarán groaned.

"I don't think I'm going to be able to tell you guys apart anyway," Shane said with a grin.

Kate found herself blushing as the bonding between the men in her life took place.

As the boys piled into the back of the car and Kate took her seat beside Shane, she felt an unexpected surge of emotion. This was how it would have been if she had stayed with Shane all those years ago and they had raised a family together. This is how it would feel going on a family excursion. It felt good. It felt warm and natural and for an instant she really believed that they were a cosy family unit.

Shane looked across and smiled at her as he fixed the buckle on his seat belt. "Okay?" he checked.

"Mmm," she nodded.

A short while later they were settling down in a row at the UCI cinema. Shane had bought massive tubs of popcorn for each of them.

"Cool," said the boys.

It was going well so far. Kate snuggled up next to Shane. Shane kissed the top of her head momentarily before returning to his popcorn. The boys were too engrossed in the latest adventure blockbuster to notice. Kate couldn't remember feeling this content in her life. Her eyes glazed over until she was rudely brought back to reality by a baby crying on the big screen of her own impending arrival. Shane would probably be really sweet about it, she pondered. But would it be fair to expect him to go through the nine months waiting and then twenty years rearing someone else's baby? He was so patient and understanding about her irrational requests. He hadn't pushed her to sleep with him even though it was obviously beginning to put a strain on their relationship. Part of her realised, however, that he still respected Natasha and didn't want to sleep with someone else until he was free. Something would have to be done sooner rather than later but for the moment she wanted to savour the experience of being Shane's partner – of being a family.

"Right, who wants to go to Casa Pasta?" Shane said, blinking as they emerged from the darkness of the cinema into the daylight.

"Me!" the boys called together. Kate had already forewarned Shane that it was the boys' favourite restaurant when they came to visit their grandparents.

"Thanks, Shane. I thought we were going to MacDonald's," Kate said as they got into his car for the short journey to Clontarf.

"This is a special day," he said. "Nothing but the best for your kids."

Kate flinched. They were her kids and not his. The fact that he had stated the obvious pulled her back into reality and out of the comfortable web she had spun around the four of them in the cinema. It convinced her even more that she had to make a firm decision about their future together and part of her felt that decision was already made.

Damien was having trouble sleeping. He had thought

that now he had made some sort of peace with Kate he would be more relaxed. For the umpteenth time he tossed and turned in the bed, images from his past flashing like light from a beacon. It wasn't what Betty deserved for her final days on this earth. It was the bitterest pill to take. He felt scared for the first time in his life. Nobody in the Royal Dublin Golf Club or on his many building sites scattered around the city would believe that Damien Carlton would be afraid of anything. But scared was the only word that he could come up with to describe how he felt. He'd been so busy working hard for the last forty years, time had raced by without giving him a chance to stop and evaluate what the hell he was doing. He had accumulated enough money not to have to work so hard. But he couldn't stand being around the house with Betty fussing and dusting around him. That was why he had put so much focus on his career. But if bricks and mortar were all he had to look forward to now, he didn't think he wanted to go on. His two children lived in different countries and he only sporadically saw his grandsons. There had to be more to life, and at sixty-two he had to make better use of the few years of good health that he had left.

He thought of Annabel for a moment. He could clearly picture her face behind the stall at the market. Beauty personified. He wished she hadn't been his daughter's friend. She had turned into a stunning woman but age wasn't something that he had thought about on the brief occasion that they were together. Her age hadn't mattered. He closed his eyes and tried to remember how it felt to hold her but couldn't, no matter how much he grappled with the memory.

He jumped out of the bed and shook himself down. Maybe a trip to the toilet would clear his head as well as his bladder.

Kate woke with a start. She looked at the clock beside the bed. It was 3.04 a.m. Something had woken her, she was sure. She pulled on a dressing-gown and went to check on the boys. Opening the door gently, she peered in. They were sleeping peacefully, their two smooth faces popping out from under the duvets. Ciarán's hair turned spiky in his sleep and no amount of brushing the next morning would flatten it. He had taken to using gel to put a shape on it. They would be teenagers soon and then off to college perhaps and they would have little time for their mother. She touched her stomach for a moment and thought about her unborn baby. Part of her longed to smell that fresh scent of talc and cuddles that only a newborn exudes. But if she had this child to look after and took her sons out of boarding school, she would be a single parent of three. It seemed too much to cope with at the moment.

Then on top of everything else she had Shane to think about. She knew she wanted him but didn't want the guilt that would come with breaking up his marriage. And would he want to take on three kids that weren't his own? Life had a habit of dishing up dollops of problems that needed solving.

As she closed the door quietly, she heard her father call her from her mother's room. She hurried to the door. Damien was crouched over his wife who was lying on the floor by the side of the bed. He looked up as Kate rushed in.

"What happened?"

"She's knocked herself out trying to get out of the bed – must have hit her head off the corner of the locker. I was awake and heard her fall."

Kate helped her father lift her mother back onto the bed. Her frail frame reminded her of a little bird. In such a few short weeks she had deteriorated more quickly than anyone had expected. There was a shallow graze at her temple but no sign of bleeding or bruising. The yellowish hue under her eyes and sunken cheeks was now a shade of deep ochre. She seemed to be breathing normally.

"We'd better ring Tony," said Damien.

Kate picked up the phone. Tony Crosby was the local GP and lived close by.

"Ask him if we should call an ambulance," said her father.

The doctor answered immediately, sounding quite alert despite the hour.

"Dr Crosby – this is Kate Carlton. I'm sorry to call you at this ungodly hour but Mum has fallen out of bed and she seems to have knocked herself out . . . we think she has hit her head off the corner of the locker . . . should we ring an ambulance?" Kate listened to the doctor's queries carefully. "No, it just happened – Dad heard her fall – and it's very slight – no real bleeding – no bruising . . ." She paused and listened. "No, no bleeding from her nose or eyes . . . yes, she seems to be breathing normally . . . Okay, thanks so much. We really appreciate it." She put the phone back onto its receiver. "He says he'll be right with us but we need to call the ambulance just in case."

"Tony has been brilliant. I only wish she had gone to see him when she found the lump at the beginning," Damien sighed. He met Tony through the golf club and was hugely relieved when the overworked GP offered to come to Betty's bedside any time day or night.

"I'll call the ambulance, then I'll wait for him at the front door," Kate said. She left her father holding on to his wife's bony fingers.

Tony Crosby tapped gently on the brass knocker that hadn't been polished since Betty had gone into Cornhill Hospital the first time. His spectacles needed a good polish too but his eyes twinkled behind them. He had whipped them onto his nose from beside his bed without giving them a wipe.

Kate opened the door immediately. The doctor smiled at her from under his bushy moustache, his hair slicked back in a duck's tail shape. Kate took his long and slender hand which gave a warm and steady shake.

"Ahh – the artist!" he asked with his west of Ireland lilting *blas.*

"That's me – come this way, Doctor."

"Call me Tony – everyone else does!"

They quickly climbed the stairs. Tony was brisk but gentle in his manner and he instilled confidence in Damien and Kate the minute he entered the bedroom.

"Damien, how is she?" he asked.

"Thanks for coming, Tony." Damien stood up and away from the bed. "She's still out but her breathing is normal."

Tony gently lifted her hair aside to check the graze on her temple, then took his stethoscope from his bag and listened to her chest. He took her temperature and she moved around slightly. "As I thought – she didn't knock herself out. She just fell from the bed and grazed her temple as she fell. She's in a very deep sleep though. She's not coping the best with the drugs." He looked directly at Damien. "It might be best to call your son. I would be concerned that she could go into a coma from liver failure."

Damien nodded, his face grave.

"Have you got a nurse for tomorrow?" asked Tony.

"Yes, and for five nights a week."

"It might be better to have a nurse every night at this stage, if that's possible.

Damien nodded. "I didn't expect her to deteriorate so quickly, Tony. Thanks for coming. I don't know what we'd have done!"

"Sure it's no trouble – I'm only around the corner from you. That's why I said 'any time'," Tony smiled. "She's settled well and should sleep comfortably for the rest of the night. Have you been minding yourself, Damien?"

"I'm fine – I have Kate here," Damien tried to smile back. "I'll be in touch soon no doubt."

Kate showed Tony to the door. "How have you been keeping?" he asked, doing his usual best at checking up on the entire family wherever he called.

"I'm fine, thanks," she replied unconvincingly.

"Be careful that you don't get ill yourself looking after everyone else."

His vast experience as a healer meant he could clearly see the signs of anxiety behind Kate's cheerful expression. She wondered if he could sense that she was pregnant as well.

"Come and see me if you need to," he said, going out the door.

"Thanks, Tony, I'll remember that."

She stood with her back to the front door after closing it. There was no way she could tell her dad's friend that she was pregnant and contemplating an abortion. But as each day passed and the longer she stayed in Dublin, she felt more strongly that she didn't want to terminate this new life and hope that was growing inside her.

Annabel opened the door to Shane with a big smile on her face.

He leaned forward and kissed her cheek. "Nice pad!"

"Thanks," she nodded. "Come in."

She showed him into her Shaker kitchen that reminded him of an interior design magazine, the Aga in the corner making the look complete.

"So how have you been since Biarritz?" she asked.

"Great, terrible and something in between!" he laughed.

"Not all at once, I hope?"

"Sometimes," he grinned. "That's what happens when Kate comes back into your life!"

Annabel felt a twinge of envy but pulled herself together. She must stay true to her strong new self. She had been able to stand up to Melissa and Colin on her own in the few weeks since her return from Biarritz. Now she would be strong about Kate.

"I was meaning to ask you about that on the phone," she said. "When did you call her?"

"A couple of weeks after you gave me her number."

"You said you've been seeing quite a lot of her?" Annabel asked curiously.

"Yes," he nodded, "but not enough – that's why I'm here. There's something odd going on – she seems to blow hot and cold – and now I can't get through to her and I was wondering if you could help."

Annabel took a deep breath that rushed all the way down to her toes. Shane used to always come and cry on her shoulder in the past when he was having trouble with Kate. Like that weekend when Kate went to London in her first year of Art College. He wore marks into her mother's living-room carpet, pacing up and down, pondering how many guys there were in her year and how many of them would be trying to get to know her more intimately. No amount of convincing on Annabel's part about the depth of her friend's feelings for Shane would placate him. That was the thing about Shane and Kate – he was more aware of what she was feeling at times than even Kate herself. Annabel wondered what his real concern was this time. Somehow she wasn't convinced that the idea of telling him about herself and Kate would be doing his relationship with Kate much good.

"We had a falling out in Biarritz and I haven't spoken to her since so I don't think I can be much help. Tea or coffee?"

Shane pulled one of the solid country kitchen chairs back from the table and sat down.

"Tea, please," he replied. "Actually, that's why I wanted to talk to you – I was hoping you might be able to throw some light on the matter of your falling out because she won't tell me about it and I was wondering whether it might account for her mood swings – well, that and the fact she has a lot on her plate with her mum's illness."

"I don't know if she would want me telling you." Or, more to the point, if *I* want to tell you. She hesitated before pouring the boiling water into the teapot.

For a moment they both watched the steam rise from the spout of the china pot. Annabel was afraid to look Shane in the eye in case he could see further than she had let anyone since revealing her secret to Kate.

"Please, Annabel," he begged. "I – I'm in love with her and I don't know where I stand – she wants me one minute, then puts the brakes on the next."

His pleas made it more difficult for Annabel to keep

from making eye contact with him. She resorted to stirring the tea bags with a small teaspoon and pondered the consequences of telling him the truth. How would Kate feel if Shane knew that her father had slept with her best friend? Would she be ruining any chance of reconciliation between herself and Kate? On the other hand Shane needed to know that he was not responsible for Kate's mood swings. She was in an impossible situation.

Annabel sucked on her lower lip and turned around to face Shane. "If I tell you, do you promise not to repeat it?" She knew that she was asking too much. If he and Kate were now lovers they would naturally share confidences.

Shane made the sign of the cross with his finger on his chest. "Cross my heart and hope to die."

Annabel poured the tea into two sturdy Denby mugs and brought them over to the kitchen table. She pulled back a chair and sat, then proceeded to add milk to her tea, drawing the moments out before telling Shane her secret. Would he think differently of her after she told him?

"Okay," she said, staring at her tea mug. "When we were teenagers I had a major crush on Kate's dad." She paused.

"She's fallen out with you for fancying her dad when you were kids?" Shane shook his head in bemusement.

Annabel raised her hand in the air but still didn't look at him. "Wait. I didn't just fancy him. I slept with him while we were all on holidays in France. I really loved him, you know."

There was a pause, then Shane said, "When was this?"

"Twenty years ago," she stalled for a moment. "I was only twenty."

Shane remained silent, unsure how to react to the news. He didn't want to seem appalled – that would make Annabel feel uneasy and she had divulged her greatest secret to him after all. He could imagine how this information would have affected Kate. She was very close to Damien and the news would have shaken her to the core.

"I've been carrying this around with me for years but under the influence of alcohol I told her about us."

"But was it such a terrible thing after all?" he asked tentatively.

She pondered for a second. "What if one of your mates had slept with your mum?"

Shane didn't reply but his expression changed. He had been fiercely protective about his mother right up until the day she died five years before. He saw it as his role after he lost his own father so young. The idea of one of his friends sleeping with her revolted him. He just didn't want to go there.

"See?" said Annabel, seeing how the idea disturbed him. "It's not that it's disgusting in itself – to me it was the most beautiful moment of my life to date – but it's only natural that a son or daughter should feel that way – all very Freudian I'm sure. I mean, teenagers and young adults can hardly bear to think of their parents having sex with each other, never mind doing it with one of their mates! That's why I kept it secret for so long. Well, I didn't have Damien's permission to tell anyway, needless to say! I should never have told her – but it's done now, and I have to confess to a certain kind of relief that it's out at last. It was a horrific strain keeping it to myself all my life – never telling a soul."

"Poor Annabel!" said Shane kindly.

"Anyway I've tried on numerous occasions to call her and she ignores me so I have to accept that she wants our friendship terminated."

"Give her some time, Annabel – she's in bits at the moment, what with Betty's illness. Hey, maybe I should take my own advice and just give her time!"

"How is Betty?" she asked.

"Not good at all – deteriorating rapidly."

"That must be having a huge effect on Kate."

Shane took a gulp of his tea. "Would it help if I got her to talk to you?"

Annabel felt in her heart that if she were to rekindle her relationship with Kate it would have to be on Kate's terms. She knew her friend well enough to know that.

"I'd love to talk to her but she mightn't like you going behind her back to see me. Might make her suspect I'd told you about Damien."

Shane nodded and they fell silent for a few minutes, each brooding on this hopeless situation.

At last Shane lifted his eyes to Annabel's and spoke. "I want her so badly."

Annabel stared at the pained expression on his face. There was no way she could help now. Kate would have listened to her before Biarritz but not any more.

"What about Natasha?" she asked.

Shane looked down at the flagstone flooring. "I'm in the total doghouse. I know I'm not being fair to her – she's the innocent party in all of this. I can't continue this double life that I'm leading. Sooner or later I'm going to have to tell her it's over."

Annabel raised her eyebrows.

"She wants to start a family and I have to admit that I never wanted kids, not with Natasha, or anyone . . . until I saw Kate again."

Annabel felt for him. She wondered what it must feel like to have that mating bond with someone. For herself and Colin the whole process of procreation had been mechanical. She wondered again how Kate must be feeling with all of these huge events happening around her.

"And what if Kate won't settle down with you?"

"I can't even contemplate that," he muttered slowly, the fear inside him showing as he carefully pronounced every syllable.

14

The house felt emptier than ever since the twins had gone back to France. Kate had heard Damien let the nurse in earlier before he slipped out to work. How many more mornings would she spend in this house waiting for the person dearest to her to die? It was unbearable. She walked across the landing on her way downstairs and paused for a moment to look in on Betty. The nurse was bathing her face gently while she slept. A dish with balm and cotton-wool buds rested beside her locker now as Betty found it difficult to take fluids orally and her lips were dry and cracking. A drip hung beside the bed where the other locker used to be. Morphine was the main substance running through the clear plastic bag. Kate couldn't believe that it was a mere twelve weeks since she had seen her mother standing upright in the kitchen that day. That meant that her baby was almost twelve weeks growing inside her, fourteen if she were to go by a midwife's calendar.

She had gone to see Dr Crosby at last. She trusted that he wouldn't tell Damien under any circumstances but he had urged her to tell Damien herself. She agreed that she would but knew that she had no intention of doing such a thing at the moment. Tony Crosby assured her that everything was going well and the cramping pains that she got sporadically were perfectly natural. It had been so long since she was pregnant with the twins that she had forgotten all the symptoms that accompanied pregnancy. She was over the most dangerous period now and was beginning to feel physically well in herself again – she had even started to have a glow about her complexion.

Still no word from Annabel, and Kate was starting to miss her sorely, despite her anger. She felt she shouldn't have let their disagreement fester and grow to the stage that it was at now. It should have been dealt with more maturely. They should have talked it out and then agreed to part company. As it was, she didn't even know all the facts. Had they only had that one night together? Did her father have genuine feelings for Annabel at that time? Did he *still* have feelings for her? Or was he simply taking advantage of a naïve teenager? Or was he the naïf one? Did Annabel seduce him, dazzle him with her youth and beauty? Kate shuddered. Either scenario was repugnant to her. She couldn't bear to think about it. But this present situation was impossible – a nightmare. It could not continue.

Then there was Shane to consider. He had been so kind and considerate through this nightmare. She had to be fair to him. The past three months had been the best and worst rolled into one. Having him in her life made her feel whole again but nursing her mum was tearing her apart – so many contradictions and emotions to handle and all so soon after turning forty.

Shane hadn't pressed too hard looking for a commitment but she could see frustration written over his face, more with each time they met. She had to be fair to him. The baby growing inside her was beginning to show and she didn't think that she could hide it from him for much longer. Deep down she knew he would accept this baby and do whatever she wished but she felt it was likely, as the years passed, that resentment would set in. She didn't want to be a burden. He was too special to play around with and he would have been happy with Natasha if Annabel hadn't given him her number on the plane. There was only one thing to do. She lifted the phone beside her bed and rang his number carefully. She loved to hear his phone ring and relished the anticipation of hearing his voice.

"Hi, Kate!" His tone was always bright when her number showed up on his phone.

"Hi, Shane. Can you come out later? Fancy a walk?" She desperately tried to sound casual but knew that Shane could pick up on her mood instantly.

"Great, I've been twiddling my thumbs here."

"About four?"

"Perfect," he said hopefully. Maybe her mood would improve in the time it took to get to Greenfield Close. "How's Betty?"

"Not good at all today."

"Can I come over earlier in that case? You probably desperately need a break." He was longing to comfort her.

"Four is best, if that's okay with you."

"Fine, see you then."

Kate went to have another look at her mother who was asleep, as she had been now for most of the last few days. It looked like she wouldn't be giving any more words of advice. Kate had heeded her lecture about her boys and had already informed the school that they would be leaving when the term was over at the end of the month.

The nurse smiled from the chair at her bedside.

"Can I make you a cup of tea?" Kate asked.

"That would be lovely, thanks – but only if you're making it."

"No problem."

She carefully negotiated the stairs and noticed that the post had arrived while she had been on the phone. The pile included several white envelopes offering Damien staggering amounts to take out on loan and a postcard from Fabian telling her not to forget him. A large A4 brown envelope was the last item of post that she looked at and it was addressed to her. She had been expecting it all week and now that it was here she was afraid to open it. She put the rest of the mail on the hall table and brought the brown envelope into the kitchen. After hitting the switch on the kettle, she carefully tore a corner of the envelope, then opened it using a kitchen knife.

It was a set of documents in French proclaiming that her marriage of eight years to Stefan Cassaux was now terminated and the settlement as agreed per separation was to be adhered to. Now that she had her freedom in her hands, she couldn't fight back the tears that welled in her eyes. She didn't miss Stefan. A divorce was the best possible option for them both but she realised that she couldn't face going through this loss again with Shane. He was too important and if she were to marry him and lose him she didn't think she'd ever get over it. The risk was too great to take. It would be easier to sort it all out now.

Shane raced up to the front door of Greenfield Close, pausing briefly to look at his reflection in the window before ringing the doorbell, as he always did.

"Hi," Kate said shortly, as she opened the door. She stepped back quickly – denying him a kiss.

He knew instantly that something was wrong.

"Come in," she said as she turned her back to him and walked into the kitchen.

Shane shut the hall door behind him and followed in Kate's footsteps. His heart was pounding loudly in his ribcage and he was sure that she could hear it.

"Tea?" she asked nervously.

"Not for me, thanks. Can we go out?" Shane wanted to change the setting – it might help change whatever Kate was going to say.

Kate paused for a moment. What she had to say would be better on neutral ground. "Want to go to St Anne's Park?" It was another of their old haunts and as she said it Kate realised that it was probably the most appropriate place to go for their conversation.

He nodded and they walked back out to the hall.

"We could take the lane and a shortcut over the Clontarf road?"

"Yeah, it's a nice day."

The summer hadn't got fully under way yet but the long evenings of June put everyone in a good mood and meant that the park was getting a lot of use.

"We used to go down this lane on my racer," Shane said, waiting to see if she recalled. "Do you remember?"

"I am scourged with a photographic memory of every day we spent together," she turned to him and for a moment her eyes glistened in the sunshine. "But that was a long time ago, Shane."

Tension was building in the space between them like some sort of invisible electricity. His stomach knotted and his breathing quickened.

"And haven't we been making new memories these past few months?" he asked hopefully. "What about the walk on Claremont beach the other night?" He desperately wanted her to relive the tender moments that they had shared since coming back into each other's lives.

Kate wished he hadn't brought that up. It had been a perfect evening and together they had found a cosy spot nestled between two sand dunes. They had watched the sunset and he had stroked her face to the slow rhythm of the waves lapping off the shore. She couldn't imagine ever feeling happier in her life than she had for those few hours. She had to pull herself together and think about the reality of the situation that she was in.

"Yes, we've had a good time," she paused. "It's been a bit like living in a time warp though. Don't you feel eighteen again going around all the old places?"

"I definitely do," he agreed.

"Well, does that not worry you?"

"Should it?" he asked in surprise.

"Maybe we're just enjoying the feeling of being young again. How different would it all be if we were in a proper relationship? Like you and Natasha."

"Kate, what are you getting at? It's not like you to beat around the bush." His face was now sullen and whatever Kate had to say he wanted to hear it sooner rather than later.

Kate sighed. There was no easy way to do this. "I think we should stop seeing each other," she blurted out, staring at the path in front of her – afraid to look at him.

He stopped in his tracks, turned and grabbed ahold of her shoulders as she bowed her head.

"Look at me, Kate!" he shouted. "Look at me! Give me that much, for God's sake!"

She lifted her head slightly until her huge brown eyes were visible under her fringe.

"What is wrong with you?" he asked angrily.

"It's what's wrong with us." It was easier to lie to him than tell him her secret.

"*What's* wrong with us? We're perfect together! Kate, there's something you're not telling me. I know you too well. What is it?"

"I just don't think you should chuck a perfectly good marriage away on the chance that we might be happy."

"I don't believe that's it, Kate. Don't do this to me, not again!" He got flashbacks to a bright summer's day twenty years ago when she told him that she was going to the States without him.

"I'm trying to take everybody's best interest into account," she said.

He didn't believe her and it was difficult to convince herself.

"Is it the boys?" he asked impatiently. "I loved the boys and they loved me. You know they did."

"It's not the boys, but there's a big difference between taking them to the pictures and being their father."

Her words stung. "I don't know how to please you, Kate. I've done everything by the book since we started this relationship. It's been all on your terms, your directions. I didn't finish with Natasha because you told me not to yet. What do you really want, Kate? Did you just want to see if you could have me again? Were you playing with me?" He couldn't believe that she was doing this to him again.

Kate gulped hard and shook her head vigorously. "Believe me, Shane, I wouldn't do that. I wish we could be together but it's too late."

"Give me a good reason and I'll leave it."

He looked deep into her eyes and pleaded for her to tell him the truth. He needed a sign, anything. They were on the brink of making the biggest mistake in both of their lives and he knew she had to be feeling the same way.

"I c–c–can't," she stammered.

He started to shake with a newfound temper. It was so surreal he couldn't believe that it was Kate in front of him. Not the woman who had brought such fun into his life again. He reached out to her and then suddenly pulled his arms back. He was too hurt to try and make up with her again – he had been through too much.

"Then you are a sad woman who deserves to be on her own. I can't take any more of your heartstring-pulling. Have a good life, Kate."

He turned on his heels and quickstepped back to Greenfield Close, leaving Kate on a road somewhere between her father's house and the park.

She watched his tall figure get smaller as he disappeared into the distance, unable to move or think. She could still see the anger and hurt in his eyes as she lied to him. Shane didn't deserve to be treated in this way. She wished she had let him down more gently. But there was no easy way to let the love of your life slip through your fingers for the second time. Nobody should lose someone they love so much twice. The tears trickled slowly down her cheeks and for an instant she felt something move inside. She put her hand to her abdomen and held it tight. The faintest fluttering vibrated inside her and, although emotionally she was more in pain than at any other time in her life, she knew she had done the right thing.

Shane was still angry as his car pulled up to Rosemount Cottage. Natasha's Mazda MX3 was parked in front of the garage. He didn't think he could face a confrontation. He was about to start the car up again when the front door opened. She stood in the doorway with a scowl painted across her pretty face. Shane sighed into his steering wheel before getting out of the car. Maybe it was time to face the music.

"Where have you been?" she frowned as he reached the front door.

"Out with a friend," he replied shortly.

"On the *northside,* I suppose?"

"There's no need to say it like that, Natasha."

Natasha hated everything about the other side of the city. She believed it to be full of drug dealers and single mothers. On the few occasions she had to travel there she had clutched her handbag tightly.

"And is this friend a girl?"

She knew his answer before he opened his mouth.

"As it so happens *she* is a very old friend but I won't be seeing her any more." His words numbed him as he uttered them. He couldn't fathom what his life would be like without Kate again. A deep hollow feeling engulfed him.

"Are you having an affair?" She had been avoiding asking him for weeks but felt she was left with no other option.

Shane didn't know how to answer. He hadn't been having an affair. Kate wouldn't sleep with him, but what they had shared was more intense than some sordid sexual affair. "No," he replied quietly and truthfully.

"Why don't I believe you? There's no other explanation for the way you've been behaving." Natasha's eyes were flashing wildly like beacons. Her temper was flaring and Shane stood back in case she took a dive at him.

"Natasha, it's nothing to do with you."

She was now incensed and started waving her arms wildly around. "I am your wife! It has everything to do with me if you're sleeping in the spare room!" She paused for a breath. "If you're not having an affair with this *friend,* then what is your relationship with her?"

Shane had never heard Natasha sound so forthright. She was more angry than upset with him. She deserved the truth and there was only one answer he could give.

"I love her."

Natasha started to shake all over with temper. She would kill this bitch if she could get her hands on her. She hadn't expected him to be so honest. She had secretly hoped he would continue to deny this other woman's existence until he got her out of his system and then come back to her repentant.

"I'm sorry," he muttered.

"I'm sorry too," she shouted, slamming the front door in his face.

Shane couldn't go back into the house. He was battered and bruised internally after Kate's harsh words earlier. He had nothing left to say to Natasha either. He wanted to be on his own. Maybe he should look for a transfer to another country that didn't have Kate or Natasha living in it. Maybe he should take a break from relationships for a while. His head was aching and he needed a drink. He sat back into the driving seat of his car and drove and drove until he was in a place that didn't remind him of Natasha or Kate, swallowing on the hard lump in his throat that was left from trying to communicate with both of them.

Natasha was still trembling as she picked up the phone to ring her mother. She paused for a moment while it rang.

"Hello."

"Mum, it's me," Natasha said sharply.

"Darling, I was just about to ring you."

"Get over here now!" She started to sob.

"Why? What's wrong, pet?"

"My bastard of a husband says that he is in love with another woman!"

There was silence at the other end of the line while her mother took the news in.

"Did you hear me? I said Shane has another woman!"

"I'll be right over. The bastard – and he looks like butter wouldn't melt in his mouth! I tell you, he will pay for this! Ring Gerard at once and tell him to get you a good solicitor. Those pilot types are all the same once they start to play away. Make sure you get every penny you can out of him!"

"Mum, my marriage isn't over. It's just a glitch."

"Let me tell you, my dear, it is over. I know this type of man. Get a solicitor while there's the chance of him still feeling the slightest bit of guilt. I'll be straight over!"

Natasha hung up and started to sob again. She didn't believe that Shane was a hard-hearted bastard. She knew him too well. But she had to think on her feet. This wasn't just some phase that he was going through. Her mother was right. She was still young and good-looking enough to find another man of means. Shane Gleason could sing if he thought she was giving up her house, car or lifestyle. He was her gravy train and there was no way she was going back to serving tea or coffee on an Airbus.

In the meantime she needed her ego massaged. She picked up the phone again and checked her watch. Josh was working late tonight. She would talk to her mother for an hour or two and then take a well-deserved trip to the gym. Josh was always there for her.

Kate pulled her duvet up to her chin and tried to make herself comfortable. It wasn't easy now that she had a bump growing steadily by the day. She closed her eyes tightly and said a secret prayer. The look of disgust on Shane's face still haunted her a week after telling him that their relationship was over. She wondered what he had done that day after he left. Did he go home to Natasha and try to act as if everything were all right? Deep down she couldn't bear the thought of him with another woman – even his wife. But there was another part that desperately wanted to do the right thing by Shane – for the first time in her life. Up until now she had always thought of herself and her own feelings first. She tried to meditate on the old proverb: if you love someone set them free; if they come back they are yours, if not, it was never meant to be. But it didn't console her.

She opened her eyes and felt the walls closing in around her. She had lived through a lot of experiences in her forty years but she could never remember feeling as miserable as she did right now. Suddenly a voice called out that caused her to sit up. It was Betty. She wondered where the night-nurse was.

Kate pulled on her dressing-gown and went into her mother's room. Her mother was wriggling restlessly under the covers. Kate sat on the edge of the bed and put her hand out to gently rub her mother's face.

"I'm here. Can I get you anything?" she asked softly.

Betty's eyes were full of tears and her mouth was quivering.

"I've been a terrible mother, Kate," she sobbed.

"Hush, I love you, Mum. Don't say such a thing. You were always there for me and Philip as kids – and adults – we are so lucky to have you."

Betty put her hand to her head and covered her closed eyelids.

"Don't die with regrets, Kate."

Kate was feeling her mother's distress and wiped away the tears that were now forming on her own cheeks.

"Mum, please don't talk about dying. I need you."

"Kate, we both know that I'm not getting any better. The pain is intense. I want to die so that it will stop."

Kate took her mother's hand into her own and stroked it. When the night-nurse came into the room Kate signalled to her to leave them in peace. She was going to stay with her mother tonight. She wondered how many more nights she would have with her and suddenly all the thoughts that clouded her head about Shane, her pregnancy and the anger with her father faded as she concentrated on minding her mother. She was the priority and for the next few days or weeks and that was how it was going to be.

15

Damien knocked gently on his daughter's bedroom door.

"I'll be out in a minute," Kate said sharply.

The tension and exhaustion of the last two weeks were now etched harshly all over her face. Caring for her mother had drained every last bit of energy from her tired body and she worried about the effect it might have had on her unborn child. Then her father's infidelity had been a shadow hanging over her those last weeks as she nursed Betty and had added enormously to the strain. In addition, even though her mother was all but oblivious to what was going on around her, Kate became increasingly convinced that deep down she was carrying some pain of her own that she hadn't shared with her.

"The car is waiting and Philip and Gloria are already in it!" Damien said, tenderly trying to hurry his daughter.

Kate stepped into her black court shoes and winced as they pinched the sides of her feet. She hoped that she wasn't becoming flat-footed, only four months into her pregnancy. Although they were only six centimetres high, she hoped that she would be able to tolerate them for the rest of the day. Glancing at her reflection in the mirror she noted how slim the black made her look – nobody would guess that she was pregnant. She lifted her jumper and looked at the neat little bulge. Hidden under my black coat is the best place for you today, little one, she said silently to her baby.

The extra weight that most women would be carrying at this stage had been kept at bay while caring for her mother. There were days when she could hardly stomach more than a few slices of toast. Everything seemed to be happening in a kind of daze. She didn't feel the incredible pain that she imagined she would after losing her mum – everything was happening in slow motion and she felt as if she was playing a part in a play. Nothing seemed real. At any moment she would walk into the kitchen to find her mother cutting the crusts from a stack of ham sandwiches and asking if she wanted tea or coffee.

Annabel was flustered. Finding something to wear to these occasions was tricky. She wasn't a member of the family so black would be too formal but a bright colour would show a lack of respect. Thankfully Maeve had rung and told her that Betty had passed away. The funeral notice was in the *Irish Independent* as she expected. Annabel hated funerals – even when she didn't know the person, they always reminded her of her father and her own loss – but Betty's ceremony would be particularly sad. Then there was the anxiety around meeting Kate again. They hadn't spoken in almost four months. There had never been a gap that long without contact at any time over the years. She could, of course, stay away from the funeral but Betty had been like another mother to her – she owed it to her as well as the rest of the Carlton family to show up. She flicked through the hangers in the walk-in wardrobe and felt around for her charcoal-grey trouser suit. That was the safest bet.

She wondered what Kate would be wearing. She wished she could be there to help her get ready, to help with arrangements and flowers and readings. That was, after all, what best friends did for each other.

A loud clattering sound came from the other side of the bedroom. Colin was pottering around the en suite like a caged animal. He had been nicer to her than usual over the past few weeks but she was disappointed that he wouldn't accompany her to Betty's funeral. It was unlike him. The fact that Damien was a successful businessman and golfer would usually have been enough incentive for him to attend.

"Why don't you have to be in work this morning?" she asked as he wriggled out of the bathroom covered in towels.

"I'm meeting a client in the Golf Club at eleven and there's not much point in travelling into the office to come back out again so soon. They can get me on the BlackBerry."

"Of course," Annabel nodded. Colin was often sending emails in the middle of dinner these days. "I'll pass on your apologies and sign the book. I don't imagine the funeral will be that big."

Betty was a popular member of the women's bridge club and she also did charity work but with such a small family and her habit of keeping herself to herself, Annabel guessed that the church wouldn't be thronged.

"Bye, Rosa!" she called to the Spanish girl who was entrenched in her room.

"Bye, Annabel!" Rosa called through the closed door.

The front door had hardly slammed before Rosa heard a tapping at her bedroom door. She didn't need to be a sleuth to figure out who was at the other side. She pulled her dressing-gown over her black lace bra and pants and tied the belt before answering.

She opened it slightly, showing only her nose and the side of her face at first. "Yes?"

"Rosa," Colin whispered, "we have the place to ourselves. I thought this might be a convenient time to get together. What do you think?"

Rosa sighed. She had to keep her part of the bargain, at least until the money came through in August. "Okay, but we will have to be quick. I have a lot of jobs to do for your wife."

"Don't worry about her. As long as I'm satisfied, the rest of the house will be happy."

Rosa wondered how Annabel put up with the pompous idiot. It was getting more difficult to carry on the charade, now that the bargain had been struck. In disgust, she took off her dressing-gown and let Colin lunge his face into her loins. The only good thing about the arrangement was his lack of staying power. The ordeal would be over soon.

Annabel was passing by the beautiful gift shop in the centre of the village before she realised that she had forgotten something. She pulled her Jeep over and searched through her handbag to be sure and then remembered that she had left the Mass card on the counter beside the breadbin. She had to go back.

Arriving there, she left the car running and ran around the back of the house. Rosa always left the back door unlocked. She ran in and spied the white envelope on the kitchen shelf. She grabbed it and turned to go. Then she heard a strange grunting noise. She stopped and listened. It was like someone in pain, moaning and groaning, and seemed to be coming from upstairs. Alarmed, she hurried into the hall and quickly climbed the stairs. The noises were coming from Rosa's bedroom. As she stood there, her heart pounding, the groans became louder and louder until they were accompanied by a banging sound – like a headboard knocking against a wall.

With trembling fingers, she slowly turned the knob on the door and pushed the door in. Nothing could have prepared her for the sight on the other side.

At first Annabel couldn't speak.

Colin stopped after Rosa tapped him on his shoulder, and suddenly realised that there was someone else in the room. He turned his head around slowly until he could see who was standing at the door, then jumped off Rosa in a panic.

"A–A–Annabel, why why – eh!"

"Don't say a thing, Colin," she said, her voice trembling. "Don't say a fucking thing, you bastard!" She spun on her heel and hot-footed it down the stairs and out the back door.

He ran outside behind her, trying to cover his nakedness with a small towel.

"Stop, Annabel. Stop!"

But she managed to get into the car before he caught up with her. She drove off. There was nothing she wanted to say to him.

St Anthony's Church hadn't been Kate's first choice for her mother's funeral but Damien had insisted. It was more convenient for anyone going on to the reception in Clontarf Castle afterwards. Betty was going to be cremated according to her wishes in the final few weeks of her life. The altar was decorated with calla lilies. White candles flickered around the back of the coffin and colourful wreaths lay on the ground around its base.

Annabel was shaking still. She didn't want to sit with her mother who would be up close to the front. She took a pew at the back of the church and hid behind a rotund man in a dark grey jacket. Her mind was still not properly registering the scene she had just witnessed in the house. How could sweet obliging Rosa be having an affair with her husband? It didn't add up. What did she see in the balding middle-aged man?

She couldn't focus on Damien and Kate at the top of the church. Her eyes were glazed over and tears streamed down her cheeks. How could she trust him again? Maybe he had been sleeping with other women all through their relationship. She remembered Nico for a moment and panicked. Kate knew about her one indiscretion in all the years of her marriage. This was different though. Colin would never meet Nico but Rosa had been living in their home.

She let out a loud sniffle and half of the congregation looked around. She lowered her head and covered her nose and the lower part of her face with a large Kleenex. Somewhere in the back of her mind she had hoped that today she would be able to go up to Kate and try and make peace with her but at the moment she felt totally incapable of doing anything other than sob as silently as she could. The quiet around the church made this more difficult.

There was a pause after the priest read the gospel. Gracefully, Kate steeped out from her pew dressed in a black linen trouser suit and walked up to the pulpit. The red highlights that had stood out so brightly in Biarritz were no longer visible against her black hair. She cleared her throat and the congregation waited in awe to see what this tall elegant woman had to say.

"Let me tell you about my mum. She was small and slim, as most of you here today know, but she had a heart as big and brave as a lioness and anyone who passed through the doors of Greenfield Close bore witness to that. There was always a plate of cake and a cup of tea on offer and God help anyone that dared refuse. She brought me and my brother Philip up with all the care and attention only the luckiest of children receive. She was my friend. Some say what goes around comes around or we get what we deserve but I can't say that for Mum. The pain she suffered with the cruellest of illnesses for the last few months was difficult to watch but she dealt with it with the same amount of dignity and good humour as she dealt with everything in her life. I'll miss you, Mum, and I know Philip will miss you too. Thank you for being there always for us."

Kate lowered her head as she took her sheet of words and returned to her seat next to her father.

Damien looked over at his daughter. Why had he been omitted from the speech? Was that deliberate on Kate's part? But why? He was after all Betty's husband for over forty years and should have at least got a mention.

The parish priest continued with the blessing of bread and wine after David and Ciarán carried the gifts up to the altar.

Kate fixed her gaze on the altar as if she were in a trance. Her eyes followed the priest in his white lace garments carrying a heavy silver burner with smoke billowing out from it. The scent of the incense was becoming overbearing and someone at the front started coughing and wheezing. Everybody knelt as the final words were prayed over the coffin.

The crematorium was a short trip away and the ceremony only involved immediate family.

Annabel hoped she could get out of the church

before anyone noticed her. When Betty's coffin was finally raised and carried by Damien and Philip and Betty's brothers out through the church door Annabel made a beeline for the side transept. She could slip out and hopefully avoid meeting anyone that knew her, especially Lily.

Her bag was shaking in her hand. She walked around the back of the church hoping there was an exit there but found she had to circle back to the front. The only way out was through the gates at the front of the church. The carpark was full and people were returning to their cars. She pulled up the collar of her jacket, ducked her head down and walked briskly through the churchyard. She thought she was home and dry when an arm gripped her from behind.

"Annabel!"

She turned around and her swollen eyes met Damien's. Would he think her tears were for Betty, or Kate? She wasn't sure who they were for.

"Annabel, are you okay?"

"Fine, Damien. I'm really sorry for your trouble," she sobbed. Then the floodgates opened and tears poured from her eyes. "I can't believe it, Damien. I'm so sorry. Please tell Kate I said sorry."

Damien took her carefully in his arms until her head rested on his shoulder. "There, there, Annabel. I'll talk to Kate. You shouldn't be this upset. Kate is doing fine. We've all had plenty of time to prepare for this."

"Of course," Annabel said, pulling away. This wasn't the time or place to be cleaning out the dirty laundry.

"I'm going through some stuff myself. Sorry for making a scene."

"You certainly are not making a scene."

"Would you mind if I called you sometime to talk about Kate?"

"Of course, I wouldn't. It would help me to talk to you about her, Annabel."

Damien's eyes were open and honest. This was the opportunity that Annabel had been waiting for, most of her life.

"Can we meet in Tammy's on Friday, about eleven?"

Damien hesitated for a moment. He had just buried his wife. He wasn't sure where he'd be on Friday. But Annabel's eyes gazed up him and were in such pain that he felt he had to do as she wished.

"It means a lot, your being here," he said quietly. "I'll try and be there. If I can't make it I'll call you."

Annabel nodded. "Thanks, Damien. See you then." She wasn't sure what she needed to talk to him about but she knew that it was something that she had to do.

Kate was watching their encounter from the other side of the churchyard. The mourners had crowded around her, backing her against the church wall. She stared over at her father as Annabel walked out of the church grounds. He was still looking after her and Kate felt a deep desire to go over and spit in his face.

Annabel was still shaking as she drove after talking to Damien. School was finishing early today for a teachers' meeting and she desperately hoped that she wasn't going to meet anyone there. She turned off the Howth Road and parked in front of the school. Folding down the mirror above her steering wheel she was able to see how blotchy her eyes were. The little ones wouldn't notice and Sam was going to a friend's house thankfully so she hoped she would get away with it. Still in a daze and at a loss about what she was going to do, she turned the Jeep into the carpark outside High Grove Primary School.

Melissa was standing in the middle of the playground with swarms of perfectly polished women cackling around her. She knew the way they operated and wondered who was getting the sharp lashes from Melissa's tongue today.

She couldn't imagine what she was going to do next. She certainly wasn't having Rosa in her house for another minute and, as for Colin, she wished she never had to see his face again. The image of the two of them on the bed was imprinted on her brain for good and she felt physically sick at the memory.

The fresh-faced children started to dribble from the classrooms around the quadrangle. Taylor and Rebecca rushed up to Annabel's Jeep without her needing to get out – much to her relief.

"Hi, girls," she smiled. "Did you have a good day?"

"That Mia Jones was pulling my hair in the playground again," Rebecca moaned.

"I keep telling you to pull her hair back!" Taylor said scornfully to her little sister.

Annabel had to make a plan and quick, to ensure the safety of her family. She had to do whatever was best for her children and put her own feelings aside.

"Fancy going to Tammy's for some lunch, girls?" She dreaded the thought of going through the doors of her home and seeing Rosa and she needed time to think and work out what she was going to say to her.

"I want to go home and watch *The Den,"* Rebecca groaned, putting her thumb into her mouth at the same time.

If Rebecca was tired then she'd have to go home. The last week of school before the summer holidays was a drudge for students, teachers and parents alike.

Rosa was standing in the driveway when Annabel arrived.

"What's Rosa doing with her bags packed?" Taylor asked.

"She's got to go home," Annabel said, feeling a wave of relief sweep over her at the sight of the packed cases.

"Why?" asked Rebecca.

"Her mummy needs her at home."

"Will she come back?" Rebecca asked innocently.

"I don't think so, darling. Rosa is very busy."

"That's not fair," Taylor complained. "She should have told us before this."

"Believe me, Taylor. It's for the best." The acid tone in her voice was impossible to conceal.

Annabel and her daughters piled out of the Jeep and the young girls ran to Rosa who held her arms out wide. Rosa was genuinely fond of the girls but just now found it difficult to display emotion in front of Annabel. But for the children's sake it was best to keep up appearances.

"Bye bye, Taylor and Rebecca. Be good girls. I have to go back to Spain."

She hugged the two girls warmly.

"We'll miss you!" they said together.

Annabel opened the front door and let the girls in, then turned to face Rosa.

"I can't say I feel the same way as my daughters," she said sarcastically. "Don't dare try and contact anyone in my family ever again, you slut!"

Rosa smirked. Annabel was a sad woman living a pathetic life with an even more pathetic husband. She was glad to be seeing the back of her *and* her husband. Rosa's plans for the summer had been ruined.

A taxi pulled up to the house. Rosa took a seat in the back.

Annabel wasn't waiting to see her off. She followed her daughters into the house and started to search for Colin. His car was still outside but then she remembered his appointment in the Golf Club. Maybe there never was one and it was all a ploy to be on his own with Rosa. Either way, despite her repugnance at the thought of seeing him, she wanted to speak to him and fast. He wasn't getting away with this lightly.

She went straight into the kitchen and took out some wraps that she had prepared earlier for the girls.

"Here, Taylor, will you take these into the TV room!" she called to her eldest daughter.

She needed privacy to make this call. She thought about ringing Lily but then remembered she would still be at the funeral refreshments. There was no point in telling her anything until she had done something proactive. Lily would just tell her to forgive Colin and carry on as before.

Colin's BlackBerry rang out. It went to voice mail and she contemplated leaving a message. She didn't know what to say so she hung up. The only other person she could think of ringing was Moira. Moira Dunne was a family solicitor and personal friend of her mother's. She was a formidable spinster who had wreaked havoc around the courts of Dublin, putting divorce settlements together. She realised she had to see her and fast. She flicked through the phone book and dialled her number with great speed.

Her call was answered by a receptionist at the other end of the line.

"Ms Dunne is with a client. Can I get her to call you back?"

"Yes, please, it's urgent," Annabel said. She gave the receptionist her details, hung up, then waited. She looked down at her hands and felt an urge to bite her nails. She would love to speak to Kate now more than anyone but, even if she agreed to talk to her, what sympathy could she have to give? Annabel was on the verge of losing her husband but Kate had already lost two and her mother. Annabel couldn't compete with that.

16

A few days after the funeral, when the mourners had offered their condolences and eaten all that was left from the buffet in Clontarf Castle, Kate was left with the unenviable job of going through her mother's clothes and personal belongings. It was undoubtedly the job of the daughter of the house though one that Kate would have happily passed on. But she had promised her mother in her final days that she, and only she, would go through her things and that she would keep the more personal of Betty's treasures for herself. This had seemed to calm her mother and lessen her anxiety towards the end.

Kate longed to get back to the Pyrénées and some sort of normality but she wasn't sure what that was any more. Her ticket was booked for the day after tomorrow but she knew that she couldn't possibly have everything done by then.

She had taken a cloth to the drawer of the almost empty tallboy when Damien came into the room.

"I'm meeting Annabel for a cup of coffee," he said casually.

Kate's dying mother's words of regret and guilt came back and hit her like a bolt from out of the blue.

"It didn't take her long to make her move," she sniped. "Mum's not even ready to be picked up from the crematorium."

Damien looked confused – and guilty. "What are you talking about, Kate? She's miserable because you guys aren't friends."

Kate turned to face him, cloth in hand. She wanted to throw it at him. Her mother was gone and her pain was so fresh and loss so strong she felt the undeniable urge to hit him in the hardest way that she could. Before she realised it the words were out of her mouth. "Don't you think you've done enough for Annabel already, Dad?" she asked sarcastically. "I mean, there aren't many fathers go to the trouble of bedding their daughter's best friend."

Damien was frozen to the spot.

"Yes, I *know*," she went on bitterly. "She told me in Biarritz, but I couldn't say anything until Mum had died. She was suffering enough without witnessing how I now feel about you!"

"So that's what the rift is about," Damien said at last with a nod of his head. He had known deep down but hadn't wanted to accept it. "I'm not going to deny what happened, Kate, but it was a long time ago and Annabel's a married woman now. There's nothing like that going on."

"I bet you still fancy her though! And Mum's only dead a few days."

Damien gulped. He didn't want to admit that his daughter was right. When he saw Annabel at the funeral his initial instinct was to run over and hold her. But Betty was still more than a memory and Kate was being harsh. His intentions were honourable.

"When did she tell you about it?"

"Only a few months ago – when I met her in Biarritz. She had kept it a secret for all these years."

Damien was stunned. If Annabel was going to tell Kate, he was amazed that she left it until now. But why tell her at all? Surely Annabel knew Kate would react in this way.

"You have to remember that I love you, Kate, and what happened with me and Annabel had nothing to do with you."

"That's not the way I see it. I'm sick of both of you. Just get out of my sight!"

Damien turned and walked away. He didn't know what he was going to say to Annabel but now that he knew for sure what the rift was about, a lot of Kate's behaviour was making sense.

Kate opened the bottom drawer of the tallboy with a new zeal. She pulled out an array of scarves and shawls that her mother had kept tucked away since the seventies. She remembered one particular stripy scarf that her mother used to wrap around her head when she was trying to look Bohemian. With the sound of her father's footsteps descending the stairs she felt the floodgates open up and held the scarf up to her face to dry the tears. It still carried the faint scent of her mother and she held it like a security blanket for ten minutes before she felt able to carry on. She began to put the scarves into a large ziplock bag. Perhaps she would keep some of them as a remembrance.

At the back of the drawer was an old chocolate box. It even had a picture of the man in the corner with his arms folded after delivering the chocolates – *And all because the lady loves Milk Tray.* Kate hesitated for a moment. It felt strange to be rooting through her mother's personal belongings – an invasion of privacy.

She opened the box and found, to her surprise, that it was full of letters. Bundles of letters all tightly bound with ribbon. The handwriting was neat and scripted but somehow looked masculine. She opened the ribbon from the first bundle and flicked through the letters, checking the postmarks. The postmarks were Australian and dated from 1980 to 1989.

Kate didn't remember her mother ever mentioning friends or family in Australia. Whoever sent these letters was obviously important in her life to have his or her letters preserved so lovingly. She opened the first letter nervously and cautiously.

Dear Beth,

I'm so glad we're back in touch. Your letters cheer me up no end. The working day is long here but at least I see the reward in my pay cheque at the end of the week. Business is booming, Damien would love the work. It means a lot that you have forgiven me. I don't think I deserve it but thanks . . .

She skipped down to the signature: *All my love, Liam.*

She opened the next one and checked the signature: *All my love, Liam.*

Dear Beth,

It was great to hear your voice last night. You sound exactly the same. Carrie has a strong Queensland accent. You two would get on like a house on fire . . .

Kate flicked through the bundle and chose a later letter.

Dear Beth,

I'm still missing you, my love. I can't believe it's only two weeks since we shared that special stolen day in Dun Laoghaire. I can still clearly imagine the boats and the harbour through our hotel window, the wonderful view we could see from our bed. Four hours wasn't enough but it was the best four hours I have spent in twenty years . . .

Kate couldn't believe her eyes. She reread the first few sentences again as the flimsy sheet of notepaper began to shake in her hand. She looked at the date: September 7th 1986.

She stared, stunned. Her head was spinning and her stomach churning. She felt she would be sick. Struggling to control an urge to retch, she opened the ribbons on the other bundles. It was all the same handwriting. She opened a few at random and looked at the signature: each was signed in exactly the same way: *All my love, Liam.*

Kate couldn't bring herself to read any more. Not only had her father had an affair but her mother had been carrying on a long-distance romance for a good deal of her married life. It explained Betty's ranting during her last days about being a bad mother. She wasn't a bad mother, she was a wonderful mother – but she may have been a bad wife. Kate wanted to rip the letters up into tiny shreds. She found she was shaking with anger but she didn't know who she was angry with any more – her mum, her dad, Shane, Annabel? She put her hand up to her forehead and tried to hold back the tears. Did this explain why she herself led such a complicated life? Maybe she had been carrying the sins of her mother and father without realising it.

Kate looked at the last bundle. The final letter was dated 1996 but it was a letter from her mother with "*Return To Sender*" stamped all over the front. Kate couldn't bring herself to open it. This was too much information for one day. The week had been traumatic enough without something like this on top of everything else. She closed her eyes and tried to imagine Shane. No wonder her mother had told her to seize the day with him. And spoke about there being only one true love in anyone's life. That could mean only one thing: she must have been in love with this Liam all her life.

But why did the letters end in 1996? She wondered if her father had discovered the affair. One thing was clear: Betty wouldn't have left the letters there for her to find, if she hadn't meant her to read them. She'd had plenty of time to destroy them. Unless she forgot about them, but that didn't make sense either – Liam was obviously one of the most important people in Betty's life. And how strange that she kept them hidden in the bedroom she shared with her husband! Wasn't she afraid he would find them? Unless she had moved them from somewhere safer only recently. So that she could find comfort from reading them in her last illness? Or because she wanted to be sure her daughter, and no one else, would find them?

She shoved them deep into the plastic bag of scarves and started to dust the drawer. It was important that Damien never got to see them. She needed to find out who Liam was but couldn't think of anyone that could fill in the gaps offhand – except maybe her Auntie Dee?

She looked at her watch – eleven o'clock – only two more days and she would be home. Forty-eight hours and she and her boys would be back in the Pyrénées – they had been through a difficult time too. She needed to sort her life out once and for all and she had a pretty good idea where she needed to start.

Annabel stirred the spoon leisurably in her tall glass of latte as she gazed pensively at the busy shoppers rushing in and out through the supermarket entrance. Was she just another one of those women who trudged their way through the chores for the rest of the family day in, day out? How would those shoppers perceive her now that she was soon to be separated? Would she become anonymous if she no longer had a man at her side? A part of her didn't care and another part of her was scared to death.

Tammy's wasn't the most alluring of coffee shops but it was halfway between Howth and Clontarf and that was why she had suggested it. She spied Damien parking up his car in the distance and felt a tingle through her body. This meeting had been all she had to look forward to since the funeral. Colin was being a complete bastard and didn't understand why she couldn't just let bygones be bygones. Nobody needed to know as far as he was concerned. A little part of her was happy with the circumstances. She couldn't see any other way out of her marriage and even though it would be uncomfortable for a time, she firmly believed that she needed to break away from Colin and the shabby existence she had as his trophy wife. She was deeply concerned for her children though. A marriage break-up could cause heavy scars and Sam would be seriously affected at the critical age he was at. Colin had little time for his daughters. All family activities were co-ordinated by Annabel and nine times out of ten he was on the golf course. But nonetheless they needed their father too.

Moira the solicitor had assured her that she would get half of the family home, the apartment in Spain and the two townhouses that they rented near the city centre. Moira said Colin would be quaking at the thought of her touching his pension and investment funds but she would be entitled to half of those as well. She would be well enough off to maintain a good lifestyle and her kids wouldn't have to suffer financially.

Yes, she was scared, but she was excited too at the prospect of independence. Her mind was already busy with plans and schemes. She could always look for the family home to be put into her name. She was entitled to stay there until the children were finished full-time education but she would rather have it permanently as her security and leave Colin the two townhouses. They were approximate in value. She was left with good options. All she had to do was convince Colin that their marriage was well and truly over. Moira said he could only live in denial for so long. She would have a settlement drawn up and sent to him sometime the following week.

"Always look for three times more than you'll settle for," the mature solicitor had said, leaning across her mahogany and leather-covered desk. Her spectacles covered half of her face. Her hair looked as if she hadn't been to the hairdresser's in years and chopped it herself in front of the bathroom mirror whenever she found the time.

Annabel's thoughts were pleasantly interrupted by Damien's arrival.

"Annabel, how are you?" he asked anxiously.

"Damien," she replied, standing up and awkwardly leaning forward as he kissed her on the cheek. "I started on a latte already." She pointed to her cup.

A middle-aged waitress briskly appeared at his side,

brushing her apron down. She had started over the minute she spotted Damien walking through the door. His presence had this effect on most women over a certain age.

"A black coffee, please," he ordered.

"And another latte for me, please." Annabel smiled at the woman – who still hadn't taken her eyes off Damien.

"It was good to see you at the funeral, Annabel. Betty would have liked it."

"Thanks, Damien. I had to go. She was like a mother to me when I was a kid."

Damien moved around awkwardly on the small aluminium chair that was more used to holding the svelte housewives of the locality rather than a man with Damien's physique.

"I was worried about you and Kate, to be honest. I had hoped you would get a chance to speak to each other." His voice was soft and soothing. "But I've only just found out the whole story."

Annabel's face whitened. She couldn't believe that Kate had told him about Biarritz. She wished for the umpteenth time that she could turn back the clock but it was hopeless and she would have to suffer the consequences. What must Damien think of her now?

"Damien, I'm so sorry. I shouldn't have told her about us. I don't know what came over me that evening." Annabel gasped as if the words were taking more out of her with each one she uttered. "She was teasing me, the way she does, sort of slighting me, and I couldn't help myself. I was full of wine and the words just fell out."

"It's okay. What's done is done. Kate is a big girl now and she will have to learn to live with it like we have for all these years." Damien looked searchingly into Annabel's eyes. "You know, Annabel, there's something else that I need to talk to you about and the whole lot is linked up in a way."

"Sure, anything." Annabel was curious.

Damien swallowed hard. It was his turn to divulge something that had been bottled up inside him for too long.

"There's something that Betty has taken to the grave with her – something I thought she might have told Kate towards the end – but she didn't. For a while though, I thought she had or that Kate somehow suspected."

"Suspected what, Damien?"

"Kate's not my daughter."

Annabel's mouth dropped. It was as if the world rocked.

Damien gazed at her with a kind of compassion – even in this situation he was clearly concerned first and foremost about her.

"But," Annabel gulped, "if not . . . is she adopted?"

"No," Damien said, shaking his head. "She is Betty's daughter but she isn't mine."

"What about Philip?"

"He is my son." He sighed before continuing. "Betty and I were in college together. I was studying engineering and she was doing Arts. We palled around in a big gang. My best friend was from Athlone and he was studying engineering too. He was going out with Betty for over a year and they seemed very much in love. I was always very fond of her as a friend but that was all. Then one night after they had a blazing row, she asked me to walk her home to her flat in Harold's Cross. She invited me in and we ended up sleeping together. A couple of weeks later she still hadn't made up with my friend and I didn't see much of her until one night she came into the college canteen and announced that she needed to speak to me urgently. She said that she was pregnant and that the baby was mine."

"Did you believe her?"

"Of course I did. It was a very different time in Holy Catholic Ireland then and young men knew nothing of women's biology. A few days later my friend ran off to Australia and Betty told everyone that I was the father of her child."

"Did you stay on in college?"

"No, we couldn't afford to, and none of our parents were very happy with the arrangement. My parents blamed her and her parents blamed me."

The waitress left the two cups down in front of the couple who were now so engrossed in their conversation that they didn't notice her.

"When did you discover that Kate wasn't your child?"

"Shortly after she was born. My mother figured the maths out. Kate weighed ten pounds when she was born and was meant to be a month premature," Damien smiled at the thought of his own naivety. "But you know what,

Annabel? The moment I set eyes on Kate I knew that I loved her more than anyone else in the world. She was and always will be my daughter. I would hate her to think that I felt any different towards her than towards Philip. If anything I probably love her more but would never admit it to him."

Annabel's head was shaking in disbelief.

"So, do you think I should tell her or not?" Despair was painted all over his face.

"Damien, the call is totally yours but my guess is that Kate has been through an awful lot recently and I don't think she would react well to the news."

"My feelings as well," Damien nodded, "but I needed to run it by someone who knew her well and you were my obvious choice."

Annabel was disappointed that Damien had this ulterior motive for seeing her. She had hoped he might have another.

"I've a bit of news myself," Annabel smiled. "I found Colin in bed with the *au pair* and we're separating."

"Jesus, Annabel, I don't believe it!" Damien's expression changed to one of horror. "When?"

"The morning of the funeral, actually. I left the Mass card in the kitchen and when I went back to get it I heard grunting upstairs."

"That must have been a terrible shock."

"It was at the time," she couldn't help smiling at the memory, "but, do you know, now that it's happened it's kind of a relief."

"Weren't you happy with Colin?"

"He's difficult to live with at the best of times. I've been doing a lot of settling for this or that throughout my life and putting other people first. Now that I've turned forty I really want to do things for me – like the market stall."

"That's a great little enterprise. You were always good at cooking, I recall."

"I love it," she agreed. "God knows I've had enough experience hosting dinner parties for Colin and his cronies over the years. If I had my way I'd have a little café of my own making natural healthy food – a kind of salad bar crossed with a country kitchen."

"That would be a great earner if you got the location right," Damien said, his brain ticking over as he spoke. "You know, I may have just such a place coming on stream near here. It's a new development with apartments on the top two storeys but it's very hush-hush at the moment. I plan to keep a number of the units and rent them commercially."

"That sounds very exciting, Damien." Annabel's eyes lit up, "but I have no experience in starting up a business. I just know that I love cooking."

"It's not going to be built overnight. We're probably looking at four or five months down the road but the prime retail unit will be the coffee shop and I could give you first option on it if you wanted to think about it."

Annabel wanted to be brave and grasp the opportunity. A businesswoman was something she had never imagined herself as.

"I can see that pretty head of yours working overtime." Damien smiled.

"Leave it with me, will you?" she said. "I'd need to come up with some capital first."

"I'd be happy to be a partner fifty-fifty. You do the work and we'll split the profits," he grinned. "I may demand the odd free slice of carrot cake, mind you."

"Damien, this is very exciting." She felt breathless. "It's a bit much to take in at the moment but I will give it some serious thought."

"Good for you!" Damien applauded her. "Maybe we should arrange to meet again?"

"I'd love that." Annabel smiled and decided to take a chance. "We could make it dinner next time."

"Absolutely," he agreed. "Why don't we say next Tuesday?"

"Tuesday's good," Annabel nodded. She'd have to ask Lily to baby-sit. "Would you mind if we tried Aqua? Colin had a row with them over a dish they served without sauce a few years ago and I've been banned from going ever since. It would feel liberating to go inside the doors of that restaurant again!"

"Good choice. Aqua it is," Damien grinned. "I'll book it as soon as I get home."

The atmosphere between them had changed in the short time since they had sat down. They were no longer there as appendages to Kate but two independent individuals, in conversation on their own terms. The fact that they had known each other for so long helped them settle into an easy kind of relationship. Annabel felt she was talking to a friend of her own rather than to Kate's father and any pressure carried from their past had dissipated.

"I'd better go and collect the kids," she said, glancing at her watch.

"I can't believe it's one o'clock!" he exclaimed.

The lunch-time customers were filing in through the doors and looking disapprovingly at the couple taking up a table, sitting over their two empty coffee cups. As they stood up Damien leaned forward and planted a gentle yet firm kiss on Annabel's right cheek.

"It was great meeting you, Annabel."

"Great to see you too, Damien." Annabel blushed as she spoke and just then, from the corner of her eye, spotted a familiar face glaring over at her.

Melissa nearly spilled her milk as she filled her teacup.

This would certainly give the local women something to gossip about. Annabel got a thrill at the thought of being one of the individuals at the centre of the local news for once.

Kate kissed Ciarán goodnight on his forehead and then leaned over and kissed David.

"Mum, is Grangran in heaven yet?" Ciarán asked.

"I would definitely say so." Kate smiled at the innocence of her son's question. "Three days is plenty of time to get there."

"Will we see her again when we die?" David asked.

"Yes, darling, but that won't be for a very long time."

Kate realised that a death in the family often got children worrying about their own mortality.

"When are we going to see Shane again?" Ciarán asked.

Kate flinched at the mention of his name. She had been trying hopelessly to wash the thoughts of him from her mind but he cropped up in her head many times a day and sooner or later she would have to resign herself to her feelings for him.

"I don't think we'll be seeing him for a long time either, boys. He's married to a lady and has to live with her."

"Why won't he come and live with us instead?" David pressed. "I mean, Stefan's gone to live with a different woman!"

"It's not that simple, boys. Adults have certain things they can and can't do." She paused. If only it was that simple. Maybe children are right and it's adults that complicate relationships. "I'll explain it all some day where you're older."

The boys groaned together and she realised that she hadn't put up a very good argument. Her reasons for her actions weren't yet visible but would be soon enough.

"Sleep tight, boys," she whispered as they snuggled into cosy positions in silence.

Kate felt a sharp cramp shoot through her stomach as she brushed her teeth. Every part of her daily routine was tedious and laborious. It wasn't just the pregnancy – nothing was as it seemed any more after reading Betty's letters. She even felt that she had been harsh in her judgement of Annabel and her father. In retrospect she had been naïve, shocked as a child would be at discovering her beloved father had feet of clay. To say nothing of her beloved mother . . .

She put on her pyjamas and curled up on the bed in the foetal position. She used to always sleep on her stomach, stretched out until she filled every corner of the bed. She was unable to do that any more as her stomach ached if she tried. She took comfort in making herself smaller.

She missed Shane more than a limb. She had no idea that she would feel so bad. He hadn't tried to call her but she hadn't expected him too either – it was after all the second time she had rejected him.

The grim realisation that she was going to be on her own bringing up this baby scared her. She wasn't a young woman any more and she recalled the physical exhaustion she felt after the twins were born. However, Tony had assured her that there was only one baby inside this time. His mini-scan equipment was state-of-the-art and she'd felt a strong maternal pull inside as the image of her unborn child flashed up on the screen. Yet again there was no father there to share the experience with her. How was she going to tell this little one about his or her father? How could she explain that he or she was the product of a one-night stand with a surfer more than a decade younger than her? She tried not to think of Brett. It had been easy to keep him out of her mind while she was with Shane and nursing her mother. But now she had begun to fret about him. Part of her was curious and anxious to find and contact him and tell him about the child that he had fathered but another was afraid to. He would probably run a mile – he had made his feelings about commitments and responsibilities perfectly clear. She felt so alone. Salty tears started to trickle down the side of her face. It could all have been so different. If only she hadn't gone to Biarritz with Annabel! Then she wouldn't have met Brett and she wouldn't have met Shane again. She'd be happy in her ignorance thinking that her father was the greatest in the world and her best friend was solid and reliable in the mantle that she had always worn. In peace, she would be painting the beautiful mountains and coming to terms with a quieter life on her own. She longed for the life she had. But her mother would still be gone and nothing could compensate for that loss.

It wasn't easy being forty.

"I have no intention of making any kind of settlement with you now or any time in the future, Annabel!" Colin shouted as he slammed his briefcase on the marble counter top. "Do you think every marriage ends after a meaningless fling?"

"Be quiet," Annabel pleaded. "The kids have only just gone to bed!"

"I won't be told to be quiet in my own home," he scowled, "especially not after receiving a phone-call like I did from that deplorable Dunne woman."

"I explained to you days ago that I wanted to separate." Annabel stood with her back to the kitchen sink and tried to remain calm.

"A separation is one thing but carving up the family home and my estate is quite another," he grunted.

"Colin, I've been unhappy for some time but I just didn't realise it. Seeing you with Rosa made it perfectly clear that you mustn't have been happy either and it is the best thing for the children that we separate before we start getting nasty with each other."

"Don't start using my own children against me, woman!"

Annabel started to shake. He had called her "woman" a few times during their marriage and each time it left her incensed. This time however she felt strong enough to answer him back.

"You were caught with your trousers down, Colin, and unless you want to be the total laughing stock of the Golf Club, more than you already are, I strongly advise you to heed the directions of Ms Moira Dunne!" Annabel was amazed at herself. She hadn't thought she had it in her to address Colin so articulately.

Colin stood gobsmacked.

The outburst had given Annabel a new strength. "Now," she went on, "you can decide whether you wish to move out tonight or over the weekend, because as far as I am concerned this marriage is over." She picked up her handbag from the countertop and stormed out of the kitchen.

She climbed the stairs with a vigour that she had never felt before. She couldn't wipe off the wide smile that had suddenly appeared on her face. Colin had been sleeping in the spare bedroom since she had found him in Rosa's bed but this was Annabel's chance to remove his clothing from the main bedroom. She took out the two biggest suitcases from the back of her closet and started filling them with his suits and shirts. With great relish she tossed his underwear and shoes along with most of his casual clothes into the cases. The whole experience was liberating. She had no idea where Colin would go and frankly she didn't give a damn.

Natasha leaned forward to get her Marlboro Lights from her tiny Sonia Reykiel handbag and lit one. She took a drag and blew the smoke out of her mouth as she turned around to face a mellow Josh who was splayed out on the couch.

"You know I hate you smoking up here."

"Don't give me any grief, Josh – I've had it up to here all day," she said, gesturing to the top of her head with her free hand. "Shane moved all of his clothes and valuables out earlier today."

Josh tried to hide the smile that was breaking through on his face. "Poor baby," he said, stroking her neck compassionately. "So he's gone for good then?"

"I don't know," she said, shaking her head. "I feel like I never really knew him. Nearly three years of marriage and I know him less now than the first day I walked onto his flight."

She took another drag from her cigarette and this time blew the smoke in his face.

"You must have really loved him." Josh was trying to figure out what was going on inside Natasha's head.

"I thought I did, but he is weak. I did everything right," she insisted. "You should see our house – I made his life very comfortable. I always employed the best staff to iron his shirts and tend to the garden."

Josh leaned back on the couch and put his hands behind his head. "He was a lucky guy."

"What do you mean, Josh? You've got a smug grin on your face."

He shook his head. He felt ill-equipped to tackle her on this issue. He had only ever lived with one woman in his life and that was a dismal failure lasting three weeks.

"Well, now you're free and . . . I'm here," he said with a roguish smile.

Natasha threw her head back and laughed out loud.

"What's so funny?" Josh was genuinely thrown by her reaction.

"You're not serious! You and me?"

"Why not?" he asked with a frown.

"Because, my dear sweet Josh," she said, giggling some more, "you haven't got a proper job and you couldn't possibly afford to be with a woman like me."

"I'm good enough to shag when you want!"

"Yes, but I couldn't honestly say that I'd be seen walking through BT's with you."

"Did you often walk through BT's with Shane?"

"Only around Christmas time but it's a litmus test I use with men. You, my dear Josh, are a pleasure model. I thought we understood each other perfectly."

Josh was disgusted with Natasha and himself. He had felt this way about several women before but now that the tables were turned he didn't like it one bit. He secretly had been delighted with the news of her separation and saw it as an opportunity to develop their relationship. But now that he knew her true feelings he felt like a fool.

"You'd better go now," he said abruptly. "I have to get back to work."

Natasha sighed. She didn't want any more hassle. "Okay. See you during the week?" she said, fluttering her eyelashes.

Josh nodded but was so disgusted by their conversation he wasn't sure how he felt about her any more.

The next morning Damien found his daughter more subdued than usual over a cup of tea in the kitchen.

"Do you need a hand with anything?" he asked cautiously. He wasn't sure what reaction he was going to get from her. She had been on a knife-edge since the funeral.

"Maybe you could take the boys out for a few hours," she said, "so I could get through the rest of Mum's stuff a bit quicker."

"Of course. It can't be an easy job."

"I've had better," Kate admitted.

"I'm sorry if I upset you by meeting Annabel. My motives were genuine."

"It's okay, Dad," Kate nodded. "We've all had a rough time."

Damien hadn't expected such a change of heart overnight but this was typical of Kate's unstable behaviour. "What time is your flight tomorrow?"

"Eleven thirty. Will you drop us out?"

"Of course," Damien replied, hurt that she even needed to ask.

Damien piled the boys into the car and drove them to the local adventure centre to burn up their energies.

When Kate was sure that they were well out of sight she dashed to the kitchen and trembled as she dialled her Auntie Dee's phone number. Kate was depending on her to come up with the information she needed to join the pieces of her mother's jigsaw puzzle together.

"Hello?"

"Dee, it's Kate."

"Kate, love, how are you doing, pet?"

"Not too bad considering," Kate replied honestly. "I've been cleaning out Mum's personal things."

"That must be very difficult for you, love," Dee said sympathetically. "Do you want me to help?"

"No, no. Look, Dee, I need to speak to you privately about some stuff belonging to Mum that I found."

"Oh? What kind of stuff?"

Kate tried to interpret Dee's tone. Did it sound a bit guarded or was she imagining that? "I'll tell you when I see you."

"Okay, pet. When do you want to meet?"

"Could you drop over for an hour, as soon as possible – I'm going back to France tomorrow."

"Well, I was going to bring my mother-in-law to the shops, the old boot. I suppose I could always say something urgent has cropped up. She's never happy no matter how much I do for her anyway."

"Thanks so much, Dee," Kate said with relief. She could picture her aunt in a smart but casual pair of trousers and crossover top setting off to sort out the world around her. She had the figure of a woman twenty years younger too. "I'll see you soon then."

"About twenty minutes, love." Dee hung up.

17

Annabel piled the last of the hummus into the cartons. At this rate she would have plenty of time to set up her stall after dropping the girls off at Maeve's house. She was such a good friend and one of the few women in Howth who still seemed to want anything to do with her since Colin had left the house. Melissa and her motley crew turned their heads so they wouldn't have to talk to her when they saw her. It went to prove how shallow most of her acquaintances were and how much she missed having Kate at a time like this. If she had been told before going to Biarritz that so much in her life would have changed in such a short time she would never have believed it. But she felt a certain pride that she had muddled through it all without Kate's help or advice.

She was surprised at how much she missed Colin and it had only been a few days. She missed the familiarity of his golf clubs strewn around the hall and the rows of neatly folded shirts in the bedroom cupboards. She had taken the

Flora margarine out of the fridge and thrown it out – he was the only one who ate it – and now she missed seeing it there..

With the last of the hummus packed she ran upstairs, grabbed her handbag and sprayed some Prada on her neck. She then went into her son's bedroom.

"Sam, honey, I'm off to the market."

Sam didn't look up from his PlayStation. He had taken to ignoring his mother since his father had left home.

"I said I'm off, honey. Will you be all right?" she repeated. "I told Granny you were here on your own and she'll be over in a bit."

The young boy's face was hidden under a mop of shaggy hair. Bringing Sam to the barber's was one of Colin's tasks and a job that had been forgotten about in the upset of the past few weeks. It was just another thing that Annabel would have to see to, now that she was on her own, and the thought left her feeling even more swamped.

"Another woman. I'm sick of women."

"Sam," Annabel pleaded, "this isn't easy for any of us. I miss your father too."

"Then you should have let him stay. I want Dad to live here with us."

Annabel ran her slender fingers through her long blonde hair in desperation. She sat down on the bed and leaned forward, forcing her son to see her face.

"Sam, I realise how difficult this must be for you, and the girls."

"No, you don't," he said, moving his gaze up until his eyes met hers. "You have no idea what it's like for me. I don't want to live here. I want to be with Dad."

Annabel felt as if she had been stabbed. Sam had never been outwardly affectionate with his father and neither had Colin been with him. She wasn't prepared for this outburst.

Sam's young eyes widened until trickles of tears became visible at the edges. He was a vulnerable small boy and for an instant Annabel saw her son as a four-year-old rather than an eleven-year-old. She felt like she had really let him down. It was only natural that he wanted his father to live at home. It was where he should be. But Annabel wondered if she would have been able to live with herself if she had let Colin stay on in the house.

"Sam, you will still be able to see Daddy whenever you want."

"Well, I want to live with him and he said I could."

This was bizarre. She knew that Colin was staying in the Jury's Hotel next to the IFSC. It was certainly not suitable for a young boy. Colin had decided to take an apartment in the city centre until he decided what he was going to do and it was absolutely unfair of him to give the lad a false hope that he could go and live with him. Sam's school and life was in Howth and his home should be with his mother and sisters. The girls had sobbed and cried themselves to sleep for the past two nights but both were clear that they wanted to stay at home with their mother.

"I don't know what to say, Sam," Annabel said gently.

"It's nothing to do with you. This is between me and Dad."

He was his father's son all right. Maybe she had sent him to too many camps. The thought of losing her son was a huge price to pay for her freedom and something she hadn't thought about.

"We can discuss this again when Daddy gets somewhere permanent to live."

Sam shrugged. "Okay, but I've made my mind up."

There was no point talking to him. He was a confused little eleven-year-old boy.

She leaned forward and kissed his forehead but he showed no reaction. As she moved to the door she looked back at him: he was intent once again on his game. Were the children going to pay too high a price for their mother's sanity and salvation?

She glanced at her watch and realised that she would be late if she didn't get a move on.

"Girls, are you ready?"

Her daughters appeared from their bedrooms. They were pleased to be spending the day with Maeve Jenkins and her family. Their own home life now lacked the regular order and stability that they were used to.

"We'll be back by four o'clock," she called to Sam as she closed the front door, but he didn't reply.

Dee reached Greenfield Close more quickly than Kate had anticipated. She felt relief as her aunt's smiling face appeared at the front door – her resemblance to her mother soothed her.

"Thanks for coming, Dee."

"Sweet Kate, how are you doing?" she said, leaning forward to give her niece a kiss on the cheek.

"I've been better. Do you want a cup of tea?"

"I've given it up but I'll have a cup of boiled water."

Kate ushered her aunt into the kitchen and put the kettle on. Dee took a seat and watched Kate as she buzzed around as Betty used to.

"How's Damien?"

"He's doing okay, I guess. Even though he had some time to prepare for Mum's death I think he's shocked now that she's actually gone."

Dee nodded her head sympathetically. "How have you been getting on?"

Dee didn't know a more subtle way to approach the subject of Betty's belongings.

Kate didn't answer for a few moments, then she said quietly, "It's something that you never imagine doing in your wildest dreams. Even when I secretly looked through her wardrobes as a child I felt as if she would pounce upon me at any moment – now that I have to sort them out because she isn't going to be using them again, it feels like a horrible invasion of her privacy."

Dee nodded sympathetically. Her offers of help had been rightly turned down. This really was something that only Kate was qualified to do and Betty wouldn't want anyone else doing it.

"I guess I sounded weird on the phone?" Kate continued.

"Kate you can say anything you like to anyone for the next few days and weeks and they will understand. You're not yourself after losing your mum and it's going to take time."

Kate filled a mug with boiling water and placed it down in front of her aunt, then made herself a mug of coffee and sat opposite her.

"Dee, I'm confused about a box of letters that I found in Mum's tallboy," she blurted out. It felt disloyal talking about her mother's private life but she had left her with no choice. "Have you ever heard of someone called Liam?"

Dee gazed into her mug of water. She hadn't heard him mentioned in years. "Why do you ask?"

"I found a pile of letters that he wrote to Mum." Kate paused. "They were writing to each other for over fifteen years. I think they had an affair. Well, it's clear they had."

Dee gulped back the piping hot water, burning her mouth. "But he went to live in Australia!"

"He came home at least once and she met up with him. Dee, did you know him well?"

"If it's the same Liam, and I'm sure it is, Betty was going out with him for a year or more when she was in college. I was still in school at the time but I remember him visiting our house. I thought he was gorgeous – I think all little sisters feel that way about their older sister's boyfriends."

Kate's face lightened. Maybe now she would get the answers that she wanted. "Were they very much in love?"

Dee took another gulp from her cup and nodded her head frantically. "Oh, very much. He was always in our house and my mother was convinced that they would get engaged. The whole family was shocked when they broke up."

"Why did they break up?" Kate asked urgently.

Dee paused for a moment on realising that this story might come as a shock to her niece. It was a pity that her sister had never confided in her daughter before this. "This shouldn't be coming from me, love . . ." She hesitated. "I guess you need to know, though."

"Tell me, Dee. I need to know what?" Kate's eager expression had turned to a frown.

Dee looked down into her cup. "Your mum got pregnant by his best friend."

The penny dropped. "Dad?"

Dee nodded.

Kate shook her head in amazement at the revelation. "That must have been a scandal back then."

"You'd better believe it. It would still be a scandal today!"

"So Liam ran off to Australia with a broken heart?"

"As far as I am aware. I had no idea that he got back in touch with your mum."

Kate rubbed her index finger over her right eyebrow comfortingly. She was truly beginning to regret giving her father such a harsh time while her mother was ill.

His relationship with Annabel had been less scandalous in many ways than her mother's relationship with Liam. And now this further revelation!

"It's strange to think of her having this lover all this time," she said.

"Well, he was really more of a fantasy, don't you think?" Dee tilted her head. "I'm surprised myself that she carried out a long-distance romance. When did the letters stop?"

"1996."

Dee sat back on the wooden chair and took a last sip from her almost empty cup. "I wonder why?"

Kate nodded. "I read a few of them but I feel like I'm invading her privacy when I open them. I was hoping you would be able to tell me more."

"I'm sorry," Dee said with a shake of her head. "I wish I could be more help. I'm as surprised as you are to find out she got back in touch with him." She paused. "Kate, you said you found them in Betty's tallboy. In her room?"

"Yes."

"But why didn't she destroy them? She must have known you'd find them."

"Yes. What's more, she was very insistent that I, and only I, sorted out her things after she died. She must have meant me to find them."

Dee nodded slowly. "So she wanted you to read them, Kate. She wanted you to know the story. Probably hadn't the courage to tell you herself."

Kate nodded silently.

Dee glanced at her watch. "Now, sorry, dear, but I really must take this old boot to the shops."

Kate stood up and cleared the mugs from the table. "I'm going back to France tomorrow. Maybe you'll come visit me before the year is out."

"I'd love that. I might come on my own and we can have a nice girlie time. Poor Kate! You've been through the mill with your divorce and losing your mum – you deserve a run of good luck now."

Kate trusted her aunt and longed to tell her about the baby growing inside her.

"I'm . . ." A little voice inside her head stopped her mid-sentence.

"Yes, Kate?"

"Nothing. I'm doing fine, Dee."

"Well, just don't be too brave and remember to call me if you need anything at all!"

Kate hugged her aunt warmly, then showed her to the hall door. "Thanks again for coming."

"If you like I can do a bit of detective work for you – see if my brothers know anything about Liam."

"Maybe, but don't make it too obvious. I don't want Dad finding out."

Dee nodded. "Whatever you think."

Kate waved goodbye vigorously as her aunt drove away. She would look at the other letters and see what they could tell her about the end of the story. Then she could decide whether to destroy them or not.

She ran upstairs and took the little bundles out. She settled down on the floor, resting her back against the side of the bed.

The last letter Liam wrote to her was dog-eared and grubby. It looked as though it had been read and reread many times.

Dear Beth,

I am missing you so much. I thought it would be enough just knowing that you are there and thinking of me but it isn't. I am so unhappy.

I made the biggest mistake of my life leaving you and you know how much I've regretted it. But we are not getting any younger. I have told Carrie that I am leaving her. I never really loved her the way a husband should love his wife. Please, Betty, I am begging you to consider leaving Damien. I will come back to Ireland or you can come to Australia. I will be happy anywhere as long as we are together. Time is running out for us, Betty. Please let me know your answer when I ring on Sunday.

All my love always

Liam x

Betty's reply was sealed and stamped with *"Return to Sender"* all over the front of it. With trembling fingers Kate started to tear at the gummed envelope. The paper inside was pristine as if it had been written only the day before.

My Love,

I didn't answer your call on Sunday because I need to write these words down. You know how I feel about you, how I've always felt about you, but your life is in Australia. I can't leave Damien now. He was the one who stood by me and has given me and the children a good life. Don't think I haven't thought seriously about your proposition – in my heart you are the one I truly want to be with. But I think we would upset too many people. I don't think I could tell Kate the truth and she would find out if we were to be together. Please believe me when I tell you how much it hurts to tell you my decision. Don't stop writing or phoning. I need to know that we can still be in touch

Forever yours,

Beth xxx

Kate felt a salty tear trickle down her cheek and stop at the corner of her mouth. She desperately wanted to know what happened next. Betty had betrayed her husband for so long. She had been living a double life with her heart on the other side of the world.

"What are they?" a voice asked from behind, making Kate jump.

Kate felt like a rabbit looking down the barrel of a shotgun.

"Dad, I eh, it's just some stuff of Mum's." Kate floundered around, fixing the letters back into a neat pile.

Damien spotted the Australian stamps. He knew they could only be from one person. It was careless of Betty to leave them around but they were probably not high on her agenda for the last few weeks. On the other hand . . . could it be that she wanted Kate to find them? He was surprised to see so many. Surely they weren't all from Liam? He had suspected that they might have been in touch once or twice but this looked like more than a passing correspondence.

"Are they all from the same person?" He was anxious to find out how much she knew.

"I don't know. I haven't read them," she lied. "I think it's probably best to burn them."

Damien said nothing. He certainly didn't want to read their contents but did want to know what Kate had learned from reading them.

"Kate . . ." He braced himself before continuing. "Are they from someone called Liam?"

Kate was startled. She didn't expect her father to be aware of his letters.

"Yes," slipped meekly out from between her lips.

Damien sat down on the double bed that he had shared with his wife for the best part of forty years. He put his elbows on his knees and sank his head into his hands. There was no right time to tell Kate the truth. Now was as good as any.

"Kate, there's something you should know."

"I know already, Dad," she interrupted.

He lifted his head in surprise. "What do you know?"

Kate moved forward on her knees and held her hand out until it rested on her father's knee. There was no easy way of telling him that she knew.

"That you got Mum pregnant before you were married. She was on the rebound from your best friend."

Damien froze. This wasn't even close to what he had to say to her.

"Who told you that?"

"Dee."

Damien swallowed hard. "It wasn't exactly like that. Kate, before I tell you this I need you to know how much I love you and have always loved you – every bit as much as Philip."

Every bit as much as Philip? What an odd thing to say! What did he mean? Kate had never seen her father so nervous. "What?" she asked.

"Kate, your mum was pregnant when we got married." Damien swallowed hard and put his hand on his daughter's for support. "But not with my child."

Kate pulled her hand away. He wasn't making sense. "What are you saying?"

"Kate, I love you like my own and I reared you like my own but your mother was already pregnant when we married. With my friend's child, Liam's child." He paused. "You are Liam's daughter."

Kate felt a thud hit her like a deep blow to her chest. She wanted to retch. Her head lightened and her stomach cramped up. Her mouth widened with disbelief.

"Kate, are you okay?" Damien asked softly.

Words totally failed her and all she could do was stare at the floor where her father's feet rested. At least she thought that this man was her father until a few seconds ago.

"Why didn't you . . . why didn't she . . . I mean, there were lots of times one of you could have told me . . ."

But still she couldn't look at Damien. She thought that she knew those closest to her – especially since Annabel's betrayal she had convinced herself that at least she had her mother's trust and confidence. The letters from Liam were difficult enough to digest without this bombshell on top of everything else.

"I should have told you. Your mother should have said something before she left us but the illness crept upon us all so quickly I guess your mother – maybe she felt that the time was never going to be right to tell you the truth."

Kate felt anger creep up from her stomach to her throat. But she wasn't sure who she was angry with any more. How could she possibly be cross with her mother after all she had been through? The anger quickly turned to regret and pity for letting her mother leave her life without getting to know her properly. While lost in her own thoughts she heard her father swallow loudly from a few feet away. This was the most difficult conversation that the two of them would ever have. She looked over in his direction and spotted a tear run down the side of his cheek. It left her feeling forlorn and in desperate need to console him. Crawling slowly over to the edge of the bed, she folded her arms around his neck and sank her head into his shoulder.

The two sobbed pitifully together for a long time. They had both been duped by Betty but they loved and missed her.

At last Kate threw her head back and took a long look at her father.

"Kate, I'm so sorry."

"You have nothing to be sorry for," Kate said, staring through eyes filled like wells to the brim. "You are my dad."

"Thank you, Kate." Damien's voice was shuddering. "You have no idea what it means to hear you say that."

Kate looked at her father with pity, all her anger evaporated. It was no wonder he had fallen in love with Annabel while her mother was preoccupied with her long-distance love affair. But she needed a question answered.

"Did you know that I was Liam's child when you married Mum?"

Damien didn't want to answer. Betty was dead and there was no point in casting aspersions. However, Kate needed to know everything. He shook his head slowly. "Betty told me that you were mine. It was some time afterwards that she admitted the truth."

"She tricked you?" Kate was shocked that her mother would do such a thing.

"I wouldn't put it like that, Kate," Damien said cautiously. "You must remember that it was a different time. We didn't have the same freedom that young people have nowadays. Betty was afraid. She didn't have many options."

"But how did you feel when you found out?" Kate needed to know that she was wanted.

"By then it was too late. I'd fallen in love with you!"

Damien's big brown eyes glowed and his eyebrows arched.

Kate's eyes filled once more but this time with relief and joy at her father's words.

"Kate, are you going to be okay?"

"Of course." Kate reached out and stroked the side of her father's face gently. "You are my dad. I never met Liam."

"Do you want to try and get in touch with him?"

"There's no point." She was in fact keen to find out more about Liam but didn't want to hurt her father's feelings.

"Maybe you should keep the letters?" Damien suggested.

Kate was amazed at the graciousness of her father. He was a wonderful man and she was very lucky to have him as a role model.

"I might put them away for posterity then," she said as she sat up on the bed beside him and rubbed the palms of her hands down her thighs. "Dad, while we are coming out with truths, I have something difficult to tell you."

Damien tilted his head. What more shocking news could they have to share?

"I'm pregnant."

Damien's mouth opened with surprise. The time for difficult conversations was obviously not over. Delicate approaches were never his forte and this was definitely one time that warranted the plain truth – especially after the conversation that they had just had.

"Who . . .?"

"Someone you don't know. It happened in France. But with an English guy."

"Are you in a relationship with this guy?"

"I don't even know where he is!"

"Kate!" It was Damien's turn to be appalled.

Kate felt embarrassed and wished she could lie. But they had shared so much already today she felt left with no other option but to tell the truth. She braced herself.

"It was a one-night stand when I was on that trip with Annabel."

Damien shook his head. "That trip seems to be responsible for a lot of upset already in your life, Kate. What are you going to do? You can't bring a child up on your own."

Kate hadn't thought the practicalities through properly but did have her answer ready. "I was on my own with the twins, remember?"

"That was different circumstances though."

Kate didn't want to go into it any further. They had both enough to deal with for one day.

"I'm big enough to look after a tiny baby. I'll be fine."

Damien caressed the side of Kate's cheek, pushing her hair back off her face. "You have had a tough time, Kate. It's a pity things didn't work out with Shane."

"He doesn't know about the baby. I couldn't have him bringing up a child that wasn't his. We couldn't be happy in those circumstances."

"It might not be such a bad thing for him, you

know." He smiled deeply as if he knew something that she had no way of understanding. "I wouldn't change my situation if I had my life to live again. I have the best daughter in the world."

Kate threw her arms around her father and hugged him tightly. "Thanks, Dad," she whispered softly, "for everything."

Annabel breezed past the stall traders. She placed a batch of hummus onto her stand and went back to the Jeep to get the rest. As she leaned across the back seat of the Jeep she heard an unfamiliar voice.

"Would you like a hand with that?"

Annabel turned around to see who it belonged to. A tall guy with shaggy blond hair smiled at her. His eyes were so blue, they were almost transparent. She looked down at his Timberland boots and black drainpipe jeans. How could anyone dress so scruffily and still look so good, she wondered.

"Em, eh, thank you." Annabel wondered who the stranger was.

"Hi! I'm new to this market but I saw you last week," he said, lifting the box from the back seat of the Jeep with ease.

"I've only been doing this a few weeks myself."

"Gary's the name, by the way." His smile was open and warm and put her instantly at ease.

"I'm Annabel, Annabel Hamilton."

"What's your speciality, Annabel?"

"Hummus and salads but I started doing quiches recently and they're doing well."

"Nice. I'm smoothies and shakes."

She wasn't surprised. He was amazingly cool and equally smooth. The two walked over to her patch of the market.

"I have to admit I love smoothies," she said.

"I'll drop one over to you later! Are you a creamy banana kind of girl or something more passionate with strawberries and raspberries?"

Annabel couldn't hide the naughty smile that was developing across her face. "Why don't you choose?"

"I just know the morning is going to fly by while I work that one out!" he said throwing her a cheeky wink.

"See you later then."

"You will indeed." He put her box of hummus onto the market stall and walked off slowly, looking back a couple of times and giving a little wave. Annabel watched him disappear into a bright orange van with fruit painted all over it.

The morning did pass briskly and Annabel found it difficult not to peek over every now and again at Gary in his fruity van. He couldn't be more than about thirty-five and he gave the impression that he was single. Annabel thought she probably gave off that impression too. She wasn't used to flirting with men. Was it because she was single now that men noticed her more? Or was it because she had a newfound confidence that came from breaking her attachment to Colin? Either way, life was certainly becoming more interesting.

When Gary did finally come over with a large pink-coloured smoothie in his hand, Annabel felt her heart beat a little bit faster. He had put a stripy straw and fresh raspberry into the paper cup.

"Hello, again!" he said, presenting the cup as if it were an apple for the teacher.

"My smoothie? Thanks! It looks gorgeous!"

"Yes, it's made from a very special recipe – it's top secret. I could tell you but then I'd have to kill you!"

"*Top Gun*!" Annabel exclaimed.

"Very good. I like a girl who knows her movies." Gary's mouth widened until his white teeth glistened, making him look really attractive, and Annabel felt as if she had been lifted off to another planet.

"So you're a *Top Gun* fan?" she asked, smiling.

"Saw it in my impressionable years – I was twelve or thirteen, I think."

"No! You couldn't have! You don't look old enough!"

"How old do you think I am?"

"Thirty-five tops."

"You've made my day," he said with a grin. "I'm forty-one."

Annabel was impressed. She discreetly looked at his left hand but there was no sign of a wedding band. "So, do you do all the markets or just this one?"

"I started out with the Phoenix Park market and then I did Malahide and before I knew it I was addicted. Gave up the full-time job in UTA insurance and I can come and go as I please. The fruit's easier to work with."

Annabel laughed. She couldn't picture this guy in a regular job.

"By the way," he said, "you wouldn't have Seán Doonan's number, would you? I seem to have lost it and need to settle up my rent."

"Sure," she said, taking her phone out of her pocket. "I'll text it to you. What's your number?" She tapped his details into her phone and sent the text.

"You're a star. That's worth another smoothie next week!"

"Maybe even a shake?" she suggested flirtingly.

Gary took the bait with a twinkle in his eye. "Maybe a smooth shake!"

He walked off slowly, looking back every few steps. The market was full of pleasant surprises. She hoped she hadn't seen the last of Gary.

"Safe journey," Damien said, giving Kate a big hug at the departure gates. "Look after your mum, boys."

Ciarán looked up from his Gameboy and gave a nod. David was listening to his iPod intently and hadn't even heard his grandfather.

"I'll see you in September," Kate assured her father. "Are you sure you don't mind flying over so soon?"

"The past couple of months have cured me of my fear of flying – life's too short. I want to see as much as possible of you and the boys from now on."

Kate wrapped her arms around her father's shoulders warmly. This had been the hardest trip home of her life.

Everything had changed. She had lost her mother, a mother it now seemed she never really knew, and her father wasn't who she thought he was either – he was neither saint nor villain nor even her biological father. One thing for sure, the bond and love between them was stronger than ever.

"Thanks, Dad. Are you going to be okay in that house on your own?"

Kate had mentioned the unthinkable. She could read his mind. It had been hanging over Damien like a heavy fog since his daughter started to pack her bags for her return to France. He dreaded the thought of returning to that house. Betty was gone and he had a solitary existence to look forward to from now on.

"I'll be fine, honestly. You're only a couple of hours away. Just mind yourself. Don't worry about me."

Damien ruffled the heads of his grandsons and gave Kate a peck on the cheek, then stood back and watched as his family walked through security. He felt as if a physical part of himself was disappearing behind the gate with his daughter. The bond between them certainly hadn't been affected by telling her the truth and she seemed to have forgiven him for the Annabel episode in the light of the greater revelations. Not that Annabel could be labelled an 'episode' . . .

He solemnly made his way to pay for his parking space. The airport was a depressing place after saying goodbye. He couldn't stand the thought of going home. The house was going to be very lonely – it was much too big for one man. He might sell up and move into one of the apartments he had built recently. The Oaks in Howth were nice.

Shane had to get his act together. He needed somewhere to live. Rob had been very good letting him stay in his apartment in Swords but it was too small and the scruffy first officer didn't rate hygiene high on his list of priorities. Shane had got used to living on the southside but it was nice to be back on the northside. Rob's place was much more convenient for work. For the time being, it seemed a good idea to stay here in familiar territory but could he stand seeing all the familiar places that reminded him of Kate every day of the week?

He took out the property section of the *Irish Times* and breezed through the lists of new properties on show at the weekend. A small development of apartments in Howth, close to the beach, caught his eye – built by Carlton developers. Good old Damien always had an eye for a good site to develop on. But he couldn't let that stop him going to see the apartments at least. He looked at his watch. It was open to the public until five o'clock today. He could squeeze a viewing in before his overnight in Köln.

He folded the newspaper and settled into the seat of his BMW. The day was warm enough to leave the roof off and he drove with the radio blaring along the coast road past Clontarf. He had to get over Kate once and for all. He had to get his own life back on track. His car seemed to know exactly where it was going. Even the scenery on the way made him feel as though he was finally going home.

Imposing electric gates led the way into the exclusive complex. A slim girl in a black business suit and severely tied blonde hair stood outside the show apartment with a batch of brochures resting in the crook of her arm. She smiled at Shane as he approached, displaying a dazzling set of white teeth.

"Hello, would you like a brochure?" she asked, holding out a shiny magazine.

"Thank you."

"We only have five units left and one of them is the show apartment."

Shane took the brochure from her and smiled as he walked through the door. He took a quick look at the guiding prices – they weren't cheap. He could realistically only afford the one-bedroom on the second floor. The two-bedroom would stretch his salary too much if he kept the payments up on Natasha's cottage as well. He could, of course, try to sell the cottage but he didn't want to cause Natasha any more distress or upset than he already had.

The show apartment was stunning. The furniture was an eclectic mix of different woods and leathers that gave the apartment a natural feel. He looked out the window at the wonderful views of the beach. It was way out of his reach but he consoled himself that he didn't need three bedrooms anyway.

"Can I see the one-bedroom?"

"It's not officially on view but if you are really interested I could give you a quick peek," the estate agent said.

"That would be great, thanks."

The blonde girl led him up a flight of stairs but assured him that the lifts would all be working within the next week. The minute he walked through the doors of the apartment he knew that he was home – a refuge in the middle of all the chaos in his life. He walked over to the huge window that looked out onto Claremont beach. He could clearly see the spot where he and Kate had sat only a couple of months earlier. He could wake to that view every morning.

He turned to the blonde girl who was looking at her watch.

"I'll take it," he said.

"Don't you want to see the bedroom?" she said with surprise. The apartment certainly didn't have the best view in the complex and the bedroom was tiny.

"Okay, but I've made my mind up," he assured her.

"Fine," the pretty blonde said. "I'll pop downstairs and get some paperwork while you look around."

Shane knew that this was where he was meant to be. He didn't believe in fate. Kate, with her bizarre philosophies, used to always try and convince him that everything happened for a reason. There was something about this place though that drew him like a magnet. Was he hankering after the past? He couldn't pretend that he was over Kate. How could he possibly move on when he thought about her now more than ever? He walked over to the window and tried to picture Kate sitting in the sunshine on the sand.

Kate felt strange as the plane descended into Toulouse airport. She didn't get the usual tingle of excitement on touching French soil. She had come to enjoy the lifestyle in Ireland that was once so familiar to her. She liked Clontarf and she would miss her father sorely. Thoughts of Liam plagued her every couple of hours but she didn't know who to talk to about it – she used to go to Annabel at times of distress but with her gone from her life there was only one other possible person that she could spill out her heart to.

Fabian was waiting in the Arrivals Hall, pristine and pampered like a turkey-cock. He waved wildly once he spotted Kate and the boys.

"*Chérie!*" he called. "Come to me, Kate. I have missed you too much! How are you, boys?"

He tapped them both on the heads and they grunted at him. He was something of an oddity and they couldn't quite make out what was so different about him. He threw his arms dramatically around Kate and kissed her affectionately on both cheeks.

"Thanks, Fabian," she said as he took the trolley from her. "How are you?"

"We have been – how you say? – plodding along, doing our French thing. Joy and Simon have made their home into a B&B and my cousin is going to jail for dealing in narcotics but apart from that you have missed nothing."

"Oh dear!" Kate said in surprise.

"It's okay. I don't like him much. Now tell me, how was your mother's funeral?"

"It went very well, I suppose." She sighed. "For a funeral!"

"And how is your father?"

"I have so much to tell you, Fabian, but maybe we can wait until we are at home," she said, nodding at the boys.

Fabian's eyebrows shot up as he wondered what other interesting news Kate could possibly have.

It wasn't until a couple of hours later with her sons absorbed in front of a computer game that Kate got a chance to talk to Fabian privately.

He poured himself a generous glass of red and placed a fresh glass of Perrier in front of her on the kitchen table.

"So, tell me about Dublin." He leaned forward across the kitchen table – all ears and interest.

"Fabian, I don't know where to start."

"What about Shane – how is your great love affair?"

"Fabian, I finished with him. I had to. I had to do what is best for him and Natasha."

Fabian frowned. "How do you know what is best for him? And what about best for you?"

"I just don't know any more! Caring for my mother

was one of the hardest things I ever had to do. To watch someone you love wilt away before you so quickly is devastating."

Fabian nodded gravely. "I can only imagine!"

"But the thing that really gets to me is how little I knew about her life and the feelings that she had. Now that she's gone I don't have a chance to talk to her about them." Kate thumped the table – her hand in a fist. "I can't believe some of the things she didn't tell me."

"Like?"

"This has been very hard for me to deal with but after cleaning out her personal belongings I found a box of letters from an old lover."

Fabian raised his eyebrows but said nothing.

"It turns out that she had a long-distance love affair with an old boyfriend for over twenty years."

Fabian's expression gave nothing away about his thoughts on the revelation.

"There's more," said Kate heavily. "That man – Liam is his name – is my biological father."

Fabian took a sharp intake of breath.

Kate nodded. "So that was something else that I had to deal with – of course I couldn't let Damien see how upset I was with the news. I still feel that he is absolutely my father but I am so curious about Liam."

"Why don't you try to meet up with him?" said Fabian eagerly.

"Because," Kate stopped and gulped. "I'm scared – but believe me I've been thinking about it."

18

Annabel was all fingers and thumbs. She fixed her hair into a ponytail and then took it out again. The thought of dinner with Damien was setting little butterflies off inside her stomach. She hadn't been out to dinner on her own with a man since before she met Colin. Her little black dress was very slimming and the Audrey Hepburn styling was very 'this season'. It was treading a fine line between looking her best and inappropriate-dress-to-be-meeting-a-new-widower-in – but it was approaching eight o'clock and too late to change now.

"Tell me again, why are you meeting Damien Carlton?" Lily asked.

Annabel turned, startled by the silhouette of her mother standing in the bedroom doorway. She hated the way her mother crept around the house and appeared at any moment. Now that Colin was gone she seemed to have taken rights over the house.

"I told you, Mum. He has a business proposition. I'm going to open a coffee shop."

Annabel returned to fixing her hair. She could see her mother shaking her head in the reflection of the mirror.

"I wish you'd have more faith in me," she said, turning once more to face Lily.

"I don't know what has got into you, Annabel. Colin rang me earlier today and is keen to patch things up. Sam is in an awful state and Rebecca is wetting the bed."

It was true. The children were taking the separation much worse than she had ever imagined.

"Please don't make it any more difficult than it already is for me, Mum."

"I just don't understand."

Annabel felt sorry for her mother. She was from a different time when it was all right for a woman to stay in a loveless marriage, under her husband's shadow – indeed, for many women today it was still enough. If she patched things up with Colin she would be back to square one. It was only now that she was away from him that she realised how much he undermined her confidence. He treated her like hired help when he wanted a particular shirt ironed or something else done and he was never around to give the children any time.

That was why she was so frustrated with Sam. She was the one who had stood at the sidelines on the cold winter mornings when he played his football matches. She was the one who had brought him and his friends to the movies. Now she felt she was getting no support back in return. But he was just a child, she had to remember that, and this was part of the grieving process that kids go through when their parents split up. It was hard, but she wanted more from life and she was determined to do something about it.

"I'll be back about twelve, I'd imagine," she said as she sprayed some Prada on her neck and picked up her little black handbag.

"I'll stay the night," Lily said.

"Thanks, Mum," Annabel said, giving her mother a kiss on the cheek.

She dashed down the stairs and out the door, slamming it behind her and jumped into her Jeep. Two minutes later she was parking outside Aqua.

The waiter took her embroidered jacket as she arrived in the foyer of the impressive restaurant. "This way, madam," he said, ushering her over to the window where Damien was already sitting at a round table covered with a crisp linen tablecloth.

Damien jumped up as she approached and tried to stop his eyes from scanning over the stunning woman who was his date for the night. He was dressed in a pale blue shirt and chino jeans with a brown leather belt, and his skin seemed more tanned than usual.

When Annabel reached him he planted a polite kiss on her cheek.

"Hi, Damien," she said with a smile. The evening had a feeling of pleasure and ease about it before it even started.

Damien pulled his shoulders back like a peacock restless in front of a peahen but fully aware that his real guise was that of a husband in mourning.

"Hi, Annabel – you look lovely."

"Thank you," she replied graciously. A tingle of excitement shot through her as she realised that she really was out for the evening with Damien. The man she had dreamed about for most of her young life and much of her adult life. She had to pinch herself to remember that he was only recently widowed and she must not read into this as anything more than a business meeting.

She sat and the waiter handed her a large colourful menu.

"The view is spectacular, isn't it?" she said, looking out at the twinkling lights from the village and fishing boats reflecting on the water.

"I love it here," he nodded.

The setting was beautiful, the scene perfect for a couple who were once attracted to each other to rekindle their feelings but Annabel felt awkward and painfully aware of Betty's presence hanging over them.

"How have you been?" she asked.

Damien swallowed and put the closed menu down on the table. "Honestly?"

Annabel nodded.

"I'm lost and lonely. Kate cleaned out Betty's things and gave them to the St Vincent de Paul. I wish she hadn't but it was under Betty's instructions."

Annabel remained silent. She remembered that her

mother had left her father's clothes hanging in the wardrobes for years after he died. Lily said years later that she thought by doing so he would eventually come back. Everyone around her understood and supported her decision. But Annabel wondered if perhaps Lily would have let the way be cleared for a new relationship by clearing out her husband's belongings – anyway it was too late for Lily now and the mention of another man entering her life had been dismissed on too many occasions.

Damien was different and a fine-looking man for his age. He had a spring in his step that resembled a forty-year-old's and an outlook that matched it. She wanted to tell him that it had been the right thing to clear out Betty's things but felt that it wasn't her place to make such a judgment.

"Has Kate gone back to France?" Annabel desperately wanted to hear any news of her friend.

"She went yesterday."

"How is she?" Annabel leaned forward on her elbows, hanging on his reply.

"She's well, considering." He paused for a moment. "Actually she has a bit of news. It came as a shock to me – she's pregnant."

Annabel sat back on her chair in surprise. "When? How?"

"Apparently it was some chap she met when she was in Biarritz."

"Brett?" Annabel's mouth dropped open.

"Was that his name?"

Annabel nodded. "What's she going to do? Has she tried to contact him?" She wondered how she would find him as it seemed he continuously trekked around the windsurfing circuits of Europe. Plus, she didn't think Kate even knew Brett's surname.

"She said there is no point in contacting this fellow. She is all over the place, Annabel. I don't think she has thought any of this through. I mean she already has the boys to look after and she's on her own now."

Annabel nodded. She found it difficult coming to terms with life on her own since Colin had moved out. Strange that for the first time in their lives she and Kate were in similar situations. It was such a pity that they didn't have each other for help and support any more.

"So what about herself and Shane?" she asked.

"She finished with him."

Annabel shook her head in disbelief. "Why?"

"She's not making sense at the moment but she said something about not wanting to put a burden on him, bringing up another man's child." Damien smiled knowingly at Annabel. "It's ironic, isn't it?"

Annabel nodded but didn't return his smile, still shocked at the revelations. "She must be in a right state."

"I'm worried about her, to be honest with you. It's been hard for her nursing Betty these past few months and she carried the knowledge that she was pregnant silently in the midst of all the mayhem."

Annabel couldn't imagine having to cope with so many ordeals at the same time.

"Maybe I could try ringing her again – but I'm not sure she'd want to talk to me."

"That would be good of you. Please try," he said with concern. "I feel she needs a woman to talk to." He paused and poured himself a glass of water from the jug in the middle of the table. "I also told her about her biological father so she has a lot on her plate."

"Oh my goodness! Poor Kate! So much to cope with!" Then she placed her hand gently on top of his. "And that can't have been easy for you, Damien."

"She was surprisingly okay about it."

"She's amazingly resilient." Annabel sighed. "I feel inadequate next to her."

Damien leaned forward on his elbows. "So, how are you doing?"

"I am keen to go ahead with the separation even though I'm getting negative vibes from all around me."

The waiter came over and presented them with the wine list.

"Would you like red or white?" Damien asked Annabel as he glanced quickly at it.

"White, if that's okay with you. I guess we'll both be having fish!"

Aqua was one of the best fish restaurants on the north side of the city and they smiled in acknowledgment of the fact.

"The Pouilly Fumé, I think," Damien said to the waiter. "Okay with you, Annabel?"

"Perfect," she said.

The waiter withdrew and Damien asked, "What's happening with Colin?"

"He has moved out. The kids are very upset naturally. It's a difficult time for everyone."

"Is there any chance of reconciliation?"

"Not the way I'm feeling at the moment," she replied firmly. "So tell me more about Kate."

"I'm seriously worried about her. She's going to have this baby and she wants to take the boys out of boarding school – so she will be on her own with three children. I wish I could help her."

They were interrupted by Annabel's mobile phone ringing. She excused herself and answered it.

"Annabel?" a man's voice asked.

"Yes."

"Hi! This is Gary from the market. I hope I'm not disturbing you."

This was a surprise. Annabel shifted around awkwardly in her seat and turned her head away from her companion. "Hi, I'm having dinner actually – but it's okay – what can I do for you?" Her tone lifted until she sounded almost like a little girl.

"I was wondering where you got the plastic cartons for the hummus. I was thinking of selling dried fruit snacks with my smoothies." His voice sounded nervous at the other end of the line.

Annabel was pleased to be getting the call but his timing was terrible. "I haven't got the phone number to hand – it's a place in Baldoyle Industrial Estate."

"Would you mind if I called you tomorrow? Actually, I was hoping to ask you out for a drink."

Annabel blushed. She couldn't believe she was sitting in a restaurant with Damien at her side and another man chatting her up on her mobile phone. This was one of the improvements in her life since she had turned forty.

"That would be fine," she replied, anxious not to sound too excited with the call and painfully aware of Damien's dark brown eyes trying desperately not to look at her from over his menu.

"Sorry for disturbing you," Gary said politely.

"Not at all. See you." Annabel switched off her phone. "I'm sorry about that, Damien."

"Don't mind me, Annabel," he said, lowering his head into the menu. "So what are you having?"

"The Dublin Bay Prawns look good for starters . . ." She paused for a second and tilted her head slightly. "Then the grouper maybe for my main course."

"Good choice. One of my favourite fish, grouper. So have you been thinking about what's going to be on the menu in our new business venture?"

Annabel smiled. The prospect of having a business grew more appealing with each day that passed.

"I have actually," she smiled. "I was hoping you were still serious – that it wasn't all a dream."

"I've never been more serious." It was Damien's turn to hide his excitement.

"Well, my solicitor thinks it's a great idea, providing I don't start before I get an agreement with Colin."

"It will be six months at the earliest."

The waiter returned with the wine, popping the cork in front of them. Damien tasted it and nodded in approval. Annabel's glass was filled.

"Do you want to order?"

They ordered and returned to discussing their business venture.

"Sounds too good to be true, Damien," said Annabel shyly. "I don't know how to thank you."

"Don't thank me – you're doing me the favour. I'm very keen to start a new business that will be run by someone else."

"Well, it's perfect timing for me."

Damien raised his glass. "Here's to a good working relationship!"

Annabel lifted her glass and clinked off his. "To a good working relationship!"

They dined in relaxed enjoyment and neither wanted their time together to end. Every time Annabel felt Damien's eyes on her she pinched herself and remembered Betty and Kate which brought her back to reality. She was in a vulnerable position at the moment and she mustn't go reading too much into the evening. This was a working arrangement they were forging together.

A whole new world was opening up for her. If she had been told a few months earlier that she would be rung by a strange man and going into business with Damien Carlton she wouldn't have believed it. She was deliriously happy and confident with nearly all the changes that had taken place recently.

"I've had a great time, Annabel," Damien said as he

drank the last drop from his coffee cup. "I've been living in such a state of stress these last few months since Betty took ill. There's been no time for normality and enjoying the simple things in life like food and conversation."

"It's been like that for me too, Damien, but on a much lesser scale," Annabel smiled. "We'll have to do this again before we start our new business."

Damien smiled back at her. The prospect of spending more time with Annabel appealed to him greatly. He was feeling very old since losing his life partner and nothing but empty nights seemed to loom ahead – until tonight.

"I'm calling a taxi – can I give you a lift?" he asked.

"It's okay, thanks, Damien. I brought my Jeep actually but I think I'm over the limit. I wouldn't mind the walk up the hill, to be honest, to work that delicious dessert off."

She had to behave appropriately in Betty's memory and she didn't want to be led into temptation.

"It's a nice bright evening – I'd like a walk myself." He saw the reservation in her eyes at the remark and decided not to push the idea. It was too soon after Betty's death for him as well to be taking romantic walks down Howth pier. Even this evening was pushing the limits of appropriate behaviour so soon after becoming a widower. At least he had the excuse of a business arrangement. He could tell himself that as he gazed longingly over at the woman who he had made love to so passionately so long ago.

He called for the bill.

"Could you get me a cab, please?" he asked when the waiter arrived.

"Of course, sir."

Annabel stood in the doorway of the restaurant with Damien as the taxi arrived.

"Thanks for a lovely evening," she said, leaning forward to give him a kiss on the cheek.

"Thank you, Annabel. You're great company."

"Talk soon then?"

"Talk soon," he said with a nod. He stepped into the black Mercedes and watched her walk along the pier as the car drove away. She was so beautiful. He felt young and full of life again being with her.

The taxi brought him to Greenfield Close. As it stopped in front of the drive, Damien realised he didn't want to go in.

"This all right for you, mate?" the driver asked.

"Yes, thanks. How much do I owe you?"

He paid the driver his dues and walked slowly up the drive. This house was too big and carried too many memories. He missed Betty's constant droning. He knew he couldn't stay in it much longer. All the warnings from his peers about staying in the family home and letting a year pass before making any major decisions seemed pointless. The Oaks on Claremont Beach were almost finished and there was a two-bedroom apartment left with a breathtaking view. He turned the key in the door and made the decision there and then that he was moving. He'd be closer to Annabel if he lived in Howth. There's no fool like an old fool, he berated himself. *Why would she be interested in you?* He went into the lonely kitchen and put on the kettle to make a cup of tea. He wished he could turn back the clock, but even if he could, he had to ask himself would he? He knew the answer was no. He had done what was best for him and for Annabel and Kate twenty years ago.

Kate woke with the most shattering pain shooting through her stomach. The clock beside the bed flashed that it was only three o'clock. She'd had a long day helping the boys move their belongings around the bedrooms. They decided that they didn't want to sleep together any more and even though Kate needed the spare room for the baby she didn't want to tell them about it yet. Her bump was almost too big to hide and it was only a matter of time before they figured out that she was pregnant. Until then the boys deserved some quality time with her all to themselves.

The pain wasn't abating and after five minutes she tried to stand up. She couldn't straighten her back and she felt like something was going to fall out between her legs. Suddenly a wet patch started to seep through her pyjamas and run down her right leg. The liquid was red and she recognised instantly what was happening to her. A dragging sensation pulled through her core. She lay back on the bed. The pain wasn't letting up and cramping spasms were coming fast and furious, making her coil up like a foetus on the bed. She needed help. She didn't want to alarm the boys but she couldn't do this alone.

"David! Ciarán!" she shouted. She felt so alone and

helpless. Again she called out, much louder this time, and knocked on the wooden headboard behind her. This time she heard a muffled response. "David? Come here, darling!"

David strolled sleepily into the bedroom. "What time is it?" he asked, still disoriented.

"Late," Kate answered breathlessly. "Could you please get Fabian for me? His number is in the little red book beside the phone in the kitchen. Tell him to come over at once."

"What's wrong with you?" David asked, alarmed.

"*Vite*, darling, I need you to get Fabian. I am not well – please," she begged.

Shock and horror crept over the young lad's face as he watched his mother toss and turn in the bed. After she pointed, speechless, to the door he turned on his heels and fled downstairs.

The pain was excruciating now and Kate didn't know how long she would last before passing out. She tried to compose herself as she heard David running back up the stairs.

"He's coming," the young boy said shakily. "What's happening to you, Maman?"

"I'll be fine."

Kate's face was now a greyish-white and she knew that David would be starting to panic. "Can you wake Ciarán up and both get – ahhh!" she screamed as another swift pain hit her. "Get dressed, love, both of you!"

David walked out of the room backwards, shaken and bewildered.

She was losing blood constantly and she prayed that Fabian would waste no time.

Quite soon a loud banging came from the front door.

"Let him in, boys!" Kate called. She could hear David open the front door and Fabian dash up the stairs.

"Kate, *chérie*!" He understood the situation in a glance. He sat on the edge of the bed and leaned in to wipe her forehead. "You have to go to the hospital. Let me call an ambulance. The boys can go to Joy – I have already called her."

"I can't move, Fabian! Don't make me move!"

The front door opened and they heard someone running up the stairs. A tall skinny woman in a grey tracksuit burst into the room.

"She's having a miscarriage," Fabian said.

"Kate, hold on!" said Joy. "I'll call an ambulance. I'll take the boys into my house."

Joy went into the bedroom and dialled emergency. The twins were standing close to each other on the landing, peering into the room, frightened and scared by whatever was happening to their mother.

"Go with Joy, boys," Kate panted. "I'll be okay."

The twins nodded, looking terrified, and under the guidance of Joy did as their mother asked.

Fabian knelt down by her side and took her hand in his. He arched his eyebrows. "You doing okay?"

Kate nodded silently. The pain was numbing and she braced herself as another wave etched its way up her spine. Her head was becoming drowsy and weak.

"Hold on a little bit more," Fabian said with a squeeze of her hand.

A few seconds later the paramedics were at the door of the cottage. Fabian felt a wave of relief as they brushed by him in their bright yellow jackets and ran up the stairs.

"What is her name?" a small woman with curly red hair asked Fabian.

"Kate, Kate Cassaux."

"Kate, can you move?" she asked gently.

Kate raised her head slowly. Then everything went black.

Shane couldn't sleep. He tossed and turned in the hard-as-nails hotel bed. Thankfully The Oaks would be ready soon and he'd have his own place to go home to after an overnight. He needed his own space. Sweat was dripping from his brow, as if he had worked out for several hours. He couldn't understand why he felt the way he did. He wanted to be sick, he wanted to cry. The physical symptoms of some sort of delirium had a hold on him and he wanted to scream. Every now and again a picture of Kate flashed before him and made him feel even worse. He had to get her out of his head. He had to do something or he was going to go mad.

Annabel woke and stretched her arms above her head. She had spent a glorious evening with Damien and felt as if the best part of her life was ahead of her. She was in her own private dream world when Taylor came running into the bedroom.

"Rebecca wet the bed again last night and Granny had to get up and change it."

Annabel knew it was all too good to be true. There was a price to pay for her newfound freedom. She felt deflated. Nothing in life worth having comes easily, she thought.

"Where's Sam?"

"Gone to George's house."

"At this time?" Annabel shrieked.

"It's eleven o'clock and you have to take me to horse-riding."

Annabel sat up quickly. She hadn't slept this late since before the children were born. "I'll be ready in two minutes. Is Rebecca with Granny?"

"They're downstairs having breakfast."

Annabel jumped out of bed and stepped into the shower. The water was cool and soothing and washed away the thoughts of Colin that crept into her head every now and again. She felt responsible for Rebecca wetting the bed. Maybe she was too harsh on Colin. The kids were reacting very badly to the split. Her emotions were changing from minute to minute. She grabbed a fluffy white towel and dried herself off.

"Annabel, are you up?" Lily called.

"Yes, Mum, I'm just out of the shower."

"I have to go to Cecilia's – I'll be back later."

"Thanks, Mum!" Annabel called as her mother pulled

the front door shut behind her. "Rebecca, get ready for tap dancing!"

She hurriedly dried herself. Soon she would be free for a couple of hours, and a brisk walk down the pier appealed to her greatly. She pulled on a pair of shorts and a T-shirt and slipped her mules onto her feet. Then she ran down to the kitchen and unpeeled a banana. She wasn't hungry after the wonderful meal that she had enjoyed the night before but felt she had to eat something.

"Are you ready, girls?" she asked her daughters, who were beautifully, if a little haphazardly, turned out. They walked out of the house but her car was gone. She was just remembering that she had left her Jeep outside Aqua the night before when her mother came back up the drive.

"I just realised your car wasn't here," she said through the open window of her Polo. "Jump in."

"You're a star, Mum," Annabel sighed. "Thanks a million."

"Are you okay now, Rebecca, love?" Lily asked as they drove off.

Annabel frowned. She wondered if her mother was playing a game with her children's emotions to try and get her to take Colin back. Had she no pride in her daughter? Did she really think that having a wealthy husband was the be-all and end-all? She decided it was best not to indulge her mother and got out of the car without saying anything when they reached Aqua.

"See you later," Lily said gravely. "I don't like you

being on your own in that big house so I'll probably stay tonight."

It was best not to make a scene in front of the girls so Annabel said nothing.

"Bye, Granny!" the girls called as their grandmother drove off.

Annabel made the drop-offs quickly, still feeling very downbeat. She was aware that her emotions were see-sawing: one minute she was high and the next minute she was rock bottom. She guessed that it was all part and parcel of a marriage break-up. Her phone rang and it was the same number as had appeared on her phone the night before. Gary.

"Hi, Annabel?"

"Gary, sorry I couldn't talk properly last night."

"I'm not going to beat around the bush. And, by the way, I've got tons of those plastic cartons, to be honest. I was wondering, what are you doing this evening?"

What would her mother say to her going out for a second night in a row – with a different man? She didn't have to tell her who she was seeing, of course, and if her mother insisted on staying the night she might as well capitalise on the opportunity.

"Tonight's okay," she replied cautiously.

"Fancy going to Findlaters?"

His tone was anxious and Annabel was flattered to think that she could make a man feel this way.

"Fine, what time?"

"I could pick you up?"

"No, better to meet down there. Shall we say nine?"

"Nine it is – see you then."

Annabel got a lift from hearing Gary's voice. Life was a rollercoaster of emotions at the moment.

Kate opened her eyes and was blinded by a tube of bright fluorescent light. She turned her head to the right and Fabian's familiar face came into focus. He was drowsing on the chair beside her bed. Slowly flashes of the night before came back to her and she realised that she was in hospital. She looked down at her arm that pinched with a strange sensation and saw that it was attached to a drip. The rest of her body was covered in a green tunic. Her legs felt numb and she was so weak she could barely lift her arm. Fabian woke immediately on hearing her move. His penetrating eagle-like eyes homed in on Kate as he leaned forward and took her hand in his.

"Fabian, have I been asleep?"

"*Chérie*, you had a haemorrhage," he said softly. "You lost a lot of blood and you must take it very easy."

Kate panicked. "Fabian, what about the baby?"

He hesitated, his face painting the grimmest picture. Kate jumped to the obvious conclusion in the haze of uncertainty that swept over her.

"I've lost it, haven't I?" she cried urgently.

"No, you didn't miscarry and the baby is still alive but it is best to talk to the doctors. We are more worried about you, Kate. We nearly lost you. You were slipping into a coma."

Her baby was still alive. Last night she wasn't sure how she was going to cope with a new baby to look after, and this morning she wanted it more than anything else in the world.

She looked into Fabian's eyes without saying a thing and felt his grip tighten on her hand. "Thank God you came when you did."

"I'm always here, *chérie*," he said with a smile.

"It's a pity you're gay."

"For me too, *chérie*," he said, scrunching his face up. "For me too."

A short nurse who generously filled her white uniform came over to the couple and gave a soft cough.

"Madame, le médecin est ici maintenant." She turned to Fabian. *"Vous êtes le père?"* She was making the natural assumption that he was the father.

"Oui," replied Fabian. He didn't want Kate to feel like she was alone and she was too dazed and confused to contradict him.

Doctor Barthez walked casually over to the side of Kate's bed. He wasn't wearing a formal uniform and he used this, along with his easy manner, to relax his patients.

"Madame Cassaux, you are very lucky – so is your little one. You came to us just in time. I need to be frank with you about your condition. You may haemorrhage again if you do not take care."

"Is my baby going to be all right?"

Doctor Barthez hesitated as he considered the best

way to tell Kate the truth about her baby's chances for survival.

"As far as we can see from our scans the baby is comfortable. It will compensate for the loss of blood in a few weeks if the placenta has not been damaged and if you do not overstretch yourself. There is however a chance of cerebral palsy and we will not know if this is the case until after the baby is born."

Kate swallowed hard. Fabian squeezed her hands tightly and watched her expression avidly. He wished desperately there was something he could do but knew there was nothing. Kate's face said it all.

For the second night in a row Annabel sat in front of the mirror at her dressing-table. The cerise cashmere cardigan and chunky silver necklace made her feel and look at least ten years younger. Tonight her hair rested in big curls casually on her shoulders.

Her mother had said nothing when she told her that she was going out again. The girls were in bed and Sam was playing quietly in his room so there was nothing for her mother to do – but she still felt guilty. Everybody blamed her for terminating her marriage. The phone had stopped ringing within days of her separation from Colin. Women who she thought were friends of hers stayed well clear. Maeve had warned her that they were afraid she would be after their husbands. Maybe Maeve was right and these people really were that insecure in themselves. Maeve was the only regular caller and she had a wonderful relationship with her husband so perhaps that explained why she was happy enough to remain friends with Annabel and even help her out.

Annabel finished her make-up off with a layer of pink lip-gloss and stood up. She hoped she wasn't imagining that she had started to look younger. There was certainly a more calm expression on her face, now that she didn't have Colin chastising her all the time. She was able to go out to a bar and meet a scrummy new man who seemed to really like her. The night before, with Damien, had been the most enjoyable she had spent in another's company since the good times she shared with Kate but as the day progressed she had resigned herself to the fact that Damien and she could never be any more to each other than business partners or acquaintances and Gary's call came at a perfect time before she fell for Damien in a more serious and damaging way than before. If anything ever happened between them there would be no chance of reconciliation with Kate. Besides, she had to accept that no doubt Damien saw her as no more than a friend of his daughter's and a woman with some sense of entrepreneurship. Despite this, she felt better about herself than at any other time in her life.

Lily was sitting in the living room reading the evening paper, the droning from the RTÉ newsreader in the background breaking the silence. She didn't look up as Annabel entered the room. She felt her daughter's recent behaviour was unacceptable. She was already highly embarrassed about the whole situation, especially going to the bridge club. She had stayed away the week after the marriage split-up but decided to face the music after Annabel accused her of being more upset about losing her son-in-law than seeing her daughter humiliated by the *au pair* affair. Lily liked the fact that Colin was a professional man of considerable wealth. It had come to mean more to her than she realised.

"I'm off now, Mum. You don't mind, do you?"

Lily lifted her head slowly. "I can't tell you how to live your life, Annabel. You're forty years of age, but maybe you should start acting like it."

"I'm *only* forty, Mum. Am I not entitled to a bit of time to myself now that I'm bringing the children up on my own?"

"You wouldn't have to be on your own if you let Colin come back," Lily said with pursed lips.

Annabel took a deep breath. "I'm not going through this again, Mum. If you don't like the way I am living my life you may as well go back to your own house. I can't take that kind of judgmental tone from you any more."

Lily stood up. "Very well. I'm tired of being used and abused. Find yourself another baby-sitter!" She took her bag and brushed by Annabel briskly as she took her keys from the hall table and slammed the front door behind her.

Annabel was speechless as she heard her mother's car start up and drive away. It was a big statement from Lily, walking out like that. She knew that Annabel was meeting someone. For all Annabel knew, she could have planned on leaving her in the lurch all along.

Now she had no baby-sitter and she didn't even feel like going out any more. Then the thought of Gary and his blue eyes made her reconsider. It was five past nine now and Gary was probably already waiting for her. She rang her next-door neighbour whose sixteen-year-old daughter sometimes baby-sat for her when she was stuck.

The young girl was having a night in, to Annabel's relief.

"I'll be there in five minutes, Annabel."

"Thanks, Lucy," Annabel sighed. "You're a godsend."

She had to send Gary a quick text so that he wouldn't think that she had stood him up.

It was nine twenty-five when she arrived at Findlaters. The bouncers smiled at her as she swept by them and entered the spacious surroundings. Large leather seats and couches were sporadically placed around the room. She spotted Gary over in the corner reading the cocktail menu. He looked as if he'd stepped out of the pages of a men's *Vogue* in his chunky jumper and bright orange T-shirt peeking out from underneath.

She walked over slowly and was almost upon him before he looked up.

"Hi," she said shyly.

He stood up and leaned forward until his lips brushed off her cheek. "Annabel, you look gorgeous."

"Thank you," she said to her own surprise. She wasn't used to accepting compliments but it felt right hearing them from Gary.

"What's your poison?"

"A glass of white wine, please."

"Won't you try a cocktail?"

"I wouldn't know what to order," she said and then berated herself for sounding so dumb.

"You are definitely a classy girl," he said. "A daiquiri for you, I think!"

Annabel liked the compliment but didn't want him deciding what she was going to drink.

"I'll just have the white wine," she said, more firmly this time.

"Whatever the lady wants, the lady must have," Gary said, bowing forward and shaking his shaggy hair.

Annabel laughed. He was a sweet guy and she mustn't think that all men were like Colin and trying to control her. A girl in her early twenties with the skinniest hips Annabel had ever seen on an adult swanned over to their table. She was wearing a pair of black trousers and a crisp white shirt, an empty tray balanced precariously on her fingertips. Her long black hair was silky and shiny and she flicked it flirtatiously at Gary. It was a fact of life when you accompanied an attractive man, Annabel guessed, but something that she had no experience of, being married to Colin for so long.

"I'll have a bottle of Miller and the lady will have a glass of white wine." He looked over at Annabel. "Any particular type?"

"The South African Chenin Blanc, please," Annabel said to the waitress, who was still staring at Gary. Annabel was chuffed that she was sitting with such a dishy date. There was something so charismatic about him.

"So, tell me all about yourself, Annabel," said Gary as soon as the waitress had left.

"I – gosh – I'm pretty boring really. I am recently separated from my husband of twelve years. I have a son and two daughters. I make hummus for a living which I have only been doing a couple of months and that's pretty much it."

"I'd say that's not even scratching the surface!" He smiled mischievously.

"What about you, Gary?"

"I share a flat in Glasnevin with a mate. I've never been married but was engaged for five years!"

Annabel straightened her back against the leather armchair as her ears pricked up.

"That was a long engagement. What happened?"

"I couldn't get up the altar!"

Annabel figured he might have a commitment problem. No one could look as good as Gary and be husband material as well. It was no wonder he was still single.

"Cold feet?"

"No, I literally couldn't get up the altar. I had a spinal injury that left me unable to walk for three years. By the time I recovered she had met someone else, with a bigger wallet and much better back. She would probably have broken mine so it was a lucky escape."

Annabel chastised herself for jumping to the wrong conclusion. It was a trait of Lily's that she was starting to develop. This guy was gorgeous and he made her laugh. She relaxed and for the next three hours his boyish manners held her in such raptures that she wasn't able to think of anyone or anything else. It was only when the waitress appeared to tell them that it was last orders that she looked at her watch for the first time all night.

"I've had a great time, Annabel."

"Me, too," she said with a wide smile.

"Do you fancy doing this again?"

Annabel definitely wanted to see Gary again and sooner rather than later. She would have liked the night to continue but felt it better to take it slowly. "Do you want to go out this weekend?"

"I tend to go out midweek because of the markets. I don't go out Friday and Saturday nights."

Annabel thought it a bit odd for a single guy like him to stay in at weekends. "Sunday?"

"Sunday is good. My favourite night!"

"Okay, where?"

"This place is good for me if you like it. We could always go straight from the market and have something to eat if it suited you?"

"I have to think of the kids. I'll get them sorted and then I'll text you."

He stood up. It was refreshing to meet a nice decent guy who wasn't caught up in the trappings of big business and his own importance. "Can I call you a taxi?"

"I'm okay – I'll walk up the hill."

"Then let me walk you home?"

"Why not?" she replied. She could think of a thousand reasons why not. Her mother might see her, or even worse Colin or some of the local busybodies.

She felt like a teenager again and shivered as they walked out into the cool night air.

"Are you warm enough?" Gary asked. "I could lend you my jumper."

"I'm fine, thanks. As soon as we start walking I'll be roasting."

Annabel walked with her arms folded casually. She took small steps that slowed down the pace of their walk. Every now and again their arms brushed off each other.

"Where is your house?"

"Up at Summit Green."

"I know those houses. Very nice. Your husband must be a high flyer!"

"He likes to think of himself as one."

"Do you see yourself getting back with him?" he asked earnestly.

Annabel shook her head. "To be honest, I've been unhappy for a long time. It's amazing how everything changes when you change one thing in your life. I started the stall and then Colin started sleeping with the *au pair* because I was around less and then I told him to leave and now my life and the people in it are all unrecognisable compared to only a few months ago. I put a lot of it down to turning forty."

"It's a great age, isn't it?" he nodded his head. "I think you only start to find yourself at forty."

The Green was upon them in no time. It didn't usually feel like such a short walk up the hill. Annabel stopped and turned around to face him when they came to the gates of her house.

"This is me!"

"Now I know where you live, you won't be able to escape me!" His blue eyes widened and glistened under the reflection of the streetlights.

"Oh dear, I'm caught then," she said with a grin. An awkward moment passed as neither knew what to do next. Annabel looked up into his eyes and felt an electricity rush through her. She braced herself as the tension between them rose.

Gary leaned forward and closed his eyes as he placed his lips on hers. Annabel felt tingles shoot up her spine. His mouth tasted so sweet and she was transported to another world. He reached out and gently rested his hands on her hips, holding her like a porcelain doll. When he removed his lips she couldn't move. She wanted more.

"I'd better go," he said. "You don't want the kids to catch you kissing a strange man!"

How thoughtful of him, Annabel thought, sighing disappointedly. "You're right. I'll see you on Sunday then."

"You will," he said dreamily. With a wink he turned on his heels and set off, back down the hill.

Annabel hid behind the large gated pillar that led to her house and watched him go. She felt like a teenager who had been kissed for the first time and was watching the boy of her dreams disappear at the end of a summer night. But she was no teenager and neither was Gary. She had responsibilities and her children must remain her priority. These new experiences were becoming too much to handle and she was wondering how she was going to cope with her new single life. If only she had Kate! Kate would be able to tell her exactly what to do. She had to talk to her.

19

Kate was glad to be home. Her stay in hospital had been longer than she expected. She rested her feet on the stool that Fabian placed in front of her.

"You can stop fussing over me," she said. "I've another four months to go. You'll be worn out at this rate!"

"I was in the hospital! I heard! You must listen to the *docteur, chérie.*"

Kate felt uncomfortable that her dear friend was sitting on his hunkers at her feet – waiting on her like a handservant.

"Fabian."

He looked up and arched his eyebrows which made his nose look even more like an eagle's beak.

"Thank you so much," she sighed appreciatively. "I don't know what I'd have done without you these past couple of weeks."

Fabian stood up slowly, looking down at Kate with his head hung like a scolded schoolboy.

"I have something to tell you, while you are in such a good mood with me!"

Kate tilted her head in surprise, wondering what it could be.

"While you were in hospital and I was here with the boys one day . . . I answered the phone."

Kate frowned. She wondered what he'd been up to.

"Annabel phoned and I told her your news."

Kate frowned more deeply. As if she hadn't enough to deal with at the moment!

"Fabian, I don't want to talk about her," she said, shaking her head frantically. "You know what she did with my father and she was chatting him up only days after my mother's funeral!"

Fabian sat down on the couch next to Kate, putting his hand on hers in an effort to calm her down. "I am your friend, Kate, and I would not tolerate anyone who upset you but I think she has a lot to say to you and it would really help you both."

"I'm not interested. Why would I want to talk to her? I have enough on my plate."

Maybe the time would come when they would talk again but this was not it. It was too soon after losing her mother and almost losing her new baby. She was washed out of any strength that she might still have for herself, let alone coping with someone else's problems – especially someone who had betrayed her.

Fabian gave her hand a tight squeeze. "Her marriage has finished."

Kate's mouth gaped open in shock as her imagination set to work. Did her father know this? "Has it anything to do with my father?"

It was Fabian's turn to shake his head. "No, *chérie*, her husband was in bed with the *au pair*."

Kate felt a pang of sympathy for her ex-friend but this was outweighed by her anxiety about Damien. "Does my dad know? Is she after my dad?" Panic reared up in her voice.

"Relax, *chérie*," Fabian said softly. "She will be opening a café with your father but it is strictly business."

Kate's brows furrowed. She wanted to believe Fabian. "What did she want?"

"To come and see you. She would like to spend some time with you before the children go back to school."

"But that would mean sometime this month!"

Fabian nodded.

"I don't know, Fabian. I still feel very raw about her."

"It is totally up to you, *chérie*" Fabian said with a casual shrug. "I said I would say it to you but didn't think you would phone her,"

Kate's eyes arched at his comment. "Am I that stubborn?"

Fabian shrugged dramatically and looked around him as if an imaginary fly needed swatting.

Kate took her hand away from Fabian's and placed it on her bump where it rested in a gesture of comfort.

Maybe it was time to make peace. Annabel had made several attempts to talk to her after Biarritz and the feud had gone on long enough . . . almost too long . . . what if she had died when she haemorrhaged?

She decided there and then that after tea that evening she would call Annabel Hamilton.

"Okay, I admit defeat, Fabian," she said. "I will call her."

At eight o'clock Annabel heard Colin turning the key in the hall door, as if he had never moved out. She felt slightly unnerved at the once-familiar sound. His heavy footsteps echoed on the wooden floor and Annabel braced herself. Getting Colin to baby-sit had seemed like a good idea at the time but now she wasn't sure. Maybe she should stay in.

"Hi," she greeted him as he appeared at the door of the television room but he ignored her.

"Hello, girls," he said as he walked in.

Taylor and Rebecca looked up with a mixture of surprise and delight. Annabel had told them he was coming but it hadn't registered until now.

Sam came bounding in on hearing his father's voice. He had been waiting all day and was wearing his new Chelsea kit. "Hi, Dad, fancy a game of football outside?"

Colin looked at his son's shirt and couldn't stop the frown from creeping across his face. It wasn't what he considered suitable clothing for his son.

"Have you got those new golf clubs I left you? We could do a bit of putting if you like?"

Sam nodded. "Thanks, Dad, they're great." He didn't want to play golf. He never liked it.

"You're welcome," Colin smiled smugly. "Let's do it in

the kitchen." He would spend this time steering Sam in an appropriate direction. He wasn't used to quality time with his son but since he had left home things had improved in their relationship. Sam wanted to live with him but that was out of the question. He didn't have time in his busy schedule to look after a young boy.

Annabel went to get her jacket, then braced herself before walking dubiously back into the kitchen.

"Well, I'll be off," she said. "Thanks for baby-sitting." She smiled in an attempt to warm the atmosphere.

Colin turned around with Sam's number seven club still swinging in the air. "I'm spending time with my children," he said squarely. "You don't baby-sit your own children."

"Of course," she replied. He still managed to throw comments that sounded like a whip cracking. She moved around from one foot to the other unsteadily. There was a high price to be paid for her new-found freedom. "I'll be back about twelve."

Sam and Colin returned their attention to the ground where their gazes fixed on a Ping golf ball. She went into the TV room and kissed the girls on the top of their heads before grabbing her bag and dashing out the front door, feeling a mixture of concern and relief.

Kate picked up the phone and started to dial Annabel's number. She didn't want to think too much about what she was doing. The phone at the other end of the line gave ten rings. She was about to put it down when a voice answered.

"Yes?"

It was Colin.

Kate recognised his abrupt tone instantly. But what was he doing there if they had split up? Maybe Fabian had made the whole tale up, or simply got his facts wrong.

"Is there someone there?" the voice asked sharply.

Kate didn't want to speak to Colin so she hung up – disappointed that her attempt to make peace had been such a failure. At least Annabel wouldn't realise that she had rung. Maybe she should think about what she was going to say more thoroughly.

She picked up the phone and rang Ireland again, but a different number this time.

Annabel parked at the entrance to St Anne's Park. It was halfway between her house and Gary's flat which she had yet to see. Butterflies started flitting around her stomach at the prospect of seeing the tall handsome man. He was patient with her and tolerant of her need for discretion and secrecy. The last people she wanted to hurt were her children and, even though they were adjusting a bit better to the new living arrangements in the house, she knew that they didn't need to deal with a new man in their mother's life. For Annabel, Gary was her secret saviour. He gave her the strength not to falter when her mother chastised her for asking Colin to leave, and gave her a reason to take time out for herself. At first she had hoped they would get to see each other often but things weren't panning out as she had expected. Still, she was happy for now with the few short hours that they managed to steal together whenever they could.

A tall broad-shouldered silhouette grew larger as it neared Annabel's Jeep, then Gary tapped on the window. With haste she released the lock on the door and let him in. Gary slid onto the passenger seat and leaned over towards her, planting a delicious kiss on her lips. The wait had been worth it already.

"Hiya, gorgeous!"

"Ditto," she sighed, licking her lips.

"Ah, *Ghost*! Not one of my personal favourites," he grinned cheekily.

"I wasn't quoting a movie, silly!" Annabel said, poking him playfully in the ribs.

"You're too cute!" he said.

Nobody had called her cute since before she left primary school. She loved it.

"Fancy coming back to my place?" Gary suggested casually.

Annabel was delighted. She had been starting to wonder what Gary was hiding in his flat – or even worse, who?

"Great." Annabel started the engine and took the car out onto the Clontarf road. She drove up tree-lined Griffith Avenue with an air of anticipation.

Gary sat back snugly on the seat, giving directions until they came to a beautiful red-bricked Victorian villa.

"This place is beautiful," said Annabel.

"Don't judge a book by its cover," Gary warned as the car stopped.

Once they got inside she knew what he meant. The leafy gardens and austere exterior hid a labyrinth of interior walls that made up eight flats. It had been some time since the landlord had invested in any sort of maintenance on the building. Some of the wallpaper they passed as they trod the stairs to the top floor looked like it had been there since the seventies.

Gary opened the thin plywood door to the attic flat. The frayed carpet covered in large yellow swirls continued from the landing into Gary's living room. As Annabel looked around she discovered that this was also the kitchen and hallway.

"I like open-plan living," Gary said lightly, in an effort to cover over his embarrassment about the pokey surroundings.

"It's very cosy." Annabel walked over to the floral printed settee and brushed her hand along the back of the cushions.

"That's a nice way of putting it!" Gary replied frankly. "It's also very small. Sit down and make yourself at home."

Annabel obeyed and tried not to grimace as a spring on the settee went ping on taking her weight. She had a clear view of Gary as he frantically searched through the cupboards one by one.

"Tea, coffee or a drink?"

"I'd better have tea – I'm in the Jeep."

Gary's head appeared above the counter that he was rooting behind.

"You could always stay the night?" he suggested sheepishly.

Annabel tried to smile. This was a man who had no concept of commitments.

"I have to be there for the kids in the morning."

Gary nodded his head, obviously uncomfortable now about his suggestion. "I'm sorry, Annabel – that was insensitive of me."

For an instant Annabel wanted to flout her responsibilities and say she'd stay. But then she remembered it was Colin who was baby-sitting, not her mother or even the girl next door. At least Gary understood that her children were her priority, especially at this sensitive time. It only made her want him even more. By the time Gary joined her on the settee with two mugs of tea and a packet of chocolate digestives under his arm Annabel was aching for him. The kiss he placed on her lips in the car wasn't enough. The fact that she was now sitting in his apartment and so close to the room where he slept each night filled her with anticipation for what might happen next. After all, they'd been together nearly a month.

Gary put his mug down on the floor and sat back with his arm loosely resting on the back of the settee behind Annabel.

"I'm sorry that I'm bringing you back to this dump. I only realise how crumby it is when I bring someone to see it for the first time."

"I meant it, when I said it was cosy. You've a lovely view over the tops of the trees from here."

"I'll be frank with you, Annabel. It's cheap and Jamie's never here."

"Jamie?"

"My mate. He has a girlfriend with an apartment a few blocks away and he only uses this place to keep his stuff and hide for refuge when they have a row."

Annabel nodded her head and gripped her mug before taking a sip. Gary had a way of making her forget herself. His arm was close but not close enough.

"Will I put some music on?" he asked.

"Okay," she said, putting the mug of tea down by her feet.

He jumped up and hit the switch on the mini hi-fi that sat on a shelf in the corner of the room. She recognised the guitar chords instantly. It had been a long time since she'd heard *Samba Pa Ti* by Santana. Damien used to play it on a cassette when he drove Kate and her home from discos when they were kids. Which reminded her – she hadn't been in touch with Damien since their dinner together.

Gary returned to her side on the couch, oblivious of the effect the music was having on Annabel's frame of mind. This time when he put his arm behind her he gently combed some of her curls with his fingers. Annabel closed her eyes and let his touch transport her. When Gary put his lips tenderly on hers she melted but with her eyes tightly shut wasn't sure if she was thinking of Damien or Gary. Eventually she opened them and she knew that she was with the right man. Gary stood up slowly and reached out his hand for her. Full of excitement and anticipation she rose and took his hand, then walked with him into the bedroom. The evening was turning out perfectly.

"Hello?"

"Hi, Dad," Kate smiled down the phone.

"I was just about to call you. I'm coming over the day after tomorrow."

She felt relief at the thought of seeing her father so soon. "Great. I'll get Fabian to collect you."

"I can get a taxi."

Kate took a lock of her hair and started twiddling it. "It will cost you a fortune."

"The plane rides are so cheap nowadays it won't make much difference. How are you feeling?"

"I've had a good day actually," she said, nodding even though he couldn't see. "It's difficult being an invalid. I can't believe I'll be like this for the next four months."

"Just take it easy," Damien said in a reassuring voice. "I'm going to sort you out with some full-time help when I get over there."

The thought of having her father there to look after her came as a huge comfort. Fabian was fantastic but family was different and Kate was getting frequent flashes, reminding her that she was never going to see her mother again.

"I'm fine, Dad. There's no need to fuss. By the way," she hesitated, "have you heard from Annabel?"

Damien hadn't and was beginning to worry about their business venture and getting it off the ground. "No."

"Apparently she rang here while I was in hospital and told Fabian that her marriage is over."

"That's right."

Kate scowled at the phone. The mere thought of her father and Annabel sharing information that she was excluded from made her feel deeply hurt.

"Why didn't you tell me?"

Damien sighed quietly. There were times when he really gave up trying to communicate with the women in his life. Betty used to frequently berate him when he tried to communicate something she didn't want to know about and then chastise him later because he hadn't told her.

"Because you said that you didn't want to talk about her ever again."

"You should have told me that, Dad."

Damien sighed again. Now was not a time to try and reason with his pregnant and flustered daughter. "I'm sorry, Kate. I don't know what I'm supposed to say or not to say to you. Your mother always did that for me!"

It was Kate's turn to feel terrible. "I'm sorry, Dad."

Damien took a deep breath. He figured, as his daughter wanted to be told everything, now was as good a time as any to tell her of his other intentions.

"By the way, I'm selling Greenfield Close."

Kate was stunned. "But why? You can't do that. That's my home."

"It hasn't been your home for nearly twenty years, Kate."

Her father was right. But she hated the thought of not

being able to stay there when she visited Ireland. "Where are you going to live?"

"Howth. I'm finishing off a block of apartments on the beach and I'm moving into a two-bedroom. I don't need much space."

"You'll get cabin fever in an apartment, Dad."

"I can't stay here. The place will go to rack and ruin if I stay in it much longer."

Kate felt a sudden desire to be in Greenfield Close. She could picture her boys and new baby in a house like that. Her thoughts jumped into overdrive as they usually did when she had a brainwave. How would Philip feel if she took the house over? He was settled in Oxford now and Gloria said that she didn't want to live in Ireland.

"Dad, if I came home for good, would you let me live in Greenfield Close?"

"Kate, you're not thinking rationally. There is nothing I would like more than to have you home but it has to be because you want to live in Ireland. Not because of a house. I am moving out regardless."

Kate's mind was working like the third hand on a watch. She'd have to talk to the boys.

"Kate, are you still there?"

"Yes, Dad. Look, I'll see you soon and we can talk then."

"That sounds like a good idea. You're very fragile at the moment. We'll sort everything out over the next few days."

"Thanks, Dad."

Damien couldn't let his daughter off the line without

asking her a very important question. "Did you say that you were speaking to Annabel?"

"I didn't say – but I did ring her earlier. Colin answered the phone and I didn't feel like speaking to him so I hung up."

It was Damien's turn to be speechless. Colin! Could Annabel have taken him back? That would certainly put a stop to their business enterprise. Or anything on a more personal level.

"Dad?"

"Yes, love."

"What time are you arriving?"

"I land at three thirty."

"Great – so you should be here by about six."

"I'm looking forward to it."

"So am I, and the boys are too. Bye, Dad." She hung up, feeling confused. Did she really want to go back to Ireland and live in Greenfield Close?

Annabel gave her hair a quick brush before getting out of the car. She checked that she didn't leave any clues on her face or clothing that would tell what she had been doing for the previous two hours. She opened the hall door like a thief, painfully aware that she had to face Colin.

He was in the kitchen, his head dug deep in the *Financial Times* and a mug of coffee resting on the kitchen table. He didn't look up as she entered the kitchen.

"Thanks for that," Annabel said quietly, hoping that he would at least acknowledge her return.

"I did it for the kids, not for you," he said, without looking up from his newspaper.

"Thanks anyway."

"When are you going to stop this charade?" Colin said, looking up at his wife this time. "I think you've made your point. I shouldn't have slept with the *au pair*. Is that what you wanted me to admit?"

Rage enveloped Annabel. Was this Colin's attempt at an apology? She managed to remain calm by silently counting to ten and then she addressed him with an inner strength she didn't know she had.

"Colin, I have been unhappy with you and your bullying ways for some time. I have no intention of going back to the way things were – not now or ever. Is that clear?"

Colin stood up suddenly, then folded his paper and looked straight at his estranged wife. "Perfectly," he replied, stuffing the paper under his arm.

Annabel was still shaking as she heard him close the front door. Gary was the reason she was able to speak to Colin that way. Gary had made her feel so good only a few short hours ago and in a couple of minutes Colin had made her feel terrible. She felt as if she was the one responsible for breaking up the family. She wished there was a way that she could make it up to her children, to make everything all right, but for them to be okay she needed to be okay herself and right now she was far from being that.

Damien's taxi stopped outside his daughter's pretty French house. It was bedecked with the flowers of summer and set against an azure-blue sky. It suited Kate. But it made him wonder if she would ever leave. He hoped she was serious about moving back to Greenfield Close but it had to be for the right reasons.

Ciarán and David heard their grandfather's taxi outside and ran out to greet him before he got a chance to ring on the doorbell.

"Boys, look at how you've grown in a couple of weeks!" Damien said as the two young boys sprang into his arms.

"Mum is better," Ciarán said with a big grin. "She was painting this morning."

Alarm bells rang in Damien's ears. His daughter was always careless when it came to looking after herself and she couldn't afford to be at the moment.

"Mum, Granddad's here!" David called up the stairs.

Kate came down the stairs with a spring in her step. "Dad! You made good time."

"Kate!" he said, holding his arms out to his daughter. "I thought you were meant to be taking it easy!"

"I am, Dad," she said, rushing over and holding him tightly.

"What's this I hear about you painting?"

Kate turned and scowled at her sons. "I was only doing a little."

"You must be in good form!" he said with a smile.

Kate slipped her hand into the crook of her father's arm. "Let's go into the kitchen, Dad."

She didn't let go until she reached the already boiled kettle.

Damien walked over to the rustic back door and opened it out to the garden. The thick walls of the gite kept the house cool in the warmth of summer. He looked out at the pretty and colourful garden set against the distant mountains.

"I can see why you love it here," he mused.

Kate left the freshly made tea to brew then sauntered over to her father. "I'll miss it," she said, leaning against the wall.

"Kate, this is very sudden. Before you left Ireland, you were adamant that you wanted to stay in France."

This was true but Kate was usually one to make sudden and dramatic decisions that changed the course of her life.

"If I don't go now, I never will. It's good timing for the boys. They're starting secondary school in September and," she let out a deep breath and rubbed her hand gently along her bump, "I want to be at home with my baby. I need a fresh start."

"What about Shane?"

Kate lowered her head and folded her arms. "I haven't heard from him. He's married, Dad. I have to think of my family, my children."

Damien nodded. He understood and was silently proud of his daughter's responsible attitude. "So, when are you thinking of making this big move?"

"I have to be quick because of the boys and school. I might even ring St Peter's later today and see if they have places for them."

"Are you sure that's the best place to send them?"

"Their Uncle Philip enjoyed his time there. If they aren't happy I can always move them. At least they will be close to me."

Damien smiled. He liked the prospect of being able to see his grandsons frequently. "What are you going to do with this house?"

"I might keep it – if you don't charge me too much for Greenfield Close, that is!"

"You know the house is yours."

"What about Philip?"

Damien knew that his son was never the most materialistic of individuals but he had no need to worry about finances for anything that he wanted to do in life. Damien had always provided well for his family.

"I can settle him up with a couple of apartments in lieu."

"Dad, I nearly lost this baby. It made me realise how much I want it."

Damien nodded and put his arm around her shoulders. "Sometimes the little surprises are the greatest blessings."

Kate felt safe and protected. She hoped the boys would be okay with the move. But the person she dreaded telling the most was Fabian.

20

Annabel was running out of people to ring. It was eight o'clock and her son hadn't been seen or heard from since school finished at two-thirty. He hadn't spoken to her at breakfast but she was getting used to his dour behaviour – it had begun long before his father left home. She had a premature teenager on her hands but all of the other mothers that she knew had similar problems with their kids once they reached eleven years of age and Sam would be twelve in a matter of days. This morning was different though. He had thought that as his father was minding him the night before he would still be in the house the next morning. Annabel had never seen an outburst like it from her son.

"I'm going to Niall's after school!" he shouted, slinging his schoolbag over his shoulder and slamming his way out the door. He had a piece of toast in his mouth at the time but that's what it sounded like.

So far she had tried every one of his friends' houses and was contemplating ringing the police. She knew that she really should ring Colin but after their words the night before she couldn't face talking to him. Lily would be hysterical so there was no point in contacting her. At least the evenings are still bright, she thought, as she looked out the kitchen window. A mobile phone rang and she desperately hoped that it was Sam. But the caller ID showed that it wasn't.

"Hi, Gary," she sighed. "I'm having a nightmare."

"What's the matter?" he asked.

"It's Sam – I thought you might be him – he hasn't been seen since two-thirty today. I think I'll ring the police."

"Do you want me to come over? Is there anything I can do?"

"Thanks, Gary, but the girls don't know you. I don't want to complicate things."

"Call the police and let me know if you hear anything."

Annabel had needed someone to give her the push and Gary's timing was perfect.

"I will. Talk later, Gary."

She put her mobile phone down and reached for the landline. Her index finger was running over the digit nine when a dark shadow fell across the back door. Annabel put the handset down and rushed to see who it was. Her first reaction was utter joy and relief to see her son shuffle up to the door but it was closely followed by shock at the state of his soiled hair and clothing. He looked up at her with blackened and hollow eyes and the smell from his breath was unmistakable.

"Where the hell have you been?" Annabel's voice was raised to a level that even she had never heard from her mouth before.

"Out," the young boy said, flicking his fringe away from his eyes. "What do you care? What does anyone care?" He continued walking across the kitchen, leaving mucky marks on the floor tiles.

"Sam, come back here when I am talking to you!"

He turned his head around slowly and threw his mother a snide glance. "No!"

It was obvious that he had been drinking but the questions raised by that fact threw Annabel into disarray. Why had her little boy run off to get drunk? Had he been on his own? It was very alarming behaviour for an eleven-year-old. The fact that he was coming home unrepentant was defiance on a level that horrified Annabel. She had heard of boys reacting badly when their dads left home but felt unequipped to handle a situation like this. She had to get to him before the girls saw him. Luckily they were in a hypnotic state in front of *The Simpsons*.

She followed the mud trail that led to Sam's bedroom where he was now lying down. His shoes stuck out over the end of the bed. As she entered the room he turned over on his side and vomited. Annabel grabbed a T-shirt off the floor and put it under his head.

Liquid foamed from his lips and he retched until he started to sob.

"What were you drinking?" she asked but realised he wasn't fit to answer.

When he was finally finished she leaned forward and kissed him on the forehead. She felt totally responsible. She must be the one who had driven him to this.

He was still groggy when she wiped the last piece of vomit from his cheek.

"Sam, love, tell me what were you drinking?"

"Vodka."

"Where did you get it?"

He pointed down at the ground.

"Downstairs? From the drinks cabinet?"

He nodded.

"How much did you drink?"

"All of it."

No wonder he vomited – there must have been a full 75cl. bottle unopened.

"Why, Sam, why did you do this?"

"I wanted to feel better."

"Well, at least now you know that alcohol only makes you feel worse."

"But I did feel better . . . for a while."

Annabel gently pushed her son's fringe off his face. "Sam, I wish you would talk to me when you feel sad. I know it must be hard for you, missing Daddy."

"Why can't he live here too? You don't have to like him but then everybody would think I had a dad."

"He is still your dad. And who is everybody?" Annabel tilted her head. "Has someone been saying something nasty to you?"

Sam lowered his head.

"Sam, tell me, did something happen?"

"Jake in school said that I won't see my dad any more. He said that you and dad were in love with other people and I would probably have to go and live with my granny."

Annabel wanted to shake the stuffing out of Jake. She wondered what rumours had been flying around sixth class, little ears eavesdropping on their parents' conversations over the dinner table. Melissa and her cronies would definitely be making up all sorts of rumours about Annabel's marriage break-up.

"Darling, sometimes people are extra nasty when we are in pain. I don't know why it is but even adults can behave badly. You are staying here with me in this house until you are old enough to leave of your own free will. Daddy will always be there for you too."

Sam's wide eyes stared up at his mother. She knew that he didn't believe her but felt utterly powerless. If only there was a way of taking her son's pain away.

"I'm okay now, Mum. Can I just be on my own?"

"Of course, but you must promise me that you won't run off like that again. Where were you?"

"St Anne's Park."

"Jesus, Sam, that's a dangerous place. You could have been mugged or abducted."

"I was okay. I just wanted to be on my own."

Annabel felt as though someone had stabbed her through the heart. Her actions had resulted in her son getting drunk on his own in a dangerous place.

"I want you to promise me that you won't drink ever again until you are much older and allowed go into a pub. Young people have died of drinking too much alcohol, and vodka is a very strong drink."

Sam nodded his head but his face showed no sign of remorse as she kissed him on the forehead and got off the bed.

"Try to sleep," she whispered as she shut the door.

She had to do something proactive to ensure something like this never happened again.

Kate put the last of her paints into the large wooden boxes.

"Won't you leave some here for when you return on holidays?" Fabian asked.

"I may have to rent the house out to keep it from getting damp."

Kate leaned back on the palms of her hands and massaged her aching back. "I will probably need the cash too – no exhibition for me this year!"

"*Chérie*, what am I going to do without you?"

Kate smiled.

"Fabian, you are going to fall in love and settle down," she laughed. "Then you won't even realise I'm gone!"

Fabian took a stack of canvases and placed them

neatly in a pile for the removal van. He brushed the dust from his hands and walked over to his friend.

"Kate, remember I am always here for you and . . ." he paused. "I might even come and visit you in Dublin."

Kate gasped. "Really? Would you?"

"I have looked up the Irish Ferries on the internet and I think I might make the trip!"

Kate threw her arms around him and gave a tight squeeze. "Please come, and sooner rather than later!"

Fabian gently leaned his head on her shoulder. He needed to reassure himself that he would be seeing her again soon. With a new baby to look after, Kate wouldn't be back in the Pyrénées for a long time.

"And who will you have for a best friend, in Dublin?" Fabian asked, gently pulling away.

Kate shook her head. "I don't know what's going to happen with Annabel. Our lives have taken huge turns in different directions and I'm not sure if we'll ever get back on talking terms. Did I tell you that Colin answered the phone when I rang her house?"

Fabian arched his eyebrows in response.

"So I don't know where she's at. Sometimes I wonder where I'm at myself. I'm scared, Fabian, and I wish my mum was going to be there – losing her has been the hardest part in all of this. It's so unfair that she is gone, now that I am finally moving home."

Fabian nodded. "*Chérie*, don't forget me!"

Kate looked at her friend's puppy-dog eyes and felt tears start to fill her own.

"Fabian, my dear friend, how could you say such a thing!"

Annabel waited with bated breath for Gary to arrive. She had been preoccupied with Sam since their last date and was grateful now for some time with him to help take her mind off things. The market had been good fun earlier. He was constantly waving over to her and bringing her samples of different juices and smoothies. The intermittent showers might have driven the punters home but they were happy in their quest to sell to the few brave passers-by.

So far there was a pattern to their dates. He brought her for a walk on Portmarnock strand – then they ate chips out of newspaper and watched the sun setting. On other nights he brought her to Dollymount strand. It felt very different to the old days with Kate and their pals. Those evenings ended up in his place and their only chances of romantic physical contact. She liked the simple unpretentiousness of their time together and he was a very sexy guy. She had psychologically shed twenty years the first time they made love in his attic flat. Her whole world had changed dramatically since then.

She hadn't spoken with Damien since their evening together in Aqua and that was weeks ago. She tried to phone him earlier in Greenfield Close but there was no reply. She reflected that Gary had come into her life at the perfect time to prevent her from making a fool of herself with Damien. If she had spent a couple more dinners like the one in Aqua she knew that she would be back to square one and in love with Damien as much as she had been all those years ago. Regarding the coffee shop, she was beginning to wonder if she was biting off more than she could chew. The stall was going well but Gary had convinced her that it was a huge step moving from a stall to a bona fide business. She might not be able for it. Gary took life easy and didn't believe in taxing himself or being around people who did. Maybe that was why he had so little to show for his forty-one years. She berated herself for thinking this way about him. She had been with a career-oriented man for long enough and that hadn't made her happy.

Gary arrived while she was deep in thought.

"Hey, gorgeous," he said cheekily as he joined her on the harbour wall where she sat.

Annabel shivered as his lips touched her cheek. "Hey, Gary!" He was fifteen minutes late but she didn't comment. "Where are you taking me tonight?" Tonight she wanted to do something different. She felt like a little luxury after her time in the market.

"Somewhere special. I thought we could go for a potter along the coast – then finish with a drink."

"It's eight o'clock in the evening!"

"But it's a lovely evening."

"I'm not sixteen, Gary!" she teased. "Can we please go somewhere nice?"

Gary shuffled around in his scruffy jacket. "We could go to the pictures if you really want. There's a new action thriller I wouldn't mind seeing."

The movies weren't exactly what she had in mind and she liked romantic comedies when she did go but something told her this was as good as it was going to get.

"Okay," she said, trying to smile.

"How's Sam getting on?" he asked as they started to walk.

Annabel shook her head. "I'm so worried about him, Gary. He's still so quiet. I can't seem to get through to him. I'm paranoid about his every move since he got drunk."

"Who's minding him tonight?"

"Colin . . ." Annabel hesitated for a moment when she saw the concern in Gary's eyes. "He's not trying to get back with me or anything. I just feel better knowing that a man is looking after him. At least he won't try and run off."

Gary put his arm protectively around her shoulder and gave her a squeeze. "He'll be all right, babe. That's the trouble with us guys – we're not very good at expressing ourselves."

Annabel thanked her lucky stars that she had Gary to lean on. He was the most positive person in her life at the moment.

Damien had returned home to Greenfield Close feeling like a new man. He was excited at the prospect of Kate's return to Dublin. Leaving his home felt like the right thing to do. It was time that the house was used as a family home again – it was what it had been built for. The Oaks were built as a development for singles and older couples and they would suit his situation far better. Living without Betty in Greenfield Close was difficult. He realised that for all the years he lived there many parts of the house remained exclusively Betty's and he was still learning how to use certain domestic appliances.

In the middle of all these positive developments were his frustrated attempts to reach Annabel. He could only presume that she didn't want to take on the business any more. He had been getting her voice mail for weeks – every time that he tried to call. There was no point in leaving a message. She knew where he was. The building was going to be finished sooner than he thought and there were plenty of people who would jump at the chance of a prime retail unit. But he still held out hope. He desperately wanted to have a common interest with her. Even though his thoughts had been with his daughter for the last few weeks he had dreamed of Annabel on several occasions. He could try to stop her creeping into his days but he could do nothing about his subconscious. There was unfinished business with Annabel and maybe that's the way it would always be.

Annabel braced herself before entering the house and facing Colin. It had been a lovely evening and Gary was such a pillar of strength – she didn't want the feelings of warmth and security to end. Everything was quiet.

"Hi, Colin."

Colin looked up from his book. He was spread out on the couch and looked very much at home.

"You're back early."

Annabel looked at her watch. She didn't think twelve o'clock was early but was pleased to see Colin so amiable. "I didn't want to hold you up," she said hesitantly.

Colin smirked. "No problem – I've taken an apartment down the road – to be closer to the kids."

Annabel wasn't particularly thrilled with the news but the way Sam was behaving maybe it was just as well. "I see." She nodded. "How was Sam this evening?"

"Stroppy, to say the least. I don't know what's got into that young fellow. I think you're much too easy on him."

Annabel felt a pang of sympathy for her son. What hope had he with such an insensitive father? "He's really missing you," she explained.

"Well, it certainly didn't seem that way this evening."

Annabel hoped that Colin hadn't made matters worse. Maybe she should have told him about the drinking episode. No, that would make life even more difficult. Colin would then be hanging around constantly.

"Did something happen?" she asked.

"I sent him to his room. He was so cheeky."

Annabel knew that she wouldn't get the true version of the story from her estranged husband. "I'm going upstairs to check on him," she said.

Colin was obviously in no hurry to move as he turned his head and put it back into his book.

Quiet snorting noises floated from Rebecca's room.

She had a habit of sleeping on her back. Annabel peeked in on Taylor who was splayed face down on the bed in a deep sleep. She slowly and carefully opened the door of Sam's room, trying not to wake her son. A gust of wind blew in from the open window. The bed was empty with his pyjamas thrown across it and his clothes were no longer on the floor where he usually threw them after changing. She was too shocked to panic. The horror of telling Colin that Sam was missing was far outweighed by the terrible thoughts of the trouble her young son could be in. She ran down the stairs and into the living room where Colin was fixed like a wax statue.

"Sam's not in his room!" she panted. "It looks like he climbed out the bedroom window!"

"What?" Colin frowned – she could have been speaking a foreign language.

"Sam's gone – his clothes are gone – he's run off somewhere!"

Colin jumped to his feet. "Don't be ridiculous, woman! I've been here all night. I'd have heard something."

"Go upstairs and see for yourself." The urgency in her voice made it perfectly clear that she was serious.

When Colin looked into Sam's room and saw the pyjamas strewn across the unmade bed he realised that he hadn't done a very good job of minding his care. He went over to the open window and stretched his head out until he could clearly see the ground. It was an easy jump from the balcony down to the top of the side wall. Sam could have climbed down onto the bins from there.

"We have to call the police," he said, bringing his head in.

"Colin, he ran away before . . . well, went missing one afternoon a couple of weeks ago."

Colin lunged forward – he was so close to Annabel that she could smell traces of garlic off his breath. "What? Why didn't you tell me?"

"I spoke to him about it and, well, there's something else," Annabel hung her head down. She really should have told Colin before this. "He got drunk."

Colin's eyes almost popped out from their sockets. "That's it. I'm calling the police."

He stomped out the door and into her bedroom to the phone. Annabel was left shaking on the landing. Her world was falling in around her. How could her perfectly manicured life have come to this?

"They'll be here in a minute," Colin said gruffly as he appeared from the bedroom. "We need to talk now, downstairs."

Annabel shivered at the tone of his voice. Silently she followed him down the stairs until they were sitting face to face over the kitchen table.

"Now, what else have you forgotten to tell me?"

Annabel shook her head. "Nothing."

"I can't trust you any more, Annabel. You're not fit to mind the children."

Even though her stomach was aching she had to try and stand up to Colin. This was what her solicitor had warned her about: many fathers were seeking custody of their children and the thought of Colin doing such a thing chilled her to the bone.

"I'm doing my best –"

"Well, your best is not good enough, Annabel."

"Let me finish," she said more sternly. "If you had spent some time with your son before we split up he might not be so insecure now – he doesn't know where he stands with either of us."

"If anything happens to Sam tonight, just remember one thing – it's your fault!"

Annabel felt as though her stomach had been speared. This was no time for blame but it came as no surprise that Colin would react in this way.

Suddenly the phone rang. Annabel rushed over to take the call, hoping that the caller would have news on her son. It was Lily.

"Annabel, have you any idea where your son is?"

This was her worst nightmare – first Colin and now her mother. But how did she know that Sam was missing?

"We've rung the police, Mum. How did you know he was –"

"He's here with me, the poor lad, and he is a very upset young man. He says that he wants to come and live with me and I can't say I blame him the way you've been behaving these past months."

Annabel let her mother's words roll off her. She could only feel relief in the knowledge that her son was safe. "I'm coming around to get him now."

"No, you are not. He would only let me call you if I promised to let him stay the night. He's tucked up in bed with a cup of hot chocolate and you can see him tomorrow."

Annabel knew there was no point in arguing.

"Okay, Mum. Thanks."

"You can tell Colin that it's time he started to take his responsibilities a bit more seriously too."

It was the first time Annabel had heard her mother condemning Colin and it came as a quiet consolation.

"Thanks, Mum. I'll let you go."

Colin stood over her as she put the phone down.

"He's in Mum's."

"I could tell that from the conversation."

Annabel lifted the handset. "I'd better tell the police he's okay."

Colin didn't move but his glare intensified until she was finished her call to the station.

"So, what are you going to do about this?" he said then.

Annabel frowned. "What am I going to do?" she asked in disbelief. "Don't fob this off as my problem. We are both in this one. We need to do something dramatic or the next time he could do something fatal."

21

The large removal truck backed up Greenfield Close and stopped halfway up the drive. Kate waddled up to the front door on hearing its arrival, looking every bit her seven months' gestation. The transition from France to Ireland had so far been flawless and, provided her painting equipment and piano remained intact in the back of the truck, she could say that the move had been easy. The boys were thriving in St Peter's school and David was showing signs of becoming an excellent football player. Ciarán had already made a connection with the music teacher who was willing to give him extra guitar lessons and they had an abundance of new pals who lived in the vicinity of Greenfield Close.

The only negative was the loss of Fabian's presence in her life. He assured her that he would visit her in Ireland and take care of the new tenants in her house in France. But she knew she couldn't find someone like him again.

If only she had Annabel! Maybe she could try to call her again.

The decorators were tidying up and getting ready to leave as the removal men started bringing in the crates and containers. Apart from the kitchen, Greenfield Close had had a major facelift, courtesy of Kate's love of flamboyant colours. She'd decided to leave the kitchen units until the baby was a little bit older. He or she would be wreaking havoc on walls and presses for the next couple of years. The back bedroom was already converted into a makeshift studio and she had plans to convert the attic in the next few weeks. That would be her bedroom and she would have lots of space. She would be able to see the mountains overlooking Dublin Bay when the skylights were put in – that was some compensation for the loss of her spectacular mountain views in France.

She went up to her bedroom for a quick lie-down.

As her head hit the pillow she could hear Damien's voice downstairs as he ordered the removal men around the ground floor. She needed a man. Her father had been wonderful but she missed having a man to take care of her and do all the jobs that men do in a relationship – like dealing with the removal men.

She sighed as she thought of Shane. She often thought of him. Every day without fail she had her Shane moments. She didn't see it as wasted time any more. It was her treat to herself. She could rest assured that she had done the right thing – but if it was the right thing, why did she feel so bad? She looked over at the bedside locker and the phone resting on it. It was the same locker that her mother had used in her last days. She missed her mum. She wished she had known her better. She wondered how well she knew anyone if the person closest to her had lived a secret life for so long. Now Betty was gone and she would never get a chance to talk to her about it. She didn't want that to happen with herself and Annabel.

Annabel owed it to Sam to try and work an amicable arrangement out with Colin. She had suggested that they met with their solicitors present but Colin had surprised her with his desire to work things out maturely. She hoped that he was serious. The docklands were a pleasant meeting place and the restaurant that Colin chose had fabulous view across the River Liffey. The super-slim waitress rushed over with a carafe of chilled water with some sprigs of mint sticking out of it.

"Would-ah you like-ah to order?" she asked. Her Italian accent was pronounced.

"I'm waiting for someone, thanks!" Annabel said, nodding approval as the girl filled her glass.

In the distance she spied Colin in a navy Hugo Boss pin-striped suit. There was something more sharp and attractive in his swagger now than when he used to walk into the hall of their house after a day's work.

"Hi," he beamed as he pulled back the chrome-and-leather seat.

"Hi, this is a nice place," Annabel said, aiming to be positive about this meeting.

"I sometimes take clients here if Patrick Guillbaud's is booked."

Annabel cringed at his name-dropping – it was one of the things that she definitely didn't miss about him.

"I hope we can move things forward today," Colin started.

Annabel felt as though she were a member of his staff about to get the sack if they didn't agree with the boss's proposal.

"What are you suggesting?" She took a sip of water from her glass to take away the dryness that was creeping around her mouth.

"I have a proposal that may suit everyone."

His cheesy grin made Annabel wonder just how off the mark he could possibly be.

"Why don't I move back home and sleep in the spare room?" Colin could see the look of defiance creeping onto Annabel's expression. "Let me finish before you say anything. I would not make any pretence that we are man and wife but the children would have the stability of both parents present in the day-to-day running of things."

Annabel started to shake her head. "Colin, do you think I went into our new situation lightly? I have been unhappy with myself and our lifestyle for years. If truth be told I can't honestly say I have ever been happy."

Colin rubbed his crinkling forehead. "Annabel, I don't mean to belittle your status or anything but things have not been very comfortable for you. Simon has filled me in on your falling out with Melissa and the other wives that you used to socialise with."

Annabel couldn't believe he could be so pompous and arrogant. She had hoped that the time on his own might have changed him.

"Then there is the matter of Sam, which is the real reason why I have come up with this suggestion. We owe it to our son to offer him stability."

Annabel couldn't disagree with Colin on this issue. Sam was in a state of anxiety and his moods were so fragile he was in serious danger of doing something else stupid or dangerous or both. "I couldn't agree with you more, but will it help Sam if we are snappy with each other and he continues to see you putting me down the way you always have?"

"I don't put you down!" Colin jerked his head back in surprise.

Annabel tried to remain calm. "But you do, Colin – all the time. In fact I don't think you even realise when you do it."

"Well, you've been rather forthright yourself recently, Annabel."

Annabel put her head into her hands and combed her hair with her fingers before facing Colin again.

"You see, this is what I'm talking about. You don't treat me as an equal partner. I am and always have been the inferior, incapable half of this relationship to you – suitable only for breeding and rearing children."

"That's ridiculous!"

"What about the first time I go and do anything for myself – like the market stall? How did you react?"

Colin sat silently.

"So you see what I mean?" Annabel's eyebrows arched in anticipation of his next outburst.

"Well," Colin mumbled, "I suppose you could keep the stall . . ."

Annabel thought about Gary. There was no way that she could carry on a relationship with another man if her husband was back living under the same roof. Gary was such a support and so different to Colin – she relished all the loving that she had been sharing with a new man in her life.

"We need to get on with each other before we can think about living with each other again," she said. "I've considered counselling and I think you should too."

Colin frowned at her suggestion. The last person he needed to see was a shrink.

"Are you-ah ready to order?" the waitress said, appearing out of nowhere.

"Dublin bay prawns, please," Annabel said, looking up at the waitress.

"I'll have the same," Colin grunted, anxious for the girl to disappear.

"Any wine?"

"No, thank you," Colin said sharply. "We're fine."

He let out a deep breath as the waitress swaggered off. Life had been uncomfortable living in the hotel and the thought of moving all of his stuff to that apartment in Howth was even less appealing. He needed to be at home where he belonged. If only he hadn't let that dreadful girl Rosa into his house – he was right all along about *au pairs*.

The tables around the couple were animated and bustling – Annabel wished that she were sitting next to Gary instead of her husband. Silently they ate their prawns but neither ordered coffee when they were finished.

"I have to go back to work now," said Colin.

"Okay."

"It's a shame we haven't moved forward."

Annabel nodded.

"You will think about my offer, though?" he said, pulling his jacket on and straightening down the collar.

Annabel nodded again. It was the easiest response.

"I'll pay for this on the way out," he said.

As he disappeared through the glass-fronted building she heaved a sigh of relief. The pressure that she felt in his presence was unnatural in a couple who had been together for so many years. How different that lunch was from the pleasant meal she shared with Damien in Aqua! She wondered where Damien was now. It was time that she told him she wasn't taking the coffee shop. There was no way that she had the strength to deal with a new venture with all the uncertainty in her life. Now was as good a time as any. Gary's words echoed in her ear as she dialled Damien's number: *"You don't need to stress out, babe! The stall is enough for you and me both!"*

Nervously she dialled his number.

"Hello?"

"Damien, I got you at last. It's Annabel."

"Annabel, hi! I've been trying to get you for weeks."

"I'm sorry, Damien. I really should have left you a message. I called a few times but was unsure of my decision until now."

She didn't need to say any more. He could tell her decision from the tone in her voice.

"I don't feel this is a good time for trying a new venture," she went on. "I'm swamped with the kids and can barely manage the stall, let alone a fledgling business."

"I understand, Annabel. There's no need to explain. I have tried to call you before now but I was too cowardly to leave a message on your voice mail."

Annabel couldn't envisage Damien being cowardly about anything in his life – and why would he need courage to ring her anyway?

"I've been really busy with Kate's move."

"Kate's what?" Annabel wasn't sure that she had heard him correctly.

"Kate has moved back and is living in Greenfield Close."

"I don't believe you!"

"Hopefully you'll get in touch before you bump into each other because it's going to happen – Dublin's too small!"

Annabel was stunned. What fantastic news! "I will definitely ring her. So she's living with you?"

"No, eh," Damien felt embarrassed telling Annabel as

she was part of the reason behind his decision to move, "I'm moving out to the new apartments I've just finished in Howth."

"You'll be only down the road from me! Oh, Damien, you'll have to visit now we're neighbours!" she giggled.

If only you knew! Damien thought silently. "Well, thanks for letting me know, Annabel, and I'm sure I'll bump into you soon."

"Bye, Damien."

That was an interesting twist. The time was well overdue for her and Kate to make amends. She beamed at the Italian waitress as she stood up from her seat to leave the restaurant. New things were happening all of the time. With feather-light steps she breezed along Custom House Quay until she came to Abbey Street. A quick trip to Eason's to get a couple of yummy indulgent novels and then she would be on the DART and home within the hour.

O'Connell Street was rippling with bodies and traffic. Annabel wondered what it must be like to face this kind of chaos day-in day-out. There was a kind of excitement around the city too that never touched the life of those who remained constantly in the suburbs.

As she approached the steps of Eason's the tall figure of an attractive man caught her eye. He was walking away from her with his arm around a slight girl with long blonde hair. Surely that was Gary? But it couldn't be him, could it? She looked again but could only make out his silhouette as he and his partner sauntered down the busy thoroughfare.

Annabel felt compelled to follow.

When she was almost upon the couple the tall man turned around and smiled at her. He had the blackest teeth that she had ever seen and a huge nose. Thank God, she sighed to herself. How could she have suspected her Gary of being with another woman? Annabel beat herself up about it. She took the latest romantic bestseller off the shelf and held it to her chest. She had the man of her dreams and she could lose herself on the way home in blissful knowledge that he was all hers.

Shane glanced at the notices on the corkboard in the operations room. There was seldom anything of interest on it apart from the odd party in Lilies Bordello. Nothing had enticed him to socialise since Kate left his life. Besides, Natasha was doing the circuit of all the hip social venues in Dublin city and he didn't want to bump into her. She still had a couple of girlfriends in Airjet that quizzed him whenever they were on his flights and dropped loaded bits of information to see his reaction. One of them in particular seemed obsessed. She had even come to his room on an overnight wearing little but a smile. He wasn't interested in sex on a plate from Natasha's friends or anyone at the moment. His only respite was on the racketball court.

"All right, Shane?"

He turned around and Tim, the generously

proportioned operations officer, beamed at him from over the top of his coffee cup.

"Oh, hi, Tim. I was just looking to see if there was anything of interest ..."

"Not unless you fancy a transfer to the States."

Shane scanned the notice-board. "Where does it say that?"

"They're looking for a couple of captains to go over and help with the training on the new routes across the Atlantic."

In the corner of the board on a small card was notification of transfers to Florida.

"When did that go up?"

"About a week ago," Tim replied.

"Sounds interesting." Shane started to think about the sun and possibilities of a whole new way of life. He could rent his apartment out in Howth.

"When's the last date for application? I can't believe I'm only seeing this now."

"There are a lot going for it."

Shane knew that the senior guys would be jumping at this great opportunity to make a lot of extra cash. It was time to move on and forget about Kate. A few months in the sun would help.

The novel was enthralling. Annabel was on page thirty-four by the time the Dart reached Bayside station. She looked out at the crisp blue sky for a moment as the train came to a standstill. Her eyes fell upon a couple on the platform wrapped caringly around each other. Suddenly she realised she recognised one of them. She blinked three times.

She was not mistaken this time. The tall figure draped around a pretty redhead was definitely Gary. This was surreal! Her previous mistake on O'Connell Street must have been some kind of premonition! Who was this girl? Could she be his sister? She didn't even know if he had a sister. The girl, who couldn't have been more than twenty-five, puckered her lips as he leaned forward and kissed them tenderly. She definitely was not his sister!

The girl waved as she jumped on the train. Gary's eyes were fixed firmly on her as she disappeared behind the sliding doors.

Annabel felt as if she had been slapped across the face. The girl sat up at the front of the carriage, blissfully unaware of the upset that she was causing. Annabel was shaking as the train continued on to the next stop and terminated at Howth. All the carriages emptied. She couldn't stomach the thought of going home or dealing with the rest of her life.

She had to find out the truth. She needed to meet Gary and soon.

Dee knocked loudly on the front door of Greenfield Close. Kate had assured her that she would be home at four o'clock. She knocked again and waited. She was about to turn around and get into her car when a vague silhouette came to light through the frosted glass.

Kate seemed disorientated as she opened the door.

"Kate, love. Are you okay?"

"Fine, Dee," Kate said, giving her eyes a rub and yawning. "I was having forty winks."

"I won't stay long. I called in to see if there was anything I could do for you."

Dee had been marvellous since Kate moved home. She was a perfect mother figure and was helping her through every step of her pregnancy.

"Go and lie down again and I'll bring you up a nice cup of tea," Dee said, ushering her niece up the stairs. "Where are the boys?"

"Dad is collecting them. I'm going to let them cycle home soon. They seem to be happy in their new surroundings."

Kate snuggled back under her duvet. Dee appeared minutes later with two mugs and a packet of digestive biscuits tucked into the crook of her arm.

"I'm going to do my mother-in-law's shopping so I thought I'd pop in and see if you need anything." Dee rested the mugs down on the locker beside Kate's bed and offered her a biscuit.

"I did a shop yesterday, thanks, Dee. You do a lot for that old woman. Does anyone else look after her?"

"Her daughters emigrated and if you met her you'd know why!" said Dee, munching a digestive. "I'm tempted to move abroad myself at times!"

"You can't do that," Kate begged. "Not now that I'm back!"

"I'm not going anywhere." Dee laughed. "But the shopping is not the only reason I called. How about this? I found out about that old boyfriend of your mum's!"

Kate sat up in the bed. She was all ears because he wasn't just her mum's old boyfriend any more. He was her father.

"It's tragic really. Your Uncle Bob heard a few years back that Liam committed suicide," Dee said in her general matter-of-fact tone as she brushed the crumbs off her trousers. "In 1996, I believe. He separated from his Australian wife and moved to the outback. He was dead for days before anyone found him. He left no family. Sad really."

Kate was shattered by her news. Now she would never get to meet her real father. "Kate? Are you listening to me?"

"I, eh," Kate felt her eyes well up, "I don't know what to say."

"It's a tragedy. Your mum knew, of course."

"How do you know?"

Dee nodded her head. "She spoke to your Uncle Bob about him several times apparently."

"Do you think he killed himself because Mum wouldn't leave Dad to be with him?"

Dee shrugged her shoulders and shook her head. "We'll never know. I have to dash, love. I'll check up on you tomorrow." She leaned forward and gave a dumbstruck Kate a kiss goodbye.

Maybe it was just as well that she would never get to

know this stranger on the other side of the world who was responsible for giving her life. Damien was her father and a wonderful father.

"Is it okay to leave you, pet?"

Kate looked up. "I'm fine thanks, Dee."

It was only after Dee pulled the front door behind her that Kate buried her face in the palm of her hands and sobbed. She wasn't sure who she was crying for. Maybe it was Liam, or maybe it was Betty. The real sad end to the whole story was the wave of loss that swept over her. Even the fact that she was on the brink of bringing a new life into the world couldn't console her. Then she realised who she was crying for – herself!

Gary was late. Annabel was wondering if the redhead had anything to do with it. In hindsight he changed slightly with each meeting. Annabel couldn't honestly say that she was getting to know him any better. She made a detour into the newsagent's beside Molly's coffee shop where they had arranged to meet. It was a far cry from Findlaters, where they had their first date. She wondered what other deceits he harboured.

Annabel picked up the new edition of *Ciao*. It was a tacky Irish magazine and one that had everybody but actual international celebrities in it. Melissa's face in the corner of the cover caught her eye. It would pass the time while she waited for Gary in the coffee shop and help keep her mind off the upset and anger she had been struggling with since seeing him at the station.

Annabel settled down at a table by the window. Autumn was here and the light was disappearing earlier as each evening passed.

"Would you like something?" the pasty-faced young waitress asked.

"A cappuccino, please."

She let her fingers flick through the pages of her magazine. The cover story was also on pages five, six and seven – Melissa and her husband Simon were walking behind the actor, Jack Owens, and his wife as they entered the Savoy cinema for the première of his new movie. Annabel cringed for a moment as she thought of the gloating that she would have had to listen to if she was still friends with Melissa. It was a relief to be away from her – but a part of her missed the social charades and games that accompanied her old life. She continued flicking through the pages until she saw a name that she thought she recognised but couldn't for the life of her figure out why – Natasha Gleason. That name rang a bell. Who was she? She was wearing a handkerchief dress adorned with diamanté studs. Her tan was flawless and her blonde hair was fixed in a loose knot at the back of her head that must have taken hours to perfect. She was resting her right hand in the crook of the arm of Dublin's most eligible bachelor. Ron Larkin was part of the multimillion-euro hotelier family. But who was Natasha Gleason? She read on and discovered that the two had recently returned from a break in Monaco where they had stayed on his yacht. *Natasha's estranged husband, Captain Shane Gleason . . .* Annabel didn't need to read any more. So Shane and his wife had actually split. But Damien had told her that Kate had finished with Shane. Maybe she didn't know that Shane had split up from Natasha. Annabel was trembling with all of this information. She longed to talk to Kate.

"Hey, babes, sorry I'm late," Gary said, pulling a chair away from the table.

"Gary, hi." She felt nauseous on seeing him – how was she ever going to tell him what she had seen?

"What are you reading?"

"It's just a trashy magazine – someone I know is in it."

Gary pushed his chair back and took a more comfortable position. "Fancy a drive or a walk?"

"I, eh, Gary, we need to talk."

His expression changed. He was usually the one who did the jilting with the women in his life and from Annabel's unfamiliar tone he knew that something was askew. "About what?"

Annabel couldn't believe that she was coming straight out with it. Inside she was trembling but now she had started she had to finish what she had to say. She needed to know the truth.

"I was on the DART today."

"Really?" He shrugged.

This wasn't going to be easy.

"Gary, I saw you kiss a red-haired girl at Bayside station."

Gary's expression changed. His eyes widened like an animal trapped in front of a loaded gun. "That's my pal Amy. She runs a stall at the Phoenix market." He frowned.

"What's your problem, Annabel. Am I not supposed to have other friends?"

Annabel knew that she couldn't back down now. She had to be firm if she was going to maintain any self-respect. "Of course, you can have friends but she looked like more than a friend."

Gary pulled his shoulders back and then moved forward on his chair. "Did I ever say that we were exclusive? I mean, you are tied up with your rugrats and I only get a look-in when it suits you."

Annabel was shocked. This was so out of character. She would never have believed that the fun-loving easy-going guy she had shared so much with over the past few weeks could turn into a monster so suddenly.

"Gary, I'm not seeing anyone else and I thought we had something special. I demand to know the truth."

He leaned forward across the table until his face was almost on top of Annabel. "Leave it, will you? Did you hassle your old man like this?" He gave a loud sigh before slouching back onto his chair.

Annabel felt his comment like a blow. She was seething inside but couldn't think of the words to launch a counter-attack. Something had gone seriously wrong since she found her new independence. "Gary, can we talk this out, please?"

Gary shrugged. "To be honest – you're a bit of a prima donna, Annabel. You're well suited to your drip of a husband. I mean, let's face it – you've friends in crappy socialite magazines. I was going to give you the benefit of the doubt but I don't need the hassle." He stood up and gave her a smug nod. Then he left her in the coffee shop with her magazine as her cappuccino arrived.

Annabel wanted to cry. Maybe Gary was right and she did suit Colin. But could she stand to go back to the way she was? She had felt like a butterfly for the last few months. Free to make all the decisions in her home and with the children. The girls were coming around even if Sam was still upset with her. She thought she was doing a good job. She had worked hard on the stall and was making a good turnover every week. Oh God, she had been so pleased about her new relationship! How could she have been so wrong?

"We're closing now," the young waitress said, startling Annabel.

She didn't know where to go or what to do. She couldn't go home – Colin was there. She needed to talk to a friend. She jumped into her Jeep. She was only a kilometre from Maeve's house.

She parked in front of the prim driveway with neat little rows of dahlias decorating the footpath. The front door was ajar and she tapped on it gently as she let herself in.

"Maeve!" she called.

Maeve came running down the stairs on hearing Annabel's voice.

"Hi, what a nice surprise! Come into the kitchen and we'll have a cuppa."

"I hope I haven't disturbed the kids."

"Don't worry about them! They take ages to fall

asleep!" Maeve went over to the kettle and put it on. "I thought you were meeting Gary tonight?"

"I was, I did, I mean . . ." Annabel sighed as she slumped down on the kitchen chair. "Why have I got such awful taste in men?"

Maeve turned around and looked at her friend's despairing face. "What did he do?"

Annabel's eyes started to water, then she sobbed. "I was meeting Colin in town yesterday and I got the DART home. I saw Gary at Bayside station," she couldn't believe she was saying the words as they dribbled out of her mouth, "kissing a red-haired girl. She couldn't have been more than twenty-five!"

Maeve cringed. "That wasn't very nice. I thought he was a dreamboat."

"There was nothing of the dreamboat about him this evening. He said he had never said we were *exclusive*."

"What does that mean?"

"That we're both free to sleep with other people."

Maeve scratched her head. "I don't know, Annabel. I'm so long out of the whole dating loop, I don't think I'd be able to cope."

"It's not easy," Annabel nodded and took the cup of tea from Maeve gratefully. "Maybe I should consider taking Colin back. He is making an effort with Sam."

"You can't take him back because Gary jilted you. You have to be sure that you want to be with him for *your* sake."

Annabel knew that Maeve was right. It was exactly what Kate would say too. But the pressure of the last few weeks was taking its toll and she didn't feel so strong any more.

22

Lily was polishing the mantelpiece with great pride and vigour.

"You are doing the right thing, Annabel. The last few weeks have been just awful for everybody."

"Mum, there's no need to do all that dusting. The new cleaner is great – she was only here two days ago."

"That Polish woman is too old. She shouldn't be taking on a house like this."

"She's at least five years younger than you, Mum."

Lily tut-tutted her daughter. "I think you should have the place nice for Colin."

Annabel threw her eyes heavenward. She had let Colin convince her that moving home was the best for everyone and after her confidence had got such a bashing from Gary she felt left with no other option. But she didn't want to let herself slip back into old routines. It might be the best outcome for the children but she still wasn't convinced that it was the best alternative for herself. The way she felt about everything had changed but things would outwardly go back to the way they had always been. Maeve had warned her to give herself more time – until she had got over the drastic Gary affair. But she had impulsively decided that she wanted stability back in her life.

The front door swung open and the crash of Colin's golf clubs against the hall floor told her that he was home. Sam had wanted to be here for his father's return but when a friend asked him to go bowling he'd decided he'd see his father later. The girls were in the television room and didn't hear the crash of the clubs in the hall.

A few seconds later, Colin peeked around the door of the living room.

"I'm back."

Lily ran forward and gave her son-in-law an awkward embrace.

Colin shook himself down after the event and nodded over at Annabel. "I'll take my things up to our room then."

Annabel didn't want Colin back in her room. They had agreed that he would stay in the spare room for the first couple of weeks. She suddenly realised as he stood in front of her that she didn't want him anywhere near her at any time of the day or night. What had she done?

Kate sat on the side of the bed staring at the telephone. Her head was full of so many thoughts – she missed her mum and even more so now that she was back living at home. She wondered about Liam – the father she would never meet – and she longed for a good chat with Fabian. Even though they had spoken a couple of days ago it didn't feel the same. She was so used to his body language speaking a multitude when they conversed and she couldn't see it over the phone.

Spontaneously Kate lifted the handset of the white telephone and dialled Annabel's number. For some unknown reason, it felt like the right thing to do. She trembled as she heard the phone ring.

"Hello?"

"Annabel, it's Kate."

Annabel was transfixed. She had dashed to get the phone so she wouldn't have to watch her mother drooling over Colin in the living-room. She certainly hadn't expected to hear Kate's voice at the end of the line.

"Kate, how are you?" she said eagerly. "Great to hear you!"

Kate felt a sudden urge to slam the phone down quickly. She was relieved with the warm reception but wasn't sure what she wanted to say any more.

"I've moved back to Dublin, permanently – I just thought I should let you know, I mean we're bound to bump into each other."

"Wow, that's fantastic news! When?" Annabel hadn't the guts to tell her that she already knew and hadn't tried to call.

"A few weeks ago."

What was she doing ringing Annabel? It felt awkward

and lots of strange feelings were haunting her as she spoke.

"Where are you staying?" Annabel sensed the tension between them and tried to lighten the tone of her voice.

"I'm living in Greenfield Close. Dad's moved into an apartment in Howth."

"Really?" Annabel was dying to ask about the baby. "How are you keeping? I heard your news – congratulations!"

Kate had a flashback to Biarritz and felt sick – but she was the one who had picked up the phone and she had to continue the conversation.

"Not bad. I had a scare a couple of months ago but I'm back on track again."

"Oh, God! What happened?" Annabel asked, genuinely concerned.

"I haemorrhaged – hopefully everything will be okay."

Annabel's heart was thumping furiously. Now that she was actually talking to Kate she felt nervous. There was so much she wanted to tell her – so much they needed to sort out. There was no easy way of bringing up the subject of Betty but she didn't want to say anything to upset her friend.

"Kate, you poor thing! You've had a terrible time, especially losing your mum."

Annabel was right, Kate thought. Losing her mum had been the bitterest pill to swallow above all else. "It seems it never rains but it pours!"

"Can we meet up for a chat?" Annabel begged. "I'd love to see you."

Kate hesitated. What had she expected? Of course they should meet but somehow the anger she had held inside since Biarritz was beginning to rear its ugly head again and grow stronger the longer she heard Annabel's voice.

"I'm housebound at the moment. The doctors warned me that I could go early."

"Well, I could come to you – whatever is the easiest," Annabel urged. She had to pinch herself – she still couldn't quite believe that she was talking to Kate at last. Even with the reservations in Kate's voice it was too good to be true.

"I guess tomorrow's good for me," Kate said uncertainly.

"Tomorrow?" Annabel said excitedly. "Will I call out to you?"

Kate felt trapped in a whirlwind of emotion. "Okay."

"Okay. Eleven? I presume your kids are in school?"

"Oh, they are."

"I'll see you at eleven then." Annabel paused. "Kate?"

"Yeah?"

Annabel wanted to kiss the phone. She wanted to tell Kate how much she loved and missed her. There were months and months of words and sentences that needed to be said. How was she ever going to make up for all that lost time apart? The gap in the conversation said it all.

"Thanks for ringing."

"Yeah, okay, see you then," Kate said hurriedly, keen to hang up.

Annabel put the phone down and couldn't conceal the wide cheesy grin that was now fixed firmly on her face.

"Who was that?" Colin asked abruptly on entering the kitchen.

"Kate," Annabel said defiantly. "I'm meeting her tomorrow."

Colin scowled. "She's in Dublin?"

"She's moved back permanently," Annabel told him gleefully.

He didn't like the thought of Kate being back in his wife's life just as he was trying to take control of her again.

"I'm off, Mum," Annabel called to Lily. "Going to the supermarket to get stuff for the stall and then getting my hair done. You don't mind looking after the kids, Colin, do you?"

She breezed out of the house as if she were floating on a cloud. Her spirit was elevated. Kate was back in her life and she was going to make sure she stayed there.

Annabel felt the jitters up and down her arms after ringing the doorbell. How would Kate be? It had been a long time.

Kate opened the door – her large bump being the first sight to greet Annabel.

"Hi, Annabel, you look well!" she said stiffly and stepped back, unwilling to make physical contact until she was sure what her feelings for Annabel were – and Annabel's for her.

"Hi, Kate! So do you. You're positively blooming."

Annabel held a bunch of white lilies wrapped in brown paper and tied with brown string. She handed them to Kate on entering the hall.

"Tell the truth. I'm like a decrepit hippopotamus," Kate said, pan-faced. "I wasn't this big after nine months with the twins. Thanks for the flowers."

Annabel smiled. Typical Kate, sharp, witty. "It's good to see you, Kate."

Kate looked down at Annabel's feet. "Come into the kitchen. I have the kettle on. Betty is still here in spirit and I now possess the antennae she had for visitors – she always knew when they were approaching."

The words dribbled from Kate's mouth as she spoke quickly to hide the anxious undertones in her voice.

Annabel walked slowly and steadily behind her friend – still unsure of where they stood with each other.

"It's terrible," she said. "I can't believe she's gone."

"It's been hard," Kate agreed. "I never realised how much you grow up when you lose a parent."

Annabel nodded quietly. Her own father was dead so long now she found it difficult at times to picture his face.

"Kate, I hope I didn't upset you by going to the funeral. I really needed to be there – I loved Betty too."

Kate nodded but said nothing. There wasn't much point.

"It's okay," she said quietly – leaving Annabel unsure how she really felt.

"How long have you left?" Annabel asked, gesturing to her bump.

"Seven weeks but the doctors think I'm going to go early. They've been watching me avidly since I nearly miscarried. I'm so unfit. I don't know how I'm going to manage the labour!"

"Plenty of gas and an epidural. That's what got me through!" Annabel said lightly.

But still Kate didn't change her expression.

"So tell me your news, Annabel. I heard you're flying solo now as well."

Annabel coughed. She felt embarrassed admitting to Kate that she had taken Colin back. "Actually, we're giving it another try."

"Oh." Kate wasn't sure how to react. "Good. Eh, I presume you are happy?"

Annabel became tight-lipped. She didn't know how to answer. "The kids seem happy, especially Sam. We had a bit of a tough time with him for a few weeks – drinking and running away from home!" Damn, she thought, Kate can see straight through me. She needed to change the subject. "Any word from Shane?"

Kate felt strange talking about him to Annabel. It's not like they had a relationship or anything. It was only a few meetings and wonderful moments mixed in with the madness and mayhem that made up the first few months of her pregnancy. If she let herself think that it was anything more than that she would burst into tears on the spot.

"I haven't seen him in months."

"That's a shame," Annabel said. "Especially as Natasha's met someone."

Kate's ears picked up. "Natasha has met someone else?"

Annabel nodded. "I saw a picture of her in *Ciao* magazine with Ron Larkin."

"The hotel Larkins?" Kate asked in surprise.

"Yeah."

Kate had been so consumed in her own feelings she never considered that Shane might have finished with Natasha on his own terms. "I had no idea."

"Does he know you're home?"

Kate shrugged. She hadn't a clue.

"I bet he'd love to see you, Kate."

"Like this?" she asked, ruefully pointing to her stomach.

"Doesn't he know?" Annabel was rather shocked. "Didn't you tell him?"

Kate shook her head.

"Shane loves you, Kate. He's always loved you."

"I wouldn't want him feeling obliged to take on a stranger's baby. He might grow to resent it."

"He could grow to love it!"

Kate said nothing. She knew Annabel was right. Wasn't that what her father had done?

"Why don't I give him a call?" Annabel suggested.

"I don't think that would be a good idea," Kate said swiftly.

"Well, if you change your mind, the offer stands."

Kate knew Annabel was only trying to be helpful but she didn't want anyone else interfering. For all she knew, he never wanted to have anything to do with her again and she wouldn't blame him. "My dad's been asking for you."

"To tell the truth, I've been avoiding him. He has been really good to me, offering premises to set up my own business. I feel bad that I can't take him up on it."

"Why can't you?"

"I wasn't in the right frame of mind to cope with such a huge undertaking for the last few months. And my not going ahead with the business venture was part of the deal Colin struck for coming back. He even wanted me to give up the stall but I was adamant that I was keeping it going. I thought I was the one doing him the favour by letting him back but he managed to turn everything around and by then I'd already told Sam that his father was coming home and it was too late."

"I think you should have your independence, Annabel."

Kate was right. It shouldn't have even been an issue. It was all about control with Colin and he wanted her in the home, working in the kitchen and running around after the kids as she used to. That was the bottom line.

"You have to put it up to him, Annabel."

Annabel smiled. This was more like the conversations

she used to have with Kate. Unbeknownst to themselves they were falling into a familiarity that they both had missed since falling out.

"I don't have the strength to fight it out with him any more. I had a bad experience with a guy I was dating and he rocked my confidence. He was a market trader as well. Thankfully I haven't seen him at the market since we last spoke – he must be taking a break."

"Annabel," Kate said shaking her head, "you do pick them! Looks like the only decent guy you ever had was my dad." Kate was smiling now for the first time since Annabel entered the house.

With enormous relief, Annabel heard her words and recognised the thaw in her expression. "Have you forgiven me?"

Kate shrugged and paused for a moment – she felt unsure whether to tell her what she had learned since Betty's death. She looked up into Annabel's open and hankering eyes and decided to open the gates of reconciliation.

"Betty was no angel either. She had a long-distance romance that she carried out for most of her married life."

"Betty?" Annabel was flabbergasted.

"I know," Kate nodded. Suddenly she felt a wave of relief rush over her. It was like some form of absolution as she smiled at Annabel and said, "I didn't lick it up from the stones, did I?"

Annabel couldn't smile in response – she was too stunned by the revelation.

"Kate, I can't believe it!"

"There's more."

Annabel suspected she knew what she was about to say next.

"It turns out Damien isn't my biological father."

Annabel did her best to act surprised.

"Damien was tricked into marrying Mum while his best friend Liam skipped off to Australia."

"Whatever became of the friend?"

Kate gulped. "He committed suicide when Mum wouldn't leave Dad for him. Well, I'm assuming that was the reason. Or at least part of it. That was after many years of a secret romance carried out mostly by mail. I have all of her letters."

"That's amazing, Kate. When did you discover this?"

"After Mum died. But I only discovered that Liam was dead a while ago. My Auntie Dee found out."

Annabel shifted forward on her chair and put her hand out until it rested on Kate's arm. "How do you feel?"

"Like I never really knew either of my parents." Kate paused. "I guess that's why I found it so difficult to digest your news in Biarritz. It shattered my image of my father. The funny thing is, the way I see everything and everyone since has changed dramatically."

"I never would have thought that Betty had a lover, not in a million years." Annabel shook her head in disbelief.

"Me neither."

"How do you feel about Damien now?"

"That's one of the positives out of all this, I guess," Kate said, nodding her head slowly. "I really love him. He has been a wonderful father to me my whole life. I couldn't feel closer to him. He's probably the reason I'm back here. I want to get back to my roots and where I belong and I need his support."

"You know you always have me," Annabel said softly. "It means a lot to be talking to you like this. There's been a thick fog hanging over me since Biarritz. I wasn't sure that falling out with you was the reason but I can see clearly now so I know that must have been it."

Kate felt the thaw flow through her hormone-filled body. Her eyes welled up and she looked deeply into Annabel's. "I missed you too. It was really hard when Betty died."

Annabel got off her seat and moved closer to Kate. She leaned down and wrapped her arms gently around her friend's neck. "Kate, please, don't let this ever happen again. I really want us to get back what we've lost. I've needed you so much over the last few months and I'm only realising now how hard it's all been."

Kate closed her eyes and rested her head on Annabel's shoulder. "I won't mention it again if you won't. You can go into business with Damien with my blessing. I'll help you organise the opening."

"Kate, what am I doing?" Annabel moved away from her friend and sat back on her seat. "Why do I let Colin bully me?"

"You're the only one that can figure that out," Kate

said wisely. "But you need to start doing what you want. Life begins at forty!"

"They weren't joking, whoever said that, were they?"

Kate shook her head.

"What about Shane then? What are you going to do about him?"

Kate felt as if she had just been given her own pill to swallow. "Watch this space. When I get out of my hippopotamus figure, I'm going to take the world on."

"You'll be too exhausted for the first three months."

"True, I forgot about that. Nature is kind, the way you forget those details, otherwise the world would be full of only children, I guess!"

Annabel laughed.

"Fancy another cup of tea?" Kate asked.

Annabel nodded. She was so happy to be sitting in Kate's kitchen drinking tea. Suddenly everything seemed much better.

23

Colin was bearable the first week he came back, he was tolerable the second, the third week he was insufferable and this week Annabel was in danger of killing him in his sleep. Sam had started complaining about him and even Lily wasn't as light in her step as she had been at the beginning of her daughter's reconciliation.

But Annabel had seen Kate a dozen times since then so she was much happier with herself and how she viewed the rest of the world. Damien gave the lease for the retail unit to a young guy who was very keen to set up a coffee-house franchise as soon as possible. Annabel regretted that her dash for freedom was now slipping away. As Colin became more difficult to live with, the loss of something that might have been became even more keenly felt.

She had gratefully talked it through with Kate and they decided that it was all down to fear. That lack of confidence that had wound its way through Annabel's life. Even with Kate back in her life, Annabel was scared to do something about it.

"I'll drop around and let the removal guy in," Kate insisted to her father at the other end of the phone.

"I told them to leave it until tomorrow," Damien said. He didn't want his daughter running around doing errands in her condition.

"Ring them back and I'll be there at three. I have nothing to do today and I'm getting so out of balance I can't seem to paint – anyway I'm too exhausted."

"Well, if you're sure . . ."

"I'm positive, Dad. I bet you're dying to get into your apartment before the baby arrives."

Damien had hoped he hadn't made it too obvious. "It's not like that, Kate."

"I know. I'm only teasing, Dad," she said with a smile. "Ring back and tell them I'll be there at three."

"Thanks, Kate."

"It's the least I can do when I'm throwing you out of your home! See you later, Dad."

Kate hung up. Now she had to find the key to the apartment in Howth. She rummaged around the odds-and-ends drawer in the kitchen and caught ahold of the key ring with *The Oaks* emblazoned across it. She had time to get petrol and a few messages in SuperValu on the way.

As she drove through the security gates of the prestigious apartment complex, she felt a tingle of energy rush up from her shoulders to the top of her head. It was a strange giddy sort of feeling and she couldn't explain it – she usually only felt it at major moments in her life like going up to receive her degree at graduation or getting married.

She had been to the apartment once, before it was painted, but she thought it was very smart and an excellent choice for her father. The hall was bright and airy and had views from all angles. She stepped into the streamlined lift to get to her father's apartment on the second floor. It was smooth and quiet and she hardly noticed it stopping.

But as the doors opened nothing could have prepared her for who was standing on the other side.

He was in full uniform with his hat balanced in the crook of his right arm. His heavy bag of flight and weather documentation was weighing down his left arm. His blue eyes fixed on Kate's as the doors stopped. Kate had to hold on to the side of the lift. Momentarily the doors started to close but Shane put his foot inside to jam them open.

Kate's mouth opened slightly but no words would come out.

"Kate," Shane said, shock etched all over his face. He looked down at her bulging stomach and back up at her face. Then he said it again. "Kate!"

She swallowed hard and tried to pull herself together before stepping out onto the landing. Shane took a few steps back to give her room.

"Shane, what you are doing here?"

"I live here. I moved in at the weekend."

"I had no idea." Kate's mouth felt suddenly very dry – she needed to sit down. "My father is moving in here."

"Really?" Shane could barely reply. "I won't be seeing much of him after next week – I'm taking a contract to the States for a year."

Kate could hardly breathe. "Oh, that will be nice!"

What dreadful timing they had!

There was an empty silence before he said, "I'm sorry I didn't make it to your mum's funeral, Kate. I didn't hear until the day after the funeral – I was away – and I didn't know whether to write or what to say."

"It's okay," Kate said, gently shaking her head. "We all knew that she didn't have long."

His eyes wandered down to her stomach again and stayed on the bump.

"Maybe this explains something for you?" she said softly, unable to look him in the eye.

"I, eh . . ." He was noticeably embarrassed by the situation.

"I'm due in four weeks."

"But who . . . sorry, that's none of my business." He shook his head and took another step backwards.

She owed it to him to tell him the truth – no matter how dreadful it sounded.

"It happened when I was away with Annabel in Biarritz."

Kate was full of surprises but nothing could have prepared Shane for this. The thought of betrayal shot through him – this was yet another example of Kate's impulsiveness, and yet she was never enticed into being impulsive when it came to their relationship. She must never have loved me the way I loved her, he thought.

"Did you know while we were seeing each other?"

"Towards the end." Kate nodded.

"You should have told me."

"I couldn't," Kate said in utter embarrassment. She stared at the floor.

He hesitated. "Are you . . . are you with the father?"

"No," said Kate, still not meeting his eyes. "I never told him. Couldn't really. Don't know where he is. It was a one-night stand."

Shane felt a surge of relief, followed quickly by a certain feeling of repugnance. *How much more shocking could she be?* He changed tack. "Are you staying here for the birth?"

"I've moved back permanently."

You really are one for surprises! "Where are you living?"

"I live in Greenfield Close now." It was Kate's turn to ask questions. She raised her eyes at last. "Where's Natasha?"

"Still living in Dalkey. She has a new man in her life!"

"I'm sorry. I only found out a couple of weeks ago that you had split up."

Shane was devastated. Why hadn't Kate rung him if she knew that he had split from Natasha? She obviously didn't want to have anything more to do with him, regardless of his single status.

"I have to get to work, Kate," he said hesitantly.

Should he ask to see her again? First he had to digest all this new information that she had thrown at him. But even as she had complicated their lives in a way that he had never dreamt possible, he knew that he still loved her. But would his heart be able to cope with more string-pulling from Kate? It wasn't the time to find out, now that he was moving abroad.

"It's been great seeing you. Take care." He leaned forward and carefully brushed his lips off the side of her cheek.

He stepped into the shiny lift, leaving Kate motionless on the other side. When she was sure that he was gone she moved shakily over to the front door of her father's apartment and tried to put the key into the lock. Her hand wasn't steady enough to get it in first go – she could barely see the keyhole for the well of tears that was building up in her eyes. She felt there was no way back now. Shane was utterly disgusted that she was pregnant and she didn't blame him. To top it all she couldn't have looked worse. Not a screed of make-up on and her tracksuit that was going straight into the bin after the baby was born. He, on the other hand, looked magnificent – but then he always did.

"And then what happened?" Annabel asked, clutching her coffee cup as if her life depended upon it.

"That was it! He went off to work."

"I can't believe it, Kate. You're the one that's the great believer in fate and if that's not enough proof for you I don't know what is!"

"All it proves is that he has good taste in accommodation."

"Nonsense!" Annabel insisted. "It's a sign. You're always going on about signs." She pointed to her tattooed ankle. "I'd never have got this bloody thing on my ankle only for you and your signs! You two have to get back together."

"He didn't give off the impression that he wanted to see me. He kept looking down at my bump and then looking away again."

"He was probably shocked and you can't honestly blame him, can you?"

Kate shook her head. "I should have told him the truth when we split up. There's no way he'd ever be able to trust me again now."

"Why don't you call him?"

"I can't. Honestly, Annabel. My hair was sticking to my head, I was wearing the tracksuit from hell and I hadn't any make-up on. I bet he thinks he had a lucky escape."

"Now you're talking nonsense. You guys know each other well enough not to be bothered by appearances. I bet he thought you looked great."

"You didn't see the way he kept looking at my bump!"

Annabel was getting exasperated with her friend. "Kate, the poor guy was in shock! Can you imagine how he felt?"

Kate knew that Annabel was right. "What am I going to do?"

"Call him!"

Kate sat back on the kitchen chair and pondered. What would she say?

"I'm sorry, Kate, but I have to go. I'm collecting the girls."

"How are things with you?" Kate asked. "I've been rambling on and on about myself all morning."

"Oh, fine," Annabel said in a tone that told Kate things were anything but.

"How long has Colin been back now?"

"Three weeks, five days and about eight hours." Annabel's expression said it all.

"I'm worried about you!" Kate said, pulling her bottom lip over her top.

"I'm fine," Annabel sighed, getting to her feet. She turned around to hide the tears that would appear if she indulged in self-pity. Life at Summit Green had become unbearable. She felt as though she were being strangled. Colin had become even more possessive and he moaned and groaned every time she left for the market. She longed for the sense of freedom that she had achieved. It had all gone terribly wrong.

"Annabel, you have to do something or you'll go out of your mind."

"Sometimes I think I'm out of it already." Annabel turned to go. "I have to pick the kids up. Talk later?"

"Yeah," Kate nodded. She got up to see Annabel to the door.

Annabel's car had disappeared from view before Kate

closed the door and returned to the kitchen. She looked over at the phone resting on the countertop. She longed to call Shane but she didn't honestly know what to say. Things had changed dramatically now that he had split from Natasha. Maybe he had someone else? She could imagine the antennae on all the air stewardesses in Airjet homing in on him like bees. With the baby due in a couple of weeks, she didn't feel in a position to do anything.

Annabel pulled up at the petrol station and started to fill her Jeep. She was in a world of her own when a deep voice called her name. Heavy footsteps approached and she turned around, almost spilling the fuel over her feet.

"Damien, how are you?" A wide smile beamed across her face as she focused on his.

"Grand thanks, Annabel." He felt awkward and embarrassed but couldn't figure out why. "And you?"

"Oh, I'm fine," she said, looking away to replace the nozzle in the petrol pump.

"I was thinking of you only yesterday!" he said.

"Really? I hope it was good thoughts." Her joke served to relax the mood between them.

"Of course. That chap who was meant to take over the coffee shop couldn't raise the cash. I was thinking it's a pity our little venture never got off the ground."

Annabel stared up at his big brown eyes. She felt so safe around him. She longed for him to hold her at this very moment.

"Are you all right?" he asked as Annabel continued to stare motionless.

"Fine, yes, Damien. It is a shame. I've been thinking about it myself. I miss doing something for myself."

"Don't you have the market?"

Annabel nodded her head. "Yes, but it doesn't feel the same any more."

"Mum, I want to go to Ellen's house!" Rebecca shouted from inside the Jeep.

"Sorry about that," she said, turning back to Damien. "Look, I might reconsider. I'll have a word with Colin tonight."

Damien smiled widely. "That would be great."

"I'll give you a call later."

"I look forward to that, Annabel."

He went back to his Saab to fill it up as Annabel went in to the cashier to pay her dues. She waved at Damien as she jumped into her Jeep and set off for home. She dropped Rebecca off at her friend's house and then made the final trip to pick Sam up from football training. He was standing at the gates of the club with two of his pals and each was as mud-covered as the other. Annabel smiled as she saw the beam across her son's face and the rosy colour in his cheeks. At least there was a positive to taking Colin back into the family home.

Sam threw his bag on the back seat and sat up into the front passenger seat beside his mum.

"How was practice?"

"Great," he said as he clicked in his seat belt. "We

have a match on Saturday and I'm striker on the A team."

"That's fantastic, love," Annabel smiled encouragingly even though the basic rules and positions of football were still beyond her – no matter how many matches she watched. "I'm so proud of you." He was coming on leaps and bounds since his father's return. "I bet you can't wait to tell Dad."

Sam shrugged. "Dad doesn't care about anything that he isn't into."

"That's not true!"

"Yes, it is, Mum. We both know what he's like."

Annabel slowed the car and looked over to see her son's expression. He wasn't complaining – merely stating a fact in an adult-like manner. "Are you not happy now that your dad is home?"

Sam shrugged again. "I guess when he left at first it made me think that you would leave too. I was confused. I know now that you'd never leave and in a way there was a lot more peace in the house when he wasn't around."

Annabel was flummoxed. Could this be her young boy of twelve years of age talking this way? "I thought you wanted us to be a family?"

"I did but . . ."

Annabel pulled the car over to the side of the road and fixed her gaze on her son. "All I want is you to feel happy and safe, love – you know that!"

Sam nodded. "I do now. I shouldn't have got drunk

and tried to run away. I was angry with you because I thought that you would leave me. I know now that was silly."

"Give me a hug," she demanded gently.

Sam nuzzled his sweaty brow into his mother's shoulder and let out a deep sigh. "I love you, Mum. I won't let you down again."

Annabel fought back the tears as she rubbed the back of her son's head comfortingly. She wouldn't upset him again but something inside told her that Sam had done a lot of growing up over the last couple of months – probably too much for a twelve-year-old. But he was going to be fine and the important thing was that their relationship was stronger than ever. She knew that there were plenty more bridges to cross as he made his way through the dreaded teenage years but they had just got through their first major hurdle and they would be a constant support for each other.

Happily she pulled into the drive of Summit Green and Sam jumped out with his sports bag in hand. Their little chat couldn't have come at a better time. She would address her issues with Colin after dinner. The fact that her son was in such good form again gave her a renewed strength.

The rest of the afternoon wouldn't go quickly enough. The more she looked at the kitchen clock, the slower the hands turned. By the time she had prepared the chicken chasseur for dinner and the aroma was wafting from the oven she was shaking with apprehension. She wanted to make a stand over something and assert her needs to Colin. The coffee shop was something that she would have total ownership of. Colin was usually on time on a Wednesday and the sooner she got to talk to him about it the better.

Shane put the wheels down on Runway One-Zero. It was his second last flight with Airjet Europe for at least a year. From now on he'd be basking in the Florida sunshine. Why wasn't he happier about his new prospects? The first officer had noticed that something was bothering him since they had taken off from Dublin Airport the day before. He parked the aircraft up at terminal B and was polite but distracted with the red-cap. He didn't know how he felt about anything any more. He just wanted to get back to his apartment and try and work things out in peace and quiet. He hadn't been able to sleep a wink in the Sheraton at Brussels Airport the night before.

"Thanks, Shane," the first officer said with a smile.

"Do you mind if I slip off? I, eh, have to be somewhere at six?"

"No problem. See you again soon. I think we're on together on Saturday."

"Are we?" Shane wasn't usually so offhand. "I'll see you then."

He walked off the aircraft without acknowledging the air stewardesses. He couldn't get home quickly enough. It was a bright day in Dublin and he put his foot down hard on the accelerator as he weaved around the coast road to Howth.

As he took the elevator to his apartment he couldn't help but picture the heavily pregnant Kate that he had seen the day before. She looked beautiful. Her eyes so bright and wide were more stunning with the life she was carrying inside her. She wore her bump like an accessory and it suited her curvy womanly figure so well. He had never thought of a pregnant woman in a romantic way before, but seeing Kate in full bloom that way made him want her even more. But how he wished the baby that she was carrying was his. If they had slept together he would probably think that it was. Maybe that was why she was so adamant that they abstained. He'd never know now, unless he got a chance to talk to someone about her.

He could always try Annabel.

Colin stamped his foot into the hard granite tiles like a two-year-old having a temper tantrum.

"What exactly are you trying to say, woman?"

Annabel's body tensed as she felt the goose-bumps rise on her arms. "I told you. I want to set up a business of my own. I was going to do it before you came back and I don't see why I can't."

"We agreed that you wouldn't do anything like that!"

You agreed that I wouldn't, she thought silently. "I've changed my mind. I can't exist like this."

Colin had to think quickly – there was no way he

was going to lose Annabel once more to some idiotic plan that she was incapable of seeing through. "What about money?"

"I don't need finance. Damien Carlton is going to put that up – it is his premises."

"Don't tell me he's willing to take you on as a partner with no previous experience, without an ulterior motive," Colin tittered. "That's ridiculous! I'm telling you he has his eye on you! The Merry Widower!"

Annabel winced. She wanted to walk straight over and hit him with a blunt implement on the head.

The telephone rang.

Neither of them moved.

"Aren't you going to get that?" Colin asked curtly.

Annabel lifted the handset – covering the sides of the mouthpiece with her hand. "Hello," she said quietly.

The voice at the other end was anxious.

"Annabel, it's Shane."

Kate braced herself as another contraction shot up her spine. They were only Braxton Hicks but hurt like hell nonetheless. "Boys, your tea's ready!" she called.

She took the pot of beans off the hob and placed them in the middle of the kitchen table. Then she heard a pop. Water gushed down the inside of her legs.

Ciarán froze at the kitchen door. Memories of the night his mum was rushed to hospital flooded his head.

"Can you get the phone, love?" Kate asked as she sat on the nearest chair and hunched over.

Ciarán took her mobile phone and handed it to her. Kate dialled her father's number. His voice mail answered.

"Dad, my waters have broken. I need you to mind the boys. Ring me when you get this message."

She rang Annabel's mobile next.

"Hello?" answered Annabel who was still on the landline speaking to Shane.

"It's Kate. My waters have broken – would you be able to bring me in to the Rotunda?"

Annabel held the two phones in her hands and looked at Colin's furious face. There was only one answer she wanted and needed to give her friend.

"Of course. I'll be right there. Where's your dad?"

"I don't know," Kate sighed. "I've left a message on his voice mail."

"Just hang on, Kate. I'll be right there!"

Annabel hung up and returned to her landline. "Shane, I can't talk now. That was Kate on my mobile – her waters have broken. I have to go. I'll call you back."

Annabel rushed past Colin with her handbag and car keys in her hand.

"Where are you off to?" he asked.

"Kate's gone into labour and I'm taking her to hospital," she said over her shoulder. "The dinner is in the oven – make sure you feed the kids."

"I'm not finished talking to you!" Colin called after her.

She swung around. "Well, I'm finished talking to you!" She came back until her face was as close as it could be to his. "I'm taking that retail unit and opening a coffee shop whether you like it or not. Now out of my way while I bring my friend to hospital." She rushed out the door, her car keys jingling.

Colin was beside himself with temper.

"Annabel, Annabel!" he called.

She was gone.

Kate was in labour. Shane put the phone back down. From what Annabel said, Kate had tried to protect him. Did she really think that he wouldn't want her if she had someone else's baby? He wondered what had been going through her head during all the time they had spent together. He wondered if he knew her at all.

Sitting in his apartment on his own wasn't going to help Kate or himself. He had to do something – he had to make a grand gesture. He grabbed his car keys and rushed down to his car.

He drove as if his life depended upon it. He didn't know what kind of a reception he was going to get but he knew that this was what he had to do. He pressed hard on the acceleration pedal of his BMW and it swiftly brought him to Greenfield Close.

He pulled up across the drive and jumped out of the car, leaving the door open. He ran up to the front door and knocked loudly. It opened and David was on the other side.

"Hi, Shane," he said, his mouth open wide in surprise. He had been expecting his granddad. "Mum's in the kitchen."

Shane walked straight in to find Kate sitting on the chair with a pool of water at her feet.

"Shane!" she said in surprise.

"I was on the phone to Annabel when you rang. Is there anything I can do?"

"You could give me a lift." Tension and pain were etched across her face.

"What about the boys?"

"Annabel can mind them when she arrives." Kate turned to her sons. "Boys, only open the door to Annabel or Granddad and stay with them until I ring, okay?"

They nodded and watched as Shane took her arm. He grabbed her overnight bag from her. She'd packed it well in advance since her last visit when her doctor had said she could go at any time – but she hadn't expected it to be this early.

"The seat's a bit low," he said, as he helped Kate into his BMW. "I didn't have this kind of situation in mind when I was buying it."

She smiled up at him as he shut the car door.

Kate grimaced and yelped every so often as they drove and Shane looked over every time.

"Nearly there," he said reassuringly, putting his hand on her thigh.

Kate smiled silently. In her wildest dreams she had sometimes imagined herself and Shane in this situation but now that it was actually happening it felt like the most natural thing in the world.

The car jerked to a stop outside the main entrance to the Rotunda Maternity Hospital.

Shane dashed around to the other side of the car to help Kate out.

They made their way towards the building.

"You can't leave that there," a grubby little man in a green uniform jacket said, pointing at Shane's car.

"I'll be back in a minute," Shane snapped. "Can't you see this woman's in labour!"

Kate had never seen him so flustered.

The receptionist sat up as they came to the main admissions desk.

"Kate Cassaux, I'm a patient of Dr Lennon's."

"Certainly, Mrs Cassaux. Can you fill out this form and take a seat, please?"

Shane was beside himself. "She's in labour!" he snarled at the receptionist.

"She has plenty of time to fill the form out, believe me," the pert little receptionist said as the smile disappeared from her lips.

"It's okay, Shane," Kate said putting her hand on his arm. "I'll be fine. You'd better move the car before you get a ticket."

Shane couldn't fathom how she could be so calm while suffering the pains. "Do you want me to stay with you after I park the car?"

"I couldn't ask you to do that," Kate said, her doe-shaped eyes looking widely into his.

"I wouldn't offer if I didn't want to," he responded.

"Okay, then. But you'll have to pretend you're the father. They're very strict."

"I'll be back in two minutes."

Shane ran out to his car and left Kate filling in the forms. He hadn't a clue what he was doing but he knew that this was where he was meant to be.

"And who brought your mum to hospital?"

"Shane," the twins replied in unison.

Annabel was surprised. But the boys didn't look like they were making it up.

"Where is your granddad?"

"He'll be here soon, Mum said."

"I'll wait until he arrives." Annabel tried Kate's number again but her phone was turned off. It was times like this that Annabel hated mobile phones. It had become so easy to contact anyone any time or place that when they didn't answer it was infuriating.

Annabel was putting the kettle on when she heard a key turn in the door. The familiar tread of heavy boots and steady steps came from the hall. Damien's silhouette became visible through the glass-paned door.

"Annabel!" he said in surprise on entering the kitchen. "Where's Kate?"

"Gone to hospital apparently. We're too late. Shane got to her first."

"Shane?"

Annabel nodded. "Do you want me to mind the boys?"

"No, it's fine. I can't seem to get through to Kate on her phone – she's not answering."

"I'll try and ring Shane – he'll be able to tell us how she is," Annabel said as she picked up her mobile and dialled his number.

"Hello?"

Annabel could hear the tension and nerves in his voice. "Hi, Shane, it's Annabel. I'm in Greenfield Close with the boys. Does Kate want me to come to the hospital?"

"No, I'm here with her. I've already been admitted and they won't let anyone else in now. I'll call you later."

He sounded anxious but in control of the situation and Annabel felt great relief that Kate had someone who had always truly cared for her at her side. She put her mobile on speaker phone so that Damien could follow the conversation.

"Damien's here too. He's going to stay with the boys."

"Okay, Annabel. I'll tell Kate that. She's being examined at the moment and some snotty matron is giving me the evil eye for talking on my mobile so I'd better go."

"Tell Kate not to worry about anything here." Annabel hung up and looked over at Damien. "Did you get that?"

He nodded. "I hope she'll be all right."

"You know Kate better than I do. She'll be fine," Annabel assured him. "Fancy a cup of tea?"

"Mmm." He felt helpless. He had secretly hoped that Kate would let him be with her for the birth. It was his job to look after her now. She might be a strong and independent woman to the rest of the world but she would always be his little girl. "I can't believe she went so quickly." Concern was etched all over his face.

"It can happen that way. She's in good hands."

Annabel sat down at the kitchen table and Damien sat on a chair next to her.

"Damien, I've been thinking about the coffee shop."

"Yes?"

"I think it's a really great opportunity. I was talking to Kate about it and we both figured out that fear is stopping me from taking the leap."

Damien shook his head. "There's nothing to be afraid of. What's the worst that can happen?"

Annabel could think of a hundred things – Colin at the centre of most of them. "I know you're right. But I've never done anything like this before."

"I have faith in you," Damien said reassuringly.

In all her years of marriage to Colin he had never used words like this. All he had done was undermine her confidence until she felt incapable of being any more than his wife and mother to their children and even in those tasks he never gave her praise.

"I told Colin earlier, before Kate rang, that I was going to take up your offer."

Damien perked up excitedly on his seat. "Really?"

She nodded. "I think it's now or never."

"Good for you. We can't go wrong," Damien smiled widely.

Annabel felt as though she was being filled up with confidence. Damien made her feel special and everything that she wanted to be. She could see a whole new world opening up before her eyes.

Kate was sweating. It was all coming back to her now. In twelve years she had completely forgotten the birthing experience but the memories started to flood back.

"You're doing great," Shane said, squeezing her hand so tightly it nearly hurt as much as the contraction.

The anaesthetist arrived, tall and casual, more like a friendly country GP or vet.

"How are we doing here?" he asked cheerfully.

"I'm coping." Kate flinched suddenly.

"Your recovery will be quicker without the epidural if you can stick it. How many centimetres are you?"

"I was four about an hour ago," Kate panted as another pain shot through her stomach. "I think I'll try it on my own."

"Kate, would you not take all the help you can get?" Shane interrupted.

"Typical dad," the anaesthetist grinned. "Too late now to be feeling bad! Well, I'll be around if you change your mind but don't leave it too long."

He exited the birthing suite, leaving Kate and Shane alone.

"Hope you don't mind," Kate said in between contractions.

"About what?"

"Having to pretend you're the dad."

"Of course not!" Shane swallowed hard and looked deeply into Kate's eyes. "I'm only sorry I'm not."

Kate's eyes filled up. "Thanks, Shane."

"Why didn't you tell me the truth? Have you any idea how I've been tortured this last few months wondering why you rejected me?"

Kate jerked suddenly and let out a yelp with the pain.

"I'm so sorry, Kate! I shouldn't be distressing you like this!"

"It's not you!" she yelled. "It's this fucking baby!"

Shane looked around anxiously. "Should I get the midwife?"

Kate nodded her head frantically.

Shane ran out to the main ward and grabbed the nearest woman in a pale green uniform. "She's in terrible pain. Please, can you come?"

The midwife hurried in. She examined Kate and smiled widely as she removed the thin rubber glove. "You're nine centimetres, Kate. Not long to go now."

Shane wiped his brow with the sleeve of his shirt. He had no idea how traumatic an experience giving birth could be.

"The best is yet to come, Dad!" the midwife said, grinning over at the traumatised Shane.

Twenty minutes later Kate was tucked up in a hospital bed with a tiny bundle wrapped in a blue blanket in her arms.

"There seems to be a run on the pink blankets tonight. I'm sure she won't mind!" the nurse had said with a smile.

Shane sat close by Kate on the black leather armchair and gazed in wonder at the little pink wrinkled face that blinked up at her mother.

"She has your hair anyway," the midwife said to Kate, pointing at the mop of black hair covering the little girl's head. "Have you any names picked?"

"I've always liked Molly for a girl," Shane said, turning to look at Kate.

Kate was mesmerised. The whole experience had been totally surreal. It was as if Shane really was the father and they were now a complete family.

"That's a nice name," Kate agreed. "I hadn't really given names any thought. I was so worried that there would be something wrong after the haemorrhage."

"That's a fine healthy baby you have," the nurse said as she bustled out the door, leaving them alone at last.

"Thanks, Shane. I'm sorry you had to go through that." The realisation of what they had been through was finally hitting her.

"Please don't say that. I wanted to be here."

"It's been quite a night, hasn't it?"

"I had no idea what it meant to bring a new life into the world. You were amazing."

Kate felt closer to Shane than at any time in her life. Lying on the bed with her daughter in her arms, she couldn't hold the tears back.

"I love you, Shane!"

He put his hand up to her forehead and brushed back the strands of wet hair that stuck to her skin. Leaning forward he placed his lips gently on hers for a brief moment – they tasted like sweet salt.

"Then be with me."

Kate blinked. Her eyes wide with the wonder of the moment. *If only things were more simple.*

"It's not just me. There are three of us – I mean four including the new edition."

Shane gazed longingly into Kate's eyes. He knew the time had finally come. From now on his life was going to be complete. He was going to be sharing it with his soul mate and he was never going to lose her again.

"Then I'm the lucky one to be getting a ready-made family! It's always been you, Kate, for me."

The baby in Kate's arms gurgled and put her hand out until it touched Shane's.

"Do you want to hold her?" asked Kate.

"Sure do," Shane said, taking the swaddled baby and carefully wrapping his arms around her.

The baby opened her eyes and seemed to gaze up at him.

"You know what?" said Shane.

"Hmm?"

"I think she's going to be a daddy's girl!"

"That was Shane," Annabel said, smiling, closing her mobile phone with a snap. "You have a healthy grand-daughter!"

Damien got up off the sofa and rushed over to Annabel on hearing the exciting news.

"Should we wake the boys?"

"It might upset them," Annabel said, looking at her watch. It was half-past twelve and they were meant to be at school the next day.

"I think you're right. We'll leave them and I'll bring them into the hospital tomorrow afternoon," Damien nodded. "Do you fancy having a drink to celebrate? I think I left a bottle of champagne at the back of that cupboard in the corner."

Damien rooted around the drinks cabinet and produced a bottle of Bollinger.

"I shouldn't really," Annabel said shyly. "I have to get back." It was already very late. The last few hours she had been entranced with Damien's company. How she had missed him!

"Well, what about if we put it in the ice-box and drink it tomorrow night – after we sign the papers on our new enterprise?"

"Oh, Damien!" Annabel exclaimed. The business was going to happen for real. Her face lit up. "I'm so excited. And I'm so happy for Kate! Do you think she'll get back with Shane?"

"I'd say after what they've just been through the answer is definitely yes – don't you?"

Annabel lowered her head shyly. Her own true love was only inches away – if only she could tell him how she felt.

Damien moved over until he was almost upon her. "She deserves to be happy. We all do!"

He felt like it was now or never. The signals he'd been receiving from Annabel all night made him confident that she felt the same way as he did. Annabel looked up until her gaze was locked firmly onto Damien's eyes. Neither could speak. The space between them was too much. They had to be closer than this. Damien reached out and gently brushed a strand of blonde hair off her face. For a moment his finger touched her cheek. She grabbed his hand and pressed it against her face, then turned her head until her lips placed a gentle kiss on his palm. They were transported back in time to another place on a rocky sea.

"We have no storm to protect us now," he said. "Are we ready?"

Annabel nodded as Damien leaned forward and tasted her honey-sweet lips.

Epilogue

Four years later

Kate sat in front of the mirror as Annabel put the final touches to her make-up.

"You look beautiful."

"Thanks to you," Kate said, rubbing her gloss-coated lips together. "Where has Molly got to?"

Annabel pointed to the bedroom door. "She's running around the house telling everyone that she's a princess."

"As long as she isn't killing the baby!"

"She loves him. I heard her say the other day that he wasn't her brother but her baby, while she was trying to put him into her toy buggy."

"She's so spoilt and such a daddy's girl!"

"Like her mother!"

"And her mother's best friend."

Annabel laughed out loud. Her relationship with Damien had been slow to take off but now that they were a bona fide couple everyone was delighted.

"Nervous?"

"Just the usual wedding-day jitters," Kate grinned. "I hope everything goes well."

"Third time lucky!"

"I know it sounds corny but it feels like the first time."

"It doesn't sound corny at all," Annabel said smiling widely. "You're only doing what you should have done years ago."

Kate nodded. "Annabel?"

"Yes," she replied while fixing her best-friend's hair.

"You do realise something, don't you?"

"What?" Annabel still didn't look at her friend's reflection in the mirror.

"There's a very good chance that some day you'll be my stepmother."

Annabel smiled. Damien and she were keeping their news until Kate and Shane got back from their honeymoon.

The End